THE GENTLE AXE

THE
GENTLE AXE

R. N. Morris

THE PENGUIN PRESS
New York
2007

THE PENGUIN PRESS
Published by the Penguin Group • Penguin Group (USA) Inc., 375 Hudson Street,
New York, New York 10014, U.S.A. • Penguin Group (Canada), 90 Eglinton Avenue East, Suite 700,
Toronto, Ontario, Canada M4P 2Y3 (a division of Pearson Penguin Canada Inc.) • Penguin Books Ltd, 80
Strand, London WC2R 0RL, England • Penguin Ireland, 25 St. Stephen's Green, Dublin 2, Ireland
(a division of Penguin Books Ltd) • Penguin Books Australia Ltd, 250 Camberwell Road, Camberwell,
Victoria 3124, Australia (a division of Pearson Australia Group Pty Ltd) • Penguin Books India Pvt Ltd, 11
Community Centre, Panchsheel Park, New Delhi – 110 017, India • Penguin Group (NZ), Cnr Airborne and
Rosedale Roads, Albany, Auckland 1310, New Zealand (a division of Pearson New Zealand Ltd)
Penguin Books (South Africa) (Pty) Ltd, 24 Sturdee Avenue, Rosebank, Johannesburg 2196, South Africa

Penguin Books Ltd, Registered Offices:
80 Strand, London WC2R 0RL, England

First American edition
Published in 2007 by The Penguin Press,
a member of Penguin Group (USA) Inc.

Publisher's Note
This is a work of fiction. Names, characters, places, and incidents either are the product of the author's
imagination or are used fictitiously, and any resemblance to actual persons, living or dead, business estab-
lishments, events, or locales is entirely coincidental.

LIBRARY OF CONGRESS CATALOGING IN PUBLICATION DATA

Morris, R. N.
The gentle axe: a novel / R. N. Morris.
p. cm.
ISBN 978-1-59420-112-9
1. Rostnikov, Porfiry Petrovich (Fictitious character)—Fiction. 2. Police—Russia (Federation)—
Fiction. 3. Saint Petersburg (Russia)—History—19th century—Fiction. I. Title.

PR6113.O758G46 2007
823'.92—dc22   2006049543

Printed in the United States of America
1   3   5   7   9   10   8   6   4   2

Designed by Chris Welch and Amanda Dewey

For my mother, Norma, who likes a good murder

ACKNOWLEDGMENTS

I would like to thank Yaroslav I. Tregubov of the St. Petersburg Historical Society, who helped a stranger find his way around nineteenth-century St. Petersburg.

And to Fyodor Dostoevsky, I can only apologize.

CONTENTS

"You are a gentleman!" they said. "You shouldn't have gone to work with an axe; it's not at all the thing for a gentleman."

—*Crime and Punishment,* Fyodor Dostoevsky, translation, Jessie Coulson

THE
GENTLE AXE

December 1866

The events described below take place approximately a year and a half after the famous case of Raskolnikov the student, in which the investigator Porfiry Petrovich played such a crucial role.

December 1866

The events described below take place approximately a year and a half after the famous case of Raskolnikov the student, in which the investigator Porfiry Petrovich played such a crucial role.

1

In Petrovsky Park

I T WAS WELL into the morning when the darkness began to fade.

Zoya Nikolaevna Petrova moved through Petrovsky Park with unthinking determination, as fat and dark in her bundled layers as a beetle. The paths, which in the summer were filled with strollers, were now hidden under snow. But she had no use for them anyway. Zoya Nikolaevna trod her own path. She was heading north, away from the frozen boating lake. Her steps were slow and uneven. Every shift in her squat frame sent a fresh stab of rheumatism shooting through the joints of her hips. Whenever she had to stoop to add a stick to her basket of firewood, it was with some effort and pain that she straightened up. But she thought of the little one shivering at home, and of the sacrifices Lilya had had to make; and was able to stoop again and straighten again and continue her steps.

The things a woman must do. It had never been easy, though some would have accused her of choosing the easy way once. But what did they know of the cost to her soul, or of the tears she had shed over the years? Tears at the start of it, when she had first felt a stranger's gaze possessing her. She had always found it harder to endure their eyes on her than their hands. And tears at the end of it, when the mirror showed her looks creased by age and a figure absurdly fat and ugly; and she felt herself worn out to the bones. Yes, tears when even that recourse was closed to her. Why should there not have been tears? That life, that way of living was all she had known, and there had been some comfort in it.

Tears came again now. But they were simply moisture drawn by the stinging cold. She felt no sadness and no nostalgia for the life she had lost, no grief for the countless miscarriages, not even for those that were accidental. Her nose ran, and she let it. It was one of the small freedoms of solitude.

She was not lonely. Not while she had the thought of the little one at home and of Lilya, who called her mother and allowed herself in turn to be called daughter by Zoya.

Who would have thought that the way out of her troubles would be to take on more troubles?

Zoya felt the land dip. Her gaze was fixed on the ground ahead of her, scanning for firewood. She had left the little one sleeping and so was anxious to get back. She couldn't bear the thought of the child waking alone. Ah, but little Vera could sleep for hours in this cold. Sometimes Zoya thought she would never wake.

She told herself not to worry. She must gather all the wood she could carry. What they didn't use themselves, she could sell. It would be a crime to go home without a mountain of fagots strapped to her back and a full basket. It would be better for them all if she took as long as she needed.

But Lilya had not come home last night, which worried her too, if she thought about it. The girl must have had a busy night. That was it. If so, she should rejoice. There would be something good to eat today. Lilya was a generous soul, and touchingly grateful. She never forgot that it was Zoya who had taught her the things she needed to know to keep from starving.

Zoya stooped to grab a scrawny twig. Nothing was allowed to escape her hunt for fuel. She felt the earth pull her overburdened torso down and braced herself to take a stand against the tyranny of gravity, forcing a clenched knuckle into her aching spine. She stood and straightened, swooning in the intense and nearly blissful shifts of pain.

And then she saw him, there ahead of her, his shoulders hunched forward, head skewed. He seemed to be waiting for her. He was a big man, tall and burly, with a massy beard that confidently matched the bulk of his person. He was dressed in an old army greatcoat. The flaps of a sheepskin cap covered his ears. He had the bloated face of a vodka drinker and cunning pinpoint eyes. His feet were plunged into tarred boots, the toes of which floated barely an inch above the white ground, a comic dancer frozen in the execution of a pirouette.

The birch trunk that bore him was bent like an archer's bow. A sudden howl of wind set the tree vibrating. A flurry of snowflakes danced as though magnetized. The hanging man spun around.

On the ground near his feet she saw something brown half-buried in the snow.

ZOYA CROSSED HERSELF with two fingers and hesitated. Drifting flakes thickened and massed, then rushed her face. The hanging man scared her. But her instincts sensed the promise of something more valuable than firewood.

She lowered her gaze and resumed her slow, shuffling step toward him.

Her foot kicked against the object in the snow. It was hard and unyielding. Risking pain, she bent to clear the snow from it with a sweep of her arm. It was a large leather suitcase.

The case was too heavy for Zoya to lift. She dragged it away from the body on the tree, leaving a broad trail.

Her fingers worked the catches, which were stiff but not locked. The lid of the case sprang upward a little, as if recoiling from what was contained within. Zoya lifted it open.

He was curled like a fetus in the womb waiting to be born. The falling snow was quick to welcome him, broad flakes laying themselves with the delicacy of a caul over a jutting shoulder.

His head, she noticed, was split open, hair roughly parted on either side of a dark glistening secret. It struck her, this head, as strangely large.

He was on his side. His left eye rebuked her. She made the sign of the cross for a second time.

She avoided the staring eye and took in the rest of him.

Oh but he is tiny! she realized. Tiny arms and tiny legs, and how did he fit all that he needed—a heart, lungs, kidney, liver—into that tiny little body? But he was a man and not a child. A dark beard was trimmed to a point on his chin.

He was dressed in a threadbare suit, the sleeves and trouser legs severely cut off and hemmed.

Without knowing she was going to do it, Zoya searched his pockets. She averted her eyes as her hands went about their business. The things a woman must do.

Her fingers closed on something hard and compact. She retrieved a pack of playing cards, still in its cardboard box. She thumbed out the first few cards. It was one of those pornographic packs, with naked girls for queens, horny satyrs for kings, and hermaphrodites taking the place of jacks. The wind snapped up a small slip of paper that had been tucked away among them. Zoya let it go. The cards were old and well used, but she didn't doubt she could sell them to some fool. She conjured them away.

The tips of her fingers probed the seams of his every pocket but came up with nothing. She was no longer aware of her fear. Something more urgent than fear compelled her.

She bustled across to the other one. She was racing against the falling snow. And she was afraid that someone might discover her. But there was something else too. A grim eagerness.

She pulled open the frozen greatcoat and gave a high squeal of horror. There, tucked into the belt of his trousers, was a short-handled axe. The blade seemed to leer at her. It was like a tongue licking the blood that stained it.

She looked up into the hanging man's face. Such a big brute. What a bully, to have killed that poor little fellow in the case. No wonder he had taken his own life. It was the shame of it.

She carried on investigating the clothing of the corpse. She thought of all the men she had undressed. They had picked her bones, and now the boot was on the other foot. She giggled. She was having the last laugh now. One hand delved into the pocket of his breeches. She felt something metallic. It was small and irregularly shaped and turned out to be a key. In itself it had no value. But who knew what treasures it would unlock? It joined the pack of cards in the secret compartments of her dress.

Her hand now burrowed into the inside breast pocket of his greatcoat and straightaway felt the contents. Two things, she judged, about the same size, one soft and papery, the other hard. She pulled out the first, a bulging envelope. It was pale lilac, unaddressed and unsealed.

Inside the envelope was a bundle of banknotes.

She darted quick glances in every direction, certain now that someone would disturb her. She took out the money, a rainbow of color in the bleached landscape, and counted the notes.

Zoya's hands trembled but not from the cold. The lilac envelope fell. She raised her face to the falling snow. Six thousand rubles! Tears now, real tears of emotion, mingled with the flakes thawing on her cheeks. She folded the cash away inside the layers of her extended being and went on her way laughing.

2

"Everything Is in Order"

PORFIRY PETROVICH TRANSFERRED the cigarette from fingers to lips, a moment of intense anticipation. It was not pleasure so much that he anticipated as clarity. Porfiry always insisted that he smoked for rational—he would even say professional—reasons.

He closed the brightly colored enamel cigarette case with a soft click and returned it to the inside pocket of his jacket.

A copy of *The Periodical* was open on the desk in front of him. Porfiry flattened the pages, seeming to stroke the words in preparation to reading them. It was an article entitled "Why Do They Do It?" An introductory line promised: "A discussion of the motivation of educated, titled, and talented perpetrators of crime and injustice." The author was given as "R."

Porfiry struck a match and leaned forward to meet its flame. As he inhaled, his blood quickened, and he felt both absorbed by and in control of his mental and perceptual processes.

The elegant syntax of the article revealed its secrets to him. He experienced it as a dance of ideas, inevitable and inexorable. He frowned, not because he was confused but for the pleasure of frowning. He was acutely self-conscious.

Something began to impinge on his reverie.

Salytov.

He felt the catalyst of cigarette smoke lose its power. His entire being was no longer focused onto the pages of the journal. He was aware now of the green leather surface of the writing desk upon which it rested. And now the rest of the room came back to him, with its government-issue furniture, the imitation leather–covered sofa, the chairs, the escritoire and bookcase, all made from the same tawny wood. But more than anything he felt the looming presence of the doors.

Salytov was shouting. Again.

Two doors led off from Porfiry Petrovich's "chambers," as this modest room in the Department of the Investigation of Criminal Causes was rather grandly known. One was the door to his private apartments, provided for him, like everything else, by the government. The other was the door to the Haymarket District Police Bureau in Stolyarny Lane.

The doors symbolized Porfiry's dilemma. Either he could take his journal and his cigarette and retreat into his inner sanctuary (although it was well past the hour when he was required to make himself available for his official duties as an investigator); or he could step out into the chaos of the receiving area of the police station and confront his colleague Ilya Petrovich Salytov.

Porfiry ground the stub of his cigarette into a crystal ashtray.

M Y DEAR ILYA PETROVICH—"

"Everything is under control, Porfiry Petrovich. There is no need for your interference." Salytov jerked his arms as he shouted, as if Porfiry were a fly he was trying to swat away. His face was red. The veins on his temples bulged. He moved constantly but without purpose. He was starting to sweat and pulled at his collar.

"Of course, of course . . . But, you know, I don't seek to interfere, merely to offer my assistance."

"I am grateful to you. However . . ." Salytov had been a lieutenant in the army. Perhaps he had learned to bluster then. But Porfiry found it hard to believe he had ever commanded the respect of his men. He had a weak mouth. The bristles of his well-trimmed sandy mustache couldn't compensate for this.

"How you scared us last time, Ilya Petrovich! We, your friends in the department, we were most concerned for your health. I've never seen such a shade of puce in nature before. And when you fainted."

"That was in the summer. It was a fearful hot day, and the smell from the Ditch was overpowering."

"But the doctor was clear that your temper had contributed to the attack."

"It wasn't an attack!"

"Were you not commanded—for your own good, of course, but commanded all the same—to avoid such excesses of passion by no less than Nikodim Fomich? Think what would happen if he were to come upon you now."

"I'm not afraid of Nikodim Fomich."

"I'm not suggesting you should be afraid of any man, Ilya Petrovich. Not even our esteemed chief superintendent. However, were you to be deprived of your position—"

"He can't do that to me!"

"A transfer, it would be called, no doubt. A move into a less stressful position. For health reasons. I know how these things work. Believe me, Ilya Petrovich, I'm on your side. I will do all I can. But surely the best course of action is to avoid his attention in the first place. Isn't there some way we can resolve this matter without all the, uh . . ." Porfiry smiled and whispered, *"Shouting?"*

Salytov gave his reluctant assent with a flinch.

"What is the situation here?" Porfiry's gently amused tone mollified the demand.

"This young hussy—a prostitute, mind . . ." Salytov indicated a small, tired-looking girl. She was handcuffed to the black-uniformed *polizyeisky,* who maintained exemplary side whiskers and an outraged expression. The girl's exact age was hard to say, but she was young. Her face was thickly made up, in the usual fashion of a streetwalker. Somehow this only made her seem more naïve. It was as if someone had explained the economic advantage of heavy cosmetics, and she had applied it in good faith. And she had donned the requisite costume too, by the looks of it handed down to her through the generations. In the glare of the police station, her red silk dress, so old and worn it was practically falling apart, appeared like a badge of poverty rather than vice. The oversize bustle and sodden filthy train invited ridicule, as did her frayed straw hat and tattered parasol. Pathetically at odds with all this, and undermining whatever effect she was aiming at, was the homely woolen shawl wrapped around her shoulders. Her build was slight. Both Salytov and the *polizyeisky* loomed over her, though Porfiry was closer to her height. The chief clerk, a pale superior type with high cheekbones, was also in attendance, seated on a stool behind the reception desk. It was clear that the girl was exhausted. Her blue eyes stared wide open in the effort to keep awake. But her shoulders continually sagged. Once or twice she leaned forward onto the desk, causing the clerk to bang down the great admissions book. She would then shoot bolt upright, betraying neither ill will nor complaisance. Necessity drove her, that was all. Every now and then a convulsion of shivering gripped her frail form, each attack more extended than the one before.

Porfiry took her in with a glance as he finished his cigarette. "She carries the yellow ticket?" he asked Salytov.

"Yes."

"And it is in order?"

"That's not the issue."

"But it is in order?"

"Yes." Salytov almost spat out the word. His face became the battleground for contesting emotions: hatred and anger on one side, the desire not to be shown a fool on the other. It was always the same when he had dealings with Porfiry Petrovich. "She stands accused of stealing one hundred rubles from a gentleman. A search by the arresting constable discovered a banknote to that denomination on her person."

"I see. And where did this alleged crime take place?"

"Alleged! Really, Porfiry Petrovich!"

"But where?"

"On Sadovaya Street."

"I see. And when?"

"In the early hours of the morning."

"Do we not know the precise time?"

"It was about four A.M., sir," put in the uniformed officer.

"I see. Is there a reason why it has taken so long to process the incident?"

"The gentleman making the charge went missing," the head clerk supplied, his tone sarcastic and amused, making clear that it was nothing to do with him.

"How unfortunate. Has he turned up now?"

"We are still looking for him," said Salytov quickly, flashing hatred at the clerk.

"Do we know his name?"

"She"—Salytov signaled the prostitute with a terse nod—"claims he was one Konstantin Kirillovich."

Porfiry turned his attention to the girl. "So this man was known to you?"

"I had met him once before, your honor." Her voice was that of a child. It was also polite—the voice of a well-brought-up child.

"Under what circumstances?"

The girl blushed and stared at Porfiry's feet. Then she escaped into another of her shivering fits.

"He was a client of yours?"

The convulsion calmed. She met his gaze. "No. Not that."

"A pimp then?"

The girl shook her head but would say no more.

"Do you know where he lives, this Konstantin Kirillovich?"

"No, sir."

"And how did you come to have the hundred rubles that were found on you?"

"He gave them to me."

"He gave you a hundred rubles? Why?"

"I didn't want to take it, sir. He forced it on me."

"He forced you to take a hundred rubles off him and then called a policeman to accuse you of stealing it? It beggars belief, does it not, child?"

"I can't explain it, sir."

"Did he want you to go with him when he gave you the money?"

"Yes, sir."

"And did you go with him?"

"No, sir."

"You refused?"

"I suppose so."

"And yet you kept the money that he gave you. Perhaps that's why he called the policeman?"

"I tried to give the money back to him. He wouldn't take it."

"Do you normally charge a hundred rubles for your favors?"

The girl made a sound halfway between a sob and a laugh. There was outrage in it and suffering, yet acceptance.

"Forgive me. But let us face the facts. You are a prostitute. You don't deny that?"

"I am legal. I have a license."

She produced the yellow passport that was her license to whore herself. Porfiry read the name: Lilya Ivanovna Semenova. She was registered as working at a brothel called Keller's at an address on Sadovaya Street.

"Of course. There is nothing to worry about as far as that is concerned. A man gives you a hundred rubles. You refuse the money and refuse to go with him. Was he very ugly?"

"It wasn't that. That has nothing to do with it, after all."

"So why wouldn't you go with him? Why didn't you want his money?"

"It was too much."

"You are a strange prostitute, to have qualms on that front."

"I was afraid of what he would expect in return."

"Ah! There are limits then? Is that it?"

"Not in the way you think."

"Please, tell me, in what way then?"

"He didn't want me for himself."

"I see. He was an agent in the transaction. And who—on whose behalf was he acting?"

"He didn't say." Her pupils, for a moment, oscillated wildly from side to side. Porfiry tilted his head to study her, a feminine gesture.

"But still it doesn't make sense. Why wouldn't you go with him? And why, on your refusal, wouldn't he simply demand the money back? Why call a policeman? Why accuse you of theft? And why, then, run off?"

"I don't know, sir."

"What has happened to the money now?"

"We're holding it as evidence," answered Salytov.

"Evidence of what? There is no complainant. We can't charge her. We can't hold her. Regarding her license, everything is in order. I suggest, therefore, that we release the girl. It is my opinion, also, that we must return the hundred rubles to her."

"But she stole it!"

"So says a man who isn't here. She says he gave it to her. There is no one to contradict that story. Perhaps it was a gift. Or we might refer to it as payment in advance for a service that hasn't yet been rendered. We can't give it back to him because he's not here and we don't know his address. There's nothing to justify confiscating this poor girl's earnings."

"But she did nothing to earn it, even if you accept her version of events," insisted Salytov.

"True. But who are we to make judgments on that account? We're here to uphold the law, not our own notions of morality. I would like very much to talk to this Konstantin Kirillovich. My dear, you don't know his family name, by any chance?"

"No, sir. I know him only as Konstantin Kirillovich."

"Ah, well. But perhaps he has reasons of his own for not wishing to talk to us. I consider it very careless of you to have let him escape, Ilya Petrovich."

"But I had no idea he would make off like that!"

"My dear fellow, can't you recognize when you're being teased? Of course I don't blame you. After all, one normally only has to confine the accused." Porfiry now turned to the head clerk. "Alexander Grigorevich, if you would be so kind as to get the money belonging to this young lady."

Alexander Grigorevich treated Porfiry to a look of open incredulity; nonetheless he slipped from his stool and sauntered into a room behind the main desk.

A moment later he returned with a brightly colored one-hundred-ruble note. The girl, Lilya Ivanovna Semenova, protested, "I don't want it. I don't want his money. You keep it." There was fear as well as disgust in her expression.

"It doesn't belong to us," explained Porfiry.

"But I don't want it. I never wanted it."

"Very well, Lilya Ivanovna. We can't force you to take it. Officer, you may release the prisoner."

The *polizyeisky* unlocked the handcuffs. Lilya Ivanovna's face was lit up by amazement. Then she frowned at Porfiry, as though he were a puzzle she couldn't solve, before turning to plunge herself into the loose crowd milling through the bureau. In her wake, she left a scent in the air.

"What do you want me to do with this?" asked Alexander Grigorevich, holding the banknote distastefully between the tips of his thumb and forefinger.

"Give it to the orphans," said Porfiry, without looking at him.

3

The Investigator's Eyelashes

LILYA SHIVERED AGAIN as she came out into a freezing fog. Restless splinters of ice penetrated her clothes and skin. Her feet were wet and numb with the cold. For a moment she had not the faintest idea where she was or how she came to be there. All she could remember was leaving Fräulein Keller's basement. And everything that had happened since seemed to have happened in a dream.

She ought to go back for her galoshes.

She walked without any sense of where she was going. She heard the lampposts singing, shaken by a wind that went straight through her, despite her shawl. Then she heard the jangle of a passing sleigh and the muted clip of hooves. The horses were almost on her before she saw them. The driver's green caftan passed in a blur, his words—whether for her or for his team—stifled by the damp air.

It was the man's eyes that had amazed her, Porfiry Petrovich's eyes. Or more specifically his eyelashes, blond to the point of transparency. Once she had noticed them, she could not look away. He blinked a lot, and there seemed to be some point to his blinking. Expectancy, or cunning, but a peculiarly feminine cunning, somehow also benign. She'd found it hard to understand what he was saying, so fascinated was she by his lashes and the effect they had on his face. And of course, she was tired.

She blinked herself, as though by imitating him she would come to understand him. Was it really true that he had let her go? And had he really meant to have them return the money to her?

Perhaps it was all a trick. If so, it was just as well she had refused the money. Ah, but to go home with nothing, after a whole night! She couldn't go home, not yet. She ought to go back to Fräulein Keller's to get what was owed her.

Zoya had come to see her. That was what she had been told. "Zoya is here for you," Fräulein Keller had said. "She wants to talk to you about your little one." But it made no sense. If Zoya had come to Fräulein Keller's, who was looking after Vera? And when she had gone out into the cold night, there was no sign of Zoya. Just him.

Lilya shivered and let the spasm take hold. She gave in to her weakness for only an instant, holding one blink of her eyelids longer than the others, and in that instant she was back home, cuddling her sweet-souled, beautiful daughter, kissing her cheeks, stroking her hair, whispering promises, never, never again will I leave you, this will last forever, this laughing, crying, clinging moment.

The fog was beginning to clear. Perhaps she had held the blink for longer than she intended. But she was relieved to find herself still standing.

Lilya pulled her shawl tight about her. She had come out into Sadovaya Street. To her right, dim shapes formed into the Church of the Assumption of the Virgin Mary across the Haymarket, above the canvas-covered stalls. She felt comforted by the appearance of the church. A bustling crowd filled the cobbled square between. But in the same way that she was able to see more, so too was she more visible. Faces turned toward her, hostile, mocking, contemptuous. And yet some of the men who pointed her out for ridicule were among those who came to the basement of the milliner's shop, at a different hour, for a different purpose.

She turned her back on the Haymarket, to face north, toward Yekat-erinsky Canal, or the Ditch, as it was known. She crossed Kokushkin Bridge over the frozen canal back into Stolyarny Lane. There was the building that housed the police station ahead of her, and she remembered again his impossible eyelashes. His eyes, she now remembered, were the color of ice, but whether that color was black or silver, she could not say. She was tempted to go back inside just to find out. And while she was at it, she would demand the money after all.

Then without her thinking about it, the rest of him suddenly came back to her. Fat—that was it. He was a fat little man, with a proud paunch out front. But every part of him, almost, seemed to have something swollen about it, from his big, close-cropped head to his plump hands. How strange and improbable those eyes had seemed in all this. How calm and unexpected and alert, but above all how kindly.

Perhaps she would go back inside. And tell him everything. But then again, what was there to tell?

She kept on walking as far as Srednaya Meshchanskaya Street. So she was going home after all, and with nothing to show for the night.

She could not face going back for her galoshes.

T HE SNOW IN the yard was stained with blood. A pig had been slaughtered there that morning. A peasant couple butchered the carcass in the open. They paused in their task to watch her across the yard. The two of them lifted their cleavers in warning, as if they suspected her of being intent on stealing their meat. Their expressions remained blank.

Lilya entered a narrow passageway at the rear of the courtyard. Its darkness shielded her from their scrutiny. She reached out one hand to grope her way along the wall, but with the first step she took, her foot kicked over an unseen obstacle, setting off an almost musical reverberation. A metal pail lay on its side, a dark stain hastening from it. Before she knew it, the peasant couple were at her shoulder, screaming abuse.

"That was our blood, you careless bitch!"

"You'll pay for it, whore!"

As she fled their stabbing fingers and careless blades, she felt a gob of hawked mucus strike her cheek. She could still hear their shouts as the door to the back stairs closed behind her.

The stench of cabbage soup and urine hung in the stairway. Even so, this felt like a refuge. The gloom welcomed and concealed her. The temperature, though chill, was a degree warmer than outside.

Lilya hauled herself up the stairs with both hands together on the grimy rail, her feet slapping on the worn-down wooden steps.

She heard the door she had just come through clatter in its frame, then hurried footsteps hammering. Somehow she managed to pick up her own pace. She did not look back.

But she was still four flights away from her landing and the footsteps were gaining on her. Then, unexpectedly, they stopped and a door below slammed.

She turned a corner and pushed her way through hanging laundry. It seemed to cling to her face, dragging her back and down. Doors stood open on this landing. Sullen, consumptive faces looked out, waiting for something but not her.

She trudged on, light-headed, her legs uncertain and aching. In a niche on the next half-landing she fancied she saw a figure hanging back, a dark shape in dark shadows. Were those eyes that flashed in the gloom, or white sparks firing in her brain? Dog-tired she was, so tired that it was not inconceivable that her nightmares had come ahead to meet her.

It felt as though the steps were moving beneath her feet now, swaying and sinking, their height increasing, so that it required the courage of a mountaineer to scale each one. And now they had no substance. Her feet sank into them. They were like the marshes the city had once been built on.

She found herself unable to go on. She looked down at her feet. The space between two boards gaped. She closed her eyes and teetered back, the wild lurch in her belly bringing her around. Her head was a dead weight. Somehow she found the strength to lift it and look up. There, ahead of her, was her own landing. The sight of her door spurred her on to a final push.

She fell into the room, gasping at the sudden heat here, but too exhausted to make sense of it. She simply allowed the hot dry air to enclose her in a swooning embrace. And now little Vera was rushing at her, cannoning headfirst in her shrieking delight at her mother's homecoming. Her daughter's unquestioning love overwhelmed her. She felt undeserving of it. At the same time she had a sense of the child, so fierce in her innocence, as being eternally closed to her, strange, other, and somehow out of bounds. And there did seem to be something different about Vera today. But again Lilya was too worn-out to pursue the impression. Instead she gave in to tears. She was wracked with the pain of pure feeling, of feeling too much for too long. She allowed herself no memories, no longer entertained dreams. She kept her ideas down to the most essential. Whole areas of moral and mental life were closed to her. All that was left was the intense feeling of the moment.

"Now, now! What's this?" cried old mother Zoya rushing up to her. She added her own embrace to the tight little cuddles of the infant. "No tears, no tears, daughter. Yes, daughter. Yes, that's right. Daughter. Don't I always call you daughter? Zoya's here. Mamma Zoya will look after you. We'll be all right. Why, my child, my daughter, my lovely girl, why—everything will be all right now. You'll see. You'll see, my sweet Lili-lilyenchka. My sweet child. No tears. Not now. Not today. Oh, my lovely lovely, you'll see. Look! Look! Mamma Zoya's taken care of everything! See! Only look, child, and you'll see. All our troubles are over. Never again! You'll never have to wear that dress again. You'll never have to go to that place again. You can tell Fräulein Keller that you're never coming back. Never! D'you hear? Never!"

Lilya pulled away, her face wet with tears. She shook her head and her eyes were tenderly accusing. She whispered her reproach: "No, Zoya!"

"Mamma, dear. Call me Mamma. Aren't I a mother to you? More than

a mother? Don't I look after you better than any mother would? Haven't
I earned it?"

Lilya shook her head and murmured, "Cruel!"

"Don't be afraid, Lilya. Don't be afraid. It's true, you see! That life
is over!"

"We'll only make it worse for ourselves!"

Zoya made a dismissive noise and arched both eyebrows in gentle,
mocking reproach. But Lilya was beyond such games, too tired even to be
annoyed. She lurched past Zoya, toward the end of the room that housed
the narrow bed she shared with her daughter. But felt a tight pinch of restraint on her arm. And cried out. Her eyes were pleading as she turned to
confront Zoya.

"Look!" commanded the old woman, gesturing to the table. Lilya
could not take it in. She saw but did not understand. The table was laden
with pastries and loaves. There were sweets too, and candied peel. There
was even caviar.

"Where did you get all this?"

"From the Shchukin Arcade, of course. Where else?"

This mystery reminded Lilya of another: "Did you come and see me
last night? They said you were at the door."

"And what kind of a mother are you, not to comment on her daughter's
new shawl?"

Lilya looked down at Vera's beaming face and frowned at the unfamil-
iar *drap-de-dames* shawl around the child's shoulders. Was this why her
daughter had seemed alien to her? She stroked the white garment as if to
question it with her fingers.

"And here! For you!" continued Zoya, holding out a dark and apparently ancient icon representing the Virgin and the infant Christ. The
gold-leaf halos flickered in and out of brilliance. As if suspecting a trick,
Lilya refused to take it. "It's all right," insisted Zoya. "It's paid for.
Everything is paid for."

"But how?" whispered Lilya, afraid of the answer.

Zoya put down the icon. She bustled to the far corner of the room and disappeared behind the curtain that concealed her sleeping area. She came back with a padlocked tin box that Lilya had never seen before. As Zoya reached the table, she let the box slip out of her fingers in her excitement. It landed with a heavy clatter. Zoya fumbled with the key, grinning and chuckling, despite her wish to appear mysterious. At last the lid was open. Zoya pushed the box toward her young friend.

The warm colors of the banknotes drew Lilya's face closer and closer. Then at the last, she recoiled, as if she were afraid of getting burned.

"Where?" she gasped.

"Petrovsky Park."

"Whose is it?"

"Ours!" cried Zoya.

"No, no. You must tell me all about it, Zoya. You must tell me exactly where you found this money. It might belong to someone, Zoya. It must, surely it must belong to someone."

"What if it does? What do we care? At any rate, the one it belongs to has no use for it now."

"What do you mean?"

"He's dead!"

"Zoya! What are you saying?"

"He was a murderer and a thief. A big ugly brute. And a bully. That's what he was. And he's dead. No use crying for the likes of him. A murderer! The bloody axe still on him, still dripping with the little fellow's blood."

"Zoya, please! I don't understand. You must start at the beginning. One thing at a time."

"I found them both. Both dead. The little dwarf. And the other one, hanging. He'd hanged himself. Out of shame."

"A dwarf, you said?"

"Tiny little man. With a tiny little suit."

"No!"

"Both dead."

"The dwarf was dead?"

"Murdered! His head bashed in. And the axe that did it was on the big one."

"What did he look like, the dwarf?"

"Tiny! A tiny little fellow."

"Was he dark? Dark hair with a beard?"

"Yes!"

"What else? Anything else about him?"

Zoya's hands retrieved something from her apron, the pack of obscene playing cards.

"He was a randy little bastard, by the looks of it. I found these on him."

Lilya gasped as if struck. "I know him! I've seen these before. He came to Fräulein Keller's. Many times. He always asks for me. Zoya, did you come to Fräulein Keller's last night? Was there something you had to tell me about Vera? Fräulein Keller said—"

"What are you talking about, child?"

Lilya took in the old woman's good-natured incomprehension. She looked again at the money in the cash box. "Zoya, we must tell the police."

"No! Don't you see? They'll want the money back."

"But Zoya, it's not ours."

Zoya's face became severe, her tone forbidding. "You must not say a word about this to anyone. Do you hear? You must swear to me on Vera's life that you will not say a word of this to a soul."

Lilya shook her head and whispered her refusal.

"On the icon, then. You must swear on the holy icon."

"But Zoya, don't you see?"

"This is a fortune," cried Zoya in desperation. "Six thousand rubles! Enough to buy property. We could have an apartment at the front. With rooms. And tenants of our own. We could have a carriage, with servants in livery. We could parade along the Nevsky Prospect, our heads held high. We'd never be afraid to look anyone in the eye. Think of the clothes, the furs, the jewels. What admirers you would have, Lilya! Oh

Lilya, think of it! Gentlemen. Noblemen. And Vera. What a future would lie before her. She could marry a prince, no less. And you, you stupid little fool, you'll throw it all away!"

Lilya backed away, in a simple reflex of self-protection, pulling her arm free of Zoya's grip. She fell onto her bed and murmured, "She lied to me." The same instant she was asleep, dreaming of the policeman's transparent eyelashes.

4

†

The Anonymous Note

T HE ENVELOPE, addressed simply to "Porfiry Petrovich," arrived on the investigator's desk with the morning's first round of mail. Its contents drew Porfiry from his rooms.

"Alexander Grigorevich, did you see who left this for me?"

Seated on his high stool behind the front desk, the chief clerk barely glanced in Porfiry's direction. He was distracted by the thin, agitated woman before him, who was keeping up a stream of tearful and incoherent complaints. Her raving drew to the clerk's face an expression of deep disgust. And yet it seemed he could not tear his eyes away from her. The woman's face was pinched and pale, with bursts of crimson on her cheeks and a deeper red, the color of raw anguish, around her eyes. Fine features had hardened into sharpness, with dark lines etched into a pattern of ravage. Her worn and dirty clothes had once been fashionable and even expensive, many seasons ago. The smell from her was strong and unpleasant. It was hard to estimate her age.

"Alexander Grigorevich," insisted Porfiry, "someone left a note for me."

"What of it?" said Alexander Grigorevich Zamyotov at last, meeting Porfiry's inquiring gaze with something close to a sneer.

More than anything, Porfiry felt a weary disappointment. He had no time for impertinence, and not because he was one to insist on the honor due his rank. "Alexander Grigorevich, you are a man and I am a man, and to that extent we are equals. I will treat you with respect; all I ask is that you do the same."

"I don't know what you mean, Porfiry Petrovich."

"I won't lie to you. I won't look down on you. I won't play games with you."

"I'm very glad to hear it, but I don't understand what bearing all this has."

"This note," said Porfiry, laying the envelope down on the counter. His voice was calm, but he was not smiling. "I ask you again. Did you see who delivered it?"

Zamyotov took a moment to study the envelope. He picked it up and turned it over and then placed it back on the counter. "No," he said, barely suppressing the pleasure he took from this little charade.

Porfiry snatched up the letter and bowed to the disconsolate woman, whose lamentations had not let up throughout his exchange with Zamyotov.

"Porfiry Petrovich," the head clerk gurgled gleefully. "This woman wishes to see *you*."

Porfiry hesitated before answering the clerk directly, without looking at the tearful woman. "I can't. Not now. An urgent matter has arisen. I must talk to Nikodim Fomich. You must tell her to come back tomorrow."

Porfiry braced himself, expecting the pitch and intensity of her plaints to increase at this announcement. But there was an alarming constancy to her behavior. It was as if she hadn't heard his decision, or didn't understand it. Porfiry realized it would be hard to get rid of her.

"Alexander Grigorevich, take a statement from her . . ." Perhaps there was some desire to punish the head clerk in this demand. Porfiry did not discount the possibility.

"A statement? I?"

"Yes, a statement. I will give it my full attention when I have seen Nikodim Fomich. If she wishes to wait, that's up to her, but I advise her to come back tomorrow."

"Porfiry Petrovich, with the greatest respect," began the clerk in a tone that contradicted his words, "what kind of a statement do you expect me to take from"—he gestured toward the woman, her face contorted by suffering—"*that?*"

"You will do your best. I am confident that it will be more than good enough."

I T'S NOT MUCH to go on." Chief Superintendent Nikodim Fomich Maximov dropped the note onto his desk. He leaned back in his chair, both hands behind his head, and looked up at the high ceiling of his office, enjoying the scale of the apartment his position entitled him to. He had learned the habit of ignoring the odd flaws in its grandeur, the peeling paint here and there, the stains of damp beneath the window, and the cracks in the plaster. For a moment his lips pursed ironically, as if an amusing thought had just occurred to him. He was a handsome man and well liked. Both of these attributes were important to him: he had an awareness of his own ability to soothe, merely by his presence. Porfiry wondered if this awareness did not sometimes affect his friend's judgment. Nikodim Fomich sometimes gave the impression of valuing an easy life above all else. "I mean to say, how do we know it's not a hoax?"

"Of course, I agree, it's probably a hoax." Under the new rules, Porfiry had the authority to command the police to pursue any matter he deemed worthy of investigation. But it was a sensitive area. It was only two years ago that control of individual cases had been taken from the police and given over to the newly created office of investigating magistrate. And Porfiry preferred to work with the cooperation of his colleagues in the police bureau, rather than with their resentful subordination. Besides, he knew that the best way to change the chief's mind was to agree with him. "I felt I had a responsibility to show it to you, that is all." Porfiry reached to take the note back.

"But if it's not a hoax?" asked Nikodim Fomich quickly. He leaned forward and grabbed the note before Porfiry could retrieve it. "If there really has been a case of 'Murder in Petrovsky Park'?" The senior police officer read the note with a heavily ironical intonation. He turned the sheet over several times. But those four words were all that was written on its entire surface. Constant rotation did not cause any more to appear. "If it were signed, it would be more credible."

"And there would be someone held responsible if it turned out to be a hoax," suggested Porfiry.

"Well, of course, a hoaxer would never sign it."

"So it must be a hoax," insisted Porfiry brightly, as if the matter were settled.

"Not necessarily," demurred Nikodim Fomich, who suddenly found himself in the position of arguing with his own original point of view. "It could have been written by someone involved in the crime in some way."

Porfiry gave Nikodim Fomich a sudden look of astonishment, as if this idea had never occurred to him. The chief superintendent frowned. Porfiry's play-acting annoyed him. He knew the investigator well enough not to be taken in. "We'll have the local boys look into it," he decided. "If they turn up anything, we'll go to the *prokuror* with it."

"Yes, yes, I agree. There is no need to trouble Yaroslav Nikolaevich until we have something definite to go on. However, if I might make a suggestion?"

Nikodim Fomich nodded for Porfiry to go on.

"Offer one of your men to assist. An officer to oversee the search."

"Isn't that a little proprietorial?"

"The note was delivered here, to this bureau."

"Did you have anyone in mind?" the chief superintendent asked.

"Lieutenant Salytov, perhaps."

"Salytov? Old Gunpowder?" Nikodim Fomich laughed with easy good humor. "At least it will get him out of the bureau for a few hours."

Again Porfiry's expression signified surprise at an idea that couldn't have been further from his mind.

"Don't overdo it, Porfiry Petrovich," said the chief superintendent, delivering the warning with a complicit wink.

S HE'S STILL HERE," called out Zamyotov accusingly, as Porfiry crossed the receiving hall. He indicated the tearful woman with a tilt of his head. "She has asked specifically for the investigating magistrate," Zamyotov confided to his fingernails, with a smirk.

"Have you taken a statement from her, as I requested?" asked Porfiry. His gaze was detached as he studied the woman. He noted that the quality and level of her keening was unchanged. He was not one of those men who are afraid to confront the tears of women, or who shy from the pain of life. But her distress embarrassed him because he felt there was something almost artificial about it. He suspected it of being a ploy, a ploy she had committed herself to and now couldn't get out of. He felt if he could say to her, in a friendly, confiding tone, "You don't have to keep that up, you know," she would instantly become reasonable. He bowed his head slightly in an attempt to engage her flitting glance with a smile. But when her eyes did meet his, for only the briefest moment, he experienced a physical sense of depression, as if something heavy and poisonous had entered his soul. He realized that her distress was not artificial after all. But it was alien to her, an infection that had taken her over. It was this terrible illness that was weeping so mechanically, perhaps even the illness that was insisting on seeing the investigating magistrate.

"Do you want me to read it to you?" said Zamyotov, referring to the statement he was now holding.

"That won't be necessary."

"I'm perfectly willing to."

"I appreciate your willingness. However, I will read it myself."
Porfiry took the statement:

> I am guilty. We are all guilty. But I am the most guilty of all. We are
> all guilty of every crime. There is no crime we are not capable of.
> There is no crime that we have not dreamed of committing. Only she
> was innocent. Only she was without sin. The sin was not hers. It was
> mine. I am guilty. I, Yekaterina Romanovna Lebedyeva, am guilty of
> her sin. I am guilty of it all. I am guilty of everything . . .

The statement continued in this vein for several more lines.

"I see," said Porfiry, when he had finished reading it. "Madam, will you
come with me?" And with that he led her into his chambers.

S O THEN, what shall we do with you?" began Porfiry, his tone kindly
and indulgent. "Shall we lock you up, Yekaterina Romanovna?"

The woman nodded briskly. Tears streamed from her eyes, transparent
trails from her snuffling nose. There was no doubting her sincerity. Porfiry opened a drawer in his desk and took out a clean handkerchief; he
kept a supply on hand for such occasions. He held it out to her. She repaid
him with a look that suggested he was the one who was raving. Eventually
she took it, though she could not be encouraged to wipe her face. Ignoring Porfiry's mime to that effect, she held the handkerchief tightly balled
in her palm.

"But on what charge, Yekaterina Romanovna? We must have a charge
to enter in the great recording book."

The woman let out a half-articulate moan, just recognizable as "Guilty!"

"Yes, but of what? You understand my predicament?" Porfiry held his
arms open across the desk as if petitioning her for help. "I have an idea,"
he said suddenly. "I shall suggest some crimes to you, and all you have to
do is nod when I get to yours. We shall make a game of it. Can you do
that, Yekaterina Romanovna?"

Porfiry smiled uncertainly at her answering nod. He could not be sure she understood him.

"Let's start at the top, I think," said Porfiry brightly. "Oh, and please don't take this the wrong way. I am not myself accusing you of anything, you understand. I am merely trying to help you make your statement a little more—how shall we say—*precise?* This is very strange, I will admit. Not the usual procedure at all but . . . there is nothing else for it, I think. So this crime, the crime of which you are guilty, is it, madam, perhaps"—and his eyes twinkled with pleasure as if he really were playing a parlor game—"murder?"

Yekaterina Romanovna let out a gasp of confirmation: "Yessss!" For the first time there was a change in the manifestation of her behavior. "Yes, yes, that's it, murder." She sobbed, her head quivering as if on a spring.

"Murder, I see. Very good. Or rather, it is not very good. But it is good in the sense that we are getting somewhere. And at least I am saved from the labor of having to go through a whole catalog of crimes and misdemeanors. Murder, you say. May I ask you—this is the form these inquiries take, you understand—may I ask you, whom did you murder?"

Again there was a development in her behavior. Her head stopped shaking, and she held his gaze steadily. "My daughter."

Porfiry sat up. The excitement he felt was no longer that of a game. "This is a very serious charge to make against yourself, madam. You do understand that, don't you? How did you kill her?"

The woman shook her head in violent denial. Her teeth were clenched, as if something inside her was determined to prevent her from saying more. Through those clenched teeth she hissed: "I refused to believe her." The effort of making this admission evidently exhausted her. She fell back into her chair.

"I meant rather, by what means, with what weapon shall we say, did you kill her? That is usually the way with murder. It is essentially a violent crime. There is usually some sort of attack. I would include poison as a weapon here. Perhaps you poisoned her?"

From her sunken position in the seat, she let out a high-pitched, cracking groan. "I accused her."

"Of what did you accuse her?"

The woman stirred and sat up a little. "I refused to believe in her innocence. But I knew. I *knew*!"

"You're doing very well, Yekaterina Romanovna. But I need to understand more. If you could take me through what actually happened, the circumstances of your daughter's death."

"Oh, she is not dead!" cried Yekaterina Romanovna pleadingly. Her eyes beseeched him.

"Then I do not see how you can have murdered her if she is not dead," answered Porfiry. He said the words slowly, trying to fathom the truth behind the woman's contradictory statements.

"I murdered her." She said this flatly, giving it an irrefutable force.

"Please help me. I need to understand." A new idea came to Porfiry. "What is your daughter's name?"

"We have no daughter." She spoke imperiously, as if announcing a sentence. Her face was set in a grim mask.

"You once had a daughter but no longer. Something you have done has brought about this circumstance."

"He cast her out."

"He?"

"Lebedyev."

"Your husband?"

She closed her eyes and nodded once.

"And you?" pressed Porfiry.

Yekaterina Romanovna opened her eyes and stared straight through Porfiry. Her face became agitated. It was as if she were watching a scene of intense and painful interest to her. "I said nothing," she said at last, in a whisper. She closed her eyes again.

"And it is because you said nothing, because you didn't intervene—it is because of this you are plagued by feelings of guilt."

"She was blameless."

"Do you know what has become of your daughter?"

Yekaterina Romanovna shook her head, still with her eyes closed.

"Would you like me to help you find out?"

She opened her eyes, this time looking directly at Porfiry. Anguish twisted her face into ugliness. A look of hatred, Porfiry felt, though who the object of her hatred was, he could not say. "I have no daughter!" she shrieked.

"Madam, I think it is a priest and not a policeman that you need."

There was suddenly a knock at the door. Zamyotov peered in.

"I beg your pardon, Porfiry Petrovich," began the chief clerk. Porfiry nodded for him to continue. "A *gentleman*"—Zamyotov broke off, giving the word ironic emphasis—"who professes to be this lady's husband wishes to be admitted." He concluded the message with his customary smirk.

"Please show him in," said Porfiry, glancing at Yekaterina Romanovna, who had just resumed her plaintive wailing. It suddenly occurred to him that her tears, and the noises that accompanied them, were a source of comfort to her, perhaps her only one.

Zamyotov bowed and backed out. The man who strode into the room now possessed the labored dignity that is common to a certain category of drunks. He drew himself upright and even beyond upright, leaning slightly backward. His movements were stilted, made with great effort and deliberation. An aroma of vodka preceded him. His florid face and the slight tremble that was perceptible in his features suggested that he was a habitual drunk. Stiff wisps of gray hair stood up from his balding head, which he held proudly erect. His eyelids fluttered gracefully, and he smiled in a show of politesse, revealing a gap where his upper incisors should have been. Porfiry was aware of the strain all this affected honor placed on the man.

The newcomer was wearing an old black frock coat with gaping seams and missing buttons. He bowed vaguely in Porfiry's direction, though his moist eyes were evasive.

"Your honor, allow me the privilege of introducing myself. I am Titular Councilor Ivan Filomonovich Lebedyev. Your honor," he repeated, "allow me the honor—ah!" He broke off disconsolately. He bowed momentarily and clenched his face into a pained rictus. He recovered with a flashing smile, marred only by the lack of teeth. "Too many honors! Your honor, what can I do?"

"You may sit down if you wish, sir."

"No sir, I do not wish." This was said with quick, haughty defiance, as if he were rebutting a slur against his character.

"How may I help you, Ivan Filomonovich?" asked Porfiry gently.

"You will allow me to address my wife?"

"Of course."

"Yekaterina Romanovna, come home with me."

Without ceasing her lament, Yekaterina Romanovna rose obediently from her seat and crossed to her husband. He signaled his approval with a delayed nod and turned to Porfiry seeking release.

"There is just one thing, sir," said Porfiry, with an air of reluctance. "Something your wife said. About your daughter."

"My wife is ill, sir. You may have noticed. She is not"—he paused and bowed and grimaced, as he had done before—"herself." He smiled again.

"But your daughter is quite well, I trust?"

"We have no daughter, your honor." Lebedyev bowed with an air of finality, then began leading his wife out.

Porfiry rose and followed them. In the receiving hall, he caught Zamyotov's eager eye as he passed him.

"It seems she has put on a similar performance in every police bureau in Petersburg," the chief clerk informed him.

"And the story of the daughter?" asked Porfiry.

"It has been looked into. There is nothing in it. I talked to Rogozhin, who transferred here from the Central District. He knows all about it. It is all a fantasy of the woman's disordered brain."

Porfiry watched the couple cross the hall toward the exit. Lebedyev had his arm around his wife's shoulder. It struck Porfiry that the gesture was not so much to protect her as to close her off from further interest and inquiry.

. . .

L IEUTENANT SALYTOV STOOD at the eastern end of Petrovsky Island, his back to the Tuchkov Bridge. It felt like the lowest point of
the city; he had a sense of Petersburg rising up behind him as if it would
bear down and crush him. A feeling of oppression was never far away
from Salytov. Ptitsyn, the young *polizyeisky* who had been allocated to
him, stood about twenty *sazheni* to his right, within sight, awaiting the
signal. Salytov looked toward the frozen, snow-covered park and was
overcome by a sudden blank hopelessness. His characteristic defense
against such intolerable emotions was rage, and he gave in to it now.

They had sent him on a fool's errand. They! There was no "they"
about it. He well knew who was behind this. Porfiry Petrovich. And what
a position he had been put in when he had announced himself and his mission at the Chestaya Street police station in the Petersburgsky District.
With what contempt they had greeted him! No wonder. Wouldn't he have
reacted in a similar way if an officer from another district had turned up
in his bureau, making similar demands, based on as little evidence?

The corporal on duty had raised his bushy gray eyebrows in an expression of mock alarm. Salytov recognized him as one of those officers of
long-standing low rank, in whom a lack of ambition had instilled the
habit of sarcasm and the vice of sloth. The man was not, however, devoid
of envy, which he directed against all those who had the power to control
his actions and curtail his ease. Superior officers, in other words, particularly those who came from other bureaus making demands. He vented his
envy by being as obstructive as possible, without risking open insubordination. "A report of murder, you say?" He had narrowed his eyes, as if
struggling to understand. Feigning stupidity was evidently one of his favorite techniques. "What kind of a report?"

"A tip-off," Salytov had spat. He had realized what he was up against,
yet still could not prevent himself from rising to the bait.

"From a reliable source, I take it?"

Salytov could have struck the fellow for that. How dare he question him, Salytov, and in that tone! Of course, what galled Salytov was the knowledge that the source was far from reliable. He regarded the corporal with hatred. "The top brass are taking it seriously. They want me to take some of your men and conduct a thorough search." It was a great strain on Salytov's patience to have to explain all this.

"We can't spare men to go gallivanting off in the park."

"You must have some men available."

"But if we are to commit resources, we must know on what basis. You must share your information with us. Besides, I will have to talk to my chief. And there is the usual paperwork."

It was ridiculous, the whole thing was ridiculous. To be put in such a position! To be made to wait! And after all that waiting to be given Ptitsyn, a mere boy!

Salytov scowled at the youth, who looked back with an expression of good-natured expectancy that was too much to bear.

"What are you waiting for, you fool?" shouted Salytov. Ptitsyn placidly waved one gloved hand, and both men began walking.

SIR, LOOK! Lieutenant Salytov, sir!"

"Yes, I see it."

The two of them broke into a high-stepping run through the deep snow, converging toward the body that was hanging from the giant bow of the bent tree.

"Is this what we are looking for, sir?" gasped Ptitsyn, breathless and rosy-cheeked, as excited as a schoolboy.

Salytov did not answer. The note he had been shown had spoken of murder, not suicide.

"Is he dead, sir?"

"Of course he's dead, idiot." There was ice in the man's beard, snow on his cap and shoulders.

"Shall we get him down?"

"No! Leave him there, do you hear? Don't touch him! Don't touch a thing."

"Who is he, sir?"

Again Salytov ignored the question.

"I've never seen a dead one before, sir." Ptitsyn looked wonderingly up into the staring eyes.

Noticing a bulge in the corpse's greatcoat, Salytov stepped up and teased it open. "So. It seems there is murder here after all," he commented on seeing the bloody axe tucked in the man's belt.

"Sir," said Ptitsyn, a frown of confusion giving his voice a querulous note. "How did he do it?"

"What are you talking about, boy?"

"I mean, how did he hang himself? You see the rope is tied around the trunk of the tree, sir. I can see how he could have thrown the rope around the tree, tied a loop, and pulled it tight. But how did he string himself up?"

There was something in what the boy said. Salytov looked up into the tree, at the point where the rope was tethered to the trunk, just below a small vertical nick in the bark. He then examined the flimsy birch branches. His eye was caught by a slip of grayish paper snagged on a twig. He beckoned Ptitsyn over.

"What is it, sir?"

"I want you to lift me onto your shoulders."

"I beg your pardon, sir?"

"Get down and lift me on your shoulders."

Ptitsyn looked momentarily bewildered, then lowered himself to a crouch so that Salytov could straddle his shoulders.

"Up!"

Ptitsyn rose shakily, crying out under the strain. As Salytov reached up to grab the slip of paper, Ptitsyn's center of gravity was thrown. It seemed for a moment as though they would fall. But by a heroic readjustment of his stance, Ptitsyn was able to right himself. Making no allowances,

Salytov cursed and kicked the man beneath him with his heels as if he were spurring a horse. "Get closer to the tree, damn you!"

Ptitsyn bellowed his response and lurched a step higher up the incline. Salytov was able to grasp his prize.

"Down!"

Ptitsyn sank groaning to his knees, losing his cap and receiving in return a face full of snow as Salytov dismounted over his head. "What have you found, sir?" he asked, when he had retrieved his cap and staggered back to his feet.

Salytov examined the paper with an expression of angry triumph. "Ha! This will show him!"

"Is it a clue, sir?"

Salytov folded his wallet over the slip of paper and scanned the ground eagerly. He noticed a mound of snow of suspiciously regular shape some way from the tree.

"There," Salytov pointed.

"Could he have jumped from that, sir? Is that what you're thinking?" asked Ptitsyn.

"What?" snapped Salytov.

"I only mean, sir—"

"I don't give a damn what you mean, you imbecile. I commanded you to investigate that mound in the snow. Are you refusing to obey my order?"

"No, sir. Of course not, sir," said Ptitsyn, stung by Salytov's severity. But he was determined to prove himself worthy of the stern officer's approval. He did not waste time wondering how the word *there* could be interpreted as a formal command. He lunged in the direction Salytov was still pointing.

Ptitsyn crouched by the mound, which seemed to have a precisely rectangular outline beneath the soft, rounded surface of the snow. He scooped away a few handfuls of the freshest fall from one side, revealing patches of brown in a sheer, smooth surface. "I think it's some kind of suitcase," he said, as he continued to excavate. "It appears to be open. There's—" Ptitsyn broke off. His gloved fingers groped into the snow and lifted what turned out to be an envelope, lilac in color. So delighted was he with this haul as he handed it to the lieutenant that he failed to notice what it had uncovered. But as Ptitsyn looked keenly into the lieutenant's face, he noticed that it had suddenly become unusually pale, as if the heat of his temper had been siphoned from him. There was no ferocity there. Following Salytov's eye line toward the spot he was staring at, Ptitsyn gasped to see the features of a man in the snow. "Did you ever see anything like this, sir?" he whispered, his eyes wide open in shocked wonder.

When Salytov answered, his voice was soft and awed. "Go back to Chestaya Street. Take a *drozhki*. Tell them what we have found."

"Yes, sir."

"I will stay here to secure the scene. You will return with more men. We will need a wagon."

"Yes, sir."

"Go then!" Salytov clapped his hands once to send the young policeman running. He watched Ptitsyn's swaying back recede as he took out his wallet once more and placed the lilac envelope inside.

5

The *Prokuror*

THREE TRESTLE TABLES had been set up in the large shed that the Haymarket District Police Bureau used to store firefighting engines. The building was next to the department's stables in Malaya Meshchanskaya Street, around the corner from the bureau in Stolyarny Lane. The wide double doors were fastened open, allowing the day's brutal light to flood the tables and their contents. On the first table were spread the various items that Salytov had recovered from Petrovsky Park. The other two held the bodies.

The bulking shapes of the fire equipment—the pumping engines, coiled hoses, and water-carrying wagons—lurked in the shadows at the edge of the hangar. With less reticence, six men stood around the tables. In addition to Porfiry Petrovich and Nikodim Fomich, present was Yaroslav Nikolaevich Liputin, the *prokuror*. In any criminal prosecution, it was his responsibility to decide if a crime had been committed and to draw up the indictment once a suspect had been arrested, as well as to prosecute the case through the courts. According to procedure, he was

Porfiry's superior, a relationship that was emphasized by Liputin's tower-
ing height. It was impossible to argue with his appearance, dressed and
groomed as he was with such consideration. Every hair, every hem, every
button knew its place in the ordainment of his presence. Also in attendance were the two official witnesses required by the new laws, in this case
Major General Volokonsky and Actual State Councilor Yepanchin; retired gentlemen, dressed now, naturally, each in the uniform of his rank.
A certain querulous confusion was evident on the face of the major general. Actual State Councilor Yepanchin hid his emotions behind a mask of
dignity. Both were quick to defer to Liputin. Finally, Porfiry had invited
Salytov, out of courtesy, given his role in discovering the bodies.

The heat from a brazier at the rear of the shed barely reached them.

"So we are waiting for?" demanded Liputin imperiously.

"The physician, your excellency," explained Porfiry.

"Physician? I don't think we need a physician to tell us what has happened here, Porfiry Petrovich."

"With respect, your excellency."

"One corpse with his head hacked in, the other hanging by the neck
with a bloody axe about his person. Really. You are not required to call a
physician, you know. Under the new laws, an autopsy is not demanded in
every case. You may use your discretion. You are able to look at the bodies yourself and draw certain conclusions. There is no need to waste our
time like this. What need do you have to involve the office of the *prokuror*?"
Liputin spoke as if this were something separate from himself. "Yes, there
has been a crime, two crimes, in fact. One murder, the other suicide. The
man wanted for both lies dead on a trestle table. The case is closed."

"Indeed, *prokuror*. But it is because I have examined the bodies—and
the area in Petrovsky Park where they were found—that I feel it is necessary to call in a physician."

Liputin's eyes narrowed minutely, almost imperceptibly.

"This flask," said Porfiry, lifting a pewter flask from the table of objects, "which Lieutenant Salytov recovered from one of the pockets of the
hanging man." Porfiry unstopped the flask and held it out to Liputin.

"Vodka," confirmed the *prokuror*, inhaling.

"Yes. And it's full. I can imagine a man intent on such deeds steeling himself with alcohol. Especially as he has gone to the trouble of preparing this flask. But to take the vodka along and not drink it?"

"You think the vodka is significant?" asked Nikodim Fomich.

"In cases like this, everything is significant."

"Perhaps it was not a question of steeling himself," objected Salytov, with some heat. "Perhaps he killed the dwarf in a fit of rage. And hanged himself in a fit of remorse. Perhaps too he was in the habit of carrying a flask of vodka about with him wherever he went. In the turmoil of the moment it was forgotten."

"It is an interesting theory," commented Porfiry. "And I am grateful to you for sharing it with us."

"But you do not hold with it?" asked Liputin.

"Look at his coat." Porfiry nodded toward the larger body. "What do you notice?"

No one risked an answer.

"Well, let me ask this of Lieutenant Salytov. Did you notice anything on the back of the coat when you cut him down?"

"Yes, there were some black marks," said Salytov. "Oil, I think."

"Yes. Oily marks on the back of his greatcoat. But on the front?"

"No oily marks," ventured Nikodim Fomich.

"It is not the absence of oily marks that puzzles me. Rather—"

"No blood!" cried Salytov.

"Quite. The condition of the front of the coat leads me to believe that even if he is the murderer, he did not kill the dwarf immediately before killing himself. At least not with the axe. The absence of blood on the old soldier's greatcoat is indeed puzzling, if we are to accept the interpretation of the evidence that the scene appears intent on forcing upon us."

"Of course he did not kill the dwarf immediately before killing himself. He took the body there in that suitcase," insisted Liputin. "The body of the dwarf was found in the suitcase, was it not?" He pointed to the moisture-stained suitcase. It lay closed on the table. Its lid bore a single large scratch across the middle.

"Yes, that's correct. And what you are suggesting is quite possibly true. It is equally possible, you must admit, that someone else carried the suitcase there. And if that is possible, it is also possible that someone else killed the dwarf."

"But why should *he* have killed himself?" asked Liputin, with an irritated nod toward the big corpse.

"That is indeed the crucial question," agreed Porfiry. He turned back to the table of objects, picking up the small grayish slip of paper that Salytov had retrieved from the branches of the birch tree. "Perhaps this pawnbroker's ticket can lead us to the answer."

"You are overlooking one important aspect of the case, however," said Liputin abruptly.

Porfiry looked up with a questioning glance.

"The self-evident inferior rank of the individuals concerned. This one is a student of some kind, I would say. Leaving aside his deformity—"

"Which of course has no bearing on the thoroughness with which the case will be investigated," completed Porfiry.

"You know, Porfiry Petrovich, that it is possible to be too zealous as an investigator. Police resources are not infinitely expendable. There are such things as hopeless cases. I mean to say, who are these people?"

"Yes. We must establish their identities. That is the first step to establishing the truth of what happened."

"Ah yes, the truth," said Liputin wearily, consulting his pocket watch. "Where is this physician of yours?"

"He will be here shortly, I am sure."

"Who is it to be?"

"Dr. Pervoyedov, of the Obukhovsky Hospital. He has served us in this capacity before. His work has always been satisfactory."

"But *this* is not good enough," commented Liputin sharply, with a glance to the official witnesses. "These gentlemen have consented to give up their time for the express purpose of witnessing this . . . procedure."

There were assenting echoes from the official witnesses.

"I am sure they are pleased to be fulfilling their civic duty."

"What about the physician's duty? You know that as investigating magistrate you have the authority to fine . . ."

At that moment, to Porfiry's relief, a red-faced young man hurried into the shed pushing a two-wheeled trolley on which a large tin trunk was up-ended. The newcomer was hatless, his long hair sticking out in unruly clumps. He was dressed in an old overcoat with a grubby plaid pattern. In many ways his disheveled and almost shabby appearance was the exact opposite of Liputin's. "Apologies, apologies, gentlemen," cried Dr. Pervoyedov. "I was delayed by syphilis. Five new cases. Five!"

Liputin pocketed his watch. His expression betrayed nothing. "That is nothing to us. You understand, I trust, your duties under the law."

"Of course, your excellency. Indubitably. In-*du*-bi-ta-bly!" The doctor settled the trolley and then cautiously rolled the trunk off so that it landed square on the ground. Despite his care, there was an alarming jangle of metal and glass. Dr. Pervoyedov hurried to unlock the trunk and open the lid. He scanned the contents urgently. "No harm done. No harm done. The jars of formaldehyde are intact. It was the formaldehyde I was worried about."

"You would achieve greater punctuality, I believe, were you able to curtail your habit of repetition," commented Liputin. "It is that, I warrant, that delays you, more than the inconvenience of treating the victims of disease."

"Ah! How very witty, your excellency. How very—"

Liputin cut in: "So our investigator, the esteemed Porfiry Petrovich, has deemed it necessary to summon you here to conduct an autopsy on these poor unfortunate wretches."

"Yes, of course, of course." Dr. Pervoyedov nodded anxiously, his face drawn and tense.

"He says of course! There is no of course about it!" Liputin turned to the official witnesses. "What say you, gentlemen? Shall we proceed with this farce?"

"Is it really necessary?" asked Major General Volokonsky.

"I myself do not see what purpose it would serve," added Actual State Councilor Yepanchin.

"But seeing as we are all here," pleaded Nikodim Fomich. "And the good doctor has brought his own equipment—"

"Well, yes, of course," said Dr. Pervoyedov. "If I did not bring my equipment, I would have nothing with which to conduct the autopsy. You might think of that, Porfiry Petrovich, next time you summon me to your service."

"The law does not require the investigating magistrate's office to equip the forensic physician," said Liputin automatically.

"But it might be more convenient if the investigating magistrate were to allow for the examination to be conducted at a hospital or clinic, where such equipment as I bring might naturally be found." The doctor smiled as he pressed his point.

"More convenient for you, no doubt," answered Liputin coldly. "Your convenience is not the main issue here."

"I shall bear your suggestion in mind in the future," said Porfiry, with a respectful bow for Dr. Pervoyedov.

"There is no need," insisted Liputin brusquely. "And I for one see no logic in the argument that just because the doctor has gone to the trouble of bringing his tools, we must allow him to use them. It remains a fruitless exercise, even with the doctor's presence."

"There is one detail I would ask you to consider," put in Porfiry, his eyelids fluttering to a close. "The tree from which this old soldier was cut down bore in its trunk a singular vertical nick . . ."

"Yes, I noticed that," said Salytov thoughtfully.

". . . consistent in size with the blow of an axe blade."

"So?" challenged Liputin.

"Who put it there?"

"What does it matter? What relevance does it have?"

"This nick was a little higher than the point at which his noose was tethered."

"Why are you bothering us with this nick, Porfiry Petrovich? I don't want to hear about this nick of yours."

"It was too high for the hanged man himself to have reached, and the dwarf certainly could not have stretched so high."

"The axe was thrown," suggested Liputin confidently. With rather less confidence, he added: "And then fell out."

"Which axe? The axe that was used to kill the dwarf? But there were no marks of blood in the nick. And the blade shows no signs of having recently made a cut. You would expect the blood to be wiped away at the tip. Unless, of course, the nick in the tree was made before the dwarf was murdered. But we have already established that the dwarf can't have been murdered at the place where the bodies were found. So it seems that another axe must have made the nick in the tree. Or the same axe made the nick, but before the wound in the dwarf's head was inflicted."

"But I repeat, what has the nick in the tree got to do with anything? It may be a coincidence. Have you considered that?"

"Certainly. It is a strange coincidence, however. I could find no other such marks in any of the other trees I examined in the area. One must at least accept the possibility that the nick is significant."

"I don't have to accept any such possibility. Porfiry Petrovich, you really are trying my patience. It is enough that I have to contest such irrelevances in the new courts. Now you are playing the part of defense counsel to a dead man."

"It is significant because it raises the question of a third party," persisted Porfiry.

"The nick could have been made at any time."

"It is a fresh incision. And even if it is not connected to the case, there is still the question, who would make it, and for what purpose?"

"If it is not connected to the case, I don't care."

"It only makes sense if it is connected to the case."

"But how? How does it make sense?"

"I don't know yet," admitted Porfiry. "But I shall."

"What questions do you wish the forensic examination to answer?" asked Dr. Pervoyedov suddenly.

Liputin let out a sigh of defeat.

"What I am interested in knowing most of all," said Porfiry, "is the cause of death in each case."

"Preposterous!" exclaimed the *prokuror*.

The doctor nodded tersely and removed his overcoat, which he handed to the actual state councilor. The gentleman received it with dumb outrage and threw it onto the floor. But Dr. Pervoyedov had already turned to the tin trunk, from which he took out a rubber apron.

"One body with the noose still around its neck! The other with a hole the size of an axe blade in its skull!" cried Liputin.

Dr. Pervoyedov nodded tersely, a scalpel in one hand now. He seemed to hold the blade toward the *prokuror* with some intent. "Shall we begin with this fellow?" he said. And although he was standing over the larger corpse, the feeling that he meant Liputin was unanimous.

L OOK AT THE EYES," said Dr. Pervoyedov.
"What about them?" asked Porfiry.

"No blood," said the doctor. "In cases of strangulation, it is normal for the eyes to fill with blood."

The rope was embedded in the soft flesh of the throat. Dr. Pervoyedov severed it with a scalpel, stroking the blade across its cords delicately, careful not to nick the skin. Then he teased it out with a pair of elongated tongs.

"Here, this is interesting," he said. "This *is* interesting!" He lifted up the beard for them to see.

His audience closed in, their heads almost touching above the corpse. They frowned over the deep furrow that the rope had left in the neck, then came up for air. The doctor found himself surrounded by blank faces.

"One moment. This will show you more clearly." He took a razor from his trunk and shaved away the beard in one place.

"Still I see nothing," said Liputin with some impatience.

"That is the point, your excellency," said Porfiry. "I think," he added, looking to Dr. Pervoyedov for confirmation.

"Precisely. Precisely," agreed the doctor.

"Will you kindly stop talking in riddles," demanded Liputin.

"No bruising," murmured Salytov, with sudden realization.

Dr. Pervoyedov nodded energetically.

"Well done, Ilya Petrovich," said Porfiry. Despite himself, Lieutenant Salytov experienced a small surge of pleasure at the praise. But immediately afterward he was annoyed with himself and hated Porfiry even more.

"Which means?" asked the *prokuror* uneasily.

"Which *suggests*," corrected Porfiry, "that he was already dead when he was suspended from the tree."

"In a live subject, bruising is caused by blood being pumped to the damaged area of the epidermis. One does see marks, analogous to bruising, occurring in corpses post-mortem. But this is simply where the blood settles as the corpse lies on the ground." As he spoke, Dr. Pervoyedov was cutting away the man's clothes with a pair of tailor's shears, splitting the cylinders of his sleeves and trouser legs, sectioning the panels covering the torso. "Otherwise, it is fair to say that dead men do not bruise." At last the corpse was lying naked on a bed of tatters.

They all saw it, the purple line around the middle of the massive belly.

"And yet here there is bruising," remarked Dr. Pervoyedov thoughtfully, pausing to record his observations in a small notebook.

"What do you make of that?" demanded Liputin.

"Nothing. As yet," answered the doctor. "For the moment, I merely observe." He touched the skin of the corpse in several places with his fingertips. This provoked an expression of distaste from the major general. The actual state councilor seemed rather surprised by it. "If one of you gentlemen could . . ." Dr. Pervoyedov mimed a pulling action as he cast a look of appeal in their direction. Neither picked up his hint. "I need to turn the body over," he explained. "I must look at the back too."

The expressions of the official witnesses turned to horror.

"Lieutenant Salytov," directed Nikodim Fomich. "Kindly assist the doctor."

"Allow me to lend a hand too," offered Porfiry. He recognized a need to touch the skin, a need to understand something through that touch. The coldness of it he expected. But its soft, yielding compliance startled him.

Between them they hauled the naked corpse onto its front. The hirsute back showed no obvious marks.

"Interesting," remarked the physician. "Very interesting."

"What now?" snapped Liputin impatiently.

"Well, as you can see, the welt does not continue around the back."

"And what conclusion do you draw from *that?*"

"It is too early. Too early, sir. My conclusions, if I have any, will be in my report. You will have that soon enough." Dr. Pervoyedov sought Porfiry's eyes beseechingly. After a long pause he added, "Your excellency."

Porfiry, Salytov, and the doctor turned the corpse back over.

Dr. Pervoyedov picked up the scalpel again and began the first incision, touching the blade to a point on the right shoulder. In the silence, Porfiry was very aware of his own breathing and of his heart pumping. He wondered if it was the same for the other men, for Liputin even. He wanted to look at Liputin. He wanted to say to him, *Are you not glad to be alive?* But he continued to watch the procedure that Dr. Pervoyedov was carrying out. The doctor drew the scalpel diagonally down to the middle of the sternum. He repeated the procedure from the other shoulder and then cut down the length of the torso, deviating around the umbilicus and completing the Y-shaped incision when he reached the dead man's groin. It left a calm wound, dark and glossy but strangely bloodless. Porfiry frowned thoughtfully and cast an inquiring glance at the wound on the head of the other corpse.

He took out a cigarette and lit it, then looked back as Dr. Pervoyedov began to peel the skin away.

6

A Theatrical Type

PORFIRY'S CHEEKS GLOWED pink from the icy air. He felt it only on his face. The rest of him was hot, swaddled in mink. His ankle-length *shuba* exaggerated the portliness of his physique, giving him the appearance of a large fur bell. The oversize *ushanka* on his head seemed to compress his form even more. The thoroughfares and open spaces of St. Petersburg were quiet and white. The buildings, both the grand stone edifices and the jerry-built wooden tenements squeezed between them, struck him as out of place. Imposed in a snowy vastness that was indifferent to them, they appeared fragile and dreamlike, no matter what arrogance or energy their construction implied.

Porfiry entered the great market of Apraxin Arcade from Sadovaya Street, near its corner with Apraxin Lane. Passing below the icon of Saint Nicholas that was suspended over the narrow wooden gate, he stepped into a dark, bustling universe. The music of a barrel organ clashed with the songs of woodworkers at their lathes and the cries of the itinerant vendors and the stallholders. Overhead, pigeons swooped with clattering wings and settled next to placid, mice-intent cats. Wooden bridges, hung with icons, spanned the passageways between the clustered booths, linking the upper stories. The areas of the market, and the trades that were conducted within them, were marked by the smells through which he wandered. The strongest aromas came as he passed the bakeries, the spice and incense sellers, the tea and tobacco traders. Then he felt the fainter but no less enticing breaths of the honey stalls and the chandlers. The fermenting complexity of the preserved fruit merchants tempted him to linger, while the dusty cough and pungent smack of the chalk and pitch dealers, their shops decorated outside with balalaikas, hurried him on. Befuddled now, he passed the harness makers, the cobblers, the metalworkers, and the jewelers. Here and there these distinct zones were complicated by the passing waft of a pastry seller, his wares balanced on his head, or by the alcoholic miasma from a tavern, or by the whiff of sanctity from the chapel next to it.

In the farthest corner, so that he had to cross the extent of the market to reach it, was the flea market, which had its own atmosphere of fustiness and must. And in the farthest corner of the flea market was Lyamshin's Pawnbroker's.

A querulous bell announced his entry. From the gloom of the shop's interior came the mingled smells of mothballs and unwashed bodies. A crowd of objects pressed in on Porfiry. He ducked the musical instruments and weaponry hanging from the ceiling. His eye was drawn equally by the precious and the worthless, the jewelry locked behind glass, the shelves of chipped and cracked pots. There were rails of secondhand clothes, from luxuriant furs to threadbare petticoats. Some men had even pawned their shirtfronts and collars. He dipped his fingers into barrels of shoes and crates of spectacles and stroked the snuffboxes and thimbles laid out on trays. It was as if these objects, left to their own devices, demonstrated some natural law of affinity, the magnetism of the abandoned. And of course, there was the fact that everything in the shop had once been part of someone's life; behind each object, however mundane in itself, was a story of despair and even tragedy.

As soon as he entered, Porfiry was aware of a booming male voice. There was something artificial about this voice and excited too: an edge of premeditated hilarity. Porfiry identified the speaker immediately, a middle-aged man with a massive paunch, his eyes shrunk by the ballooning of his ruddy-complexioned face. The man's gesticulations drew the attention as much as the delivery of his words. His face seemed almost paralyzed into joviality, and it seemed he felt the need to compensate by making the rest of his substantial body as expressive as possible. Porfiry realized the man was reciting a speech from a play, for the benefit of the pawnbroker. The actor, for Porfiry had him down as a professional of the boards, kept his eyes cast down. He was capable of achieving a curious effect in his vocal performance. The speech had the character of a surly mumble, yet every word was clearly enunciated. More than that, his voice filled the shop. The pawnbroker, a skeletally thin individual who evidently believed it bad taste to appear too prosperous or well fed before his customers, waited for the recital to finish with his head on one side, a strained smile frozen on his features. His hands, in fingerless gloves, rested on a seven-stringed gypsy guitar that lay on the counter in front of him.

At last the speech came to its end with "Holy God, what I wouldn't do for a bowl of cabbage soup! I'm so hungry I could eat a carthorse. Whoops—someone coming, must be his lordship."

Porfiry clapped his hands four or five times and called, "Bravo!" The pawnbroker, however, merely grimaced and turned the guitar over.

"Osip's monologue, from *The Government Inspector*," said Porfiry. The theatrical type acknowledged the applause with a bow, his face gratified and friendly. There was a waft of vodka about him.

"I played the part in 'fifty-six, in the revival at the original Mariinsky Theater. You are an aficionado of the dramatic arts?"

"I am an admirer of Gogol."

"Twenty rubles," growled the pawnbroker, setting the guitar resonating as he put it down sharply.

"Twenty! You thief! You bloodsucker! You Jew! It cost me ten times that. It belonged to Sarenko."

"Twenty rubles."

"The speech alone was worth twenty rubles."

"I can't sell the speech. If you can prove it belonged to Sarenko, I'll give you twenty-five."

"You have my word."

"Twenty-two."

"Twenty-two! The man has a heart of stone," cried the actor, appealing to Porfiry.

"You know how it works," said the pawnbroker. "I can only give you what I think I'll get for it."

"You'll get more than twenty-two for this. One hundred at least."

"Twenty-two. Take it or leave it."

"Very well. Be warned. He will suck the blood from you," said the actor in a loud aside to Porfiry. The actor took his money and withdrew a step but did not leave. It was as though he were waiting for something. Porfiry was aware of his presence behind him as he handed the ticket to the pawnbroker.

The gaunt face across the counter regarded him suspiciously. "You have the money?"

Porfiry laid down a red ten-ruble note. He looked over his shoulder to see the actor watching him intently. The other man gave a reflex smile and made his face bland. The pawnbroker came back with a bundle of books, tied together with string.

"You're not Virginsky," said the pawnbroker.

"Could you cut the string for me, please? I wish to examine the books more closely."

"You're not Virginsky," repeated the pawnbroker.

"Who is Virginsky?"

"The man who pawned these books."

"Does it matter? I'm paying his debt. I have the money to redeem the pledge on his behalf. Please cut the string."

The pawnbroker hesitated, sucking in even farther the cheeks of his death's-head face. All his vitality was concentrated in his eyes, which were locked on Porfiry as he slipped a penknife under the string.

The first four books were Russian translations of, in turn, Moleschott's *The Cycle of Life*, Büchner's *Force and Matter*, Vogt's *Superstition and Science*, and Dühring's *Natural Dialectics*. The fifth book, in maroon cloth binding, bore the title *One Thousand and One Maidenheads*.

"Ah," came the voice at Porfiry's shoulder as he investigated this last one, "I see you are an acolyte of Priapos." Porfiry closed the book hurriedly. He gave the actor a stern, questioning glance. "Priapos," his new friend explained, "my favorite publishing house." Porfiry saw that this was the name of the book's imprint. "There is nothing quite like the thrill of cutting the pages of the latest Priapos. If ever, my friend, you feel the need of another's hand to guide your blade, I have much experience in such mutually advantageous manipulations."

"Sir, I believe you are laboring under a misapprehension."

"What's wrong with two gentlemen enjoying a gentlemanly pursuit together? It is the same as if we were to share a bottle of fine wine or, as the redskins do, a pipe. But why stop at breaching virgin paper when there is virgin flesh to be sundered? There are girls, sir, yes, fresh, sweet, compliant girls . . . You have only to say. These things can be arranged."

"I have no wish."

"Of course, I understand. The unique pleasure of the solitary method, if I may put it like that. There is the question too of hygiene, not to mention speed. It is the rational choice. But still, a helping hand would not go amiss, I venture to suggest. Between friends, it is often the most civilized way, I find."

"Sir, I am outraged."

"And I am at a loss. From your other reading matter, I took you to be a rationalist and a materialist. With such an outlook, what objection could there be?"

"I have not come so far in my freethinking."

"Then I am sorry for you."

"And I for you."

"Please do not be."

"I am a magistrate."

"Ah!"

"I am here on police business."

"I bid you—" But the theatrical gentleman flew the shop without completing the farewell.

Feeling strangely compromised by the encounter, Porfiry turned back to the pawnbroker. The man met him with a look of open impertinence. Those eyes, intense, dark, and fiercely alive, seemed momentarily more obscene than anything in *One Thousand and One Maidenheads*.

"This Virginsky," began Porfiry.

"Pavel Pavelovich."

"You understand now that it is a police matter."

"I know nothing of that."

"Can you give me a description of him?"

The pawnbroker shrugged.

"Is he particularly tall or—how shall I put it?—diminutive?"

"Not particularly."

"I see. So there is nothing especially distinctive about his appearance?"

"He has a pale complexion and a generally disreputable appearance. But among the students of Petersburg, I dare say there is nothing distinctive about that."

"And from your familiarity with him, I take it he is a regular customer of yours?"

"Regular enough."

"Do you happen to know Pavel Pavelovich's address?"

"I do."

Porfiry added another red note to the first still on the pawnbroker's counter.

"You have only to go to Lippevechsel's Tenements. And ask there for Pavel Pavelovich Virginsky."

The pawnbroker picked up the two banknotes and held the second one out to Porfiry. "This is a legitimate credit business. The debt is paid."

Porfiry bowed and held the bow.

"I am a Jew, yes, but I am also a law-abiding citizen."

Porfiry lifted his head, looked the pawnbroker in the eye, and met the anger there without flinching. He took back the note that he had offered.

"Would you please tie up the books for me again?" he said, as he folded it into his wallet. The pawnbroker breathed out sharply through his nostrils before complying.

7

The Gamble

LIPPEVECHSEL'S TENEMENTS in Gorokhovaya Street was one of those sprawling apartment buildings that seemed to have grown like an organism rather than been built to any rational plan. Ramshackle and crumbling, its various fronts and wings clustered around a series of dirty yards into which sunlight never penetrated. When the wind blew through it, it was felt by every occupant, even those huddled around one of its stoves or samovars, even one buried under a mound of rags or bent double in a cupboard. Close to Kameny Bridge, the building overlooked the Yekaterinsky Canal, which was frozen now but in the summer served as an open drain. The stench, in those high hot days, seeped in through the gaping cracks in its walls and spread throughout the building. It mingled with the smells of cooking, insinuating itself into the lives of the residents, so that it shared their intimacies and infected their dreams.

The interior of the building was divided by flimsy partitions and lit here and there by oil lamps. Doors hung open or were lacking altogether. Families lived side by side and almost on top of one another, every room divided and sublet to meet the rent. From one side of a curtain came the cries and cracks of a beating, from the other the frenzied thump of copulation. Everywhere in the background could be heard a gentle snagging sound, as regular and constant as the lapping of the sea, an anonymous, muffled weeping.

Porfiry, still carrying the bundle of books in one hand, stood at the threshold of an endless twilit maze. He took off his fur hat and breathed in a damp atmosphere that was heavy with the smell of waste. Clotheslines were strung across the corridors. Ragged, shrieking children ran beneath them, without any sense of the invisible boundaries of so many abutting lives. Somewhere, out of sight, a card game was in progress. Porfiry could hear the laughter and abuse, the slap of the cards, the jangle of coins.

As he sought vainly for the source of these sounds, he saw a figure emerge from one of the crisscrossing corridors. It was a girl. He couldn't be sure because she was moving briskly with her face angled down and swallowed by gloom, but he felt that he knew her.

He called out. His cry drew her gaze. But when she saw him, a look of panic came over her face. She turned and ran, disappearing from his sight. Porfiry cradled the books to his chest and gave chase. In the moment that her face had been lifted toward him, he recognized her. It was Lilya, the young prostitute who had been brought in to the bureau.

He followed the heel of her shoe and the hem of her swaying skirt, which was all of her he ever saw as she vanished around succeeding corners and even through vaguely partitioned rooms. His pursuit invaded privacy after privacy but without provoking a single complaint. It was almost as if he were invisible. The only time his presence was commented upon was when he stumbled into the table of card players, who swore at him for upsetting their piles of coins. His apologies delayed him long enough for the trail to go cold. When he peered around the next corner, there was no sight of any part of her, however fleeting, just her scent in the air.

He returned to the card players.

"Gentlemen, if I may interrupt your game for a moment." A collective growl arose from the table. But no one looked up. They were too intent on their cards. There was a grumbled joke and a crackle of harsh laughter at Porfiry's expense, but essentially this was a grim endeavor for them all. He had the sense that his use of the word *game* had been ill judged. "The young lady who just passed through here," he pressed. "Did any of you happen to see . . . ?"

But they were ignoring him now, not even bothering to make him the butt of their jokes. There was a nearly empty bottle of vodka on the table, and most of the men smoked pipes. Nothing outside the absorbing tobacco fug had meaning for them.

Porfiry pulled over a rickety chair and joined the table, placing the books on his lap. He waited for the game to play itself out, then said, "I'm looking for Pavel Pavelovich Virginsky."

A significant look was passed around the table and settled on one of the players, a stubble-jowled man with silky black hair, a greasy frock coat, and dirty nails. He was the only one not dressed in workmen's overalls. His sharp, calculating eyes assessed Porfiry for a good minute. "Do you know Schtoss?" said this man, at last.

"Schtoss? Who is Schtoss?"

Loud, unrestrained laughter erupted around the table. Some even banged their fists. The hilarity died down. They watched the man in the frock coat with nervous expectation.

"Schtoss, my friend, is not a man. Schtoss is a game."

"I don't know it," said Porfiry. "I'm not much of a card player."

"No matter," said the other. "Schtoss is a game of luck. There is nothing to it but luck."

"I see. How do you play it?"

"It's very simple. Alexei, give the gentleman the pack." A young painter, to judge by the specks of color on his overalls, handed Porfiry the cards. "You have that pack," said the man in the frock coat, "and I will have this one." He withdrew a second pack from one of his pockets. "First we must agree on the stake. The game is between you and me. If you win, I will tell you where you can find Virginsky."

"And if I lose?"

"If you lose, you will swap your fur *shuba* for my frock coat." There were murmurs of amused dissent. The feeling seemed to be that the man had gone too far.

"That is hardly fair," said Porfiry. "This is fairer. If I win, you tell me where I can find Virginsky. If I lose, I send out for a second bottle of vodka to be shared among you all." Porfiry's view was that even if he lost the bet, he would win over the company. One of the others, looking favorably on his generosity, would be sure to tell him what he needed to know. The proposal was met with such a cheer that Porfiry's opponent was forced to bow his agreement.

"Very well. We will play. Pick any card you like from your pack, and place it facedown on the table without letting me see it. Very good. Now then, this is my pack. Here, I want you to cut my pack for me. You know what it means to cut the cards, I take it?"

Porfiry nodded and obeyed.

"Thank you." The other man put the two halves of the pack together. "In this game, the game of Schtoss, I turn over the first two cards from my pack. The first card goes on the right, the second on the left. Like so." He dealt up the nine of hearts followed by the three of spades. "If the number of your card matches the first of my cards—that is to say, if it is a nine of any suit—then you lose. If it matches the second—the card on the left—then you win. If neither matches, we deal again, a third and fourth card, and so on until we encounter a match. Are you willing to play?"

"Yes."

"Then, please, be so good as to turn over your card."

Porfiry turned over the queen of spades.

"No match," said his opponent. "No matter. We keep going."

He dealt two more cards, the six of diamonds followed by the ten of diamonds. Again Porfiry's card, the jack of clubs, failed to produce a match.

The man in the frock coat nodded grimly and dealt two more cards, neither of which was matched by Porfiry's.

The two players stared unflinchingly into each other's eyes, as if this would have a bearing on the cards they dealt. Porfiry's hands shook. His palms began to sweat. And yet he did not want the game to end. In each turning of a card, he felt the heavy hammering of his heart, reminding him with renewed insistence that he was alive. Whatever the outcome of the game, he knew he would miss this feeling.

It was about ten deals later when Porfiry turned over a seven of clubs, matching the seven of hearts on top of the left-hand pile of cards.

"I win, I believe," said Porfiry. It was as he had expected. His delight at winning was tempered by regret that the game was over. He wanted to play again.

The other man nodded, admitting defeat. "To the left, over there, past that woman with the cough. There is a door. It leads to the annex. Virginsky lodges in there, on the ground floor, with the cabinetmaker Kezel."

After the tension of the confrontation, the mood returned to the earlier one of brash amusement. The laughter now, however, was at the expense of the man in the frock coat, who took in good humor their jibes at his failure to secure them a fresh bottle of vodka.

Porfiry left the table reluctantly, almost disappointed; depressed, despite his success. He had the sense that they had finished with him. And all that he had to turn to was his duty.

T HE NAME KEZEL was chalked on the door.

Kezel himself was not in, but his wife—a silent, cowed woman whose face bore the marks of her last beating—showed Porfiry to the door of the tiny cell occupied by the student Virginsky. He was as the pawnbroker had described him, pale and shabbily dressed. He was also, Porfiry noted, underfed to the point of stupor. His glazed eyes were sunk in dark circles of exhaustion. He was shivering. It struck Porfiry that Virginsky showed no sign of surprise at his arrival. It was almost as if he had been expecting him. But perhaps he was simply incapable of registering any emotion. As soon as Virginsky admitted Porfiry to his room, he fell back on the bed. As there was nowhere for Porfiry to sit other than on the bed, he remained standing. He sniffed the air, which was—unexpectedly—scented.

Porfiry looked down at the pitiful figure of the young man and felt the stirrings of a deep anxiety. He couldn't help being reminded of the student double-murderer whose case had so engaged him the year before.

"You are Pavel Pavelovich Virginsky?" His voice sounded harsher than he had meant it to.

"Yes."

"Allow me to introduce myself. I'm Porfiry Petrovich. I'm an investigating magistrate. I've come here from the Department of the Investigation of Criminal Causes."

Virginsky made no comment.

"Do you recognize these books?"

Virginsky glanced apathetically at the books and nodded.

"Do you know to whom they belong?"

Again Virginsky nodded. "How did you get them?" he roused himself to ask, his voice hoarse and lethargic. But Virginsky showed no real curiosity about the answer. In fact, he closed his eyes.

"I redeemed them from Lyamshin's," said Porfiry.

"Impossible," said Virginsky, without opening his eyes.

"Why do you say that, Pavel Pavelovich?"

"Because I have the ticket."

"You have the ticket?"

Virginsky nodded.

"Please, this is very important. Could you show me the ticket?"

Virginsky finally opened his eyes. For a moment, Porfiry saw in them an engaged intelligence that eased his fears for the student. But this look did not last. The eyes swam. An instant of confusion gave way to simple blankness.

"Pavel Pavelovich," said Porfiry sternly. "When did you last eat something?"

"Eat?"

"Yes, eat."

"I . . . do you have food?"

"No. But I can get some."

Virginsky managed four rasps of empty laughter. It was as if he were laughing at the folly of a man who promised him infinite riches.

"I have only to talk to your landlady."

"She . . . I owe . . . rent."

"Of course, but it is a question of common humanity. She will not let you starve."

"Her husband." Virginsky raised one hand hopelessly and let it fall.

"I understand," said Porfiry, laying down the books on the edge of the bed. "I will arrange it."

Porfiry found Madame Kezel in the kitchen stirring a large pot of broth. She flinched away from his gaze.

"That boy," he began. "How can you let him starve when there is food in the house?"

"My husband forbids it."

"But your husband is not here."

"He will find out."

"How will he find out?"

"He always finds out. Pavel Pavelovich tells him."

"How much does Pavel Pavelovich owe you?"

"My husband knows."

"If Pavel Pavelovich paid all the rent that is due, your husband would allow you to feed him?"

The woman nodded.

"I am a magistrate. I undertake to pay Pavel Pavelovich's debts to you and your husband. Please, in God's name, take him a bowl of broth."

"My husband has forbidden me to go into his room."

"Give me the broth, and I will take it to him."

"You are a magistrate, you say?"

"Yes."

"And you will leave money?"

"Yes."

Madame Kezel fetched a bowl from a cupboard and ladled in the brown fatty broth. She handed it to Porfiry with a spoon and a crust of stale bread.

"If you could ask Pavel Pavelovich not to express his gratitude to my husband . . ."

"I understand."

"Or to myself. There is no need for his gratitude."

Porfiry carried the broth back to Virginsky's room. The student lay with his eyes closed, his face torpid and drained. But gradually his expression changed as he became aware of the savory aroma. His nostrils twitched. He licked his lips and swallowed. A smile showed. It seemed he was dreaming of a marvelous feast. Then the point came where he was able to disassociate the smell of food from his dream, and he understood that this tremendous, overwhelming sensation was real. A look of wonder, almost of fear, showed as he finally opened his eyes and looked around.

"Can you sit up?" asked Porfiry.

Virginsky lifted himself up on his elbows and allowed Porfiry, now perched next to him on the bed, to spoon-feed him. Every now and then he took a mouthful of the bread, which he was only able to chew by soaking it well in the broth. By the time he had eaten the last spoonful, he had regained his strength enough to wipe the last remaining piece of bread around the bowl.

Porfiry set the bowl aside on the floor. There was nowhere else to put it. Virginsky gave a small burp of satisfaction. "Who are you?" he asked Porfiry, evidently fortified by his meal.

"I have told you. I am Porfiry Petrovich. We were talking about the books." Porfiry indicated the pile on the bed.

"My books!" exclaimed the student in delight.

"They are yours?"

"Yes. But how did you get them?"

"I have already told you. Don't you remember?"

Virginsky frowned. "Now I do remember, I think. But it doesn't make sense." Virginsky rose from the bed and stood swaying before reaching out to the wall opposite. The room was so small that he could touch any side from this spot in the middle. He lifted a loose flap of wallpaper, revealing a large empty hole beneath. This discovery seemed to shock him. Then a wry downward smirk twisted his face, and he started laughing. There was a warmth and richness to his laughter now, unlike the frail spasm that had gripped him earlier. "That bastard Goryanchikov," he said at last.

"Who is Goryanchikov?" asked Porfiry.

"Stepan Sergeyevich Goryanchikov," answered Virginsky. "The son of a whore who stole my pawn ticket. I kept it in here."

"But why would anyone want to steal a pawn ticket? It amounts to the same thing as stealing a debt."

"Oh, Goryanchikov would do it. Goryanchikov is capable of doing anything." Now Virginsky picked up the books and scanned the spines. "I see they are all here," he said, blushing as he got to *One Thousand and One Maidenheads*. "Thank you for returning them to me. I am grateful. You have saved me the expense of redeeming them myself."

"I'm sorry. I can't let you keep the books. At least not yet. They are evidence in an ongoing police investigation."

"What investigation?"

"Perhaps you would be good enough to give me a description of this Goryanchikov."

"Goryanchikov? Has he got himself into trouble? He's a good fellow really, you know. All this, the pawn ticket, the books—I didn't mean to accuse him. I'm sure it's just one of his jests. I've warned him, but that's what he's like. He will have his jokes."

"Please, I must press you for a description of your friend."

"Yes, he is my friend. I know I insulted him, but he is my friend. If it's a question of debts, I can write to my father. I wouldn't do it on my own account, you understand, but for Goryanchikov."

"The best way you could help him is to tell me what he looks like."

"Well, he has dark hair and a scrawny beard. His eyes, if I remember rightly, are dark and set slightly wide in his face. You might justifiably describe his nose as prominent. He has a large mole on one of his wrists—his left, I believe."

"And that is all?"

"Oh, no!" cried Virginsky, as if suddenly remembering. "One other thing. He is a dwarf." Virginsky smiled, pleased with himself for the joke.

"Pavel Pavelovich, I believe I have some bad news for you. The body of such a gentleman was found in Petrovsky Park."

"Body? What do you mean, body?"

"Circumstantial evidence would lead me to conclude that it is the body of your friend. The pawnbroker's ticket was found on him."

Virginsky dropped back onto the bed and sat with his head in his hands. "How?" he groaned through his hands.

"We believe he was murdered."

"Oh no, please God, no!"

"I'm sorry."

"I have warned him. I warned him so many times."

"Of what did you warn him?"

"He takes pleasure—took pleasure," Virginsky corrected himself. Then he rubbed his eyes as if to rouse himself from a dream. "He took pleasure in provoking people. Goading them. I knew it would end badly."

"I see. He made enemies?"

"Oh, but surely no one!" Virginsky looked imploringly into Porfiry's eyes. "God knows he has provoked me enough times. Once or twice I could have happily throttled him myself."

"We will need someone to confirm—" Porfiry broke off.

"You revived me for this!"

"I'm sorry."

Virginsky looked down, catching sight of the books on the bed. He picked up Büchner's *Force and Matter* and stroked the cover absently. Then he dropped it on top of the others, as if it had suddenly become hot. "But these books can have nothing to do with his death, surely? It is a mere accident that he had the pawn ticket on him when he was murdered."

Porfiry said nothing to confirm or contest this. "I have agreed with your landlady to settle your debts here. Will this cover it?" Porfiry presented the student with fifty rubles.

"Why would you do that for me?"

"Because I believe you have the potential for great good. But I fear that poverty and hunger may lead you into acts you will regret."

"How can you know so much about me? You have only just met me."

"But I have met someone very like you before."

"Do you believe I killed Goryanchikov?"

"I should warn you, we found another body near where that of your friend was discovered. It may be that you can help us in identifying that person too. If it was someone known to Goryanchikov, there is a chance you knew him too."

"Must we go now?"

"If you feel strong enough. In my experience it is better to get these things behind one as soon as possible."

Virginsky nodded tersely and raised himself to his feet. His first attempt at a step sent him lurching forward. Porfiry was quick to catch him. With his face close to Virginsky's, he breathed again the scent he had noticed when he first came into the room.

"How long have you known Lilya?" Porfiry murmured gently.

"Lilya?"

"She was here. Just now. She is a friend of yours?"

"Yes. Do you know her too?" There was a bitterness in Virginsky's voice.

"Not really. Not in that way. She was brought in for questioning."

"She is a good person."

"I'm sure she is," said Porfiry, picking up the books and holding them in one arm, so that he was able to support Virginsky with his other hand. He sensed a stiff resistance in the other man as they started walking.

8

At the Obukhovsky Hospital

THE HUNGER HAD GONE, but now it was back. The city danced around him in the falling snow. There was a sense of finality to the snow. This was how it was going to be from now on. He was light-headed. It was the hunger, he told himself. But it was something else. He felt himself to be on the brink of something. How did he come to be in this jangling *drozhki*, sitting next to this stranger, this strangest of strangers? The plump little fellow with the blinking eyes lit a cigarette and watched him closely.

"Porfiry Petrovich," he heard himself say.

"Yes?" said the man next to him, exhaling smoke.

"I'm cold," he told the man.

The man nodded and rearranged the furs that lay over his lap. "We'll soon be there."

"Where?"

"The Obukhovsky Hospital. Don't you remember?"

"Am I ill?"

"Possibly you are ill. There is a doctor there who will examine you. But that is not why we are going."

Pavel Pavelovich Virginsky shivered and tried to think. "Why are we going?" he asked at last.

"You're going to help me. You have a duty to perform. It's not a pleasant duty, I'm afraid."

He realized now where it came from, this feeling of being on the brink. "The city will never look the same to me again," he said, as they glided over the frozen Fontanka between two lines of birch trees placed there to mark the route. Beyond the trees, men were loading a sled with blocks of ice hewn from the river.

Porfiry Petrovich did not answer.

"Are you a policeman?" asked Virginsky.

"I am an investigator. A magistrate."

"And he is really dead?"

"I believe so."

As the *drozhki* slowed, he caught sight of the bronze bust of Catherine II on the side of the hospital she had founded. He had the feeling she was waiting for him.

"Porfiry Petrovich."

"Yes?"

"I'm cold."

P ORFIRY, still with the books under one arm, led Virginsky along the crowded corridors of the men's hospital. Some men were slumped against the walls, others lay where they had fallen on the floor. A few paced. All were dressed in ragged and dirty clothing. The Obukhovsky was a free hospital.

Occasionally, one of the men turned toward them and watched them pass with a kind of hostile expectancy that stood in place of hope.

Virginsky experienced a heightened sensitivity. The sound of cough-ing resonated in the joints of his bones. He was aware of the smell of his own body and how it reacted with the other smells around him. He drifted in and out of physicality.

"It's like a magnet, a great stone magnet, it draws them to it," he mur-mured, in one of his lucid moments.

Porfiry met the observation with an expression of mild inquiry.

"This building. It's like a magnet for their misery. And God knows there is enough of it."

"You speak as if you're not one of them."

"I have no right to. I have been drawn here too. By my misery."

"Your case is slightly different. It's more a case of sorrow, I would think."

"Does that imply less suffering?"

"Perhaps. Perhaps you have it in your power to end your suffering whenever you wish."

"It's not in my power."

"You spoke of your father."

"I don't remember. I must be ill. It's not like me to speak of my father."

"Is he a landowner?"

"What's that to me? He won't give me a single kopek." They ap-proached an elderly man supporting himself with one hand on the wall. He was in the grip of a hacking cough. "And why should he help me?"

"Because he's your father. He's bound to you by blood."

"There are other bonds, stronger, more important."

"Such as?"

"Love."

"Ah. Lilya," said Porfiry gently.

"No," said Virginsky quickly. "I mean, perhaps, I don't know. It's not . . . She has a child, you know."

"I didn't know."

"Yes."

"Are you . . . the father?"

"Certainly not. There has never . . . There has never been anything like that between us."

"Who is the father, do you know?"

"No. I don't know. She's never told me. Why are you interested?"

"There is quite a little mystery concerning your friend Lilya. A man, one Konstantin Kirillovich, family name unknown, accused her of stealing a hundred rubles. She says he gave it to her. She was brought in for questioning, but her accuser having disappeared, she was released."

"I can tell you now, she is no thief."

"I believe you. She didn't want the money when it was offered to her. Have you ever heard her speak of this Konstantin Kirillovich?"

"No."

"I should very much like to talk to Lilya again."

Virginsky offered nothing in return.

"I believe I might pay her a visit. What was the name of the establishment she works at? Something German. Keller or Kellner. It was there on her license, I remember," said Porfiry.

"Keller. The madam is a German woman."

"Is that where you met her?"

Virginsky winced, as if in pain. He came to a stop. "Once, with a group of friends—no, not really friends, acquaintances. People from my school days. There had been a dinner. Drinking. I was taken to that establishment. She was there. Something about her touched me. I saw how young she was. I couldn't go through with it. I gave her money and left. I—I met her again by chance in the street. It may seem unlikely to you, but we became friends."

"On Sadovaya Street, isn't it?"

"Beneath a milliner's. These places usually are."

"Can you remember anything else about it?"

Virginsky shook his head, and they continued in silence, until they came to a closed door that bore the sign PATHOLOGY.

. . .

THE SMELL OF formaldehyde overwhelmed everything else. The room was large, with high workbenches running its length. Virginsky had expected to see cadavers and body parts scattered about. But if there were any, they had been hidden away. The surfaces and instruments were gleaming. He saw jars and bottles of various sizes, as well as enamel basins and test tubes in racks. Microscopes were distributed regularly about, at some of which stood men in white laboratory coats. One of these, a young man with unruly hair, looked up. His face showed recognition, and he came toward them.

"Ah, Porfiry Petrovich! Our esteemed Porfiry Petrovich!" he cried, shaking Porfiry warmly by the hand.

"Dr. Pervoyedov, good day to you."

"You were right, Porfiry Petrovich. There can be no doubt about it, you were right!" The physician beamed with excitement.

"You have finished your report?"

"No, no! You've seen the corridors? The beds are taken up with influenza victims. There's no time for writing reports."

"I understand. But I fear others may not."

"The *prokuror* will get my report in due time. But don't you want to know what I've discovered?"

"Of course I'm interested in your preliminary findings. However, there is a more pressing matter. This gentleman"—Dr. Pervoyedov bowed to Virginsky—"may be able to identify the victims for us."

Dr. Pervoyedov's face became grave. "I understand." He addressed Virginsky directly: "What you are about to see . . . you must prepare yourself."

"I am prepared," said Virginsky.

Dr. Pervoyedov addressed the next question to Porfiry: "You have told him what to expect?"

"I have told him everything that's necessary," Porfiry answered with a flutter of his eyelids.

The doctor stared intently into Virginsky's eyes. "I'll get you a seat.

It's better if you sit down." He dragged a stool over. "I'm afraid the pathology laboratory is not furnished for comfort."

Porfiry took Dr. Pervoyedov to one side. "Do you think he's up to this?"

"Will it make any difference to you, Porfiry Petrovich, if I say he is not?"

"Of course. I will postpone the identification."

"Give me a moment."

Dr. Pervoyedov returned to Virginsky, who was now perched unsteadily on the stool. He passed a hand in front of the student's face, then said, "Open your mouth, please." With a wooden spatula, he pulled back Virginsky's lips and examined his teeth and gums. "Hold out your arms, please." After a moment's delay, Virginsky complied. "Could you bend your right arm?" The doctor gripped Virginsky's bicep. Virginsky winced as he bent the arm. "That hurt?" asked Dr. Pervoyedov.

Virginsky closed his eyes on the pain.

"Any other joint pain?"

"I don't know. I suppose so. I hadn't noticed. Not much. Sometimes." Virginsky opened his eyes with a challenging look.

"Straighten your arm again, please. Keep it out in front of you. Now push up against my hand."

Virginsky was unable to move the hand that the doctor had placed on top of his own.

"Relax now." Dr. Pervoyedov's expression for Porfiry was critical as well as concerned.

"Well?" asked Porfiry.

"There are signs of malnutrition. Slow reaction times. Joint pain. Muscular atrophy. Weakness. Really, I put no effort into holding down his hand. And dizziness, of course. You can see for yourself how he's swaying. His teeth and gums are in a shocking condition." After a pause the doctor added, "It's the sort of thing I see every day."

"He has eaten recently. I saw to it."

"Then possibly it is the best we can hope for."

"Pavel Pavelovich," said Porfiry to Virginsky, "do you feel able to proceed?"

"What is the alternative?"

"We could come back. Another time."

"But there is no escaping it." He said this with fatality.

Even though it was not a question, Porfiry nodded.

"I'll do it. Now."

"I'll get them then," said Dr. Pervoyedov. The doctor crossed to the far end of the laboratory and returned pushing a trolley, on top of which were two large specimen jars. As the trolley got nearer, Virginsky saw the eyes in the first jar, staring out of a murky amber liquid.

His first impulse was to deny that this thing had any connection with him, even on the most basic level. It could not be what it seemed to be. It could not be a head, a human head. Then he saw the gaping mouth and the strands of hair and beard. But that was not hair or beard, there. That was something else trailing, something sinewy and dark. And what was that above the eyes? It seemed to be a second, cruder mouth set vertically in the forehead. He looked into the colorless pulp revealed there.

"Do you recognize him?" asked Porfiry.

Virginsky nodded.

"It is your friend Goryanchikov?" pressed Porfiry.

Virginsky could not take his eyes off the wound in the preserved head. He gazed at it with urgency, as if he hungered for the sight of it and was afraid that it would be taken from him. It was obscene, but like all obscenities it pulled at his soul. "It *was* him," he said at last.

"I am very sorry," said Porfiry. He nodded to Dr. Pervoyedov, who wheeled the trolley around so that the second specimen jar was at the front. "Do you recognize this man?"

Virginsky felt calm now. In fact, he was conscious of his calmness and astonished by it. He felt capable of the utmost callousness.

"It's not a man. It's a head," he said.

"But do you recognize it?"

"It's Borya."

"Who is Borya?"

"It's strange. If you look. Goryanchikov's head fills its jar more completely. His head really was big. I always thought it an illusion, caused by the smallness of his body. Borya's head is tiny in comparison."

"Please, I need to know more about Borya."

"He was not a great thinker, so perhaps it should not surprise us." Virginsky began to giggle unpleasantly. "Goryanchikov, on the other hand, thought too much. As we can see, it has had an effect on his brain. What is the word for it when something grows too large? Hypertrophy?"

"He is delirious," observed Dr. Pervoyedov.

"On the contrary, doctor. I have never felt more lucid. To see this, to be granted this, I thought it would sicken me. I find I am not in the least nauseous. My appetite, I have not lost my appetite at all. Should I be sad? Goryanchikov was a friend, I loved him as a friend, but he was a difficult man to like. And Borya, Borya—who could not love Borya?"

"He was a popular man?" asked Porfiry.

"I would call it a privilege. To be granted this, this vision. It is not given to everyone to see such wonders."

"The two men were known to each other?"

"I'm not sad. Isn't that strange? Not sad at all. I find myself feeling quite . . . almost, you might say, happy. No, not happy. I'm not happy. But I am glad. I shall say that much. What does it mean? Does it mean I have no soul? Does it mean I'm not a man?"

"Why are you glad, do you think?"

"I think I'm glad because it's not my head pickled in one of those jars." Virginsky began to shake. He could not stem the sudden flood of tears over his face. "I'm crying for myself, not for them," he insisted. "I'm crying because I'm a man without a soul. Because I'm not a man. Because I can look at the severed heads of my friends and still live and still breathe and still rejoice to feel my heart beating. Because I'm a bastard, the bastard son of a bastard father, the last in a long line of worthless cowards, and knowing this doesn't change a thing. I will eat and sleep and write a letter to my father, and one day perhaps I will marry. And looking at their

pickled heads won't change a thing. I'm not a great man. I have no great-
ness of soul. I'm not great enough to be enlarged by this. If anything, I
will be shrunk by this."

"I don't think so."

"You don't know a thing about it!" snarled Virginsky.

"I know enough to recognize a man who is in deep shock. Would you
not say so, doctor?"

Dr. Pervoyedov nodded solicitously.

"For all you know, I killed them."

"Is that a confession?"

"I know how you people work. The fact that I knew them both makes
me a suspect."

"You are sick. I will arrange for you to be taken home."

Virginsky fell off the stool and staggered forward, grabbing the trolley
for balance. "I can find my own way home. I don't need any help from
you." He gave the trolley a push. The two heads glided away, rotated,
then slowed to a halt. "Thank you for showing me this, these . . . You
have shown me myself."

"You hate me at this moment. You would do better to hate whoever
killed your friends."

"You are quite the psychologist."

"Who is Borya?"

"Whatever he was, he is nothing anymore."

"Please. Sit down. You can't go like this."

"Are you arresting me?"

"I'm asking for your help. "

"Aha!"

"Borya . . . ?"

"Was the yardkeeper at Goryanchikov's building. Now will you let
me go?"

"And the address? Of Goryanchikov's building."

"How can I be expected to remember these details? What difference do
these details make, now, after all this?"

"It's very important. It may help us find whoever killed these men."

"He lodged with Anna Alexandrovna and her daughter. In a house on Bolshaya Morskaya Street."

"The number?"

"Yes, there was a number." Virginsky pinched the bridge of his nose. "You are quite right, there was a number."

"Did you go to the house?"

Virginsky looked down disconsolately at his feet. "I need new shoes."

Porfiry followed his gaze. "I couldn't agree more."

"Seven. The number of the house. It's come back to me. It has a seven in it. It's either seven or seventeen, or seventy. Or seven hundred and seventy-seven." Virginsky laughed wheezily. "No. There's only one seven, I'm sure of that. At any rate there is a sign."

"Thank you."

"Will you write to my father and tell him that I've done my duty as a good citizen?"

"Do you wish me to?"

"Not particularly."

"You should go home now."

"And the shoes?"

"Don't worry about the shoes."

"He was my friend, Goryanchikov. As for Borya . . . Borya was an innocent. Of course, they hated each other. It's strange that it should end like this." Virginsky bowed farewell, took one step toward the door, and fainted.

T HE TWO MEN came toward Virginsky and bent over him.

"How are you feeling?" asked Dr. Pervoyedov.

"What a shock you gave us, Pavel Pavelovich," said Porfiry.

Virginsky began to lift himself up.

"Please," protested Dr. Pervoyedov. "Don't try and get up."

"I'm quite all right," insisted Virginsky. "It was the shock."

"Of course. A quite understandable reaction," said Porfiry.

"I was not expecting—" Virginsky broke off. His face was gray. He was standing now. He turned to Porfiry with a look of hatred. "You didn't warn me. That it would be heads. Just heads. In jars. Was that how they were found?"

"No. The heads were removed and preserved by Dr. Pervoyedov. I'm sorry if it shocked you."

"It was cruel of you. Why did you do it? Is it part of your technique?"

"I'm truly sorry," said Porfiry. "This is what we deal in. This is our currency. Perhaps we become inured to it and forget the effect it has on others."

"I do not believe you are one to forget anything, sir. I know what you were trying to do. You were trying to shock me into revealing something."

"You speak as though I suspect you. But surely you see I can have no reason to suspect you of anything."

"And did it work? Your nasty little trick? Did I reveal anything?"

"Very well, I'll be honest with you. You're an intelligent young man. I like you, Pavel Pavelovich. I did hope to break down any barriers you might have erected in your mind, which might have prevented you from cooperating fully with the investigation. Not because I suspect you, but because you see me as a figure of authority and it's natural for you to resist me. In the same way that you resist your father. There may be something you know that could be crucial to the solution of this case, but you may not realize you know it, or you may not realize that you are keeping it from me. I hoped, in the aftershock of this discovery—"

"It's not that. It's just that you're cruel."

Porfiry did not answer this charge.

Virginsky addressed his silence: "I would have told you what I know about the damned house."

"I believe you would. I had to be sure. However, I'm not required to explain myself to you." Porfiry narrowed his eyes. "You remind me of someone. A student. He was poor. And proud. Perhaps too proud."

"A poor student has no grounds for pride at all? Is that your opinion?"

"Pride can be a dangerous thing."

"You're wrong about me. I have no pride."

"There are other similarities. A certain tension in your demeanor. A certain unpredictability. A wildness, you might almost call it."

"May I go now?"

"Of course. I will look in on you tomorrow."

"You have already said as much. There is no need. But I understand you have your own motives for wanting to do so."

Virginsky gave a curt bow to Dr. Pervoyedov. He then strode with surprising firmness of step to the door.

Porfiry felt the doctor's disapproval. With some annoyance he said: "So, Dr. Pervoyedov, what have you discovered concerning the causes of death? You were eager to tell me, I believe."

The physician seemed startled by the demand, as if he could not understand its relevance.

At last Porfiry turned his gaze toward Pervoyedov. Unusually, he held it without blinking. "There is something you wish to say?"

"Very well, very well. I will say it. With all respect, with the utmost respect indeed, I wish it to be known that I detest your methods."

"Naturally. You are a doctor. I am a criminal investigator. We have different purposes, after all. But I ask you, as a physician, would you rather I employed the old methods of extracting information?"

"To replace one form of brutality with another is not progress."

"I wish I could afford the luxury of your fastidiousness. But when you are investigating brutalities—"

"Do you think he is the murderer?"

Porfiry smiled and now fluttered his eyelids. He took out and lit a cigarette. "Now, Dr. Pervoyedov, what were you saying about your discoveries?"

"Ah. I understand. Yes, yes, of course. I am merely the physician. You are the investigator." Dr. Pervoyedov shook his head ruefully. He moved along the workbench and opened a drawer set beneath its surface. "It's true, I have discovered something interesting," he said, taking out a cardboard file.

Porfiry nodded encouragement.

Looking down at his notes, Dr. Pervoyedov continued: "Well, let us start with the big fellow."

"Borya."

"Yes, yes. Indeed. You remember I drew attention to the absence of bruising around the neck. That naturally made me suspicious. When examining the lungs, I noticed that although the lungs themselves appeared to be healthy, the covering of the lungs was inflamed. And then, when I came to test the stomach contents—"

"What did you find?" interrupted Porfiry eagerly.

"Vodka. A hell of a lot of vodka in there. That of course masked the smell."

"The smell of what?"

"Of prussic acid."

"I see."

"Yes. The test for prussic acid was positive. A deep and rather beautiful blue."

"He was poisoned."

"It appears so."

"How was it administered, do you know?"

"I'm inclined to think it was in the vodka."

"His own flask was full," mused Porfiry.

"Exactly. The vodka in his stomach could have been given to him by person or persons unknown."

"Who then strung him up on the tree in an attempt to make it look like suicide. I wonder if the line of bruising around his abdomen has anything to do with that?"

"Very likely, Porfiry Petrovich. Very likely."

"Excellent work, Doctor. And what about Goryanchikov?"

"I am more or less certain that the wound in the head was administered post-mortem."

"The lack of blood over his face led me to suspect as much. How did he die, then? Was he poisoned too?"

"I have detected no traces of any known poison. However, sections of the lung parenchyma reveal ductal overinsufflation consistent with asphyxia. And I retrieved something very interesting from his larynx." The doctor held up a small feather, taken from the file.

Porfiry crossed to where the trolley had stopped its glide. He bent down and stared into the first of the jars. Goryanchikov's head stared back at him, its mouth and the mouthlike wound in its forehead gaping in supplication. "Someone held a pillow over his face," said Porfiry.

9

Beneath the
Milliner's Shop

VIRGINSKY TRUDGED THROUGH the wet snow lying along the southern Fontanka bank, heading northeast. The sprawl of the Apraxin Market lay ahead of him, across the frozen river. The ice seeped into his soul from his feet, through his gaping uppers.

It would be so easy to end it all. One letter to his father was all it required. If the old man knew what misery he was living in, he would be sure to send him some money. There would be no need to grovel for forgiveness, or—even more unthinkable—grant it. Merely to explain the facts, that was all that was required.

> Father,
> You are my father. I am your son. I am badly in need of new shoes.
> I have no money for food or rent.
> Your son,
> Pavel.

That was all that needed to be said. Perhaps he could add, in a spirit as it were of magnanimity:

We will talk of other things at another time.

Yes, that seemed to hint at reconciliation. He was throwing out a few crumbs of hope to the old man, without committing himself to any concessions or admissions.

But of course, he knew that he would never write the letter.

Perhaps the investigator was right. He was too proud after all. He often felt himself humiliated, especially in his present circumstances. The two things went together, he believed: a heightened sensitivity to humiliation and excessive pride. If only he could shake off them both. Independence of means was the only way to do it, and a letter to his father would not help him there. He could not bear to owe his father anything, not now, not after all that had happened. If he could not have independence of means, he would at least have independence of spirit or, failing that, independence of behavior. No one would tell him what to do.

He imagined composing a different letter to his father:

Sir,

You are not my father. I am not your son. I am badly in need of a new pair of shoes. I have no money for food or rent. And yet I want nothing from you. If you choose to send me money, that will be your decision. I do not ask for it. I do not expect it. I shall not consider myself in your debt. If you choose not to send me money, it will be for the better. I will not think of you again and ask you to do the same regarding me.

Yours,

The human entity who is known by the name Pavel Pavelovich Virginsky without acknowledging kinship to any other man bearing that name (i.e., you).

How he hated his name.

Of course, there was another way to end it all. It had been in his mind all along. Simply to lie down in the snow now and wait for the cold and hunger to do their work. The end would come soon enough, and there would be no pain.

It was a comforting fantasy, but he kept on walking. He realized he was walking away from the investigator's damnable jars and all that they entailed.

He was suddenly certain that the whole ridiculous, tawdry mess had gone on long enough. It *was* time to bring it to an end; and what was more, he would do it by the second of the two means he had considered. But first there were matters to attend to. He hastened his step as he turned onto Gorokhovaya Street, crossing the Fontanka by the Semenovsky Bridge.

I T WAS DARK by the time he reached Sadovaya Street. He walked with his head bent down, not meeting any face, looking only at his shoes kicking through the sludge. It was easy to imagine that those feet did not belong to him. He didn't feel the cold anymore, nor his exhaustion, his hunger, or his pain. His certainty of purpose had overridden everything.

He had to see Lilya.

But it was harder than he had imagined to find the milliner's shop. Admittedly, he had hoped that a mysterious force would draw him straight to it. The one other time, long ago, that he had been there, it had been dark and he had been drunk. He was as good as blindfolded. When he had fled from it, he quickly became lost in this city, which had never truly been his home.

He was aware of a presence ahead of him. His cowed glance took in a dark, bulky figure. He had a sense of a dim orange glow bobbing around it and then soaring up into the darkness. A streetlamp flared and lit the workman beneath. In his refusal to look the city's lamplighter in the eye,

Virginsky recognized a puzzling mixture of defiance, humility, and fear. The lamplighter passed on into the darkness at Virginsky's back, leaving a trail of illumination. The transformation wrought by his restless wick was so sudden and complete that it was difficult to believe in it. Virginsky felt himself to be entering a realm of deception. His instinct was to shun it. But to speak to Lilya—as another, more urgent imperative demanded—he had to press on into the light, crunching diamonds underfoot.

He knew from Lilya that Fräulein Keller's establishment was on Sadovaya Street, but where exactly she had never revealed. She didn't like to talk about the place, to the extent that she had begged him never to mention it.

He thought he remembered a side entrance to the shop he was looking for, and iron steps there leading down to the basement. None of the shops he saw now had that configuration.

He heard voices. A group of young cavalry officers, already in their cups, were exchanging ribald jokes. The deceptive light glinted coldly on the buttons and decorations of their greatcoats. He recognized in their voices and their leering grins the same harsh appetite that had once drawn him to Fräulein Keller's, in the company of a similar group. Perhaps, he conjectured, they were heading to that very place now! He hung back before following them.

Their progress was slow and interrupted, but Virginsky matched their pace, careful always to remain at the same distance from them. He kept to the edge of the streetlamp's glow, out of its brilliance. All the same he felt sure that they would notice him. He tried to imagine what he would say if he became the object of their contemptuous attention. But no words came to mind, and the only outcome of the adventure he could envisage was a beating for himself. He would not resist. He would surrender himself to their violence, as if he deserved it. He wondered, in fact, if he were not trying to provoke it by following them. He seriously considered calling out insults to them. A belief in his own invisibility suddenly overcame him. It was a giddy and dangerous moment. He was prevented from doing anything reckless by a sudden outburst from one of their number, who fell to his knees and began singing "One Night of Gladness" in a perfectly acceptable tenor voice.

"Like a moment you passed,
Night of gladness I knew . . ."

The interlude was enough to give Virginsky pause. He remembered his original purpose and was amazed how close he had come to jeopardizing it. He was following the cavalry officers because he believed they would lead him to Lilya. The thought of Lilya in connection with these young men inspired in him an overpowering disgust. At the same time it confirmed him in his mission. He had to find Lilya, now. There were questions he had to ask her.

He had come close to asking her questions before: "How many men? How many times?" And other questions, which he could barely frame in his mind. But her anguished reticence had always touched him. And yet if he was honest, he would say that part of what touched him was anger and part of that anger was directed against her.

The musical soldier began the next verse:

"She despises my grief,
She is heartless and cold,
She has bartered her youth
For splendor and gold . . ."

These men, these drunken, loathsome men, with their grins and buttons, to say nothing of their sentimental hypocrisy—it was men like these Lilya went with. (How he hated the euphemism—he knew full well what it stood for!) Perhaps tonight, this very night, they would be her customers. His mind forced an image of Lilya into the midst of these privileged hooligans, her clothes falling away beneath their manicured pawings. Her face fluctuated between childlike innocence and meretricious depravity. He had only ever seen the former expression on Lilya, his

Lilya. He had seen it the first time he met her, even there, in the depths of Fräulein Keller's establishment. But he did not doubt the existence of another Lilya, with another face. He hated that Lilya as much as he hated these men.

The singer was hoisted to his feet and cajoled into moving on. His fellows were evidently impatient. Virginsky continued to track them as they made their veering way along the Prospect, the lyrics of the folk song trailing in the crisp air:

"Earth and sky, fare you well,
To the river I go,
Where the waters are deep,
O'er my heart let them flow . . ."

Virginsky was disproportionately agitated by the words. Of course, the river was not flowing at this time of the year. But allowing for that one small change of detail, he could almost believe that the oaf had read his mind and sung his thoughts.

It wasn't long before they came to a stop again. A new tone to their laughter, a gunshot excitement, alerted Virginsky to a significant change in their mood and roused him from his preoccupations. He looked around to see hats floating in a callously illuminated shopwindow. He could hear the officers discussing money. Virginsky was in no doubt. This was the place. And there to confirm it was the wrought-iron stairway at the side.

The financial negotiations became heated and drew in all the officers. Virginsky took the opportunity to slip past the jostle of smooth backs and down the stairs. He sank into darkness, stumbling the last few steps. Was this really the place? He heard the cavalry officers move on and felt the certainty drain from him.

A paneled door formed itself in front of him as his eyes became accustomed to the gloom in the stairwell. He groped for and found the bellpull. There was no answering sound.

He filled the silence with doubts. The questions now were for himself.

Why had he allowed himself to be led by the cavalry officers? He saw that there was no logic or consistency to his behavior. This irritated him, and yet he got some satisfaction from the fact that he was still capable of objectivity in his self-analysis. If this did turn out to be the place, perhaps it would also turn out that he had always known how to get here. He had wanted to involve the cavalry officers in his own guilty knowledge; he had wanted, in fact, to pass it on to them and in so doing absolve himself. But it was possible that they had never had any intention of coming to Fräulein Keller's. It was merely another coincidence that they had led him here. The sinfulness and hypocrisy were all his. They, perhaps, were as innocent as babes, at least in this respect. If so, he hated them even more.

A panel in the door opened, and a beam of light projected into Virginsky's face. There was a scornful cackle.

"Hello?" Virginsky called out, shielding his eyes.

"What you want?" came a deep, heavily accented female voice.

"Is Lilya there? I must speak to her."

This was met with more of the same laughter. Virginsky suddenly felt that the beam of light and the laughter were one and the same. The laughter existed only inside the beam of light. With their harsh, corrosive force on his face, he had never felt himself more exposed.

"Tell her it's Virginsky."

The panel closed; a moment later the door itself was opened, and the small frail figure of a girl was pushed out.

"Pavel Pavelovich, what are you doing here?"

"Lilya? It is you, Lilya, isn't it?" Virginsky had only caught a glimpse of her, momentarily silhouetted in the doorway. But even in that moment he had noticed something different about her appearance.

"Yes, of course it's me. What's the matter? Why do you ask?"

"You have a new coat."

"Yes."

"It's trimmed with fur."

"Yes. What of it?"

"Business must be good."

"Please, Pavel Pavelovich. Please don't be cruel. It's not what you think."

"How does it feel when they touch you?"

"Please, Pavel Pavelovich."

"You must get some pleasure from it. I can't see that you would be able to do it at all if you didn't get some pleasure from it."

"Why do you want to make me suffer?"

"Nonsense! Can there never be candor between a man and a woman about such things? Can't you see? It's not my intention to judge you. I have no right. It's just hypocrisy I hate. I want to understand. I want to know the truth. The truth about it all."

"And then? When you have the truth? What will become of me?"

"No, Lilya, you can't ask me that. Or rather, you can't hold me to my answer. But you must understand this: we cannot proceed on the basis of lies and hypocrisy. I must have the truth."

"And what do I get?" The force of her anger surprised him. "There's only one thing I will tell you. This door has closed behind me for good. I am never coming back to this place or this life. I will kill myself and my darling Vera before I go back in there."

Her weight was nothing as she pushed past him, and yet he was buffeted by the force of her repulse. He noted, with that remarkable objectivity that he had already admired in himself, that he wanted to hurt her even more than before.

"Goryanchikov!" he called after her.

She was halfway up the stairs when she stopped to face him. Looking up, he saw her haloed by a streetlamp. "What of him?" she demanded.

Virginsky did not know what he was going to say next. He wanted to tell her that he had seen Goryanchikov's head floating in a jar. Instead he said: "He was one of them, wasn't he? I saw it in your eyes when you were together. The look of fear that he would betray you. And in his eyes, something else, something nasty and possessive."

"All that has nothing to do with you."

"You're right. None of this has anything to do with me. I have no right to interrogate you in this way. I'm surprised you allow it. It's up to you what you do with your body, who you sleep with, for what reasons. It's nothing to do with me."

"Very well then." But she stood for a moment without turning from him.

"Lilya."

"What?"

"He's dead. Goryanchikov is dead. That's what I came to tell you."

He couldn't see the details of her face as she took this in. "I have to go" was all she said. The tread of her galoshes set off a muted ringing.

Virginsky hid his face in his hands.

10

†

Beneath the Milliner's Shop Again

PORFIRY PETROVICH LIT a cigarette. He was appreciative of the opportunity the flaring match gave him to take in his surroundings. The paneled door that briefly appeared was unexpectedly impressive. He shook the match out before it burned his fingers. The details of the door faded. Porfiry blinked, as if testing the darkness with his eyelashes. He coughed once as he waited for the unheard bell to be answered. He felt that he need not have coughed, or that the cough had a psychological rather than strictly physiological origin. The truth was, even in the impenetrable blackness of this night, he felt himself spied upon. And whenever he experienced this sensation, all his actions struck him as false.

At last a small panel in the door opened. Light fled the interior as if scandalized.

"Yes, *mein Herr*?"

"Fräulein Keller?"

"Do I know you?"

"I would like to make your acquaintance."

Her laughter revealed the indecency as well as the absurdity of his idea. "I always like to make new friends, especially when they are a handsome gentleman like you." She held the door open for him, treating him to a smile that was more ironical than coquettish. Even so, and despite her age (he judged her to be past the midpoint of her fifth decade), that smile set his heart thumping. It was not that he found it attractive. But there was knowledge in it, and experience. Her face was wearied by habits he could only guess at. Perhaps the most wearisome of all: this habit of opening the door to strangers, of assessing their predilections and facilitating fulfillment. Her smile stripped him bare but did not even show her teeth.

There was nothing of the bawd or the courtesan about her appearance. Her dress was fashionable and tasteful, even demure. All that it revealed was that she had kept her figure. He sensed a certain affectation in the way she carried herself, but was almost reassured by that. It seemed only human and certainly was to be expected. If he slapped her once, very hard, she would perhaps be cured of it. But he knew that he would, on balance, regret its loss.

Porfiry was admitted to a corridor decorated with more propriety than he had anticipated. He had expected crimson plush. The walls were in fact painted pale green, which struck an oddly prim note, as did the framed prints of racehorses. Only the narrowness of the corridor seemed indecent, due to the physical proximity it forced on those who passed in it.

Fräulein Keller held out her arms for his *shuba*. Porfiry was shocked by the gesture. To take off one's coat in such an establishment was not an innocent activity. It expressed a certain intention. Besides, the coat seemed to afford some protection, not least from that smile. It was strange too how he felt the need to escape from this place as soon as he had entered it. No, he would keep his coat on; he had a perfect right to, after all.

He saw his tortured mental processes mirrored and mocked in her smile.

"Fräulein Keller, I am an investigating magistrate."

"And so you cannot take off your coat. I understand."

"No, no. The point is I'm here on official business."

"A bird may be known by its flight. Is that not what you say?" Fräulein

Keller laughed at her own cleverness, then, catching that Porfiry did not share her amusement, became serious: "But we are all legal. There is nothing to investigate here." As if to prove her point, Fräulein Keller opened one of the doors from the corridor, seemingly at random. She showed Porfiry into a parlor paneled in highly varnished yellow wood. There was a hint of excess in the style of some of the furnishings. Porfiry was oppressed by the number of mirrors in elaborate frames. A fire was blazing, suggesting that someone other than the fleeting reflections on the walls had just occupied the room. "You will be too hot if you insist on keeping your furs on."

"I am looking for a girl."

"Of course."

"In connection with an investigation."

"*Ja, ja,* I understand."

"Her name is Lilya Ivanovna Semenova. I believe she works here."

"No longer. She has retired from the business."

"I see."

"It happens. The girls find themselves a rich patron. They settle for a while, but it never lasts. Soon they come back, knocking on my door. 'Fräulein Keller! Fräulein Keller! He has thrown me over! He has taken up with a dancer! Fräulein Keller, please! Let me in!' They cannot escape the life. It is in their blood. They are born whores."

"When was the last time you saw Lilya?"

"Today. She came back for her galoshes, the little fool. Does she not realize her new friend will buy her all the galoshes she desires?"

"She told you of this . . . *patron?*"

"She didn't need to. It's obvious. How else could she afford to retire?"

"Perhaps she has found other employment."

Fräulein Keller laughed cynically. "It is a wonder you catch any criminals, you are so innocent."

"The girls who work for you—they live here in the brothel?"

"And now you say dirty words to prove how worldly you are."

"Where is Lilya now, do you know?"

"It is not my concern."

"She had a child, didn't she? Who looked after the child when she was working?"

"I know nothing about these things. Perhaps it would profit you more to talk to one of the girls. I can arrange for you to be introduced. It would be my pleasure. You may pick one to examine more closely, in private. And that will be your pleasure, I am sure."

Fräulein Keller once again held out her arms for Porfiry's *shuba*.

"What if I wished to talk to them all?"

"That would be very greedy of you, *mein Herr.*"

As if this answer decided him, he finally began to take off his fur coat.

E VEN THOUGH THE heat from the fire had dried his throat, Porfiry declined the champagne.

"So the Widow Cliquot is not to your taste?" asked Fräulein Keller archly.

Porfiry also refused the brocade-upholstered chair, with its ornately carved "Second Rococo" frame, ignoring the care with which Fräulein Keller had positioned it.

"I will stand," he said curtly.

Four "girls" filed in through a second door in the parlor and stood in front of him. He did not step back or flinch under the force of their under-dressed presence, but he wished he had accepted both the drink and the seat. His own breath seemed intoxicating to him. It accelerated and en-larged his pulse. A kind of heavy sickness seemed to have entered his be-ing, as if his soul were solidifying. The cause of this strange excitement was the sudden knowledge of what he was capable of.

He lit a cigarette without knowing he was doing so.

Porfiry looked into the eyes of each of them in turn. And something about the way they returned his gaze suggested that he had broken the one taboo of the house. But in their eyes he saw no depravity, only detach-ment. This was all they had in common. In other respects, they presented

different faces behind their makeup: boredom, fear, stupor, and desperation. They affected expressions of licentiousness, but mechanically.

It was immediately apparent that Lilya Semenova would have been the
youngest and prettiest of them.

"This is all of them?" asked Porfiry, with an exhalation of smoke.

"All that are available. Is none to your taste?"

"You know it is not a question of that."

"If you say so, *mein Herr*. Who then will you choose? We have Olga.
Nadya. Sonya. Raya." A succession of ragged curtsies broke out along
the line, the satirical nature of which was confirmed by a further embel-
lishment from the final girl. She pulled down her chemise to bare one con-
ical breast for Porfiry's benefit.

"Please. There is no need for such exhibitions."

"Raya is very exuberant. Everything is natural to her." And yet it was
Raya in whose eyes Porfiry had detected fear.

Porfiry sighed heavily. "Very well. I choose Raya."

H ER HANDS WERE on his face. He removed them methodically.
The bed filled the room, so much so that one was practically
forced onto it as soon as one entered. There was a screen on the far side of
the bed, embroidered with kingfishers in flight. A silk kimono was slung
over the top of the screen.

"Do I not please you?"

He took in the fact of her naked skin. Her blond hair seemed distilled
from its pallor. "You're not Russian?"

"I'm Finnish. I am sorry."

"There's no need to be sorry. Do you know Lilya?"

"Yes, of course. But she doesn't work here anymore. Fräulein Keller
says—"

"How old are you?"

"How old do you want me to be?"

"I am a magistrate. You must answer honestly."

"I am twenty-seven."

"And how long have you been a prostitute?"

"I can't remember. I don't count the years."

"Do you know Konstantin Kirillovich?"

"What is this about?"

"Have you heard the name Konstantin Kirillovich?"

"I don't know."

"Think carefully."

"I think perhaps I have."

"Who is he?"

"A photographer. He takes photographs of the girls sometimes. And prints them up."

"Has he ever taken your photograph?"

"No."

"Why not?"

"He likes them younger."

"Has he taken photographs of Lilya?"

"Once, I think."

"It's not so bad, having your photograph taken. There are worse things, I should imagine."

Raya shrugged. She did not give any indication of resenting his eyes on her.

"Konstantin Kirillovich. Konstantin Kirillovich. What is his family name? I have forgotten."

"Everyone knows him only as Konstantin Kirillovich."

"That must be why I can't remember it." Porfiry smiled and blinked. "You touched my face. Why did you touch my face?"

"I don't know."

"Perhaps it is because you wish me to touch your face?"

"Yes, that's it."

Porfiry placed a hand flat against her cheek. Her skin was hot, and the makeup on it greasy and granular. He closed his eyes. Then felt her hand on his thigh.

"No," said Porfiry, pulling his hand away and standing up. He distanced himself from Raya's lingering touch.

"Why did you come?" asked Raya, looking up at him in wonder. Her eyes were very blue, he noticed.

"Where will I find Lilya, do you know?"

"It's Lilya you want?"

"I wish to ask her some questions. Do you know a student called Virginsky?"

Raya shook her head. Her silk-fine hair opened and closed like a fan.

"How about Goryanchikov? The dwarf?"

"I know the dwarf. He's a regular here. He always asks for Lilya. Perhaps he is her new boyfriend?" she wondered.

"Impossible. He's dead."

The alarm in her eyes intensified.

"It's likely that he was murdered."

"You think it was Lilya?"

"Where will I find her?"

"She'll be with Zoya Nikolaevna, I should think."

"Who is Zoya Nikolaevna?"

"The old prostitute who looks after Lilya's child. They share a room and Lilya's earnings."

"Did Lilya not board here?"

"Not during the day. Fräulein Keller would not allow the child here." Raya shivered. She was dressed only in underwear. However, it was not cold in the room.

"Cover yourself up," said Porfiry.

Raya reached across the bed and pulled down the kimono from the screen. Slipping it on, her face was confused as well as fearful.

"I will tell Fräulein Keller that you pleased me," he reassured her.

"I don't understand. Do you want nothing more of me?"

"An address? For Lilya."

"I don't know it. How would I know it?"

"No matter."

"Zoya lives somewhere near the Haymarket, I believe."

"Thank you. That is very helpful."

"Are you sure you want nothing more of me? Fräulein Keller says I am to do whatever you ask."

"Is it not a relief to you?"

"It makes no difference to me. It's why I am here, after all."

"Are you really so indifferent?"

She reached out and lifted one of his hands to her face again. He pulled it away. Her reaction was as if he had struck her.

"Please, there's no need."

Her habitually cowed expression changed into one of cunning. "Why *did* you come here?" she asked again.

"I'm looking for Lilya."

"Lilya is the only one who can please you."

"Not in the way you think. I merely wish to speak to her."

"I don't believe you. You're a man. And I know why you won't sleep with me. It's because you want my gratitude."

"It makes no difference to me." There was something pointed in the way his intonation, as well as his words, matched hers. To soften this, he added, "I would prefer it if you're not grateful. You have nothing to be grateful for, after all."

"Will you go now?" she asked, as if his presence made her uncomfortable.

He came close to telling her that she hadn't the right to dismiss him. Instead he said, "What are you frightened of, Raya?"

The question took her aback. "The same as everyone," she answered after a beat. "Getting old. Losing my looks. Not being able to work."

"It frightens you that you will one day be free of this place?"

"Hunger isn't freedom."

Porfiry lit another cigarette and smoked it through completely in silence. "You're an intelligent girl," he said at last. Then he looked into the blue of her eyes and left.

11

A Well-Ordered Household

THE FOLLOWING MORNING, as he had promised, Porfiry Petrovich called for Virginsky. He brought with him a pair of laborer's boots. They were not brand-new but they were in good condition.

Virginsky sat on the edge of his bed and looked down at the boots between his feet. His toes poked out of threadbare stockings. The nails were overgrown and yellow. The skin in places burned an angry red.

"Why have you brought me these?"

"You are in need of a stout pair of boots."

"I am in need of many things. Do you consider it your duty to provide me with it all?"

"I need your help. I want you to come with me to the house in Bolshaya Morskaya Street."

"I told you enough to find it, didn't I?"

"Yes, but I think it will be interesting for you to come."

"Is this part of your investigative technique?"

"You're very suspicious. Are you studying law, by any chance?"

"I was. I hope one day to resume my studies. When my finances allow it."

"And have you considered what you will do when you've graduated?"

"I imagine I will be a lawyer. An advocate in the new courts."

"So you believe in the rule of law?"

"I believe I will be able to exonerate the guilty as well as the next fool."

"You're not so cynical as all that."

"What else is one to do with a law degree?"

"You could be a magistrate. An investigating magistrate."

"In that case I'll be performing the opposite function. Incriminating the innocent."

Porfiry smiled indulgently. "I take it back. You are a cynic."

Virginsky put one foot tentatively into a boot. "It's too loose."

"You could put extra stockings on."

"Do you have extra stockings with you too?"

"Of course not. Surely you . . . ?"

"I am wearing all the clothes I own."

"It's not necessary for you to live in this way."

Virginsky ignored the remark and tried the other foot. "Where did you get these boots from?"

"Where do you think?"

"I think they came from a dead man."

Porfiry pursed his lips with amusement.

"They're not too bad after all," said Virginsky, standing.

THEY WALKED NORTH along Gorokhovaya Street. The Admiralty spire glinted ahead of them, a fine gold blade piercing the bright sky, like the memory of an inescapable crime in the city's heart. The great thoroughfare glistened and smoked. Huge apartment buildings squatted on either side, presenting rows and rows of windows diminishing into the distance. Porfiry had a sense of all the lives lived out behind those blank panes. For some, such vistas brought to mind a theater backdrop. But for

Porfiry, the city's uniform facades were more like an impenetrable stone curtain. The tragedies took place behind rather than in front of them.

Virginsky smirked with private amusement as his boots pushed firmly through the recent layer of snow.

"What is it?" asked Porfiry.

"Oh, nothing. Except you have bought me for a pair of boots. That is how cheaply I have bartered my soul. Not that I have a soul."

"You don't believe in the soul?"

"I didn't say that. I just said I didn't have one. But no, seeing as you asked, I don't believe in the soul. Or in God. Or the devil. Or any of that superstitious rot. Just as well really. If Mephistopheles himself were to come before me with an offer, I don't reckon much for my chances of holding out."

"So you compare me to Mephistopheles? But it's not a question of selling your soul. You want to find out who killed your friends, don't you? And you talk of becoming a lawyer. Really, you can't be both a nihilist and a practitioner of law. Your position is fraught with contradictions."

"Yes. Which is another reason why I despise myself."

"Do you like your boots?" asked Porfiry after they had walked another few paces.

"I like the fact that they don't let in the snow."

"That is a perfectly reasonable position."

"Tell me," began Virginsky with some diffidence.

"Yes?"

"Am I not a suspect?"

Porfiry thought for a moment, then replied, "I don't have a suspect yet."

"Let's say I am a suspect. Does it not complicate the issue, involving me in the investigation like this?"

"Let's say you are a suspect. I will learn something from watching you react to the people in the house where Goryanchikov and Borya lived."

"So I am a suspect?"

Porfiry gave his pursed smile again.

"This is a game to you," said Virginsky accusingly.

"But let's say you're not a suspect. I much prefer to say you're not a suspect. Even so, both victims were known to you. It is possible that the murderer is also someone known to you, perhaps someone who lives in the house, who may be there this morning. Your presence may provoke an interesting revelation. Oh, by the way, I may as well ask you this. It could save me a lot of trouble. Do you have any idea who could have killed them?"

"Do you think I would have kept it to myself if I knew?"

"Of course not. But you once said Goryanchikov had many enemies. How about Borya?"

"The only enemy Borya had was Goryanchikov. Ironic, isn't it?"

"Not really. Whoever killed them wanted to make it look like Borya had killed Goryanchikov and then killed himself. I expect I shall hear much about how the two men hated each other."

"It's true, though."

"Last night I went to Fräulein Keller's," said Porfiry abruptly. Virginsky faltered in his step. Porfiry watched him. "The boots?" asked Porfiry blandly.

"They're still a little loose."

"Your friend Lilya wasn't there. It's Fräulein Keller's opinion that she's found herself a rich protector."

"Is that how it is?"

"If you believe Fräulein Keller."

"Why are you so sure that Lilya has something to do with this?"

"I'm not. But Lilya herself presented me with a small mystery. The mysterious Konstantin Kirillovich." Again Porfiry watched Virginsky closely. "It is a coincidence that Lilya should come to our notice the night before an anonymous note was received alerting us to the two bodies in Petrovsky Park. A coincidence that I should see Lilya at Lippevechsel's Tenements when I came over to see you yesterday. As an investigator, one learns to mistrust coincidences. I discover she is known to you. And you, I'm afraid, are the only person I have so far whom I can link to the two dead men. So Lilya is also linked."

"But it's all nonsense. It means nothing. It could lead you nowhere."

"Yes. But so far it's all I have to go on."

"Besides, there are lots of other people who knew them both. It's just you haven't met them yet."

"Today I hope to rectify that," said Porfiry, as he came to a halt. They had reached Bolshaya Morskaya Street. "Now then. Seven, seventeen, or seventy? Which is it? I wonder."

"It's that one," said Virginsky. He pointed out a pink house in a three-story terrace on the other side of the street. The building was recently built, within the last twenty years. It was highly ornamented with lion's-head relief panels set into the stonework, ionic pilasters on the second story, and even caryatids—massive female sculpted figures—framing the passageways that led to the courtyards behind.

"An elegant building," commented Porfiry, though his voice lacked the warmth of approval. "Who would have thought it was home to two victims of murder? Perhaps the caryatids provide a clue. I always think of murder victims when I see the stone inhabitants of Petersburg."

"That's very fanciful of you."

"No doubt. It must be something to do with my occupation. Too many unsolved cases, I'm afraid. I seem to see the dead appealing for justice everywhere I look. And yet their faces seem strangely calm, do you not think? As if they are reconciled to their fate."

"Who could be reconciled to such a burden?"

"You mean the burden of supporting the upper stories?" asked Porfiry with a smile.

"I mean the burden of being a woman. They are women, aren't they?"

"These ones are. One does see men, of course. Technically, the male figures are atlantes. Shall we go in?"

Looking from the house to Virginsky, Porfiry noticed that the student's face showed signs of sudden agitation.

"You can't force me to." His eyes were fixed on the pink house, but his head was leaning backward as if subject to a force of repulsion.

"My dear friend, I wouldn't dream of it."

"Well then, I won't do it. I've brought you here. I've pointed it out. That's enough." The force of repulsion acted now on his whole body. He began to edge away from Porfiry. The next moment he turned on his heels and broke into a wide-paced run. Without slowing his step, he called over his shoulder, "Boots! Excellent!"

Porfiry had the impression he was grinning.

T HE NUMBER OF the house turned out to be 17. An additional sign indicated that the house belonged to the widow of State Councilor S. P. Ivolgin.

The door, which was to the left of the central caryatid-framed passageway, gave directly onto the street. The maid who opened it was dressed in a neat gray dress with a well-starched apron over it. Her hair was tied up inside a clean white cap. She had an attractive, intelligent face. Porfiry sensed a spirited independence that he could imagine crossing over into pride or even impertinence. Her eyes were questioning without being suspicious. There was a slight impatience in her demeanor that suggested he had dragged her away from some important work. He guessed her age at around thirty.

"Good day," began Porfiry. "Is this the home of Goryanchikov, the student?"

"Yes?"

"May I speak to Goryanchikov?"

"He's not here. He hasn't been here for several days."

"Have you any idea where he is?"

Porfiry felt himself subject to her scrutinizing gaze.

"I'm Porfiry Petrovich, an investigating magistrate. It is to do with a serious criminal matter." Porfiry looked away down the street, then back into her undaunted gray eyes. "Perhaps it would be better if I came inside."

The maid agreed without hesitation, bowing slightly as she closed the door behind him.

Porfiry looked down at a highly polished parquet floor. The hall was warm and comfortably furnished without being ostentatious. Rugs from the Caucases hung on the walls, and one lay on the floor. A faintly spicy smell pleasantly stimulated his nostrils.

"I think you had better talk to Anna Alexandrovna."

"Your mistress? The Widow Ivolgina?"

"Yes."

"Of course. But I would like to talk to you first. What is your name?"

"Katya."

"When was the last time you saw Goryanchikov, Katya?"

"Stepan Sergeyevich. His name is Stepan Sergeyevich Goryanchikov."

"I see. So when was the last time you saw Stepan Sergeyevich?"

Katya thought carefully before answering. "Four days ago."

"Is it normal for him not to come home for so long?"

"No. Sometimes we don't see him for a day or two. But four days is unusual."

"Did you think nothing of it?"

"I was beginning to think something of it."

"What were you beginning to think?"

"He'd done a moonlight flit. He owes Anna Alexandrovna a fortune in rent."

"I see. And what was Anna Alexandrovna's view?"

"She thought the same. We thought we would never see him again. And that she would never see the money. What's all this about?" Katya asked abruptly.

"I am afraid Stepan Sergeyevich Goryanchikov is dead."

Katya's brows came together in a frown as she took in the news. Then an expression something like horror opened up on her face. "Borya!" she cried.

"Why do you say that?"

"Borya killed him, didn't he? They had a row. Borya threatened him with an axe. It was shortly before Stepan Sergeyevich disappeared." Her head was trembling perceptibly.

"What was the argument about?"

"I don't know. What do men ever argue about?"

Before Porfiry could answer, another female voice called from a room at the back of the hall: "Katya! What is it, Katya? I need you in here." The appeal was followed by the muted clatter of pots.

Katya gave Porfiry a quick look that seemed to have something accusing about it, as if he were to blame for bringing all this on them. That glance left him in no doubt of the depth and force of her protective feelings toward her mistress.

A moment later this lady herself came out from the kitchen, her head tilted upward, poised between inquiry and annoyance. When she saw Porfiry, her expression became guarded. She looked to Katya for some explanation. The maid returned a warning but, in contrast to her mistress, seemed unabashed.

Anna Alexandrovna was dressed simply. Her dark hair was neatly pinned. Her face was still youthful, with a flush of color at her cheeks. Hers was a soft beauty, its malleability such that every touch of experience had compromised rather than enhanced it. Looking into her eyes, which she allowed him to do only for a split second, Porfiry saw that she was older than he had first thought. He saw a glance complicated by caution and disillusion. Porfiry remembered Virginsky mentioning a daughter and wondered briefly what kind of a man State Councilor Ivolgin had been; wealthy certainly, judging from the house he had left to her. The same house also hinted at his ambition and even pretension.

"I did not realize we had a visitor," she said, dipping her gaze below Porfiry's face. "I was grinding cinnamon. I needed Katya's help. I didn't realize . . ." Porfiry was touched that she was flustered on his account. She brought with her another scent besides the cinnamon, the faint hint of her perfume. Porfiry was aware of how different it was, in intent and effect, from Lilya's. It was a clean, uncomplicated fragrance.

"This gentleman is a policeman," said Katya sternly.

"A magistrate. An investigating magistrate," corrected Porfiry, with an apologetic smile. "Porfiry Petrovich, madam," he added with a bow.

"What is it about?" asked Anna Alexandrovna anxiously.

"Stepan Sergeyevich," answered Katya, her voice strained. "He's dead."

Porfiry watched the quick transitions of Anna Alexandrovna's face with interest. It was difficult to be certain about the precise emotion this news inspired in her, but Porfiry felt that genuine grief was part of it.

"I'm afraid that's not all," said Porfiry. "Borya—your yardkeeper, I believe—is also dead." Porfiry glanced guiltily toward Katya.

Anna Alexandrovna shrieked. "Oh, this is terrible! Terrible!" she cried, a hand coming up to her suddenly white face. Katya rushed up to her and embraced her.

Porfiry's bow was contrite. "There is no easy way to break such news."

"Oh, poor Borya," cried Anna Alexandrovna, pulling herself away from her maid's support. "It's all right, Katya. I'm all right." But she staggered as Katya released her. Porfiry held out a hand that was rejected with a shake of the head. "Please, sir . . . ?"

"Porfiry Petrovich," Porfiry reminded her.

"Please, Porfiry Petrovich, would you accompany me into the drawing room?" She gestured toward a pair of double doors. "There is a samovar there. Katya, will you serve us some tea, my dear?"

THE SAMOVAR GURGLED and hissed agitatedly. Porfiry Petrovich and Anna Alexandrovna turned away from it as though with discretion. She gestured for him to sit on a gold and maroon Russian sofa. As he did so, a gust of wind rattled the panes.

The drawing room was lined in pale blue brocatelle, with gilt work on the rococo moldings. The air was humid with tea-scented steam. Silk curtains of the same blue were draped in swooping sections across three large windows. The light that filtered through cast a milky sheen over Anna Alexandrovna's dark dress. Within a marble fireplace, short, quick flames peeped shyly out of a mountain of glowing coals.

"It's such a shock," said Anna Alexandrovna, looking out of the window, as if she were commenting on the sudden violence of the weather. "How did it happen?"

"I'm afraid it seems as if they were both murdered."

"No!" She searched his face for a different answer.

"Their bodies were found together in Petrovsky Park."

"Petrovsky Park?" There was no doubt about it. The mention of Petrovsky Park had startled her. But now her expression became guarded. She leaned back slightly from Porfiry. He watched her expectantly, but she gave nothing more away.

Porfiry accepted a glass of tea from the tray Katya held out to him. He slipped a sugar crystal between his teeth to sweeten it. He placed the glass on the low mahogany table that was in front of the sofa.

"Katya informed me that Borya and Goryanchikov—Stepan Sergeyevich, that is—quarreled shortly before Stepan Sergeyevich disappeared."

"Yes. That's right. Everyone heard it."

"Everyone? Who else lives in the house?"

"My daughter, Sofiya. And Osip Maximovich. And Vadim Vasilyevich. However, Osip Maximovich was not here on the day of the quarrel."

"Who are these gentlemen?"

"Osip Maximovich rents the second floor. Vadim Vasilyevich lodges with him and serves him in the capacity of a secretary. He also has a manservant, Artur."

"Is there anyone else in your household?"

"Yes, there is Marfa Denisovna. She was Sofiya's nurse when she was younger. She lives with us still. And Lizaveta, our cook."

"You have a cook, and yet you were grinding your own cinnamon?" Porfiry teased her.

"There are some jobs I like to do in the kitchen, both because they give me pleasure and because I don't like to leave them to others."

Porfiry nodded his understanding and tried to make up for his gentle mockery by blinking repeatedly. Anna Alexandrovna seemed startled. "We will want to speak to everyone in the house," he said more seriously. "One of my officers will come back this afternoon to take statements."

"But Osip Maximovich and Vadim Vasilyevich will be at the publishing house."

"The publishing house?"

"Osip Maximovich is a publisher."

"I see. You said that Osip Maximovich was not here on the day of the argument. Do you know where he was?"

"He was staying in a monastery in Kaluga province."

"Optina Pustyn?"

"That's right. He was on retreat."

"When did he leave for Optina Pustyn?"

"Oh, weeks before. I mean, possibly two weeks before."

"Did he go alone?"

"Yes. Vadim Vasilyevich took him to the station and saw him off."

"But Vadim Vasilyevich was here in the house at the time of the argument?"

Anna Alexandrovna thought for a moment before replying: "I think so, yes. It's hard to say for sure."

"And when did Osip Maximovich return?"

"Last night."

"Only last night? I see. And as for Borya . . . when did you notice that Borya was missing? Presumably you had noticed that Borya was missing."

"Yes, of course, but . . . Borya often disappears. He can go missing for days."

"He is a drunkard," put in Katya, whom Porfiry was surprised to discover had not left the room, merely withdrawn into the peripheral gloom.

"Was he drunk when he argued with Stepan Sergeyevich?"

"When wasn't he drunk?" commented Katya without concealing her disgust.

"Katya!" pleaded Anna Alexandrovna. Her eyes widened in admonition.

"Anna Alexandrovna, can you tell me what Borya and Stepan Sergeyevich argued about?"

"They were always arguing. Stepan Sergeyevich took pleasure in goading Borya. Stepan Sergeyevich was an intellectual. He questioned everything. Borya was a simple man. A man of faith. Everything he believed in, Stepan Sergeyevich ridiculed."

"But what brought it to a head?"

"I don't know that it was brought to a head. Why do you say it was brought to a head?" There was evasion in her question.

"Katya informed me that Borya threatened to kill Stepan Sergeyevich."

"Borya would never kill anyone," protested Anna Alexandrovna feelingly.

"But would you say this row was any worse than any of the others they had had?"

"Oh, things were said, certainly."

"What things?"

"Please! How can I be expected to know?"

"Where did the argument take place? Can you tell me that?"

"In the yard. Borya was in his shed. Stepan Sergeyevich was in the yard, shouting into the shed."

"What was he wearing?"

"I beg your pardon?"

"Stepan Sergeyevich, what was he wearing?"

"His *shuba*, I think. Yes, I'm sure of it. He would have been. He never went out without his *shuba* on. He was very proud of it. He had it made specially, of course. To fit."

"That's interesting. He owed you money, I understand. And yet he could afford to have a fur coat made."

"From time to time Stepan Sergeyevich would do work for Osip Maximovich. Translations. He was paid most generously. But the money never lasted."

"I hope you will forgive my next question, but it occurs to me and so I must ask it. That is the way it is with investigations."

Anna Alexandrovna looked anxious but said nothing.

"How did such a man as Stepan Sergeyevich Goryanchikov come to be living in your house?"

"He came to us when my husband was still alive."

"I see. It was your late husband's wish that Stepan Sergeyevich reside here?"

"My husband agreed to it, and so I suppose he must have wished it," said Anna Alexandrovna.

Porfiry blinked excessively again as he took in the tension in her expression. At last he said: "I would like to search Stepan Sergeyevich's room. And also to have a look in Borya's shed. Did Borya have an axe?"

"Yes, of course. He had many axes."

"Of course, what yardkeeper doesn't have a good collection of axes! Even so, it is useful to have it confirmed. Especially as I expect that I will find one of his axes missing."

"He killed him with the axe!" cried Katya.

"An axe is involved in these crimes, that's true," said Porfiry, turning to Katya. "But I'm curious to know why you are so convinced that Borya killed Stepan Sergeyevich. I have not said that."

"And Borya was murdered too, Katya." Anna Alexandrovna appealed to Porfiry: "You did say that they were both murdered?"

"Apparently."

"Was it with the axe?" pressed Katya.

Porfiry smiled but didn't answer. "Perhaps you would show me to Stepan Sergeyevich's room?" He placed the glass on the tray and stood up.

P ORFIRY STOOPED TO enter the room, a tiny space with sloping walls in the apex of the house.

"It's very cramped," he observed to Katya, who had shown him up.

"Stepan Sergeyevich was comfortable enough," she answered from the doorway. There was not room for them both inside. "He didn't need anywhere bigger. He never complained."

Porfiry took in the details of the dead man's lodging: the child-sized bed tucked beneath the eaves, the desk and single chair, both sawed off at the legs. The other furniture consisted of an enormous-seeming ottoman and an ornately carved trunk of dark wood. Through a small dormer window he looked down on Srednaya Meshchanskaya Street. The sky was darkening. It seemed that there was a blizzard thickening in the air. But the room was warm: the heat of the house rose into it. Unlike the highly varnished parquet of the lower apartments, the floor was of rough boards. The room was clean, however. Porfiry looked around for an icon on the white-painted walls but did not see one.

On the desk, there was a neat pile of paper and an open book. Porfiry lifted the book to glance at the cover. It was the first volume of Proudhon's *Philosophie de la misère*.

"The Philosophy of Misery," said Porfiry aloud. The book was open on page 334. A phrase from the middle of the page, underlined in red ink, drew his attention: *"J'insiste donc sur mon accusation."* Porfiry returned the book to the desk. He picked up the top sheet from the pile of paper. He saw that it bore—written in a flamboyant hand and also in red ink—a Russian translation of the page he had just glanced at. In it, the phrase "I insist therefore on my accusation" was also underlined. In the Russian version, the words immediately following this were: "The father of Faith will be the destroyer of Wisdom." Startled by the strange statement, he checked the original French text. There, after the underlined phrase, he read: *"Sous le régime aboli par Luther et la révolution française, l'homme, autant que le comportait le progrès de son industrie, pouvait être heureux . . ."* The Russian translation of this phrase—"Under the regime abolished by Luther and the French Revolution man could be happy in proportion to the progress of his industry . . ."—came only after the interpolation concerning the father of Faith.

Porfiry placed the sheet back on top of the pile and turned to Katya with a smile. "And you keep it tidy for him. It seems to me Anna Alexandrovna runs a well-ordered household. She is a good mistress, I would say."

"The best."

"Tell me, did anything else unusual happen on the day of the argument? Did Goryanchikov or Borya have any visitors, for example?"

"There *was* a boy," answered Katya with surprise.

"A boy? What boy is this?"

"I don't know. I had never seen him before. It was strange. He insisted on seeing Stepan Sergeyevich. And on his way out he called on Borya in his shed. Soon after that they had their argument. And soon after that Stepan Sergeyevich went out."

"Wearing his *shuba?*"

"Of course . . . as Anna Alexandrovna has said."

"And how soon after Stepan Sergeyevich went out did you notice that Borya was missing?"

"Well, of course, the yard needed clearing. We couldn't open the door for the snow. We had to ask Osip Maximovich's man Artur to do it for us. He wasn't happy about that, I can tell you. Considers himself above such tasks."

"And who has kept the yard clear for you in Borya's absence?"

"Anna Alexandrovna has come to an arrangement with one of the neighbors' yardkeepers. He sometimes helps us out when Borya goes missing."

"This boy interests me. Was he a friend of Anna Alexandrovna's daughter perhaps?"

"No!" cried Katya, outraged at the suggestion. "He was a scruffy little urchin. Sofiya Sergeyevna would have nothing to do with the likes of him. Besides, he was only about ten years old."

"And how old is Sofiya Sergeyevna?"

"She was thirteen at her last birthday."

"I see. Tell me more about this boy. Did you speak to him?"

"I answered the door to him. And I would have shut the door in his filthy face too if Stepan Sergeyevich hadn't come down and seen him."

"Did Stepan Sergeyevich know the boy?"

"I don't think so. But he heard him asking for him by name."

"So he had the boy admitted and brought him up here to his room? How long did the boy stay?"

"Not long. Ten minutes at the most. If that."

"Does Stepan Sergeyevich give lessons as a tutor?"

"Not anymore. And this boy was not the sort of boy to have lessons. He had a stupid face."

"You took against the boy, I can see."

"He left a trail of dirty footprints throughout the house. It was a job to get them out."

"And what about Stepan Sergeyevich? Did you like Stepan Sergeyevich?"

The question went unanswered.

"Katya?"

"One should not speak ill of the dead."

"He was a difficult man to like, though, wasn't he?"

"He was a devil."

"Do you know a friend of Goryanchikov's called Pavel Pavelovich
Virginsky?"

"I believe there is a gentleman of that name who visited from time
to time."

"Did he visit on the day of Goryanchikov's disappearance?"

"No. However, it's strange you mentioned it . . . He called to visit
Stepan Sergeyevich yesterday."

"Yesterday? What time was this?"

"It was late. Very late. Anna Alexandrovna and her daughter had both
gone to bed. He knocked the whole house up."

"And he asked to see Stepan Sergeyevich?"

"He demanded to be admitted to his room."

Porfiry fumbled in his pockets for his enameled cigarette case. A severe
frown from Katya deterred him from opening it. Nonetheless, in this instance, he found the touch of it stimulating enough.

OUTSIDE, Porfiry finally lit the cigarette he craved. The blizzard he
had seen massing from Goryanchikov's room had blown itself out.
But the courtyard had already been cleared. Porfiry felt sorry for Borya,
whose death had been so quickly and easily compensated for, as if erased
beneath a snowfall.

Inside the yardkeeper's shed it was as if the objects of his life were
shaping themselves around the fact of his death, around his physical absence. There was an old paint-spattered wooden chair, its seat worn and

polished by many sittings. It was crammed in next to a folding card table, the baize threadbare and stained. The samovar on it seemed to possess an air of mournful disappointment. Chipped cups milled around it without purpose. The sawdust had settled on the floor, around an assortment of bricks and logs. The bottom of a barrel was propped up against one of the shed's sides. Life continued only in the cobwebs that grew heedless over the tools and tins of his occupation.

Porfiry backhanded a line in the air, a conjurer's gesture, as he checked off the row of hanging axes. But of course, he did not need to do this. He could see perfectly well where the missing axe should be. He could judge too, from its position in the hierarchy of axes, that its size matched that of the bloodied axe found on Borya.

He stared at the gap and wondered at the mind that had chosen this axe over the three others hanging there. The second-smallest axe had been taken. The chances were that it was snatched in haste. But even so, some exercise of intent must have been involved, whether conscious or unconscious. Why, for example, was the smallest axe not taken, which would surely have been more convenient? The axe, or rather the absence of this particular axe, had to point at something. It was in precisely such a detail that the killer would betray himself.

Porfiry brought his hand back and in the air drew a vertical line up and then back down the gap formed by the missing axe. He realized that he had crossed himself. His hand came to rest on a small birch box that lay on the shelf beneath the axes. He picked up the box and discovered that it was locked.

I N   A N   U P S T A I R S   A P A R T M E N T, seated alone at a card table, Marfa Denisovna looked down at hands disfigured by warts. She laid out the cards for a game of solitaire. She accepted the fall of the cards in the same way as she had accepted her warts, and all the other things sent by God. Without pleasure or complaint.

Marfa Denisovna was sixty-six, as old as the century. It was a convenient coincidence, because if she ever forgot her age, she only had to ask the year.

Deep peach-stone whorls lined her face. She lacked lips entirely and showed as little as possible of her eyes. Her body was wiry and compact. There was not much to her physically, but she was far from frail. The passage of time had worn away all softness from her, leaving a human kernel. Her shoulders were draped in an enormous black shawl. A delicate lace bonnet seemed out of place on her tightly pinned-up, almost metallically hard gray hair.

She did not look up as Anna Alexandrovna came in.

"Has he gone?"

"Yes."

"Who was he?"

"An investigator."

"What did he want?"

"They have found Stepan Sergeyevich and Borya."

Marfa Denisovna moved the ace of spades up.

"Dead. They are both dead." Anna Alexandrovna's voice was distant and empty.

Marfa Denisovna moved the seven of hearts across, placing it on the eight of clubs.

"Marfa Denisovna? Did you hear me?" Now there was an edge of panic to the younger woman's voice.

"I heard you."

"He asked about the argument."

"What did you tell him?"

"I told him what I had to."

"So. Stepanushka is dead. Poor Stepanushka. Ah well, it was meant to be. God did not look favorably on his life. His deformity was a punishment."

"But why should he have been punished? It was not his sin."

"He was not the only one punished." Marfa Denisovna laid down the cards and spread out her fingers. There was not one that was without a wart. In places the clusters of nodules distorted the shape of the finger. It had not escaped Marfa Denisovna's notice that her affliction made it harder for her to place her hands together in prayer. She picked up the cards again and dealt out the next three.

"They will be back. The authorities. A policeman will come to take statements from us all," said Anna Alexandrovna hurriedly.

Marfa Denisovna at last looked up at Anna Alexandrovna, though with eyes that were barely visible. "I have always taken good care of this family. You need not be afraid on my account."

"I'm not afraid."

Marfa Denisovna continued playing in silence. At last she said, "I took care of things before, didn't I? And I will take care of things again. God's will be done."

12

The Testimony
of a Prince

O F C O U R S E , you must have expected it," said Chief Superintendent Nikodim Fomich.

"I expected nothing of the sort," answered Porfiry.

"Porfiry Petrovich." Nikodim Fomich spread the fingers of both hands
out on his desk as if he were taking precautions against its levitating. He
pressed down firmly once and then sat back. "The *prokuror* has decided—"

"The *prokuror* is an arrogant fool."

"In his opinion, the case is closed. The dwarf was murdered by the
yardkeeper. The yardkeeper committed suicide. Your own investigations
have uncovered several independent testimonies alluding to a violent argument between the men. Lieutenant Salytov has now interviewed all the
residents of the house. A number of them have testified to the fact that the
yardkeeper was heard to threaten the life of the dwarf."

"But the medical evidence—"

"In the *prokuror*'s opinion, the medical evidence is flawed. 'Suspect,' I
believe, was the word he used."

"Dr. Pervoyedov said that he had never seen a clearer case of poisoning by prussic acid."

"Those were the words he used?"

"Something like that," answered Porfiry uncertainly.

"The *prokuror* is not impressed by Dr. Pervoyedov."

"But that's outrageous."

"Another doctor, a doctor appointed by the *prokuror*, is of the opinion that the prussic acid traces were due to a contamination. Dr. Pervoyedov has been very overworked at the hospital. It is unlikely that the *prokuror* will allow you to call on his services again. He feels that Dr. Pervoyedov should be fined for incompetence, due to the contamination that has occurred. The facts of the case, as the *prokuror* understands them, are not consistent with poisoning by prussic acid."

"No, no, no, no, no! That's insane!" protested Porfiry.

"Be careful, Porfiry Petrovich. This is not like you."

"But you must see the illogicality of the statement you just made."

"Porfiry. This is Russia. We are governed not by logic but by authority. You know that as well as I. In fact, your friend Dr. Pervoyedov is getting off lightly. The *prokuror* was at first of the opinion that he had falsified the results deliberately to further his career. I managed to persuade him that that was not the case."

Porfiry slumped in his seat. He could not speak for some time. At last he murmured, "What do I do now?"

"You must let it drop."

"But the dead men? What of the dead men?" He saw in his mind an image of Goryanchikov and Borya transformed into masonry figures bearing the upper stories of an imaginary building. But unlike the real atlantes and caryatids of St. Petersburg, they writhed and groaned under the strain.

"They are dead. In the opinion of the *prokuror*, they should not be allowed to disrupt the smooth running of the judicial system."

"Why didn't he tell me this himself? I report to him, not to you."

"Shall I tell you what I believe? I believe he is afraid of you. You're cleverer than he, you see, Porfiry. All he has is his ambition and his power. You have more. You have cleverness and compassion."

The compliments depressed Porfiry. "I'm surprised to hear you say I have compassion. Dr. Pervoyedov would not agree with that, I think."

"But if you didn't, you wouldn't care who killed these men."

"It's not compassion that makes me care who killed them. I don't have compassion for the dead. It's no use to them. What are they going to do with my compassion?"

"I know what drives you, Porfiry. I know for whom you have compassion."

"If so, you know more than I do."

"The perpetrators. The poor, miserable sinners."

Porfiry clasped his hands together and placed the knuckles of his thumbs against his lips. The gesture was prompted by agitation, but it looked a little like he was praying. "You're thinking of that boy." There was a note of denial in his voice. He would not look at Nikodim Fomich.

"Not just of him. It is for their souls, for the souls of them all, that you do it."

"You're talking nonsense. Why should I care about anyone's soul but mine? I might have said such things in the past. But it was just a ruse. A technique. To get the confession. The confession is everything."

"That's my point!"

"But not for the reason you think. They can all go to hell for all I care. I can have no compassion for a cold-blooded murderer."

"But you can, Porfiry. And you do. And that is what separates you from our esteemed *prokuror*."

The tension flashed in Porfiry's eyes. His expression oscillated between wounded and angry. "You're wrong. You're wrong about everything. It's for the glory that I do it. I am as ambitious as the *prokuror*." Still he would not look at Nikodim Fomich, as if he were afraid he would find confirmation in the other man's gaze.

. . .

T HE CLERK ZAMYOTOV was waiting for Porfiry at the door of his chambers. Porfiry was in no mood to confront Zamyotov's sly insubordination. However, he sensed something unwonted in the other man's expression. Zamyotov seemed distracted, almost rattled, and this caused him to abandon any pretense. The angry impatience with which he greeted Porfiry was openly impertinent.

"Porfiry Petrovich! Where on earth have you been? How am I expected to fulfill my duties if you do not inform me of your whereabouts and movements? This gentleman—"

Porfiry frowned at a slightly built young man seated on one of the chairs reserved for witnesses and suspects waiting to see the investigating magistrate. The fellow's eyes locked onto Porfiry's desperately and beseechingly. His tie was fastened in a large looping bow. An overcoat trimmed with silver fox was draped over his shoulders. Beneath it he wore a mustard-colored suit and emerald waistcoat. A beaverskin top hat perched on his lap, kid gloves folded neatly on top of it. His hair lay in tight curls around his collar. He was clean shaven; in fact, Porfiry suspected his cheeks had not yet felt the razor. In the angle of his head and the needful intensity of his gaze, Porfiry saw some connection with Zamyotov's flustered mood.

"—a personage of indisputable rank and influence."

The young man smiled appealingly as Zamyotov spoke.

"Indeed," said Porfiry drily. "It is not like you to be impressed by rank and influence, Alexander Grigorevich."

Zamyotov pursed his lips as he weighed up his response. "I don't know quite what you are implying. I know only that he will not go away until he has seen an investigating magistrate. It concerns a matter requiring the utmost sensitivity. Having acquainted myself somewhat with the essentials of the case, I felt that you, Porfiry Petrovich, would be the person best—"

"Please, Alexander Grigorevich, your flattery is making me anxious."

Porfiry smiled as he caught the look of confusion on the clerk's face. He felt him close on his heels as he entered his chambers.

"But what am I to tell him?" demanded Zamyotov.

Porfiry looked up from behind his government-issue desk and calmly assessed the clerk's angry insolence.

"A matter requiring—what was it? Sensitivity? But is it a criminal matter, Alexander Grigorevich? If it is not a criminal matter, I don't see how I may be of service."

"I believe it is a complicated case," said Zamyotov, frowning distractedly. It seemed that Porfiry's tone escaped him. "Obviously, not being an investigating magistrate, I am myself not qualified to judge legal issues."

"My goodness! Such humility, Alexander Grigorevich!"

Zamyotov's frown sharpened into annoyance. "It is your job to decide whether a crime has been committed, not mine."

"Quite so."

"Will you see him or not?"

"I feel, almost, that it is my duty to see him. Please, show the gentleman in, Alexander Grigorevich."

The young man entered with a tentative step. Hat and gloves in hand, he had something of the air of a supplicant.

"You may go now," Porfiry said to Zamyotov, who was lingering expectantly. The clerk challenged the peremptory dismissal with a glare. He slammed the door as he left. Porfiry turned to the young man, indicating a chair. "Please." The young man moved with deliberation, almost gingerly, as if he were afraid the seat would not support him. And yet, as Porfiry judged, there was hardly anything to him. "You are?"

The young man seemed surprised by the question. He hesitated, as though he were unsure about the wisdom or necessity of supplying his name. At last he said, "Makar Alexeyevich Bykov." His voice was high and strained. As the name seemed to make no impression on Porfiry, the young man added in a whisper, "I am Prince Bykov."

"*Prince* Bykov." Porfiry's emphasis was satirical.

"You have heard of me?"

Porfiry allowed a beat before admitting, "No."

"It's just that I have written some plays."

"You are a playwright?"

"They have caused quite a stir in certain circles. Perhaps they have come to your attention in an . . . uh . . . official capacity?"

"No. I have not heard of you or your plays." Porfiry smiled in a way that he hoped was reassuring.

The young man seemed dubious. "Of course, I do not believe there is anything seditious in them myself. My works are inspired by a profound patriotism."

"That's all right then," said Porfiry.

"Were they ever to be performed, however, there is a danger that they might be misunderstood. Willfully misunderstood, I mean. The meaning of the plays is clear enough."

"I would hope so."

"Alexander Grigorevich led me to believe that you would be able to help me."

"I can't help you with your plays. I am a magistrate, not an impresario."

"It is not to do with my plays that I have come to see you."

"Ah—I misunderstood."

Prince Bykov was overcome by a sudden turmoil of emotion. It was as if he could hold himself together no longer. His voice was breaking as he blurted out, "Ratazyayev is missing."

"Ratazyayev?"

"Yes." The prince nodded violently, knuckling away his sudden tears.

"Who is Ratazyayev?"

"He is"—Prince Bykov closed his eyes, steeling himself—"a very dear friend of mine." Prince Bykov opened his eyes again to see how Porfiry had taken this declaration. His look was raw and exposed but not timid and had about it no pretense. Whatever else he was, Prince Makar Alexeyevich Bykov was an honest man and a brave man too, Porfiry decided.

"I see," said Porfiry. At that moment he decided also that it was time to take Prince Bykov seriously. "Please," continued Porfiry, taking and lighting a cigarette. "Please tell me how it came about that Ratazyayev went missing."

"I blame myself. It was all my fault. We quarreled, you see."

"What was the quarrel over?"

Prince Bykov's expression became pained. "Ratazyayev came suddenly into some money. I was suspicious. I accused him of certain things. He said he had an engagement. An acting engagement. Ratazyayev is an actor, you see, although he has not performed on a public stage for many years. I'm afraid I didn't believe him. I accused him of many things. The engagement was supposed to be in Tosno. It was for a week, apparently. Precisely one week. But what theater is there in Tosno, tell me that? And what kind of a run lasts for just one week? One week! What can you do in one week? Was he not required for rehearsals? But then, no, it's not a week, it's two weeks. It was a private acting engagement. There was to be only one performance. The two weeks included the rehearsal time. It was in honor of Prince Stroganov-Golitsyn. You know the Stroganov-Golitsyns have their estate near Tosno. It was to be held on the prince's birthday. A special performance, arranged by his friends. Very well. What play? Well, first it was to be *A Feast During the Plague*. A very appropriate play for a birthday celebration, would you not say? So then, no, it's not *A Feast During the Plague*, it's *Little Snowdrop*. My goodness, Pushkin must give way to Ostrovsky? So no, it's not *Little Snowdrop*, it's *Boris Godunov*. The whole thing? You can have a passable production of *Boris Godunov* ready in two weeks? No, no, no. Not the whole thing. Scenes from *Boris Godunov*. Scenes, only scenes. And what part is he to play? Why, he will take the title role! But if you know Ratazyayev, you will know he would be hopelessly miscast as Boris Godunov. The whole thing was a pack of lies from beginning to end, it was obvious. But when I challenged him, he became angry. He packed his case. He was going to Tosno. I could not go with him. He would not let me carry the case out to the carriage. Would not let me even touch it. So I was not required. That is all very well. I will accept that. I will accept that Ratazyayev is a free man. If he wishes to go to Tosno, I will not stand in his way. But to lie to me! That I will not stand for! And it is a lie! What he doesn't realize, you see, is that I was in the Cadet Corps with a cousin of Prince Stroganov-Golitsyn's. Whom I happened to meet at the English Club. And whom I happened to ask about this marvelous theatrical birthday celebration. At which point I discover that the prince's birthday is in the summer—in August. Surely there must be some mistake. But no. The cousin is quite certain. He went to the party for the prince's last birthday. And there was not a theatrical performance. There were open-air tableaux. The cousin himself took part in one. A scene from the Trojan War. He was Patroclus, I believe. I decide not to confront Ratazyayev with this. I can't bear to. I can't bear to hear more lies. I can't bear to see the man I—" Prince Bykov broke off. He looked at Porfiry queasily. "A man I greatly admire . . . humiliate himself with lies." Prince Bykov regarded Porfiry with a genuinely tortured look. "Perhaps I should have done. Perhaps if I had confronted him, Ratazyayev would be with me today. Instead I chose, to my shame, to employ subterfuge. I spied on him. I disguised myself and followed him to the Nikolaevsky Station, where he was to take the train to Tosno."

"You disguised yourself? How did you disguise yourself?"

"Is it important?"

"It may be. If he saw you and recognized you, it could have a bearing on the case."

"He did not recognize me."

"How can you be so sure?"

"I disguised myself as a woman."

"I see."

"He looked straight at me and did not see me."

"And so you followed him to the Nikolaevsky Station."

"I stood behind him as he bought his ticket to Tosno. I heard him say the destination. I saw him take the ticket."

"You were so close, and he didn't recognize you?"

"He had no idea. I bought a ticket to Tosno myself. I took the train. I did not sit in the same compartment as him, but I had a good look at him. He was on the train. I saw him on the train."

"So what happened?"

"I got off at Tosno. I was one of the first to get off, I swear. I saw everyone who got off that train."

"And?"

"Ratazyayev did not get off the train."

"He decided to continue his journey?"

"But here is the thing that is strange."

"Go on."

"I saw a man, a man I had noticed in Ratazyayev's compartment, get off at Tosno, and he was carrying Ratazyayev's case."

"But it was not Ratazyayev."

"Precisely."

"I see. Can you be sure?"

"I was not sure at the time. I doubted the evidence of my own eyes. But now I am sure of it."

"Why are you sure of it now?"

"Because Ratazyayev has not returned. From wherever he went, he has not returned. He should have been back, he promised me he would be back, two days ago. But he has not come back, and I have not had a single letter from him for the whole time. That is not like him. I know we quarreled, but he would not punish me so much. We have quarreled before, and he has always come back. There have been tears. And reproaches. But forgiveness also. He knows I would forgive him. And he would forgive me."

Porfiry paused to allow the prince to master himself. Then he asked, "Can you describe the case?"

"It is a brown case." Prince Bykov mopped his cheeks with an enormous handkerchief. "A brown leather suitcase."

"But how can you be sure it was Ratazyayev's case? There must be many people who have brown suitcases."

"It was the same size and shape, and it was scratched in a certain way."

Prince Bykov watched expectantly as Porfiry finished his cigarette and stubbed it out in his crystal ashtray. "It is inconclusive," he announced.

The young prince became crestfallen. "However, if you bear with me for one moment, I would like you to look at something."

I T TOOK SEVERAL minutes for the case to be brought. There was some doubt as to its whereabouts, whether indeed it was still in the station. Lieutenant Salytov put his head around the door at one point to challenge Porfiry's order. "You are aware that as of today this investigation is officially over?"

"I am aware of that, Ilya Petrovich, though I am grateful to you for bringing it to my attention. However, this is to do with another investigation. This gentleman—a prince, no less—has reported a missing person. His testimony makes mention of a piece of luggage. In order to get a more accurate impression of this particular article of luggage, I wished to compare it to the suitcase that you found in Petrovsky Park. That is all."

Salytov seemed dubious, suspicious even. And no doubt the necessity of instigating a search was inconvenient to him. But in the end the case was tracked down. It had left the room in which evidence is stored, but not the station, and was found under an officer's desk. Clearing out the old case files that had been temporarily stored in it took only a few moments.

Prince Bykov nodded tensely when the case was put on Porfiry's desk. "That is it. That is Ratazyayev's. The scratch on the front is the same."

13

A Strange Document

A s porfiry entered the main headquarters of the St. Petersburg City Police Department, he was impressed not so much by the grandeur of the building as by its immaculate preservation. The contrast with the Haymarket District station was marked. The very uniforms of the policemen, even when they were of the same rank as the men in his own bureau, seemed crisper and smarter. He had the sense of visiting wealthier relatives and felt that he should be on his best behavior.

The building was situated at 2 Gorokhovaya Street, close to the Admiralty. Prokuror Liputin's chambers were on the third floor. Porfiry walked slowly up the stairs. The echoing clip of his heels drew disapproving glances from those coming down.

He was kept waiting, as he knew he would be, for over an hour before being admitted to an office similar to his own, except larger, cleaner, and with newer furniture. The *prokuror* was seated at his desk, his head bowed as he studied a case file. When he finally looked up, his face was puckered by a scowl of displeasure.

"Porfiry Petrovich." He made the possession of such a name sound like a crime.

"Your excellency."

"What is this about?"

"I wish to apply for permission to reopen the investigation into the murder of Goryanchikov."

"The dwarf?"

"New evidence has come to light."

"What are you doing seeking new evidence?"

"I did not seek the evidence. It came to me."

"What is this evidence?"

"It is the testimony of a prince. As you know, our law makes clear that the rank of a witness has a bearing on the reliability of his testimony. The testimony of a prince cannot be discounted."

"Who is this prince?"

"Prince Bykov."

"What is his testimony?"

"He has identified the suitcase in which the student Goryanchikov was found as belonging to an associate of his. One Ratazyayev. This Ratazyayev is now missing."

Liputin screwed his face up in distaste. "How did he come to see the suitcase?"

"I showed it to him."

"You showed it to him!"

"There were certain details concerning Ratazyayev's suitcase, which is itself pertinent to his disappearance. I felt that if Prince Bykov saw the case found in Petrovsky Park, it would help him to describe the missing man's luggage."

"You were playing games, Porfiry Petrovich."

"I was pursuing a connection."

"Who is this Ratazyayev?"

"An actor."

"An actor!" exclaimed Liputin disdainfully.

"A very good friend of Prince Bykov, who is himself accepted within the highest echelons of our society. He speaks warmly of the Stroganov-Golitsyns."

"The dwarf was killed by the yardkeeper. The yardkeeper committed suicide," recited Liputin.

"Perhaps that is true. But still the question remains, how did Goryanchikov's body come to be found in Ratazyayev's suitcase? And where, indeed, is Ratazyayev?"

"How can he be sure that it is the same case? It is a nondescript kind of brown suitcase. There must be thousands of them in circulation in St. Petersburg. No, it is not enough. You may only investigate the disappearance of Ratazyayev. You may not assume any connection between the cases." Noting the look of disappointment on Porfiry's face, the *prokuror* added with an insincere smile: "I am only protecting you from yourself, Porfiry Petrovich. The last thing I want is for you to make a fool of yourself over this. Besides, it's not like you to be seduced by a minor member of the aristocracy."

T HAT NIGHT PORFIRY dined in his chambers: fish soup, sturgeon and beans fetched from the Palais de Cristal restaurant on the corner of Sadovaya Street and Voznesensky Prospect. Or rather, the food was laid in front of him by Zakhar, the aged manservant provided for him by the government. Zakhar took it away hardly touched.

"His nibs is out of sorts," Zakhar confided to himself as he carried the tray away, swallowing down the anticipatory build of saliva. "Well, I have done my duty by him," he decided. This was the license he needed to devour the remains.

Porfiry had not asked for wine to be brought. The month before

Christmas was, after all, a period of fasting in the Orthodox calendar. But he had consented to a pot of strong black coffee. And although he relinquished the food, Porfiry let out a warning yelp when Zakhar threatened to take the coffee. That was the only communication he had all evening with the human being who shared his apartment.

Spread out in front of him were the books he had redeemed from Lyamshin's. He also had the French book that Goryanchikov had been working on, together with Goryanchikov's unfinished translation. He felt that he should continue to examine this text for its discrepancies with its source. But a sullen lethargy possessed him. Perhaps it was not lethargy; he had after all been forbidden from working on the Goryanchikov case. Perhaps it was submission. At any rate, he was beginning to feel the over-stimulating effects of the coffee. Why had he let Zakhar take the sturgeon away? He lit a cigarette to quell the hunger pangs and aid his concentration. But even smoking, he was not up to conducting a close textual comparison between a French philosophy book and its handwritten Russian translation.

He halfheartedly turned to the other philosophical titles, the Russian editions of *The Cycle of Life, Force and Matter, Superstition and Science,* and *Natural Dialectics.* But his study of these books only went as far as the title pages, where he discovered that they were all published by the same house, Athene. There was a St. Petersburg address given: 22 Nevsky Prospect.

But then he surrendered completely to his mood and turned to the other book. He was aware that he had been avoiding this book, aware too that it disgusted him, but equally aware that he had wanted to look at it ever since it had been put into his hands by the pawnbroker. He was salivating every bit as copiously as he knew Zakhar to have been.

Of course, he could not now pretend, not since his interview with Liputin, that his reasons for looking at *One Thousand and One Maidenheads* had anything to do with the investigation. But in a way, that interview freed him. He was like the officer who had appropriated Ratazyayev's suitcase to store paperwork. The books no longer counted as evidence. They had belonged to a man who was now dead. It would not be frowned upon if he used them for his own purposes.

The title page of this book gave no address, only the imprint, Priapos, and the name—or rather pseudonym—of the translator. An inscription read: "Translated from the French by 'Alcibiades.'"

The pages of the book were uncut. And he found himself strangely reluctant to take his paper knife to them. It was not, however, the kind of book that required its pages to be cut for its qualities to be appreciated. At a little under two hundred pages long, Porfiry calculated an average of five maidenheads per page. There was not much room left for narrative complexity, or even continuity. And yet even from the truncated version he allowed himself to read, Porfiry found that the author had quite cleverly constructed the story to avoid monotony and build interest. Although the first maidenhead was breached on page one, the episode itself covered several pages, as the erstwhile maiden quickly acquired a taste for the activity responsible for the loss of her virginity. For the whole of the first third of the book, as far as Porfiry could tell, all the deflowerings occurred consecutively. By the middle of the book, it seemed the hero was able, somehow, to increase the number of virgins who were willing to share his bed at any one time. The final climactic episode took place in a private girls' boarding school, when the remaining tally of three hundred and twenty-one maidenheads was accounted for in one endless white night and twelve exhausting pages; the final maidenhead being that of the school's headmistress, a sixty-three-year-old virgin, who wept uncontrollably at the discovery of what she had missed out on for so many years.

So engrossed was he in this touching denouement that Porfiry parted the last pair of uncut pages, so that he could continue reading what was written in their closed faces. His eye was caught by a folded sheet of paper that had been slipped between the pages and was adhering to the side that he was interested in reading. He widened the paper sheath and teased out the sheet. Unfolding it, he read the following document, drawn up by hand:

Being a legally binding and legitimate contract entered into freely and willingly by the parties of both parts, the undersigned:

Pavel Pavelovich Virginsky.

[followed by Virginsky's signature]

Stepan Sergeyevich Goryanchikov.

[followed by Goryanchikov's signature]

On the twentieth day of the eleventh month of the year of 1866, the party of the first part Pavel Pavelovich Virginsky confers ownership of his soul on the party of the second part Stepan Sergeyevich Goryanchikov, unconditionally and in perpetuity; excepting upon the death of Stepan Sergeyevich Goryanchikov whereupon ownership shall be transferred to the heirs of Stepan Sergeyevich Goryanchikov; or if there are no heirs existent ownership of the soul of Pavel Pavelovich Virginsky shall revert to the abovementioned Pavel Pavelovich Virginsky provided Stepan Sergeyevich Goryanchikov has not otherwise disposed of said possession being the eternal soul of Pavel Pavelovich Virginsky through his last will and testament or any other legally binding document.

Signed before the presence of witnesses:

Konstantin Kirillovich Govorov.

[followed by Govorov's signature]

Alexei Spiridonovich Ratazyayev.

[followed by Ratazyayev's signature]

S O YOU HAVE come back to us, *mein Herr*!"

Porfiry nodded but did not meet Fräulein Keller's eye. He could sense her mockery without having to look for it.

"And you have removed your lovely fur coat this time! Will you have some champagne, I wonder?"

Again Porfiry nodded without speaking.

"This time, perhaps, you are not here in an official capacity?" teased Fräulein Keller as she served him the chilled wine.

"Has Lilya Semenova been back here since my last visit?"

"No, not Lilya, we have seen the last of Lilya. But there are other girls, *mein Herr*. You would like to spend some time with Raya again? Or perhaps Raya was not to your taste?"

"Do you not have anyone younger?"

He felt Fräulein Keller's laughter resonate with his own corruption. He was sickened by it but joined in. "We don't have any virgins, if that's what you mean!"

"Lilya was the youngest of your girls?"

"Lilya, oh, Lilya, it always is Lilya with you! But even Lilya, you know, is not a virgin. And what is it you Russians say? Better a dove on the plate than a wood grouse on the roof?"

"That is not quite right, but all the same, if I wanted a really young girl, a virgin, is there someone you know who can arrange it for me?"

"What would you have me do? Snatch a girl off the street?"

"Is that how it's done?"

"There is also your saying about curious Varvara's nose, no?"

"Curious Varvara's nose was torn off."

"That's right. I would not wish that should happen to you."

"Do you know a man called Konstantin Kirillovich Govorov?"

"In my business one hears so many names."

"How about Ratazyayev?"

Fräulein Keller shook her head. "No. I think I would remember that one."

"Do you know the old prostitute Zoya Nikolaevna, who looks after Lilya's child?"

"Lilya's child? But she is very young, *mein Herr*. She is not yet five."

"Naturally, I would pay."

Even Fräulein Keller's eyes started at the coolness with which this was delivered. "It might have been possible once, *mein Herr*. But now that Lilya has found her rich protector, I doubt that you could persuade her, for any price. You can't break through a wall with your forehead."

"But Zoya. Perhaps she would be amenable to negotiation? There will be something in it for you too, of course, if you lead me to the old whore."

"You are a determined man. I misjudged you." Fräulein Keller narrowed her eyes assessingly.

"Not everyone who wears a cowl is a monk," said Porfiry. He avoided Fräulein Keller's admiring gaze and bowed his head to his champagne glass. But he found that he was suddenly chilled to the bone, and the thought of the champagne in his mouth was nauseating.

14

†

The Man Without a Soul

IN HIS DREAM, the cabinetmaker Kezel was constructing an interminable twisting staircase for the tsar's new palace. He wanted to explain that he had no experience or knowledge of building staircases. But it was as if someone had nailed his tongue to the floor of his mouth. The timber was white oak from the Terskaya region, conveyed to Petersburg at great expense. He knew that the quantity of wood had been precisely calculated to build the staircase according to the plan that he had been given. He could not afford to make one mistake. All this had been made clear to him. But a draft of wind kept lifting the plan and folding it in two so that he repeatedly had to break off from his work to lay it flat. In the end, he decided to abandon the plan. He was sawing the wood and fitting it together from memory. To begin with, everything went well. It was as if he weren't working in the heavy, unyielding medium of his craft. He hefted and chiseled beams without any effort at all. Dovetailed joints slotted together at the touch of his finger. Doweling plugs sank into wood as if into butter. But then something made him look up, and he saw that the staircase he was building was diverging hopelessly from the landing that was awaiting it. And now the pieces that he had shaped would no longer fit together. Joints that he had carefully measured refused to marry up. He was forced to fasten the pieces together with enormous nails. But no matter how hard he hammered the first of these nails, he couldn't drive it into the wood. He hammered and hammered on the head of the nail. With each hammer blow, he felt the nail advance minutely, only to see it a moment later retreat, as if the sundered timber were healing itself and in the process forcing the nail out. Now there was an air of desperation to his labors. The hammer blows fell faster and harder. But it made no difference. The evil nail would not go in.

Frustrated by the dream, and losing patience with its unreasonableness, Kezel woke up, only to hear that the sounds his dreaming mind had interpreted as hammer blows were in fact coming from the front door of the apartment. It was pitch-black and cold. Caught between fear and anger, he was little inclined to get out of bed to answer the pounding. But suddenly the issue was decided for him as the door crashed open. A lantern beam lit up the apartment and was in his eyes. Behind the beam he could make out a huddle of men in dark uniforms.

"The student Virginsky!" one of them shouted. "Where is he?"

Kezel pointed at the door to Virginsky's room.

Two men separated themselves from the huddle and rushed the door, shouting. Their shouts were inarticulate, the tension of their act finding voice. The door flew open. The shouting continued inside Virginsky's room.

Another man strode into the apartment now, a short, stout individual wrapped up in a *shuba*. He bowed gravely to Kezel, without speaking.

Virginsky's voice could be heard: "All right! All right! Let me get my boots on!"

A moment later he was hauled out by the arms. The unfastened laces of his boots whipped out as he kicked his feet in protest.

He was taken before the man in the *shuba*.

"So first you bring me presents. Now you have me arrested!"

"That is the man," said Porfiry Petrovich, blinking rapidly. "That is Virginsky."

V IRGINSKY WAS GIVEN something to eat and then taken to Porfiry's chambers. An armed *polizyeisky* was stationed at the door.

Porfiry laid the contract on the desk in front of him. Virginsky read it in a few seconds and then snorted derisively, "It was a joke. The whole thing was a joke. You think I killed him because of this?"

"Who are these men? Govorov and Ratazyayev?"

"I don't know. They were friends of Goryanchikov's. Goryanchikov knew all sorts of people. They were just two men who happened to be in the tavern at the time. I'd never met them before. They were actors, I think. Or had been."

"They were both actors?"

"I think so. I can't really remember. I was drunk at the time. That's how they knew each other, I think."

Porfiry looked down at the document. "Konstantin Kirillovich. A strange coincidence. Yet another strange coincidence concerning your friend Lilya. I asked you once if the name meant anything to you, do you remember?"

"I don't know. I suppose so. I can't remember." Virginsky gave a sudden angry scowl and came back fiercely: "No, actually. I don't remember. I don't remember you asking me that. What you asked me, I seem to remember, was if I had ever heard Lilya mention him."

"Ah! You *would* make a fine defense counsel. A nice distinction. It does not, however, persuade me of your innocence. First you say you can't remember, and then you seem to remember only too well."

"It just came back to me. I'm tired. I was dragged from my bed. You can't expect me to be in full control of my faculties. But of course, that's exactly the way you want it, isn't it? That's why you do this, to catch me napping."

"I don't pretend to understand what you thought you were doing when you entered into this contract."

"I was drunk. We had been gambling. I owed Goryanchikov a lot of money that I didn't have. I didn't want to renege on the bet. There is such a thing as honor. He suggested this way out. I thought, why not? It was either this or writing to my father. This seemed the lesser of two evils."

"Where was the contract drawn up?"

"Some filthy drinking den near the Haymarket. Where did you find it?"

"It was tucked away in the pages of one of those books you hocked."

Virginsky quaked with wheezing laughter.

"I take it you didn't put it there?" said Porfiry, a note of incredulity in his voice.

Virginsky shook his head.

"So how did it get there? Do you have any idea?"

"I imagine Goryanchikov put it there."

"Why would he do that? Why would he put it in one of your books?"

"They weren't my books. They were his."

"But you pawned them?"

"All right, I confess. I will admit to a crime. I stole them from him. I stole the books from him and pawned them for the money. I would have redeemed them and given them back to him, I swear. Once I'd got the money together."

"How did you intend to get the money? Your father?"

"No, I—I don't know. There are ways. Goryanchikov always seemed to manage. I had thought of journalism."

"I think perhaps Goryanchikov took the contract rather more seriously than you. That is why he stole the pawn ticket from you. Because he was determined to get the contract back."

"Perhaps he simply wanted the books back because they were his. I mean, because he had translated them."

"He translated *all* the books?" Porfiry raised an eyebrow.

"I know that he translated the philosophy books. He was hired by that fellow."

"What fellow would this be?"

"The one who lodged in Anna Alexandrovna's house."

Porfiry nodded. "Osip Maximovich. So he is responsible for publishing the Athene books?"

Virginsky gave a half shrug in answer.

"Your father must be a terrible monster," said Porfiry abruptly.

"Yes. You're right. The worst kind of monster." Virginsky was not inclined to elaborate.

"And you have got yourself into an awful mess because of your unwillingness to accept help from him."

"I will never accept anything from that man."

"Some would say your feelings for him are unnatural."

"Shall I tell you what is unnatural!" cried Virginsky hotly. "A father who steals from his son all hope, all possibility of happiness."

Porfiry raised his eyebrows to ask the question how.

"There—was—a girl," said Virginsky heavily.

"Ah."

"I loved her. There! What do you say to that? He knew. He knew it all. But he—he wanted her. He wanted to consume her in the same way he consumes everything. And the fact that I, his own son, was in love with her, only added spice to his appetite."

"But what of the girl? What did she want?"

"She . . . I could not compete with his lies. Or his wealth. They married. My mother has been dead for many years."

"It seems to me this girl is not worthy of you. And perhaps it's because you realize this that you are so angry with your father. You blame him for her imperfection."

"And is that why I murdered Goryanchikov, according to your . . . psychology?" Virginsky sneered sarcastically.

"It was why you were able to enter into this bizarre agreement. You had reached a point of such despair, of such nihilism, that this seemed preferable to asking your father for money."

"But this is nothing. It's a worthless scrap of paper."

"And yet you returned to the house in Bolshaya Morskaya Street two nights ago to try to retrieve it from Goryanchikov's room."

Virginsky winced and looked away in embarrassment. "I went there. I admit it. I went there to try and get it back. I don't believe in it. I don't believe in any of it. I'm a rationalist. You might call me a materialist, and I wouldn't argue with you. But still, I felt easier having it in my possession."

"And that was why, on the following day, you wouldn't go into the house with me. The maid would have said something. You would have been discovered."

"I had nothing to be ashamed of."

"Except that you had pretended to Katya that Goryanchikov was still alive when you knew perfectly well that he was dead." Porfiry pursed his lips when he put this to Virginsky, as if he disapproved of this lie most of all.

"I wasn't thinking straight. I panicked."

"Let us return to Konstantin Kirillovich. The man was known to you. You can't deny that. And yet you did not say so when you had the opportunity."

"I tell you, I didn't know him as Konstantin Kirillovich. I didn't know him by any name. He was just some loathsome old lecher Goryanchikov bumped into."

"A girl at Fräulein Keller's told me that he takes pornographic photographs."

"I can believe it."

"Of very young girls."

"Why are you asking me about this? I know nothing about any of this."

"This document is highly incriminating. There are some who would see in it a motive for murder."

Virginsky shook his head.

"They would say you murdered Goryanchikov and framed Borya," insisted Porfiry. "This fellow Ratazyayev is also missing. It is conceivable that you murdered him too. And Govorov, the other witness to your contract? Where is he? The motive is certainly here. A case could be made that it is in your interest to eradicate everyone connected with this strange piece of paper."

"But it's not true," said Virginsky wearily.

Porfiry shrugged. "Ah, the truth! If ever you do become a lawyer, Pavel Pavelovich, you will quickly learn not to rely overmuch on the truth."

THE SNOW-COVERED pavement of the Nevsky Prospect was mottled with black footprints. Porfiry kept his head bowed as he walked, looking at the footprints, following them, as if he expected the footprints to lead him to the solution of the mystery; to the murderer, in other words. But really he was looking at the pavement to avoid looking at the sky, for the sky above this great broad strip of openness was too much a reminder of the infinite. He felt the mediating presence of immense buildings. He was aware too, in a similar way, of the wooden cross that hung around his neck and touched his skin.

It was late morning, but the gloom of a northern winter clung to the city. The shopwindows glowed. Carriage lights trailed in the damp air. The crowds, in places, stretched across the pavement. Sometimes he felt himself jostled along and had to match his pace to the tread of those around him. Sometimes the pedestrians coming toward him were like the ranks of an opposing army.

Tiny sharp snowflakes began to swirl in the air and fell over them all.

Number 22 was a three-story building on the north side of the street, identical twin to number 24, on the other side of the Lutheran church. In the summer this would have been the sunny side. But there was no sunny side today. The ground floor was taken up with a number of shops, a delicatessen, a grocery store, its facade brightly painted, a furrier's, a gentlemen's outfitter's, and a shop selling various mechanical devices. The floors above and behind were given over to business premises. It was here that the famous publishing house Smyrdin had its offices. It was also the address given as the home of the publisher Athene in the title pages of the philosophy books Porfiry had redeemed from Lyamshin's.

He left his galoshes in the marbled foyer, under the steady gaze of the senior commissionaire, an immovable mound of a man around whom, it seemed, a monumental desk had been built. He concentrated his vitality into his eyes and could convey enormous meaning in a single blink. His more energetic colleague, a wiry old soldier whose face showed the strain of enforced inaction, leaped up to escort Porfiry to the Athene offices. "You'll never find it, your excellency," he cried gleefully, as if this were something to celebrate. "Never in a thousand years."

Of course, there were stairs to be climbed and corridors to be tramped, corners to be turned. And rows of numbered doors, some of them also bearing the names of the businesses conducted within. "You see, it's as well that I came with you, your excellency," commented the energetic commissionaire. But it was soon apparent that he himself was lost, although he would not admit it. His pace, however, did begin to flag. At last he angrily accosted a young man hurrying toward them with a sheaf of papers under one arm: "Athene?"

"Next floor down. Suite seventy-two."

"Ah! They've moved, have they?"

"Always been suite seventy-two," shouted the young man over his shoulder, picking up his step.

"Young fool doesn't know what he's talking about," said Porfiry's escort snappily. "They were on this floor the last time I came along here."

They retraced their steps, this time with Porfiry leading.

The door to suite 72 was open. Before they drew level with it, Porfiry could hear the voices inside, two male voices, the first light and relaxed, the other a forced baritone. The debate was passionate but good-natured. Porfiry had a sense of the friendship, the mutual fondness even, between the two men.

". . . but I insist a philosopher's thought is enwrapped in his language."

"What you are saying, more or less, is that the endeavor of translating philosophy is either futile or impossible."

"If it is the latter, it is also the former."

"But it is the endeavor to which you have devoted your life. It is what we do. It is our business."

"There is nothing nobler than to devote one's life to a futile enterprise." This was said after a slight pause, with a cheerful, almost mischievous lilt.

Porfiry dismissed his guide with a deep bow and stepped into the doorway. He drummed his knuckles lightly on the open door, and the two men looked up.

They were as he had imagined them from their voices, almost exactly. The younger man was tall and thin, his legs especially so. He had a high-domed forehead and thinning hair. Perched on the edge of a desk behind which his companion sat, he looked up at Porfiry over a book, the pages of which he turned distractedly with long fingers. His face was pale, his expression somewhat severe: a small pinched mouth was drawn together in readiness for denial. His eyes were gray and cold. The seated man was portly but neat. He kept his beard trimmed, and his hair, though thick and long, was tidily combed. His age was approaching fifty, and he wore silver-framed reading glasses. Behind their glinting lenses, his quick black eyes shone with intelligence and humor. Though his figure was spreading and his face filling, he was still a handsome man, or at least he was still able to carry himself like one. A long straight nose gave his face strength in profile. Viewed frontally, a small cleft at the tip arrested the gaze. His mouth, which was generous in comparison to his companion's, curved into a ready smile, whereas Porfiry noticed the other man's frown deepen.

"Good day. This is the office of Athene publishing, is it not?" asked Porfiry.

"It is" came simultaneously from them both.

"And if I am not mistaken, I have the pleasure of addressing the two gentlemen who lodge at the house of Anna Alexandrovna Ivolgina, that is to say Osip Maximovich and Vadim Vasilyevich."

The two friends looked at each other uncertainly.

"You do," said the older man, who turned out to be the source of the lighter, higher voice. "I am Osip Maximovich Simonov. You have the advantage of us, sir."

"I am Porfiry Petrovich." Their faces were blank. "I was the investigating magistrate on the case of Stepan Sergeyevich Goryanchikov. I believe he occasionally did work for you?"

"Ah! So that's what this is about," said Osip Maximovich. "Please sit down." But every spare seat in the office was already taken with a jerry-built tower of books or papers, or sometimes both.

"We've already given statements to the police," said Vadim Vasilye-vich, raising the book he was reading so that it covered his face. He also shifted the position of his gangling legs, swinging one knee across and turning his body away from Porfiry.

"Yes, you spoke to Lieutenant Salytov, I believe. I have read your statements. But this is not about that case. That case is closed."

"I read about it in the gazettes," said Osip Maximovich brightly. "Isn't it your theory that Borya killed Goryanchikov and then took his own life? Poor Borya. Poor Goryanchikov. A tragic waste. He was one of our most inspired translators. You see, translating philosophy is not an exact science. As we were just discussing, the translator needs to engage his imagination. He must first understand what the philosopher means to say, before he attempts to render that meaning into another language. Take Hegel. He was not even understood by the Germans. He said himself, 'One man has understood me, and even he hasn't.' But really, is it any wonder? Language, the only means we have available to us for expressing thought, is a far from perfect medium. We can say for certain that there are things that exist for which we have no words. Words simplify and reduce the universe. There is, moreover, a gradation of ideas that is not reflected in the divisive and categorical nature of language. Hegel showed, I think, that it is possible for an idea to contain within itself its opposite. A word cannot do the same. Yes, indeed." Osip Maximovich broke off, suddenly morose. "An invaluable talent that boy had."

"You said in your statement that the two men quarreled?"

"No," said Osip Maximovich calmly. "I know nothing about it. I wasn't here. I was eight hundred versts away. It was Vadim Vasilyevich who heard the argument."

Vadim Vasilyevich fidgeted at the mention of his name.

"Ah yes, Osip Maximovich," said Porfiry. "I remember. Anna Alexandrovna told me. You were on retreat in Optina Pustyn. You are a believer then?" Porfiry noticed the icon mounted high up in one corner of the room.

"Should I not be?"

"I would hazard a guess that some of the authors you have published are not."

"Why if the case is closed are you asking us all these questions about it?" asked Vadim Vasilyevich with sudden hostility. It seemed his voice sank even lower when he was agitated.

"My dear Vadim Vasilyevich," said Osip Maximovich smoothly. He smiled, but his eyes were stern.

"I was not asking questions about that case," said Porfiry, with a flutter of his eyelids. "I was merely asking questions out of interest. You are right, that case is closed. But I have come here to talk to you about another case. I am here investigating the disappearance of one Alexei Spiridonovich Ratazyayev."

There was a moment's silence. Then Vadim Vasilyevich said, "We don't know anyone by that name."

"How about you, Osip Maximovich? Perhaps you would care to answer for yourself."

"I think I may have heard the name Ratazyayev. Wasn't he an actor? I may have seen him in something. Before your time, dear boy," he added to Vadim Vasilyevich. "Ratazyayev, Ratazyayev. Yes, I think he was quite a celebrated actor at one time. And then something happened to him, I think. Drink, or some other scandal."

"Well, he has disappeared now."

"What has this to do with us?" asked Vadim Vasilyevich, finally standing away from the desk and exhibiting his full height.

"His name was found on a document belonging to Goryanchikov. Along with the name of another gentleman, one Konstantin Kirillovich Govorov." Porfiry studied the two men closely for their reactions. Vadim

Vasilyevich slammed his book with a sigh. Osip Maximovich smiled blandly. "Goryanchikov is linked to you because of the work he did for Athene publishing. He was working on a translation for you at the time of his death, wasn't he?"

"Ah, yes. Proudhon. *Philosophie de la misère*," sighed Osip Maximovich regretfully.

"He also owned a number of philosophical volumes published by Athene. I believe they were copies of the books he had translated."

"Moleschott, Büchner, Vogt, and Dühring," said Vadim Vasilyevich. "Those are the authors he has done for us."

"Yes, those are the ones I am referring to," said Porfiry with an appreciative nod. "So you see, Ratazyayev is linked to Goryanchikov. And Goryanchikov leads me to you."

"You say that Ratazyayev has disappeared," said Osip Maximovich thoughtfully. "But surely people disappear all the time? He may simply have tired of living in St. Petersburg and moved to Moscow. One does not even have to look so far. Perhaps he is living in the Vyborg District. Not wishing for his old acquaintances to spoil his new suburban life—perhaps even ashamed of it—he is simply lying low. Perhaps he is no longer living the disreputable life of an actor but has joined the service. He may even be teaching in a girls' school. Alternatively, he may have drunk himself into a stupor, fallen over in the street, and died from exposure. It is the sort of thing that occurs daily in our great city."

"These are all interesting theories," said Porfiry with a smile. "And indeed plausible. However, there are circumstances surrounding his disappearance that incline us to treat it as suspicious."

Vadim Vasilyevich shifted nervously. "If you will excuse me, I have duties to attend to." Vadim Vasilyevich bowed.

"By all means," said Porfiry. "But I will wish to talk to you again before I go."

Vadim Vasilyevich's small mouth twitched into an uneasy smile, and he crossed into an adjoining room off to one side.

"There are just the two of us here," said Osip Maximovich, by way of explanation. "Unlike our illustrious neighbors, Smyrdin, we must do everything ourselves. We have an urgent order to prepare for the University of Moscow."

Impatiently, Porfiry nodded his acknowledgment, then asked, "Is it customary for you to go on spiritual retreat?"

"No, this is the first year that I have done it. And I discovered it is something I have been longing to do all my life. To begin the Christmas fast with a penitent's retreat. Perhaps it is something to do with getting older. One reaches a certain age. The issue of mortality becomes more pressing. One's death is no longer an abstract proposition, it is an imminent reality. You were right to question my belief, by the way. I have not always been a believer. As you have probably worked out, I am the son of a priest. I was myself educated in a seminary, and it seemed at one time that I too would follow the path of my father. But like so many of my generation, I discovered philosophy. And science. And doubt. It used to be my opinion that faith and knowledge were irreconcilable opposites. To embrace faith by definition meant rejecting the truths that one had acquired through knowledge. Hard-won truths. I could not in all conscience do the latter, so it was impossible for me to do the former. I was too much under the spell of logic, so I reasoned myself out of my faith. But now I think I have found a way to reconcile them."

"And how did you do that?"

"I read Hegel. I discovered that true knowledge, the true subject and object of philosophy, is the spirit knowing itself as spirit."

"I have never been to Optina Pustyn."

"You should go. I mean, really you should. From the longing in your voice, I can tell that it is what your soul craves. For me there was an added impetus, in that one of the monks there, Father Amvrosy, taught me as a seminarian. He also taught my father. He is an old, old man now. He will die soon. There was a chance that if I did not go this year, I would never see him again in this life. He is without doubt the holiest man in Russia."

"It is a long way to Optina Pustyn."

"For sure. One must take the train to Moscow. From there one travels to Kozelsk. But there is no road to the monastery itself. One must approach it on foot or by river, or as I did."

"And how is that?"

"On my knees."

Porfiry sighed. "Perhaps one day I shall go. One day very soon."

"I would urge you to."

"What was the date you left St. Petersburg?"

"Let me see, it was the twenty-eighth, I believe. The twenty-eighth of November. The train left at twenty minutes past eight in the morning. Isn't that a strange coincidence?"

"You arrived in Optina Pustyn?"

"On the evening of the following day."

"And you returned to St. Petersburg when?"

Osip Maximovich's eyes flitted briefly as he calculated. "Two days ago, was it now? I have been so busy since returning, and this existence is so different from the spiritual calm of the monastery. It seems a lifetime ago since I left there."

"Thank you, Osip Maximovich. You have been most helpful," said Porfiry with a bow. "Now there is just one question I would like to ask Vadim Vasilyevich."

Porfiry moved quickly to the adjoining room. His sudden appearance seemed to surprise the secretary, who tried to give the impression that he was busy wrapping books, and had been for some time. It was obvious, however, that he had been listening.

"Vadim Vasilyevich, on the day Osip Maximovich took the train to Moscow, you accompanied him to the station, did you not?"

"Yes?"

"Did you see him onto the train?"

"I saw him onto the train and waved him off."

"And you remained in St. Petersburg the whole of the time that he was away on retreat?"

"Indeed."

"Thank you." Porfiry bowed and was about to leave, but there was something in the other man's expression that sought to detain him.

"May I ask you," began Vadim Vasilyevich hesitantly. "The work that Stepan Sergeyevich was doing for us, the Proudhon translation—do you know what has become of it?"

"It is in my possession."

"We would appreciate it very much if it could be returned to us. We have a book to prepare, you understand. And we must find another translator to complete Stepan Sergeyevich's work. Possibly I will have to undertake the task myself, or Osip Maximovich. It would be helpful to know how much Stepan Sergeyevich managed to complete."

"I'm afraid that will not be possible just yet. I have not finished analyzing it. It may turn out to be important evidence."

"How long do you think you will need it for?"

"I can't say."

"I don't see what possible use it could be to you."

"That is for me to determine."

Vadim Vasilyevich stared at Porfiry for a long time. His eyes narrowed but did not blink. "Osip Maximovich is a saint," he said at last.

Porfiry bowed, as though in gratitude for this information.

15

An Abundance of Icons

S HE MOVED THROUGH the Apraxin Arcade with the same inflex-
ible determination with which she had crossed Petrovsky Park,
only a few days before. Those who saw her coming stepped aside.
Those who didn't felt the buffet of her shoulder or the swipe of her arm,
and skipped out of the way with an angry sidelong glance at the force that
had impelled them. They saw an old woman bundled in layers of ragged
clothes, a strange, sealed expression on her face. It was almost a smile, but
cunning prevented it from going so far. If anyone studied her face for
long enough, they would reach the conclusion that there was a secret contained in it. But whatever that secret was, it could not escape through the
tight slits of her eyes.

She reached the corner of the market where the icon dealers were to be
found. Her approach stirred the sheepskin-clad traders into an exchange
of nods and winks. There was something conspiratorial, but also compet-
itive, in the way they bristled at the prospect of her. They vied for her

custom with friendly cries and waves: "Hello Granny!" "Madam!" Those
who knew her name called out, "Zoya Nikolaevna!"

But she chose today, as had done on previous days, a dealer who made
no effort to get her attention or her business. It was his face, and more
specifically his eyes, that drew her. He had the eyes of Christ the Redeemer. And just like the Christ figure in one of the icons he sold, his long
hair fell around his shoulders in ringlets, and his beard was divided into
two soft points. He was a young man, the youngest of them. His face
was always serious, giving the impression that he was well aware of
the solemnity of his trade. The others hawked their icons like half-kopek
cakes.

He acknowledged her presence at his stall with a silent upward tilt of
his head. Her greeting in return was an involuntary twitch of the mouth.

She scanned the banks of icons, arranged according to the holy personages represented and the manner of representation. Here the Christs:
Christ Immanuel, Christ Redeemer, Christ's Descent into Hell, Christ of
the Fiery Eye, Redeemer with Moist Beard, Redeemer Not Painted by
Human Hands. Next to the Christs were the Marys (although, of course,
both figures were featured in depictions of the Nativity): Virgin of Compassion, Our Lady of Vladimir, Our Lady of Kykkos, Our Lady of Refuge
and Succor. And then the saints: Saint Nicholas, Saint John, Saint George,
Saint Paul, Saint Demetrius. The lights of the market glinted softly in the
gold paint and jewels.

As well as those on display, there were deep baskets filled with icons.
Zoya stood over one and closed her eyes. She held out one hand and let it
hover. Then she dropped it to caress the varnished surfaces, before forcing her fingers down. It was a question of wheedling and teasing, of flex-
ing her fingers to engineer minute shifts in the abutment of edges. She was
able to plunge her arm all the way up to her elbow before withdrawing
it. And then, at last, she opened her eyes and inspected her forearm. It
seemed strange to her that no visible change had been wrought upon
it; that it was not glowing or dripping with gold.

The young icon dealer tolerated all this without comment, too polite even to give any indication of noticing. Zoya, however, chose to see something other than politeness in his gently averted eyes. In them she saw infinite compassion.

Looking back to the icons that were hung up around his stall, her eye was drawn to one she hadn't seen before, a heavily jeweled representation of the Savior. His halo was formed from circles of pearls, alternating with settings of sapphires and lapis lazuli, all on a base of beaten silver. Seeing it for the first time, she felt the breath leave her body in amazement. It was not simply the beauty and richness of the jewels and precious metal that impressed her. She understood that this was meant to represent Christ's splendor. Her soul grasped too the inadequacy of any earthly treasures to convey it. The Savior's face remained unmoved by the riches surrounding him. And it was the face she stared at, the face that humbled her.

Finally she addressed a remark to the dealer: "Haven't seen this one before."

His eyes flashed toward where she was pointing. "It came in today."

"Is it old?"

"Seventeenth century."

Zoya's eyes narrowed further. She seemed to find this information discouraging. "It's not the oldest I've seen. Was it in a church?"

The young man nodded.

"How much is it?"

"It's very precious. The jewels alone are extremely valuable."

"How much?"

"One hundred rubles."

Zoya clicked her tongue. "I don't care about the jewels."

The icon dealer shrugged, as if to say, *Don't buy it then.*

"It's not the jewels I want," insisted Zoya. "If I wanted jewels, I would go to Fabergé."

"I know what you want from them." His eyes confirmed his understanding. "I have one here that also came in today. I put it aside for you." He bent out of sight and returned holding a tiny, dark rectangle of wood, on which was painted an image of the eternal Mother of God holding the

Infant Christ. He held it out for her to examine. She took it and felt its power in the quickening of her heart.

The gold paint of the background was peeling off. The age of the varnish flattened the details of the clothing. But the intensity and directness of the Virgin's gaze was undimmed. Zoya felt the tears trickle down her face. She thought of all the men who had squirted their seed into her, the seed of life, of all the unborn, unbaptized babies she had carried, but not to full term. She realized that she could have no secrets from those eyes. The Virgin's gaze knew everything, understood everything, and forgave everything. It promised intercession and redemption. It promised hope. Those eyes looked into her soul without flinching.

"This one is twelfth century. It's over six hundred years old. Imagine."

She nodded as she dabbed the tears away.

"Imagine how many people have thrown themselves down before it. Imagine how many prayers have been said to it. Six hundred years. Imagine how many miracles it has performed."

"I'll take it," said Zoya. She did not ask the price. "I'll take them both." And all the gilded saints and angels and all the varnished prophets flickered their blessings on her purchase.

A GROUP OF children was playing in the snow in front of the apartment building on Srednaya Meshchanskaya Street. One of them, a little girl of about three or four, wearing a *drap-de-dames* shawl, caught Porfiry's notice. Somehow he knew that she was Lilya's child. She was less ragged than her playmates, dressed in smart new clothes and boots, which seemed to confirm Fräulein Keller's story about Lilya's rich provider. He could see something of Lilya in her wide blue eyes and the shape of her head. Her lips reminded him of Lilya too. It was only the nose that made him doubt, rather stronger than the insignificant nub typical of children her age. It had a distinct double tip, which was reddened by the cold. Like the rest of her face, it seemed familiar to him, and so perhaps it was more like Lilya's than he remembered.

As he watched the children play, he thought of the price he had paid for this lead. He felt as though he was defiling them by his gaze.

As much to cut short these reflections as to advance the investigation, Porfiry called out, "Hey! You lot!" The children turned, their faces startled but not afraid. "Who can take me to Zoya Nikolaevna's flat? A shiny five-kopek piece for the one who can!"

They ran up to him, arms outstretched, calling for the money. But Porfiry kept his gaze on the little girl he had noticed earlier. Her eyes had widened even further and her mouth gaped in wonder.

"Do you know Zoya, little one?"

"She's my granny!"

"And what's *your* name?"

"Vera."

"Hello, Vera. Would *you* take me to Granny Zoya's?" Porfiry bent down and held the five-kopek piece in front of her amazed eyes. He fended off the protests from the older children with an upheld palm.

"She's gone out," said Vera simply. Porfiry winced at her trusting innocence.

"So there's no one at home?"

"Mamma's at home!" This was said with that good-humored indulgence that children reserve for the stupidity of adults.

Porfiry nodded thoughtfully and gave her the coin. The other children began to drift away. "Mamma? I see. Is your mamma's name Lilya, child?"

The little girl nodded energetically.

"Let's go and see her, shall we?" The child became grave, affected by the responsibility of her commission. But she saw nothing strange in it. He felt the tug of childhood in her hand.

T HE DOOR OPENED narrowly. The mother's blue eyes peered out, uncomprehending and mistrustful. Her face shocked him, somehow. And then he realized. She was not wearing her streetwalker's makeup. Her pale exposed skin confronted him with her undeniable humanity. The makeup, he saw, protected both of them.

"Lilya? Do you remember me?"

Of course she remembered him: her eyes showed recognition clearly enough. But she did not understand his presence there. And when she saw her daughter holding his hand, her expression of general anxiety changed to one of fear.

"Vera? What have you done?"

"It's all right." He tried to reassure her with his smile. "I just want to talk to you. It would be better if I came in."

Obedience was clearly a habit with her, yet she resisted widening the gap of the door. Her eyes begged for release, for him to let her be. She had the conflicted look of one who has something to hide but longs to confess it. Her face was momentarily panic-stricken as she glanced at her daughter; then finally, as he knew she would, she began to open the door.

Little Vera ran around his legs to get inside. Porfiry caught the complex of apology and indulgence in her mother's loving eye.

As Porfiry stepped inside, *ushanka* in hand, he gasped audibly. Candles burned everywhere, hundreds of them, of every size and type, some in gold candelabra and elaborate jeweled stands, others simply placed in bottles or on saucers. And then he saw the walls, and a second, more self-conscious gasp escaped him. A multitude of holy faces looked out, though their gaze eluded contact. The oil-fueled flames that flickered in front of these faces both illuminated and excluded, creating a glowing screen that seemed to float in front of the dense glittering of icons. They were the blessed ones in paradise; those in the room, the unredeemed on earth. Every square inch of the walls was covered. The icons butted up to one another, frame against frame. The air was thick with burning beeswax, oil, and incense.

Hardly able to believe his eyes, Porfiry looked to Lilya for confirmation. She bowed her head, shamefaced. She could look him in the eye when they talked of prostitution, but this excess of religious sentiment embarrassed her, it seemed.

"I have never seen so many icons," murmured Porfiry. "Not even in a church."

"Oh, you will see this many and more at the icon dealers' stalls."

Porfiry searched her face for an explanation.

"They're not mine! I didn't buy them!" she cried in protest.

Vera ran between the candles shrieking. The child threw herself onto the floor and began to recite a prayer, in childish imitation of something she had evidently seen many times: "Merciful Mother of God, look down with pity on us sinners . . ."

"Zoya Nikolaevna?" Porfiry suggested. Lilya nodded. "But how? I mean, where did the money come from? Forgive me, but what I mean to say is, I can't imagine that she has money to spare on such . . ." Porfiry gestured sweepingly. He refrained from defining the expenditure as folly.

Lilya didn't answer. But the tension in her expression was revealing.

"There are some questions I need to ask you, Lilya Ivanovna." Porfiry's voice was heavy with significance. For the first time, he noticed her new and fashionably simple clothes. She wore a dark blue silk skirt with a brocade hem and a contrasting chemisette of white muslin.

Lilya nodded and led him over to the stove, away from where Vera was now playing with a new porcelain doll. She gestured for him to sit down at the table.

"I went to Fräulein Keller's," he began. The color flooded her face. "She told me you'd come into money. She says you've found a rich protector. A new boyfriend."

Lilya shook her head hotly. "Fräulein Keller can only see things through her own eyes."

"That's true enough," said Porfiry, with a half laugh. But then his face became serious as he remembered the depths he had sunk to in order to get information out of the madam. "But Lilya, I look at all this, I look at your dress, at Vera's toys. When I saw you at the police bureau, you were dressed in hand-me-down rags."

"I wore what I needed to wear."

"Yes, of course. But tell me, where did all this come from?"

"Zoya found . . . some money. That's all."

Porfiry noticed the hesitation and frowned skeptically. "She was indeed lucky. But I wonder, did she not think it might belong to someone?"

"You've never been poor. You've never known what it's like."

"I am not here to investigate or judge Zoya Nikolaevna."

"Why are you here?" It was the same question Raya had asked him at Fräulein Keller's.

"You know the student Pavel Pavelovich Virginsky." It was a statement, not a question.

Lilya stared at his strange, colorless lashes. "Yes."

"We are currently holding him in connection with a possible crime."

She gave an inarticulate sob of protest. Her eyes questioned and challenged him.

"Anything you can say in answer to my questions will help him."

"You don't believe he . . ."

"I don't believe he what?"

"Is it to do with Goryanchikov?"

"You know about Goryanchikov?"

"Pavel Pavelovich told me. And . . ."

"And what?"

Lilya could not meet his flickering eyelashes. She looked away to answer: "Zoya found him. She found him and another man. Dead. In Petrovsky Park."

"She has a habit of finding things, your Zoya."

"The money, she found the money there too. It was on the other man. In his pocket."

"How much?"

"I don't know. I . . ." She tried to lie. Then saw his eyelashes. "Six thousand rubles," came heavily.

Porfiry whistled. And began to laugh. "And she has spent it all on icons and candles, I see."

"She has been g-generous to us."

Porfiry smiled at the significant stammer. "It's easy to be generous with someone else's money."

"But he's dead. The man it belonged to is dead!"

"The man she found it on," corrected Porfiry deliberately, "was a yard-keeper. How do you suppose a yardkeeper came by six thousand rubles?"

"I don't know."

"But you see, it has a bearing on the investigation. The police should have been told about this. When you wrote me your little note, you could have mentioned the six thousand rubles." Lilya started in amazement. The investigator's face chided her with gentle irony. "I see my shot has hit the mark. I'm grateful to you for the information you provided, incomplete as it was. Though if Zoya had come forward herself, it would have saved us a lot of trouble, I believe."

"How did you know?"

"Murder in Petrovsky Park?" Porfiry repeated the words from the anonymous note in a melodramatic whisper. "I didn't, until you told me that Zoya had discovered the bodies." Porfiry's expression became pained as he contemplated his next question. "Was Goryanchikov a client of yours?"

Her shocked expression demanded an explanation of him.

"When you mentioned Goryanchikov, there was something about the way you said his name. And he must have been known to you, otherwise why would Pavel Pavelovich tell you of his death, and how would you know that the body Zoya Nikolaevna had found was his? I'm afraid I asked the question in the way I did because, well, it seemed the most likely way in which any man might be known to you."

"He came to Fräulein Keller's. He always asked for me."

"And what about Virginsky?"

Her brows came together. Her lips seemed to tremble. "It was never like that with Virginsky."

"But did he know about Goryanchikov? Is it possible that he was jealous?"

"If he was jealous of Goryanchikov, why should he not be jealous of them all?"

"Perhaps he was. In some way."

"Didn't the other man do it? The big man hanging from the tree. Zoya said he did it. She found an axe on him. There was blood on it, she said."

Porfiry sighed wearily.

At that moment, the door to the flat opened. Porfiry looked up to see a round ball of a woman waddle into the room. Her small wrinkled face appeared to have been pinched out of the headscarf that surrounded it. She was carrying a parcel wrapped in brown paper, tied with string.

"Babushka!" cried Vera. She abandoned her doll and jumped up, throwing herself at the old woman, whose solid form absorbed the force of her love. Vera made a great fuss of her Babushka, patting and stroking her and smiling up at her with a face that had its own, child's, cunning. "Babushka, Babushka, my lovely Babushka! What have you brought for me today?"

The old woman, who had by now noticed Porfiry, chuckled but threw a self-conscious glance toward the kitchen table. "Now, now, child, that's no way to greet your granny." But she was looking at Porfiry as she said this.

Vera pawed at the brown paper parcel the old woman was holding. "Is it for me?"

"No, darling, this one's for Granny."

"Leave Mamma Zoya be, Vera."

But the child clung to the old woman, pushing a cheek into the soft padding of her body. Zoya too seemed reluctant to release the child. There was defiance in the way she placed one arm around Vera's head. With the other, she lifted the brown paper parcel to her bosom.

Porfiry rose to his feet and bowed to Zoya. She picked up the nervousness of Lilya's movements. She saw that there was something guilty and yet obstinate in the girl's expression. Things had been said, she knew. She pulled Vera into her for protection.

"Ah, this must be the lady about whom I have heard so much. Zoya Nikolaevna, I presume?"

Zoya was not taken in by his "lady." She tilted her head slyly in answer.

"I am Porfiry Petrovich."

"This gentleman is a policeman, Mamma Zoya."

"No. I am an investigating magistrate." Porfiry smiled. "But no matter. You could say I am a policeman."

"What is this about?" Zoya clasped her parcel tightly, as if she were afraid he was going to snatch it off her.

"I am investigating the disappearance of a man called Alexei Spiridonovich Ratazyayev."

Lilya seemed thrown by the announcement; Zoya, relieved. Porfiry noted that she even allowed herself a small grin.

"I don't know anyone by that name."

He noticed Lilya frowning at him doubtfully, as if she had suddenly lost faith in him. She seemed almost angry. He met her frown with a smile. "I believe him to be an associate of someone known to you, Lilya Ivanovna." Alarm showed in her eyes. "Konstantin Kirillovich. Whose family name, I have discovered, is Govorov. Wasn't it a certain Konstantin Kirillovich who accused you of stealing one hundred rubles?"

"Yes."

"Konstantin Kirillovich Govorov. The mysterious man who accused you of theft and then ran away before charges could be brought. Why did he do that, do you suppose?"

Lilya shook her head without looking at him.

"Perhaps he believed," continued Porfiry, "as many do, that it would be enough for a gentleman to accuse a prostitute. That the authorities would naturally take his side. That there would be no need for the formalities to be completed. If so, he is unaware of the changes wrought by our legal reforms. We have juries now, and courts. And defense advocates. It takes more than an accusation to have someone sent to Siberia, even a street girl. But then Konstantin Kirillovich is no gentleman, is he?"

"I don't know what it means, to be a gentleman," said Lilya, finally challenging Porfiry with her gaze.

"There are only men!" agreed Zoya Nikolaevna with a high, harsh cry. "There are no gentlemen."

"Konstantin Kirillovich took photographs of you, didn't he?"

"I allowed him to." Her voice came from somewhere dead.

"But a photograph is not so terrible. At least it does not involve—"

"Oh, it involved the worst that you could imagine!" cried Lilya despairingly.

"And you were young, you were very young?" His question offered mitigation.

Lilya nodded rapidly. She dabbed tears out of her eyes and looked toward her daughter. "It was . . . in the beginning."

"But you did it," said Porfiry. His tone was flat, not accusing. It was as if he were speaking her thoughts for her.

"Yes." The word came heavily. "I did it." She searched his eyelashes for some sign of understanding; or more: redemption.

"This time, however," pressed Porfiry, "was different. What was it that he asked of you this time?"

Lilya shook her head. Her eyes were red-rimmed now. She would not look at any of them. Like the faces in the icons that surrounded them, her gaze was fixed on another world. But it was not heaven that she was contemplating.

"Leave her alone!" barked Zoya Nikolaevna threateningly.

"I need to find Konstantin Kirillovich Govorov," insisted Porfiry calmly, without apology. "Lilya, can you tell me, when he took the photographs of you, where was it?"

But Lilya was lost to him.

"You will look after her." Porfiry's command drew an eager nod from Zoya Nikolaevna. "Is there anything *you* can tell me about this man?" This time she shook her head, with equal resolution. "About the money you took . . ."

"I found it, fair and square."

"On a dead man. It is a punishable offense to disturb police evidence. More important, there is the issue of to whom it belongs. There is every chance the money was stolen."

"Yes! That's it!" cried Zoya, startling Lilya out of her trance. "He stole it off the dwarf. That's why he killed the dwarf, to get his money. So it doesn't matter! The dwarf is dead. What can the dwarf want with the money now?"

"Please don't call him that," sobbed Lilya, suddenly. "He was a man. His name was Stepan Sergeyevich."

"I hope to God you haven't spent it all on these?" Porfiry threw a dismissive hand toward the edges of the room. He glared at Zoya. "What they need, what you all need, is provision in *this* world. If you're worried about the next world, you can pray. Prayer is free, after all." There was an edge of exasperation in his voice.

Zoya Nikolaevna hung her head. "But they are so beautiful."

"If she ever has to go back to Fräulein Keller's, I will pack you off to Siberia so fast—"

"We'll give the money back!" cried Lilya. Zoya shook her head warningly.

"I would dearly love to know," said Porfiry, ignoring Lilya's interjection, "what else you found in Petrovsky Park. Was there anything, anything at all, other than the money you took?"

"There was a pack of smutty playing cards I found on the dw—" Zoya broke off and bit her bottom lip contritely. "On the little fellow."

"Stepan Sergeyevich," supplied Lilya.

"But I sold them," continued Zoya. She gave a little penitent shrug and smiled at Porfiry in a way that was almost schoolgirlish.

"Anything else?"

"Just this." She took her arm away from the child's head and delved into her layers with one hand. A moment later she pulled out a small key.

"Where did you find it?" asked Porfiry, taking and examining it.

"On the big brute."

Porfiry pocketed the key and took out his cigarette case. With an unlit cigarette in his mouth he regarded Zoya for some time, as if deciding what was to be done with her. He looked down at the little girl who was still clinging to her Babushka. The child's face was taut with fear.

"Who is the child's father?" he asked at last.

There was an anguished cry from Lilya.

"She's never told me," said Zoya, meeting Porfiry's gaze steadily. "And she won't ever tell you."

Porfiry nodded. He bent over one of the candle flames and lit the cigarette. "Why not? Doesn't she know?"

"She will not speak of it," said Zoya through tightly clamped teeth, as if she were uttering a curse. "She will not speak of it." The repeated words had the passionately felt but unthinking intonation of a liturgical chant, rising in intensity until a third, final: "She will not speak of it."

16

The Perfumed Letter

THE PETER AND Paul Fortress cannon signaled midday with an irrefutable boom. As though to escape the impact of the distant shot, Porfiry hurried his step as he pushed open the door to the building in Stolyarny Lane, shivering in from the cold. The Haymarket District Police Bureau was on the fourth floor. Cooking smells came from the open doors of the flats he passed on the way up. The stairs were steep. He paused at the landing of the second floor to light a cigarette. The smoke thickened the gloom of the stairwell. It was narrow here, and he had to stand to one side to let porters and police officers go by in both directions. These purposeful men regarded him with suspicion. But he took his time. He needed to feel the tobacco smoke's stimulating influence spread throughout his body before he could go on. When he did finally move, it was as if he were borne up on the swirling wisps.

As he entered the bureau, he caught the look of avid expectancy in Prince Bykov's eyes, and his heart sank. The young nobleman ran toward him with quick, clipping steps. "Porfiry Petrovich!"

"Prince Bykov. How delightful to see you again."

"Porfiry Petrovich, I have something that I believe will be useful to you in your investigation. Alexander Grigorevich said it would be all right for me to wait."

"Alexander Grigorevich?" repeated Porfiry, with a quick, arch glance to Zamyotov. "I did not realize you two ... *gentlemen* were on such terms." The clerk's answering glare was characteristically insolent. Porfiry bowed and clicked his heels as he took the photograph that Prince Bykov was holding out to him. It was a studio portrait of a striking man of about forty years of age. His face possessed traces of the masculine beauty that had once defined it: the strong, flaring nose, the heroic chin and sculptural cheekbones. Somehow these were what came out to the viewer and not the slackened flesh around them. Yes, he was running to fat and, it could fairly be said, had his best years behind him. The hair was receding, but its blond glow and defiant length signaled a former glory, and the angle of the forehead that was increasingly exposed was finely determined. More than anything, there was a compelling intensity to his eyes. They glared out of the picture and fixed the observer with an unflinching openness that combined power and vulnerability. The man's pose was artificial, theatrical even, but some quality of amused intelligence in his face seemed to acknowledge this. Beneath the superficial artifice, Porfiry detected the hint of a deeper honesty. He was not a man to be trusted, a man capable of lying, certainly. But neither was he a man who lied to himself. He must be lively company, was Porfiry's thought.

"This is Ratazyayev," said Porfiry.

"Yes," confirmed Prince Bykov.

"He's older than I imagined." Porfiry lifted his head and watched the prince thoughtfully. He was thinking of the bond between the young prince and the aging actor.

"How is the investigation going?" demanded Prince Bykov abruptly.

"Makar Alexeyevich." Porfiry Petrovich used the time it took to say the name and patronymic to consider the many responses available to him. Finally, he settled for: "It is making progress."

"But you have not found Ratazyayev?"

"Does the name Konstantin Kirillovich Govorov mean anything to you?"

"Govorov? I have heard the name, I think."

"He is a known associate of your friend Ratazyayev's."

The prince blushed. "Alexei Spiridonovich has many friends. I have not been introduced to them all."

"Would you be able to tell us where we can find this Govorov? We are very interested in speaking to him. We think he may have information relating to the disappearance of your friend."

"I can't help you. Other than to provide you with this photograph."

"What of Virginsky? The student Pavel Pavelovich Virginsky? Do you know him?"

Prince Bykov's face remained blank.

"Ratazyayev's name was found on a document pertaining to Virginsky."

"I have never heard of a Virginsky."

Porfiry shook the photograph distractedly. "Thank you for this. It will help, I'm sure." But his shoulders sagged in disappointment, and he was already looking past Prince Bykov.

ALEXEI SPIRIDONOVICH RATAZYAYEV, the missing actor," said Porfiry as he laid the photograph on Nikodim Fomich's desk.

The chief superintendent took up the photograph. "I believe I may have seen him in something. Many years ago."

"I have the *prokuror*'s permission to investigate his disappearance."

Nikodim Fomich nodded.

"I would like one of your officers to take the picture around the taverns in the Haymarket area. Ratazyayev signed a document that was drawn up in a drinking dive near the Haymarket, according to Virginsky. Whoever is assigned should start from the Haymarket and move out."

"It sounds like a job for Salytov."

Porfiry fluttered his eyelids and gave the slightest bow. "He could mention the name Govorov too, when he is making his inquiries."

"Very well." Nikodim Fomich nodded back, then pursed his lips thoughtfully. "Speaking of Virginsky," he said at last, "he is demanding to be released, you know."

"He is a strange, unpredictable youth," said Porfiry, as he lit a cigarette.

"It's not so strange to want your freedom."

"But what is *his* freedom? The freedom to starve? He is fed here, isn't he?"

"He is a law student. It seems he has attended enough lectures in his time to know that he has rights. You have not charged him. Indeed, there is nothing, technically, to charge him with. As far as the disappearance of Ratazyayev is concerned, you don't need me to tell you, Porfiry Petrovich, that you have not established a crime. And if you are holding him in connection with the affair of the dwarf, it's my understanding that that case is closed."

"I want him close to me," said Porfiry abruptly. He frowned at the cigarette burning down between his fingers.

"If Prokuror Liputin—"

"Please don't bring Prokuror Liputin into this. I will speak to Virginsky."

Nikodim Fomich noticed the strain in his friend's voice. He saw too the dark patches beneath Porfiry's eyes. "You're smoking too much," he said.

Porfiry held the smoke in his lungs. His eyelids quivered closed. He was light-headed, near to swooning. Finally, he let the smoke out in a sudden, noisy gasp and looked Nikodim Fomich in the eye. "It helps me think."

Y OU CAN'T KEEP me here."

Porfiry sighed and looked down at Virginsky. The student was stretched out on the pallet bed of his cell. His eyes were closed complacently, arms folded behind his head. His cheeks had filled out and picked up color. He had evidently put on weight.

"That's true," agreed Porfiry. "I have come to tell you that you are free to go whenever you wish."

This seemed to disturb Virginsky, who looked up doubtfully. "Very well," he said at last and sat up.

"I want to believe that you are innocent," continued Porfiry. "So let us proceed on the basis that you are. If you leave here, you may be putting yourself in danger. The person who killed Borya and Goryanchikov is still at large."

"I thought the official story was that Borya killed Goryanchikov and then killed himself."

"That is the official story. I say again, the person who killed Borya and Goryanchikov is still at large. This is a dangerous individual. He may kill again. At least while you are here, you are safe."

"But why should they kill me?"

Porfiry gave a vague shrug. "Let me put it another way. While you are held here, as our chief suspect, the real murderer will believe himself to be in the clear. He may drop his guard. He may even reveal himself through some careless mistake. If we release you, he will feel himself to be under suspicion once more. It is natural, the natural neurosis of a criminal. He will begin to wonder what you have said, or what you could say. He will look for connections. He will wrack his brain, running over every conversation he has ever had with you, until he remembers the one time when, perhaps, he let slip that one incriminating detail."

"And what if I don't know the fellow?"

"Oh, be under no illusions, my friend. The murderer is someone known to you. Someone you know, someone who knows you."

"You can't be certain of that."

"I feel it very strongly."

"What would you have me do?"

"I am asking you to remain here a while longer. Voluntarily, you understand. We will make your stay as pleasant as we can."

"Why should I?"

"It would help me. It would help me find the murderer of Goryanchikov and Borya. There will perhaps come a time when I will ask you to undertake a more dangerous commission."

"What would that be?"

"To leave here. In so doing, you may help us bring the murderer out into the open. But you could also be putting yourself at risk. That is something you will have to face, but it is not necessary that you face it yet."

Virginsky touched the fingertips of both hands to his forehead, then pushed them back through his hair. He looked up at Porfiry. "No," said the student at last. "I would rather die a free man than live forever as a prisoner. Besides, there are things I need to attend to."

Porfiry's nod was unsurprised.

BACK IN HIS own chambers, Porfiry placed the box that he had taken from Borya's shed on his desk. The box was made from burled birch, most likely Karelian, wonderfully smooth to the touch, and honey-gold. The hinges and lock were brass. There was a brass emblem in the shape of an eagle inlaid into the lid.

He tried the key that Zoya had given him, the key she had found on Borya. It turned easily in the lock, and the box opened. Inside he found a single crisply folded sheet of ivory-colored writing paper.

Porfiry lifted the sheet to his nose without unfolding it and breathed a scent he recognized. He opened the paper to read a short handwritten note:

Do you remember the summer? Do you remember the day we met in Petrovsky Park this summer gone? Do you remember the place near the boating lake, the dip in the land surrounded by birch? How could you forget it? I will hate you if you have forgotten. But you will not have forgotten. I saw from your eyes that you would never forget. It is there, recorded in the map of your heart. I saw so much from your eyes. I saw your goodness. I saw your fear. But do not be afraid. Trust in your goodness. Meet me there tonight at midnight. There is a way

forward in all this. If you love me, which I have never doubted, you
will come.

The note was signed: "A.A." He held the paper to his nose again. The
scent, he was sure, was Anna Alexandrovna's. Despite its wholesome
freshness, he found the effect of it was not conducive to thought. But he
had no desire to swap it for one of his cigarettes.

He was suddenly aware of high-pitched shouting coming from the station. With hurried guilt, he placed the note back in the box, closed the lid,
and locked it. The shouting continued. It was getting louder, approaching
his chambers. Porfiry looked up to see his door burst open and Katya—
Anna Alexandrovna's maid—come in, holding by the ear a very dirty-
faced boy of about nine or ten, dressed in grubby livery. The boy was
screaming in protest: "You're killing me! Let go!"

"This is him! Here he is!" cried Katya, and all the determination of her
character seemed to be expressed in that grimly triumphant cry. "The
boy!" She gave a vicious twist of the hand holding his ear, screwing the
boy's head down. The boy tipped forward and squealed in pain.

"Ah!" said Porfiry, rising from his chair. "You mean the boy who came
to visit Goryanchikov?"

"He came back. I caught him spying on the house."

The boy's shrill screams had not let up: "You're pulling my ear off!"

"Could you not let go of his ear? You appear to be hurting him."

"If I let go, he'll run off. You watch. I brought him all the way here
like this."

"Good heavens. I really would like you to let him go. Testimony ob-
tained under duress is not admissible in the new law courts." Porfiry
crossed to the door and locked it. "There, now," he said, dropping the key
into the hip pocket of his frock coat. He nodded sternly to Katya. She
frowned uncertainly, still reluctant to let go.

"You don't know this one," she said.

"The door is locked. He can't escape."

Finally she released the ear. It seemed, from her wary dismay, that she believed he would vanish the moment he was out of her grip. But also there was the sense that she had relinquished the source of her own confidence and momentary power. She seemed to find herself superfluous now that she had let him go. Noticing this, Porfiry bowed and thanked her. "I beg you to stay while I question him," he said. The boy stood up straight, rubbed his ear, and regarded Katya with a look of vindicated innocence.

"You're not out of here yet," she warned him.

"So, boy, tell me, what is your name?" asked Porfiry.

"I've done nothing wrong," the boy answered.

"No one is accusing you of anything. But it is possible that you may be able to help us in a murder investigation."

The boy's eyes widened in his coal-smudged face. "Murder!"

"Yes."

"Is there a reward?"

"You will have the satisfaction of knowing that you have done your duty as a loyal subject of the tsar."

"That's not much of a reward."

"Perhaps I should explain to you how the legal system works. It is not so much a question of rewards for doing your duty as penalties for not. If you do not provide me with the information I require, I can have you locked up."

"And flogged," added Katya, with a threatening nod.

"That may not be necessary," corrected Porfiry. "The loss of liberty in itself is considered to be a sufficient deterrent. Of course, if I feel that you have rendered us exceptional help, I can recommend that your services be recognized. There is the possibility of a citation or even a medal."

"What's a citation?"

"It's a piece of paper with your name on it, outlining the extent of your contribution."

"What use is a piece of paper?"

"It will be sent to the tsar."

"And what will the tsar do with it?"

"He will be gratified."

"Will he give me money for it?"

"He will not lock you up and have you flogged," said Porfiry, rather wearying of these negotiations. "And he may recommend that you be given a gold medallion. But it all depends on how much you help us. Of course, nothing can happen if you don't tell us your name. We can't write the citation if we don't have your name."

"Dmitri."

"Very good, Dmitri. At least that can go on the citation. And where do you live?"

Dmitri narrowed his eyes suspiciously.

"So that the tsar knows where to send the gold medallion, should he decide to award it."

"The Hotel Adrianopole. I am the bellboy there."

"Very good. And where is the Hotel Adrianopole?"

"On the Bolshoi Prospect. Vasilevsky Island."

"Thank you. Now, please, Dmitri, could you tell me why you were spying on the house of the Widow Ivolgina, in Bolshaya Morskaya Street?"

"I wasn't spying."

"He was," insisted Katya.

"I was waiting for the dwarf."

Porfiry exchanged a significant glance with Katya and nodded minutely to Dmitri. "I see. The dwarf. Why were you waiting for him?"

"I wanted to ask him how he did it."

"How he did what?"

"The trick."

"Perhaps you had better start at the beginning. You admit that you have met Stepan Sergeyevich Goryanchikov—the dwarf, as you call him—before?"

Dmitri seemed unsure how to answer. He looked mistrustfully between Porfiry and Katya.

"This lady says you came to the house, the house where Goryanchikov—the dwarf—lived, and visited him."

"All right, it's true."

"Why did you go there?"

"A gentleman sent me."

"What gentleman?"

The boy shrugged.

"How did you know him?"

"He was at the hotel."

"A guest?"

"Yeah."

"Why did he send you there, to the house?"

"He had a message."

"For the dwarf?"

The boy nodded.

"And so you delivered the message?"

He nodded again.

"And?"

"And what?"

"Well, I'm trying to establish why you came back to spy on the house. The trick you mentioned. Can you tell me more about that?"

The boy frowned uncertainly. "Well, he came to the hotel."

"Who did?"

"The dwarf."

"I see. The message that you delivered was an invitation then? So what happened when he came to the hotel?"

"He went into the gentleman's room."

"So what happened next?"

"He was such a little man. He was much smaller than me, and yet he was a man."

"Yes. But what happened after he went into the room?"

"The gentleman quit his room. The ordinary-size gentleman, I mean."

"And the dwarf?"

"He didn't come out. The other man paid his bill and paid for another week in advance as well. A whole week in advance! He said the dwarf was taking over his room and would want it for another week. But this is the thing, you see. I went back to the room. To see if there was anything the dwarf wanted. I knocked on the door. No answer. I opened the door. Nobody there. The room was empty. There was no sign of him."

"He must have gone when you were with the other gentleman."

"I would have seen him. There's only one way out. Down the corridor and past the reception. He hadn't been that way, I'm telling you. I was watching all the time. I wouldn't have missed him. Even though he was such a tiny fellow." Dmitri became heated in his insistence.

"He must have climbed out of the window then!" said Porfiry.

"No!" shouted Dmitri, amazed at Porfiry's stupidity. "There is no window. It's the room under the stairs."

"I see. Very interesting."

"He must be some kind of goblin, don't you think?"

"I would incline toward a more rational explanation."

"A wizard then? Or some such."

"Tell me, did you carry the gentleman's luggage out for him?"

"No!" The boy cried out in remembered indignation. "He wouldn't let me. Insisted on carrying it out himself, didn't he? Wanted to do me out of a tip, I'm sure."

"I believe he may have had other reasons," began Porfiry with a pleasant flicker of his eyelids, "for holding on to the suitcase so jealously."

The boy's look of indignation turned slowly to one of horror. "He was in the case! The dwarf was in the case!"

"The guest, the gentleman who sent you on your mission and whom the dw—the smaller gentleman, Goryanchikov, visited . . . you don't happen to remember his name, do you?"

"Did he murder him? Did he murder the dwarf? And put him in the case?"

"It is a possibility."

"And what if he comes back to murder me?"

"If you help me catch him, I shall make sure he cannot come back and murder you. I shall make sure he can never hurt anyone else again."

"That's what you say."

"It is indeed what I say. Now, please, can you remember the guest's name?"

"Govorov."

Porfiry felt somehow that he had expected this. He believed he was not surprised. And yet he felt his pulse quicken at the mention of Govorov.

"Now you will write that thing for the tsar," said Dmitri. "I should get a gold medal for this. I've risked my life."

Porfiry blinked himself into concentration. "The citation? I shall be glad to. But first I have just one more question for you. After you had delivered your message to Goryanchikov, you then stopped off at the yard-keeper's shed. Is this not true?"

Porfiry watched in amazement as the boy's face colored and collapsed beneath an overwhelming surge of emotion. He had forgotten that this was a child he was dealing with. Thick streams of sudden tears ran from Dmitri's eyes, clearing tracks in the dirt on his face. He howled his unhappiness: "It's not fair. I've answered all your questions, then you ask me more questions. I've done nothing wrong. You can't keep me here. You promised me a medal. Give me my medal."

Porfiry cast a glance of appeal toward Katya. But she was having none of it. She scowled suspiciously. Her hand was reaching out as if to grab Dmitri's ear again. Porfiry stepped forward and reached out to restrain her.

In that instant, Dmitri's hand flashed into the pocket of Porfiry's frock coat. Then, in the tail of the same instant, he was at the door and opening it. Porfiry suddenly felt the truth of Nikodim Fomich's observation. He was rooted to the spot by age and by his tobacco-shortened breaths. The boy's sudden move had not just taken him by surprise, it had left him winded, his body incapable of responding to the excited chemicals surging through it. His first impulse had been to light up rather than give chase.

At the door, thrown open by the fleeing Dmitri, Porfiry's cry of "Stop him!" was smothered in a coughing fit. It turned a few puzzled, a few curious, but mostly blank faces. One elderly *polizyeisky*, surely long past retirement age, seemed to grasp what was going on. He saw the young, filthy urchin running full tilt toward him, away from the investigating magistrate. The *polizyeisky* dropped eagerly to a catching posture, spreading his feet and stretching out his arms. Something kindled in his eyes: sport and the memory of a youthful energy. Bobbing with anticipation, he possessed the narrowed space between two desks, effectively blocking Dmitri's only escape route. But the boy did not slow his pace. If anything he accelerated, hurtling straight toward the human obstacle. Then, at the last minute, as the elderly *polizyeisky* reeled and readied himself for impact, groping the air and masticating nervously, the boy leaped to one side, vaulting onto one of the desks. It was a startling feat—fearless and marvelously athletic. There was no break in the fluidity of his movement. The sweep of his boots sent paper fluttering, upturning an inkpot that bled a quick puddle of black over the desk. He rose from his leap with perfect balance, head high, legs kicking. In two thundering steps he was across the desk and off the other side. The clerk behind it threw up his hands in impotent outrage, but the *polizyeisky* blew out his cheeks, spontaneously admiring.

In the time that it took to accomplish all this, Porfiry lit a cigarette.

"You let him get away," accused Katya, when Porfiry turned back into his chambers. "After all the trouble I went to to bring him in. And I don't suppose I'll be getting a medal from the tsar."

Porfiry licked a loose fleck of tobacco from his upper lip as he considered her antagonism. "I know where to find him," he said nonchalantly. "I remain grateful to you, Katya. And as a representative of the state, I am confident the tsar is grateful too." He bowed solemnly, blinking, as if he had been officially authorized to reward her with the rapid oscillation of his eyelids.

17

The Elusive Govorov

A FOOL'S ERRAND, it was another fool's errand.

Lieutenant Salytov descended into the seventh tavern that day. How the smell of these places sickened him. The air, abrasive with hard spirit, licked his eyes into weeping. He was jostled on the stairs by two drunks leaving. Nothing malicious—it was simply that they could not control their shoulders. They seemed to be attracted to him magnetically.

The rub of their filthy coats, the sense of their awkward humanity beneath, disgusted him. The unshakable absurdity of it disgusted him.

His rage made it difficult for him to speak.

"Oaf." With leather-gloved hands, he pushed one of them away and was horrified by the heavy, beseeching roll of the man's eyes and the grim, clownish slapstick of his tread. "You—" Salytov's throat tightened around the words he could have said. "People!" It was all he was able to squeeze out. But he was satisfied by the word. He felt it placed a distance between himself and such individuals.

The drunk's answer was a deep and inarticulate growling.

His companion gripped the handrail of the stairs and swayed as if he were at the prow of a listing ship. He swallowed portentously. His body lurched dangerously after Salytov as he passed. But the sober policeman moved too quickly for him. He left them on the stairs and did not look back.

Wan candle flames glimmered on the half-dozen tables and along the bar. The uncertain light, pocketed in gloom, seemed to encourage introspection among the isolated drinkers. Not a single face turned toward him. In one corner of the room, a woman wrapped in a grubby shawl was squeezing random notes out of a ruptured concertina. The anxious expectancy that these sounds induced was incompatible with conversation. There was no laughter, no voices raised in conviviality; only groans and sighs of despondency sounded in the gaps between the instrument's wheezes.

Salytov pushed through his own resistance to the wooden bar, where a skinny adolescent potboy was intent on smearing glasses with a dirty rag. The youth paused now and then, prompted somehow by the irregular rhythms of the concertina. It was as if he couldn't continue his task until the next note had sounded. He wore a soiled and belted *rubashka*, the embroidery of which was coming apart.

"Who's in charge here?" The boy responded to Salytov's abrupt demand with a look of stupefied amazement. "The landlord, idiot!" Salytov brought a fist down on the bar. The noise it made was less impressive than he had hoped, but still it was enough to startle the boy a second time. It seemed also to silence the concertina player, at least temporarily. "Why are you staring at me like that? Why will you not speak? Are you a mute? Are you an imbecile?" Fear bloated the boy's eyes. This only infuriated Salytov more. "Can you people not understand——?" He broke off, unable to voice what it was he wanted to be understood. His sense of contamination was incommunicable. He resorted to announcing: "I am Lieutenant Ilya Petrovich Salytov of the Haymarket District Police Bureau." And now the boy's mouth was gaping. "Don't you understand Russian? Where is he?"

"Who?" came finally, in a cracked voice that managed to span several octaves in one word.

"The landlord, you idiot!"

"He's in the other room."

"Call him then! Don't you people understand anything?" He could feel it on his scalp now, the contamination. It had spread over the surface of his body and was now seeping into him. Every second he was forced to spend in these places deepened it. A shudder of loathing passed through him. He scanned the floor for cockroaches and looked back at the boy as if he had found one.

But without the boy calling, a rotund man with indolent eyes appeared behind him. His face was dirty, his hair and beard knotted. His pear-shaped body bulged beneath a greasy leather apron. "It's all right, Kesha." There was a note of suspicion in his bass voice. Wariness flickered in his eyes as he took Salytov in.

"You are the proprietor of this"—Salytov looked around as if he would find the word he was looking for daubed on the walls, then settled for a sarcasm—"establishment?"

The landlord nodded minimally.

"Lieutenant Salytov of the Haymarket District Police. I am conducting an official investigation. You must cooperate or face the consequences." Salytov reached into the pocket of his greatcoat, then passed across the photograph of Ratazyayev. "Do you recognize this man?"

The landlord studied the photograph without comment. He blinked once with great emphasis, making his face a mask of imperturbability. "We get a lot of people in here," he said finally, handing the photograph back.

"But do you recognize him?"

"Not particularly."

"Not particularly!" shouted Salytov with sudden spluttering rage. "What on earth do you mean by not particularly? Either you recognize the man or you do not."

"In that case, I should say, all things considered, I do not."

"Are you trying to make a fool out of me? Is that your game? I warn you, do not try to make a fool out of me."

One of the landlord's eyebrows rose and fell eloquently.

"Do not raise your eyebrow at me! You dare to raise your eyebrow at me? Impertinent—" Salytov struck the man across the face with the back of his hand. The potboy jumped back in shock. But the landlord hardly turned his head and swung it back immediately as if eager for another blow. He faced Salytov now with lowered eyes. "That will teach you to raise your eyebrow at me."

The landlord nodded in meek penitence.

"Now, I ask you once again, do you recognize this man? Look at the photograph carefully." Salytov thrust the picture into the landlord's face, so that he had to lean back to see it.

"Now that I think about it, perhaps he has been in here, once or twice." The landlord's voice was flat and calculated. He spoke deliberately, without a trace of fear.

"He is known to frequent the filthiest dives in the Haymarket area. Why would he not come in here?" When it seemed the witticism would not receive the appreciation it merited, Salytov continued his questioning. "When was the last time?"

"I don't remember, your excellency." Despite his readiness to use the honorary title, the landlord's tone remained dangerously neutral. Salytov eyed him suspiciously, even nervously.

"Today? Has he been in here today?"

"No, your excellency."

"Last night?"

"No. We haven't seen him for a while, your excellency." A new note, of strained impatience, crept into the landlord's voice. He flashed a decisive glance at Salytov and risked: "Or the other one."

"The other one? What other one?" The kindling of Salytov's curiosity relaxed his aggression. He dropped the hand holding the photograph.

"He often comes in with another man."

"Name?".

"I don't know, your excellency. It's not my business to inquire into the names of my clientele."

"I could have you pulled in as the accomplice to a very serious crime." But Salytov was distracted. The threat was delivered without conviction, almost out of habit. "You are guilty of aiding and abetting men wanted by the police," he added sharply, as if remembering himself.

"I didn't know they were wanted by the police, your excellency." The landlord spoke with measured guile. "If I had, I would have made sure I got their names. As it is, I don't know the names of any of these people." He gestured toward the stupor-frozen faces peering out of the gloom. "They come in, they drink, they leave. I don't interfere with them. Perhaps Kesha can help you." The landlord nodded permissively to the pot-boy, whose face was suddenly stretched by panic at the prospect of having to talk to the police officer.

A slow sneer writhed over Salytov's features. "Very well. You. Talk." Kesha's gaze flitted anxiously between the landlord and the policeman. Salytov held up the photograph. "So you know these men?"

Kesha nodded.

"Speak!" barked Salytov.

"Y-y-y-yes."

"Names? Did you ever hear them address each other by name?"

"I think s-s-s-so."

"Good. So what are their names?"

"That's Ra-Ra-Ra-Ra. . . ." The boy's stammering dried up.

"Ra-Ra-Ra? What sort of a name is Ra-Ra-Ra, you imbecile?"

"Ra-Ra-Ratazyayev!" The name came out, eventually, in an angry rush.

"I know it's Ra-Ra-Ratazyayev, you idiot. I don't need you to tell me it's Ra-Ra-Ratazyayev. I want to know about the other one. The man he comes in here with."

"Govorov." This time, the name was produced without stammering, in a sudden, involuntary regurgitation.

"Govorov? Are you sure?"

Kesha nodded frantically.

"So. Govorov. What can you tell me about this Govorov?"

Kesha's shrug was anything but nonchalant. It was as much a wince anticipating pain as a gesture of helplessness. He was desperate to know what it was Salytov wanted to be told about this Govorov. Then he could get on with telling it. But only one thing came to mind: "He has photographs."

"Go on."

The boy's lips rippled uncomfortably. Another spasm of a shrug shook him.

"Tell me more about these photographs. What were they of?"

"Stupid."

"What is so stupid about them?"

"Just . . . stupid."

"You are the stupid here, boy. Tell me exactly what you saw when you looked at the photographs."

"Girls."

"Girls? What is so stupid about that? Don't you like to look at photographs of girls?"

"They had no clothes on."

Salytov let out a great "Ha!" of amusement. "What's wrong with you? That's not stupid, that's . . ." The word eluded Salytov. "Do you have any of these photographs?"

Kesha frowned and shook his head. "I didn't like to look at them."

"Come, come! A boy of your age! Listen, I will not arrest you for looking at a few smutty photographs. Tell the truth now, Kesha." The boy was startled to hear his name from Salytov. "What did you do with the photographs?"

"I wouldn't take them! I wouldn't look at them!" insisted Kesha hotly.

"Why ever not? Are you a *skopsy*? Have you cut off your balls and dick, is that it? Or are you—" A look of horrified disgust came over Salytov.

"It's nothing like that. It was their faces. They looked afraid."

"They're just whores."

"They were—some of them—they were just little girls. I have a little sister. It's not right."

"They are born whores, girls like that. Why else do you think they do it?"

"I didn't like to look at them."

"You have a saint here, cleaning your pots," Salytov joked to the landlord.

"He is a good boy, Kesha is."

"He is a liar. I know boys. He is a liar, or worse." Salytov looked at Kesha distastefully. "Tell me, *skopsy*, did he show these photographs to anyone else?"

"He was always showing them to people. He would sell them to whoever would buy them, and—" There was a warning look from the landlord. Kesha broke off.

The fire returned to Salytov's complexion. "Damn you! What's this?"

"I remember the man myself, now," put in the landlord quickly. "Once he tried to pay for his *kvas* with some of these pictures."

"Strange how your memory returns. Did you accept the pornography as payment?"

"He told me he was an artist. They are what he called artistic poses. Nobody said anything about pornography."

"Get them."

The landlord moved slowly, reluctance thickening his torpor. His eyes were the last part of him to turn.

"Hurry it up!" barked Salytov. He smirked at the landlord's waddling gait as he hurried into the back room.

Approximately the size of playing cards, the photographs were no worse than many he had seen. True, the faces had a certain bewildered quality, but he found that only added to the piquancy. He shuffled through them briskly, ruthlessly, careful not to dwell on any one image or to betray an interest other than professional. And yet the luminous pallor of the flesh, the crisp darknesses of exposed and in some cases immature genitalia, drew his eye and hardened his pulse. He recognized, in among the stilted pageant, the young prostitute who had been brought into the station, accused of stealing a hundred rubles. In the instant that her photograph flashed before him, he assessed the fullness of her breasts.

There were men in some of the photographs. Their faces were always turned away, cropped off or blurred by movement: never shown. Unlike the women, the men were clothed, although in some cases their sexual organs, in varying states of rigidity, were exposed. In one instance, the male subject had been captured at the moment of his self-induced ejaculation. The beads of his semen hung in the air; their trajectory seemed to be toward the female model's abdomen. She viewed their approach without enthusiasm.

Salytov turned the photographs over and shuffled through them again. An address was written on the reverse of one.

"This. What is this?" said Salytov, laying it down on the counter.

"Three Spasskoi Lane," read the landlord.

"Is this Govorov's address?"

"I suppose it must be. I never noticed it before now." The landlord avoided Salytov's eye.

"I find that hard to believe. It's more likely that he wrote it for you deliberately. So that you would know where to go if you wanted more of the same."

"Well, I don't remember. Besides, I don't spend much time looking at the backs of photographs."

"This is police evidence now," said Salytov with a provocative grin. He pocketed the photographs. The landlord didn't offer a protest, unless a slight hunching of the shoulders could be read as such. "If you see either of these men again, Ratazyayev or Govorov, send Kesha to the police bureau on Stolyarny Lane. Detain them until we get here. Is that understood?"

Salytov didn't wait for an answer. He delivered a warning nod with the precision of a hammer blow. The concertina player started up again. Salytov had the fanciful idea that her playing was not just mournful but diseased. In his mind, tuberculosis floated in the ragged notes. He turned suddenly and fled. The sense of contamination pursued him, even as he took the steps two at a time.

S EVENTY-TWO, SEVENTY-THREE, *seventy-four, seventy-five* . . .
Virginsky counted his steps. But no matter how far he walked, he couldn't put any distance between himself and his humiliation. It was always there with him, staring him in the face, in the form of the boots Porfiry Petrovich had given him. So it had come to this: he was a charity case. And to accept charity from such a man! Virginsky had not forgotten how they came for him in the night, nor the words with which the magistrate pointed him out: "That is the man. That is Virginsky." And then this same Judas had the nerve to argue that he should relinquish his freedom voluntarily!

That man is the devil, he said to himself. *To think I nearly went along with it.*

He realized that he had lost count of his steps. It was difficult to count and think at the same time. That was the point, of course—the point of the counting. If he could only concentrate on his counting, he wouldn't have to think about his humiliation. He picked up from the last number he could remember, not knowing how many steps he had missed.

Seventy-six, seventy-seven, seventy-eight . . .

He was walking along the side of the solidified Yekaterinsky Canal, toward the Nevsky Prospect. It was not a day to be out unless you had good reason. The cold wind assaulted his face and mocked his tattered overcoat. The ice cut into him and spread along his nerve fibers with greedy, destructive haste. There was a bend in the canal. The towpath kinked sharply northward. On his right was the Imperial Bank, turning its curved back on him jealously. *You shall not have any of this,* it seemed to say. On the other side, across the canal, loomed the massive bulk of the Foundling Hospital. It struck him as an ironic juxtaposition.

Virginsky stopped to consider the significance of it. He felt weak, unable to think. And yet it was suddenly pressingly important to him to work out what it meant to be standing between the Imperial Bank and the Foundling Hospital.

As he stood there, a man even more destitute than he shuffled past, his meager jacket and trousers padded with straw and newspaper. The tramp seemed to have come from nowhere, his footsteps almost silent. There were many such individuals in Petersburg, anonymous and interchangeable. As one died, another would appear. Virginsky did not attempt to meet his eye, though he did look at his feet. The man wore an old, disintegrating pair of felt boots, soaked and filthy.

Virginsky acknowledged the superstitious dread that had prevented him from looking into the man's face. He was remembering a story he had once read about a man haunted by his double.

He let the tramp disappear around the bend in the path before starting his steps again.

Seventy-nine, eighty, eighty-one . . .

When he turned the corner the tramp was not in view.

Eighty-two . . .

The canal path brought him into the Nevsky Prospect alongside the Kazan Cathedral. The width and prosperity of the street intimidated him. He felt that the wind that purged it would destroy him, deliberately. Only the affluent, layered in furs, could venture into it.

Virginsky decided to shelter in the colonnade of the Kazan Cathedral. Though he would describe himself as an atheist, he had always liked this place. The semicircular sweep of the colonnade was vaguely reminiscent of arms held open for embrace. He responded to the grandeur of the design without being awed by it. It seemed to contain within it something welcoming and benign. He believed the humanity of the peasant stonemason shone through.

The wind had blown between the columns a light scattering of snow dust, which every now and then it moved around or added to. Looking at the palimpsests of footprints on the paving stones, Virginsky's mind went blank. He was suddenly unable to count his own steps.

His humiliation came back to him and the dim memory of a resolve to end it. He remembered a plan, conceived in a police cell or possibly even before then. He seemed to spend his life reaching the same resolve, drawing up the same plan. Would he ever find the courage to put it into action?

But already he had forgotten what the plan was and would have to wait for it to come back to him. In the meantime . . .

One, two, three . . .

He set off again, walking the colonnade.

It was not that he was simpleminded. It was just that he was hungry. If only he could find a solution to that, the hunger, and the humiliation that came with it. But that was it, he suddenly remembered. That was why he was here in the Nevsky Prospect. To bring an end to the hunger.

Four, five, six . . .

He noticed that he was following one particular set of footprints. These seemed to be both the most recent and the most indistinct, lacking any clear heel or toe definition. At times they smudged into long lines, as if the walker had been dragging one foot or the other. Virginsky looked up but saw no one. All the same, he did not believe he had the colonnade to himself. He sensed another presence, concealed behind the shifting blinds of the columns.

Seven, eight, nine . . .

Then he saw the man—the same tramp from beside the canal—darting across the aisle between two columns.

He moves quickly, thought Virginsky. *Yet to look at him, he must be in a worse state than I.*

And it was not that Virginsky had found the courage to move away from the Kazan Cathedral. It was just that he could no longer bear the tramp's proximity. His terror had crystallized. He was certain now that if he came face to face with this other, he would see his own features staring back at him.

He stepped out into the Nevsky Prospect, his gaze fixed on a square three-story building on the other side of the street. Fortunately the road was clear of traffic. But the wind shrieked gleefully as it battered into him.

I WISH TO see Osip Maximovich."

Vadim Vasilyevich's cold, gray eyes looked down on the bedraggled individual who had just presented himself at the offices of Athene Publishing. His small mouth drew itself into a tight pucker of distaste. "And who are you?" The question was strangled by the man's forced baritone.

"You know me. You've seen me at the house of Anna Alexandrovna. I am Pavel Pavelovich Virginsky."

"What is your business here?"

"I wish to see Osip Maximovich."

"He's a very busy man. You can't just walk in here demanding to see whomsoever you like."

"Tell him I was a friend of Goryanchikov's."

"You will have to do better than that."

"I am a writer. Well, a student. But I have written . . . essays."

"Petersburg is full of writers."

"Goryanchikov said that I could get work here. Goryanchikov said he would vouch for me."

"Unfortunately, Goryanchikov is dead. He can't vouch for anyone."

"Please. Let me see Osip Maximovich. Goryanchikov told me—"

"Goryanchikov told you what?" A second, higher voice, leavened with relaxed good humor, took over the interrogation. Osip Maximovich himself had just come into the room. A twinkling flash danced across his spectacle lenses.

"About the work he was doing for you. The translation. The Proudhon. We talked about it."

Osip Maximovich took off his spectacles. His face was serious as he assessed Virginsky with his penetrating black eyes. "You talked about Proudhon?"

"Yes."

Osip Maximovich replaced his spectacles. The optical effect was to retract his eyes. "And you think that qualifies you to take over Stepan Sergeyevich's work?" He had seemed to be on the verge of asking something else entirely, but the thick lenses masked his intentions.

"We talked about other things."

"What other things?"

"Philosophy in general. Philosophers. Hegel."

Osip Maximovich pursed his lips as if impressed. "You talked of Hegel."

"Please. I want to work for you. Give me a section to do. If you're happy with the result, hire me to complete it. I will work for half what you were paying Goryanchikov."

"Is that because you are only half as good as him?" quipped Vadim Vasilyevich.

"I'm not greedy. Just hungry."

Osip Maximovich's smile expressed his approval of the answer. He transmitted some of his beaming pleasure toward Vadim Vasilyevich.

"There is no point," said Vadim Vasilyevich bluntly. "The police have confiscated the text of Goryanchikov's translation. We don't know how far he got."

"I know he didn't finish it," said Virginsky.

A sudden change came over Osip Maximovich's mood. He sighed despondently. "Poor Stepan Sergeyevich. His death was a terrible blow to us." He smiled forlornly to Virginsky. "He was like a son to me."

Virginsky frowned. "I wonder why people say that. It doesn't mean very much."

"I . . . miss him."

Virginsky said nothing.

"Did he ever, I wonder, speak of me . . . warmly?" pressed Osip Maximovich.

"Would it make any difference to you to know he hated you?"

"He said that?"

"No. But those are the feelings I have toward my own father. If he was like a son to you, you should have expected the same from him."

Osip Maximovich laughed abruptly. "I think you will make a very good translator of philosophy. We will try you out with the final section of Proudhon. If you make an adequate job of that, you can have the section before the last. And so on in reverse. With any luck, when we get Goryanchikov's version back from the police, the two will meet in the middle."

"Madness," said Vadim Vasilyevich, throwing up his arms.

"Now, now, Vadim Vasilyevich. We'll find out soon enough if he's up to the task. Do you accept the commission, my friend?"

"What about money? We haven't agreed on the money."

"That depends on the quality of the work. If it isn't up to scratch, I'm afraid we won't be able to pay you anything."

"But I need some money now." Desperation made Virginsky's tone aggressive. He quickly softened it. "For materials. Paper . . . pens . . . ink . . . candles." After a moment Virginsky added, "Et cetera."

"Et cetera? What et cetera can there be?" smiled Osip Maximovich.

"Food."

"This is beggary," commented Vadim Vasilyevich.

"Well, I'd rather deal with a beggar than a—" Osip Maximovich's lips closed on the word he had been about to say. "Some other kind of scoundrel."

Vadim Vasilyevich averted his eyes, as if Osip Maximovich had just told an off-color joke.

"At any rate, we can't let our translator starve," decided Osip Maximovich brightly. "We'll give you fifty kopeks in advance. If the work is adequate, you will receive a further five rubles and the next section, that is to say the preceding section, to translate. If the work is not adequate, the fifty kopeks will serve as a severance fee, and we will never see you again. Is that agreed?"

Virginsky nodded without looking Osip Maximovich in the eye.

"Vadim Vasilyevich, the money box, please."

Vadim Vasilyevich was shaking his head as he withdrew into the back room.

O UT IN THE OPEN, with the cold air piercing his face, Salytov began to feel cleansed. It didn't last. He saw a man vomit orange paste into the gutter. Another argued with the wind. At the northeast corner of Haymarket Square, where it spilled over into Spasskoi Lane, a shivering woman offered her headscarf for sale. The thought occurred to him that she would get a better price for it than for herself.

Students clustered around the racks and tables outside the secondhand bookshops on Spasskoi Lane. He had little patience for them. In fact, the sight of them infuriated him. He had no doubt they would consider themselves superior to him, as if their rags for clothes, their battered, crooked hats, even their starving bellies should be objects of envy. What kind of inverted table of ranks was this when the trappings of the most abject poverty were held to be a source of pride? They were no better than the ignorant peasants who scavenged for crusts and rags. No, they were worse, far worse. At least the peasant had a sense of his duty to himself. The peasant too had his soul intact. These educated fools had squandered theirs.

Salytov imagined himself kicking over the book displays, a kind of Christ among the moneylenders.

The entrance to number 3 hung open. Salytov skipped up the steps and pulled the door behind him, but it would not close. It was dark in the hallway and rapidly becoming darker. He could just about make out the looming rectangles of the apartment doors on the ground floor. He kicked the front door wide open. It made little difference. Outside the afternoon was dissolving into gloom. He sensed rather than saw the stairs ahead of him, in the same way that he sensed his hand in front of his face.

Before he lost the light completely, Salytov knocked briskly on the first door he came to. Minutes passed. He knocked again, with renewed urgency. His raps echoed in the dark. He had the sense of a great emptiness behind the door.

He wondered if perhaps he had made a mistake. Was he wise to have come here alone or at least without informing anyone at the bureau what he was doing?

He thought about turning around. He imagined himself outside, running, yes, running like a coward away from this place. But he imagined other things too: a knife coming out of the darkness and plunging into his midriff. He imagined a figure stepping out of the shadows. The face was a smooth blank. At the same time Salytov felt a retrospective anger at the way Porfiry Petrovich had tried to make a fool of him over the disappearance of the prostitute's accuser, the man they now believed was Konstantin Kirillovich Govorov. But it had had nothing to do with him. The man had absconded before he became involved.

He would show Porfiry Petrovich. He would bring Konstantin Kirillovich Govorov in alone.

But more than anything, it was Salytov's fear that persuaded him to stay.

He could hear footsteps in the ground floor apartment now. In a moment he could be dead.

The door cracked open. The glow of an oil lamp held at chest height flared upward, illuminating a single dark eye, set deep beneath a sprawling, highly animated eyebrow.

"Govorov?" The hoarseness of his own voice surprised Salytov.

"Upstairs." The eyebrow wriggled as if from the effort of producing the word. A waft of pickled cucumber came with it.

"Show me."

The eyebrow plummeted heavily. The movement expressed angry refusal.

"I am a police officer. It will be better for you if you cooperate."

The door swung inward, allowing the halo of light to spread across the hall. The oil lamp was held by a short, balding man of about fifty. The first thing Salytov looked at was his eyebrows. He was impatient to dispel a superstitious sense of evil. Seeing them in the context of the full person only partially reassured him. He remained disturbed by their apparent unruliness and independence. He had to force himself to take in the rest of the man's face. His skin was sallow, features Asiatic, his face skeletally gaunt beneath high, sharp cheekbones. A large bald head tapered acutely into a pointed beard, like an inverted onion dome.

"I don't want any trouble," said the man. "This is a respectable house."

"I'm glad to hear it. You are?"

"Leonid Simonovich Tolkachenko. I am the yardkeeper here."

"You have keys to all the apartments?"

"Yes."

"Bring them."

The light went with Tolkachenko as he withdrew. Salytov felt Govorov's presence fill the darkness.

"What has he done?" said Tolkachenko sternly, returning with the bobbing light and the keys.

"It's no concern of yours," said Salytov to the caretaker's back as he followed him up the creaking stairs.

"I knew it would end badly," Tolkachenko threw over his shoulder.

"What are you talking about?"

"I told him it had to stop."

"What?"

"He brought girls here. He denied it. But I saw them and heard them. He tried to sneak them up the stairs. But I know the creak and groan of every step. And there is a board outside his door that calls out to me."

They reached the first landing. Tolkachenko pointed to the door on the right and nodded. Salytov gestured for him to open the door.

The flat was in darkness.

Tolkachenko cast the lamp's unfocused glow about the room. "He's not here." Tolkachenko seemed surprised. "He *was* here." The caretaker crossed to the window and held up the lamp to look out. He tested the window and found it locked. "How strange."

"Perhaps he slid down the banister," said Salytov, grinning in the darkness. "Bring the light over here," he added sharply. He was aware of an undefined dark shape hovering at shoulder height. "Give me that!" He took the lamp and allowed its flare to wash over the shape, which he was able to identify as a camera on its tripod. "So this is where he takes the photographs," muttered Salytov. In that instant he hated Govorov. His desire to catch him and see him punished—for something, he didn't care what—solidified.

The swing of the sputtering oil lamp gradually revealed the room as a series of unrelated fragments: a sofa draped in a satin throw, a table littered with breadcrumbs and dirty crockery, an unmade bed, an open escritoire, a shelf of books, and propped up beneath it, a seven-stringed gypsy guitar. The escritoire demanded closer examination. Even at a distance Salytov recognized its contents as more of the genre of photographs he had confiscated from the tavern owner. In fact, it contained multiple copies of the same photograph. It was that girl again, the prostitute who had been brought in for stealing the hundred rubles. She was lying naked on Govorov's sofa, her arms behind her head, her legs at right angles to each other, one knee sticking straight up, the other pointing out. Salytov felt his mouth contract with dehydration, sticking slightly to his teeth. The insistence of the image, repeated on every card he looked at, was dizzying.

"Filthy whore," commented Tolkachenko, with a heavy swallow. "And to think, all this has been going on above my head. Wait till I see Govorov."

"Say nothing. Do not arouse his suspicions. Do you understand? He may well be dangerous. This is a murder investigation. The moment he returns, send word to me. I am Lieutenant Ilya Petrovich Salytov of the Haymarket District Police Bureau. The Stolyarny Lane station."

"I know it. Not that I have ever been in trouble with the police," added Tolkachenko quickly.

"What hours does he keep, this Govorov?"

"It is hard to say. He is not what you would call a regular gentleman. Sometimes he sleeps all day. Sometimes he is out all night."

Salytov crossed to the shelf of books. The volumes were all roughly the same size and shape, all in the same maroon cloth binding. He scanned the titles: *Hareem Tales, The Adventures of a Rake, Pandora's Awakening,*

White Slaves, A Sojourn in Sodom, The Gentleman's Privilege, The Whip and the Whipped, The Pleasure of Purple (Being a Sequel to The Whip and the Whipped), Flesh and Blood, She Gave Herself to Gypsies, One Thousand and One Maidenheads, The Monk and the Virgins. Each one bore the imprint Priapos.

Salytov gave an emphatic nod of triumph. It was not for the benefit of the caretaker, to whom he had nothing to prove, and whose presence he had anyway forgotten. He was imagining that he was showing the books to Porfiry Petrovich.

18

The Hotel Adrianople

THE *DROZHKI* SPED north across the Neva over the Bizhevoi Bridge. The driver stood to whip the horse, a bay stallion. The beast's neck arched and writhed. Its back rippled beneath glistening skin. Steam rose from its flanks. It turned its face sideways into the sharp oncoming air. Under the driver's cries, the horse's snorts, and the constant jangle of the harness bells, Porfiry Petrovich could hear the hiss of the runners over the smooth ice. He folded down his fur collar so that the moisture from his breath would not dampen it.

It was good to be sitting in an open *drozhki* wrapped in furs, hurtling into the coldest, clearest day of the winter so far.

"Fools," muttered Salytov.

Porfiry turned to see what had provoked the remark. Salytov's gaze was locked onto a wooden sledding hill built on the frozen river. It was Saturday morning, and the thrill-seekers rushed four abreast up the steps of the great tower. Their shrieks as they came down the other side hung high in the emptied air. It was mostly boys and young men, but there were some girls there too, their faces flushed and intent on excitement. Porfiry smiled. He felt vicariously the stomach lurch and the soul's vertiginous untethering.

He did not feel inclined to push Salytov for the source of his misanthropy. "You did well, Ilya Petrovich," he commented instead, shouting over the noises of transit. The sledding hill was behind them now, though the yelps of pleasure and fear could still be heard.

Salytov did not reply. His expression was hidden from Porfiry.

"Finding Govorov's lodging was a breakthrough."

"It was nothing but methodical old-fashioned police work. A lead was bound to come eventually. It came sooner rather than later. I was lucky." Salytov did not face Porfiry as he shouted his reply. The investigator had to strain to catch his words.

"You know as well as I do, you make your own luck in this game."

Salytov grunted.

"Of course, the question raised by your discovery is, why should a man who has permanent lodgings in Spasskoi Lane take a hotel room on the Bolshoi Prospect?"

Salytov's refusal to face Porfiry became pointed.

Porfiry frowned. "Ilya Petrovich, if I have offended you in any way . . ."

Salytov half-turned in Porfiry's direction. But he could not bring himself to look the other man in the eye. "You have not offended me," he said in a stiff tone.

"I'm glad to hear it. Then may I ask—" Porfiry broke off. "But no, I may be mistaken." Porfiry's reticence failed to elicit the openness he had hoped for from Salytov. He watched the other man closely before pressing: "Do I detect a certain antagonism in your demeanor, Ilya Petrovich?"

Salytov sighed deeply, making sure it could be heard, then faced Porfiry at last. A fierce and undisguised bitterness showed in his eyes. "I know my place. I am a simple police officer. I do whatever is required of me by the office of the investigating magistrate. If you have any complaints concerning the way I have fulfilled my duties, I suggest you take them up with my superior, Nikodim Fomich."

"I have no complaints, Ilya Petrovich. I merely wonder why you dislike me so much." Porfiry's throat felt tight from shouting. His voice sounded hoarse.

"It is not necessary for me to like you. Or for you to like me."

"Of course, but what I think you do not realize is that I have enormous respect for you. I specifically requested you to be assigned to this case so that we could work together." Salytov's expression was suddenly outraged, as if Porfiry had insulted him. "What have I said now?" demanded Porfiry.

"You do not know?"

"No." Porfiry's eyes pleaded.

"You insist that I tell you?" Salytov's demand received a nod from Porfiry. "Very well. I know that you make fun of me. I know that you send me off on fools' errands. You intrigue to get me the worst jobs. And here you have the boldness, the effrontery to say that you respect me!"

"You are wrong, Ilya Petrovich."

"No, Porfiry Petrovich. I am right. I know that you are not to be trusted. You use the same tricks and techniques on your colleagues as you do on the criminals you interview. With me, it is flattery and disingenuousness. No doubt you would call it psychology."

"Is that really fair, Ilya Petrovich?"

"You cannot even be straightforward with me now, when you have demanded honesty from me."

Porfiry exhaled audibly through his nostrils. "Perhaps you're right. It is interesting to see myself illuminated by your perception. Not a very flattering portrait you paint."

"*I* do not flatter."

"I know, I know. That is my method. Forgive me then. I will own up to everything you accuse me of. Obviously, I am not as subtle as I like to think."

Salytov regarded Porfiry's ingratiating smile coldly. He then leaned toward Porfiry, so that their bodies were pressed together. "You have never forgiven me," he murmured, though he was close enough for it to be heard.

"Forgiven you? What is there to forgive?" Porfiry too spoke more quietly now.

"That it was to me that he confessed," Salytov hissed with intimate antagonism.

"I really have no idea—"

"That student. Raskolnikov. He sought me out and confessed to me!"

"But I was pleased that it was so, Ilya Petrovich. I was glad that he was able to confess at all. It does not matter to whom. The important thing is he confessed."

"Hypocritical nonsense! It was a blow to your vanity. Admit it. Have the decency to admit it."

"I see that I will not be able to persuade you of something you're so determined not to believe."

"You cannot persuade me of your sincerity, if that's what you mean."

"Hmm." Porfiry pulled away and flexed his brow. "I'm sorry you feel this way. It is painful to me."

Salytov shrugged.

"We must simply agree to ignore our differences and concentrate our efforts on the case," said Porfiry, as brightly as he could.

Salytov closed the gap between them again. "But will you be honest with me even in that?" His challenge had a pleading edge to it. "Will you honestly share with me all that you have discovered? Or will you—hold something back?"

"If I am guilty of holding things back, it is only because I have nothing certain to disclose. I have discovered nothing. The solution evades me as much as it evades you."

"But you have your suspicions?"

"Perhaps. But suspicions at this stage of the investigation are worthless."

"You see! You will not even share your suspicions with me!"

"I will say this. I do not believe that Borya killed Goryanchikov—or himself."

"That is obvious. You have given me nothing."

"As for the student Virginsky—"

"You let him go."

"I had no choice in the matter. I believe that he provides the key to the mystery somehow. Everything comes back to that contract. At the very least it provides him with a motive. But I need more than a motive. And I suspect there is more to it than meets the eye. At any rate, I have put a tail on him. I think it is as well to know what he is up to. It may even save his life."

"You think he is in danger?"

"If the murderer believes he can incriminate him."

"Who do you think the killer is?"

Porfiry Petrovich sighed despondently. "I do have a fault, you're right. It's a very Russian fault. I'm superstitious." Porfiry's glance was momentarily shy, almost apologetic. "Did you know I come from Tartar stock? On my grandmother's side. She was born into a Kezhig tribe. Married a Russian subaltern. In my more fanciful moments, I like to imagine she was the daughter of the tribal shaman. Perhaps that accounts for it, my superstition. At any rate, it is that which is to blame for any reticence you may have noticed in me. Nothing more. Incidentally, contrary to what you may think, I do not believe these mysteries are solved rationally, through the exercise of a cold, deductive reasoning. The thing that terrifies me—sometimes, when I allow myself to think about it—is that I don't know how they are solved. One must go to a place within one's self. It is a kind of Siberia of the soul. In the criminal, it is the place where these deeds are conceived and carried through. But we all have a similar place within us, or so I believe. I know that I have. I can't speak for you, of course."

"What's your point?"

"My point is, one cannot see clearly there. One gropes one's way. Occasionally figures come toward one. Perhaps one is able to glimpse the features of a face."

Salytov relaxed heavily. He threw himself back and sat for a while considering Porfiry's analogy. "Nonsense," he shouted, at last. "You're still trying to hoodwink me. You just want to guard your secrets in case I get there first. I must disclose everything I learn to you, but you can keep everything back."

"This has been a very diverting conversation," said Porfiry. He took out his brightly colored cigarette case and held it open toward Salytov. The policeman snorted his refusal. The *drozhki* began to slow. Porfiry put away the case without taking a cigarette.

V IRGINSKY SAW THE tramp huddled in a doorway on Gorokhovaya Street, a coarse sack pulled over his head. He knew from the ragged felt boots sticking out at the bottom that it was the same man.

He was relieved that the man's face was hidden. It saved him from confronting the fear that now obsessed him: that he would recognize himself in the stranger's features. Somehow the idea had entered his mind that this figure dogging his steps was nothing other than his future self. The absurdity of it did not escape him. That he was incapable of religious faith but was prepared to entertain this stupidity as a literal truth.

I am mad! He almost laughed out loud.

His self-awareness offered hope.

I think I am mad, therefore I am not mad.

He sensed a movement in the sacking as he passed. But did not look. He was torturing himself with the notion that the instant he looked the tramp in the eye, he would merge with him. He would become his future. What a ludicrous and humiliating—yes, humiliating, everything about his life was humiliating now—superstition! And yet he believed in it enough to keep his eyes fixed firmly ahead.

With the tramp behind him, he allowed himself to think about the meal he would soon have in a cheap restaurant. Perhaps that should have been humiliating too, given the means he had used to acquire the money for his dinner. He had not just begged; he had lied. Virginsky had no intention of attempting a word of the translation. He had gone there simply to see what he could get out of them. But he found that he was not ashamed or humiliated. He felt no compunction at all.

He was almost grateful to his hunger, as it enabled him to look forward to a five-kopek meat pie as if it were a banquet. It also excused any behavior.

He had just one more errand to run before dining. Glowing spheres of color drew him. He approached the lights in the window of Friedlander's the apothecary. He was momentarily touched by wonder, although he knew that they were just big bottles filled with colored liquid and lit from behind. Unconsciously, his gaze went back to the doorway where he had last seen the tramp. He was dismayed to see that it was empty.

THE HOTEL ADRIANOPLE was a low wooden structure that squatted heavily at the side of the Bolshoi Prospect, a brooding shadow compressed beneath the featureless sky. In places, its timbers were charred, as if someone had tried to set light to it.

It was dark inside, and deserted. The reception area was minimal. A rack of keys was suspended behind a high desk at the start of a narrow, low-ceilinged corridor. Dirty yellow wallpaper absorbed the weak light.

Porfiry pushed the bell on the desk. It gave a broken chime.

A stubble-faced porter eventually appeared through an arch in one wall. He was wearing a grubby uniform undone to the belt, revealing a discolored vest. The porter assessed the two of them with an insolent expression. "A room for the hour, is it?"

"How dare you!" shouted Salytov. The speed with which he attained his rage astonished even Porfiry.

"We are looking for the boy Dmitri. It is police business. I am an investigating magistrate. This gentleman is a police lieutenant."

"What has he done, the little gypsy?"

"Tell him we wish to give him his reward. From the tsar."

The slovenly man stirred himself into a frown and then roared, "Dima!" without taking his eyes off Porfiry.

In an aside to Salytov, Porfiry murmured, "Please, Ilya Petrovich. Remember he is a child." To Salytov's look of startled outrage, he added, "There is nothing to be gained from scaring him."

Salytov shook his head in angry impatience.

"You mentioned a reward," said the porter, an unpleasant eagerness in his eyes.

"For Dmitri, yes," insisted Porfiry.

The porter countered this detail with a cynical leer. "Leave it with me, your excellencies, and I will make sure that he gets it. There is no need for your excellencies to be inconvenienced. You could be here all day hanging around for that wastrel."

"You want his reward? I'll give you his reward!" Salytov closed in on the porter with a raised hand. Although he was protected by the desk, the porter backed away from the policeman's threatening advance. He flashed a quizzical appeal toward Porfiry and shouted for "Dima" again, this time embellishing the diminutive with abuse.

A moment later the boy's face peered out from the archway. It was every bit as filthy as the last time Porfiry had seen it. He had a grimy pillbox hat pushed back on the crown of his head. His eyes widened when he saw Porfiry, and it looked for a moment as if he might make a run for it.

"Ah, Dmitri, my friend! How good to see you again! I have something for you—from the tsar himself." Porfiry held up a shiny silver ruble. It drew the bellboy out into the open. But just as Dmitri reached for it, Porfiry closed his fist around the coin.

"It's not gold. It's silver," said Dmitri dismissively.

"Ah, but it's freshly minted—just for you. It has the tsar's picture on it."

"Give it to me then."

"You've almost earned it. If only you hadn't run away when we were talking before, it would be yours already. Why did you run away, my friend? There was nothing to be afraid of."

"I wasn't scared."

"Then why did you run away?"

"You ask too many questions."

"It's my job." Porfiry took out and lit the cigarette he had put off smoking in the *drozhki*. Dmitri's watchful envy inspired him to offer the boy the case. Dmitri took a cigarette eagerly and sucked in his cheeks as Porfiry lit it for him.

"Turkish?" he asked with his first, delayed exhalation.

Porfiry nodded. "You like it?"

Dmitri shrugged.

"We were talking about the yardkeeper, remember? When you delivered your message to the dwarf Goryanchikov, you called in at the yardkeeper's shed. Did Govorov give you a message for him too?"

Dmitri bit the inside of his mouth. "He gave me a note, yes."

"So? Why not tell me that before?"

Dmitri held the cigarette between thumb and forefinger and studied the glowing ash. "Dunno." He took a long draw. "Something he said, maybe" came out with the smoke.

"What did he say?"

"It was nothing really." Dmitri steadfastly refused to look Porfiry in the eye.

"Yes, I'm sure you're right. It's bound to be nothing. A pity. If it proved to be useful . . ."

"'Be careful with it.'"

"'Be careful with it'?"

"That's what he said. 'Be careful with it.'"

"Anything else?"

The boy shrugged. "It was the way he said it. His smile. The way he looked at me." The boy shuddered at the recollection. In that moment, and in the distant narrowing of his eyes, he seemed curiously ageless, beyond all consideration of age, as if he were remembering something that had happened a hundred years ago. "It sent a shiver down my spine."

Porfiry pursed his lips. He glanced quickly to Salytov for a reaction. The policeman was frowning thoughtfully. "Interesting," conceded Porfiry.

"So do I get it now?" Dmitri held out his hand.

Porfiry winked and produced the silver ruble. He reasoned that he would not get much more out of the boy on the promise of the coin alone. "You've done well. The tsar will be pleased." He handed over the prize.

Dmitri flashed a proud glance around, but seeing the grubby porter, his expression became wary. He hurried the coin into a pocket. "Do you know the tsar?" he asked Porfiry.

"Not personally. But I will communicate your cooperation to my superior, and he will communicate it to his superior, and so on until it reaches the tsar. I am confident he will be pleased."

"He's playing with you, you little fool," sneered the porter suddenly.

"I assure you, that's the way the system works," said Porfiry, blinking calmly. "His Imperial Majesty's gratitude—or *displeasure*—is passed back down." He lowered his head to menace the porter with significance. "It could be a beating as easily as a coin." Porfiry turned to Dmitri with a smile. "Now, my friend, there is one more thing I would ask you to do for me. I would like you to show us the room that Govorov occupied."

Dmitri drew from his cigarette with a manly grimace. "We'll need a candle," he said.

V IRGINSKY SCANNED Gorokhovaya Street as he came out of Friedlander's. He couldn't see the tramp. But it was getting dark, and the air was thick with swirling snow. It was difficult to see anything. He had the sense, however, that the man was out there somewhere waiting for him. Perhaps he was one of the vague shapes huddled around the yardkeepers' fires that punctuated the pavement on both sides of the street.

Virginsky's stomach growled painfully. Big snowflakes streamed toward his eyes, hungry for his tears.

He started walking south. His new boots served him well on the slippery surface. He felt them grip but also sensed within his step the heart-lurching point at which they would fail him, and he measured his gait to stay the right side of it. Then, as a closed carriage passed him heading in the opposite direction, he turned sharply back on himself and ran in its lee. He was exhilarated by his ability to stay upright. He surprised himself by the maneuver but was comforted by it all the same, not merely because the carriage sheltered him from the weather. If the tramp was still on the other side of the street, the moving vehicle would act as a further blind, in addition to the nascent blizzard. As he came to the first corner, he turned right into Morskaya Street. The carriage continued straight on. Virginsky ran a few more paces and then abandoned himself to a slide that took him, arms windmilling, a couple of *sazheni* along the pavement. His arms came up, and he ducked into a quick walk, casting a single glance over his shoulder.

With the same impulsiveness that had prompted him to turn on his heels in Gorokhovaya Street, he suddenly lurched toward the door of a shop. He did not look at the name of it and had formed no clear impression of what it sold.

There was a smell of new felt and cologne, which had to it an elusive familiarity. He had been here before, once, a long time ago. In fact, his last visit to the German hat shop on Morskaya Street had been soon after his arrival in St. Petersburg. In those days his own apparel was equal to the expensive hats on display. It had seemed the most natural thing in the world to hold his head high as a shop assistant measured its circumference. Then he had inspected the shop's wares as if they already belonged to him, and he had not been afraid to look himself in the eye in one of the many looking glasses. His face beneath a German topper had not struck him as preposterous. Far from it. He had bought the hat, though it was long since hocked, the pledge surrendered.

Now the mirrors crowded in on him oppressively. He flinched away from them as if from a public shaming. And to try on one of the hats would have been as impossible as to dance on the ceiling.

Virginsky moved far enough into the interior to be partially hidden from the street, but not so far that he could no longer look out through the window of the door. He was anxious also to avoid the attention of the shop walker. Fortunately, the staff all seemed to be busy with other customers.

He didn't have long to wait before the tramp shuffled into sight. In fact, the man's sudden appearance on the pavement outside the shop took him by surprise. He had not had time to prepare himself for what now confronted him: an unimpeded view of the other's profile. The greatest shock was that he did not recognize the face. It was certainly not his own. This was so unexpected that he stared blankly at the man, scarcely believing that it was the same tramp. He looked down at the stranger's feet for confirmation. He was still wearing the old felt boots. But Virginsky noticed he now had a pair of good rubber galoshes over them.

The man hesitated briefly on the pavement almost directly in front of Virginsky, casting searching looks up and down Morskaya Street. It seemed it did not occur to him to look inside the German hat shop. It was clearly inconceivable to connect the object of his search with the interior of such an establishment. The man moved on. Once again his speed and purpose impressed Virginsky.

"Can I help you?"

Virginsky turned. A sleek, elegantly dressed man of around thirty stood before him. He tilted his head back so that he could look down at Virginsky more effectively.

Virginsky thought of all the things he could say to the fellow as he took in the details of his appearance, the long oiled hair that curled solidly at his collar, the crisp black frock coat, beneath it the taut waistcoat, as glistening and bright as a polished mineral, and the finely tapered, beetle-black shoes. Everything was sharp and unassailable, a hostile elegance, even the needle-scent of his perfume.

"*I* bought a hat here once," said Virginsky, putting as much defiance as he could into the claim.

The shopman disdained to comment but pivoted backward at the waist, as though reeling from the words.

"My father is a landowner," blurted Virginsky. He bowed his head and left the shop, burning with a hotter, deeper shame than he had ever known.

D MITRI LED THEM down the dingy corridor. It was so narrow, they were forced to proceed in single file. Uninvited, the ragged porter brought up the rear. There was a watchful stupidity to his expression. His heavy-lipped mouth hung open. He evidently didn't want to miss anything.

It was hardly a room at all, just an odd bit of space left over after the construction of the rest of the hotel, an airless cell crammed into the last corner beneath the stairs. The door had a corner cut out of it to accommodate the sloping ceiling. Dmitri's candle showed up the grime that lay over everything. The wallpaper was yellowish, though it seemed more likely that it owed its color to age than to any printing process. There seemed to have once been a pattern to it. The single bed almost filled the floor space. Next to it a wooden stool doubled up as a bedside table. There were more candles on a dark, oversize chest. Dmitri lit them from his own candle.

"Who'll pay for those?" demanded the porter.

"You may present me with a bill. I will pass it on to the chief of police for approval," answered Porfiry.

"The chief of police!" scoffed the porter excitedly. But seeing the seriousness of the others, including the boy, he became discouraged and sullen.

Porfiry handed a candlestick to Salytov and took one himself. The two of them examined the room closely. Porfiry looked under the bed, where, unsurprisingly, he found a thick drift of dust. In places, it seemed, the dust had adhered into heavy clumps. Porfiry removed one glove and tested one of these clumps with a fingertip. It was not dust after all.

Porfiry rose to his feet stiffly, with a pinch of the substance between his thumb and forefinger.

"What is it?" asked Salytov.

Porfiry sniffed it. "I can't say for certain, but I think it's horsehair."

"Horsehair?"

"Yes."

Salytov sank down onto his knees to take a look beneath the bed himself. Porfiry turned to Dmitri. "Is there anything you can remember, any detail at all, that struck you as odd, from the time that Govorov was staying in this room? Did you hear any cries, for instance?"

Dmitri shook his head.

"Did Govorov ask for anything? Did he eat? Did you bring food to his room?"

"Yes, he ate. Of course he ate."

"What did he eat? Can you remember?"

"Veal. Hors d'oeuvres. Tea."

"Did he ask for anything else?"

Dmitri thought for a while. "He didn't want vodka. I asked him if he wanted vodka, and he said no."

"That's interesting," said Porfiry. He gave Salytov, who was now back on his feet, an inquiring glance.

Salytov nodded pensively. "Yes, I would not have had our Govorov down as an abstemious gentleman," he confirmed.

"Perhaps he brought his own vodka?" suggested Porfiry. "Let's see," he began to recap. "He declined the vodka but accepted the veal—even though this would have been within the Christmas fast, would it not?"

Dmitri nodded.

Porfiry continued: "Obviously not a strict observer of the Faith."

"Who is these days?" said Salytov. "Besides, I am surprised you expect a murderer to observe the fasts."

"We don't know he is a murderer," said Porfiry with a provocative smile.

"It's all we have," said Dmitri abruptly. "If you don't eat veal, you don't eat here."

"We've never had any complaints," said the porter aggressively.

"And there was nothing else?" pressed Porfiry.

"Only veal and hors d'oeuvres," said Dmitri.

"I meant anything else at all out of the usual."

"Well," said Dmitri, letting out a huge sigh and frowning thoughtfully. "He did ask for a needle and thread. And a pair of scissors too."

"Ah!" cried Porfiry. "That is interesting. Was this after Goryanchikov had joined him or before?"

Dmitri's expression was blank.

"The dwarf," prompted Porfiry.

"Oh, the dwarf was here. It was *because* the dwarf needed a patch in his suit."

"Really?"

"That's what he said. He said, my friend needs to patch his suit."

"So it was Govorov who made the request? Did you *see* Goryanchikov—the dwarf—at this point?"

"No. He was inside the room. The gentleman came out to speak to me. He kept the door closed behind him."

"That is very interesting. And it could be significant. Ilya Petrovich, do you remember a patch on Goryanchikov's suit?" Porfiry asked.

Salytov shook his head.

"Neither do I. Let us look at the bed, for a moment," continued Porfiry. He pulled off the coarse blanket and gray sheets and threw them on the floor.

"Do you mind!" objected the porter.

Porfiry ran a finger along the seam of the mattress. "It's been sewn up," he said. "Rather badly, by the looks of it." He picked at the large stitches with his nails. They unraveled easily. Salytov, Dmitri, and the porter, each holding a candle, pressed in at his shoulders, craning to see what he was doing.

"Please be careful not to set fire to the bed," pleaded Porfiry drily. "You may destroy vital evidence."

Porfiry pulled out a length of thread and folded back the corner of the mattress covering. There was a chorus of gasps behind him.

Inside the mattress, lying flat on top of the horsehair wadding, was a small fur coat suitable for a child. The arms were folded over neatly, reminiscent of a corpse laid out in a coffin.

Porfiry opened his cigarette case. He took one out and put it in his mouth. There were eight left. These he gave to Dmitri.

19

Govorov Returns

ORFIRY SAW PRINCE BYKOV before Prince Bykov saw him. The young nobleman was sitting on one of the chairs outside Porfiry's chambers. His expression was pained but patient, self-consciously stoical. With one hand he fondled his fur-covered top hat as if it were a lapdog.

Why is he *here?* thought Porfiry. But the desperate neediness in the prince's eyes was clear, even from a distance. He came to the police station because he was compelled to. It was the last link he had with his vanished friend.

Porfiry experienced a mild spasm of guilt, the kind that comes when one is reminded of a duty deliberately ignored. But there was a kind of arrogance to his presence too, an aristocratic failure of imagination. Such a man was evidently incapable of understanding that Porfiry had anything better to do than investigate the causes of his unhappiness.

Porfiry was about to turn on his heels when he heard his name called out.

The clerk Zamyotov had seen him. At his loud, piercing "Porfiry Petrovich!" Prince Bykov looked up.

Porfiry blinked several times and squeezed his lips into a smile.

The prince rose to his feet, his hat in one hand, the other extended vaguely as if to grasp something.

"My dear prince," said Porfiry, walking briskly over to him as if he could not be more delighted to see the prince. "How opportune it is that you should present yourself here! There is an important question I must ask you."

Prince Bykov tossed his head so that the dark tight curls at his collar shook. Confusion, and the effort of thinking it through, gave his face an antagonistic edge.

"Please." Porfiry held open the door to his chambers for the prince. "We have been pursuing a very significant lead."

"You have found Ratazyayev?" Now Prince Bykov's expression shone with trusting expectation.

Not for the first time, the young man's emotional openness embarrassed Porfiry. He gestured for the prince to sit down. "No," he said, taking his own seat behind the desk. He averted his eyes, so as not to have to witness the disappointment that would inevitably cloud the prince's features. "But we have tracked down Konstantin Kirillovich Govorov. Do you remember that I asked you about him?"

Prince Bykov frowned at the name. "Has he told you what happened to Ratazyayev?"

"Ah. The fact is, we haven't actually spoken to him yet. But we know where he lives. We are hoping to speak to him very soon. The yardkeeper at his apartment is very cooperative. He will inform us the moment Govorov returns."

"What if he doesn't return?"

"Let us hope that he does," said Porfiry with a strained smile. He leaned back in his seat to light a cigarette.

Prince Bykov watched him disapprovingly. "You said you wanted to ask me a question."

Porfiry closed his eyes. "The student Virginsky described both Govorov and Ratazyayev as actors. Please think back to the circumstances in which you heard the name Govorov. I believe you once told me that you had heard the name. Is it possible that it was in connection with Ratazyayev's acting career?"

"I really don't know. I suppose it's possible."

"You will have to do better than that," said Porfiry sharply. In truth, he was weary. "For instance, can you tell me the last professional production in which Ratazyayev performed?"

Prince Bykov seemed hurt rather than offended by Porfiry's harsh tone. He composed himself and considered his answer. "It was hard for him to come by roles in recent years. His friends, or rather former friends, had turned against him."

"Why was that?"

"He was thought to be unreliable. But it was . . . not fair. There had really only ever been one incident."

"What incident was this?"

"But surely you know?"

Porfiry shook his head, his mouth turned down.

"He got drunk once. Very drunk. During a production. He went on stage drunk and—oh, I can't believe you've never heard of the time the famous Ratazyayev . . ." Prince Bykov placed a pale hand over his eyes. "They have never forgiven him for it."

"What did he do?"

"Must I say it?"

"It may be significant. It may very well be significant."

"He relieved himself into the orchestra pit during the performance."

"I see."

"And then he fell off the stage. It caused a scandal. He . . . ran away. He was not seen or heard of for a year."

"So he has disappeared before?"

"Yes, but this was a long time ago. Before I met him. Of course, I had heard the story—who has not?"

"I had not, until now. But tell me, what was the production in which this unfortunate incident occurred?"

"It was a revival of *The Government Inspector,* at the original Mariinsky Theater."

Porfiry was silent for a moment. "In 'fifty-six?" he asked distractedly.

"So you do remember it?"

Porfiry didn't answer the question. "That was a long time ago. Ten years. How has he managed to earn a living since then, if not through acting?"

"He has relied, to a large extent, on the goodwill of his friends. He still has friends."

"Govorov?"

A wrinkled anguish disfigured Prince Bykov's face. "I see, sir, that you are determined to force me to speak about that individual. Let me say first that I have never met him, that I will not meet him. I do not approve of him. I will say that he has been loyal to Ratazyayev. However, I also believe that his is a loyalty Ratazyayev would have been better off without. The loyalty of a viper is poisonous."

"You admit that he is a friend from Ratazyayev's acting days?"

"He was to blame! It was he who got Ratazyayev drunk! More than that, he goaded him on."

"I see. And recently?"

Prince Bykov closed his eyes on a shudder. "Through Govorov, he became involved in certain . . . vile activities."

Porfiry opened a drawer in his desk and produced the photographs Salytov had taken from the innkeeper. He spread them out and pushed those that featured male participants toward Prince Bykov.

The prince compressed his lips in disgust and nodded. "Yes. That is Ratazyayev. It is Ratazyayev in them all."

Porfiry gathered the photographs up.

Prince Bykov looked away, trembling. "He also occasionally acted as a distribution agent for a publishing company. This was through Govorov also."

"Athene?" The name escaped without conscious thought. Porfiry did not know why he made the assumption.

"No." Prince Bykov was definite. "I have heard of *them*," he added thoughtfully. "But this was not a respectable house."

"Priapos." It was not offered as a question.

The prince dropped his eyelids in confirmation.

L EONID SIMONOVICH TOLKACHENKO felt the turmoil of too many pickled cucumbers eaten too hastily.

He was sitting in his armchair reading *The Northern Bee*. He had to hold the candle close to the newspaper. There was no light from the window. It was past three in the afternoon. Soon he would have to go outside and attend to his duties.

Tolkachenko lived alone in a small apartment at 3 Spasskoi Lane, the building where he worked as yardkeeper. He had never married. Once, many years ago, when he was still a young man, he had come close to declaring his feelings for the daughter of Devushkin. This Devushkin was a clerk in the Ministry of Internal Affairs, where Tolkachenko worked at the time as a courier. Tolkachencko had also lodged with the family, subrenting a room hardly bigger than a cupboard in their tiny apartment. The girl, Mariya Alexeyevna, was sixteen when it started. He left gifts for her that he could ill afford and feigned an interest in literature. But despite the family's poverty and the father's alcoholism, her parents were proud. They talked frequently and loudly of a very important personage from whom they imminently expected a proposal. Tolkachenko grew discouraged, even though the proposal from the important personage was not forthcoming. He stopped buying bonbons and lace. He went back to reading *The Northern Bee*. Mariya Alexeyevna ceased to be sixteen. In his eyes, she ceased to be many things. Her father lost his position. Her mother died, it was said, from disappointment. Mariya Alexeyevna began to look at Leonid Simonovich with big pleading eyes. Now she left gifts for him, books that he never read. She suggested a walk along the Fontanka in one of the city's white summer nights. But he had remembered, with a mixture of shame and revulsion, the estrangement from himself that he had suffered at the height of his passion. Perhaps he had wished to punish her for that. Perhaps he had been afraid of experiencing such feelings again or, even worse, of not experiencing them. Or perhaps he had simply awakened from a strange dream. He did not meet her at the appointed time. Instead he put his few belongings into a carpetbag and walked away from the Fontanka. He did not look up once into the brilliant night sky. Nor did he ever make inquiries to find out what became of her.

Thirty years on Leonid Simonovich Tolkachenko sat alone in the dark, reading *The Northern Bee* by candlelight. Since the policeman's visit, he felt a more direct connection with the news accounts. Until now the wives beaten to death, the trampled drunks, the fathers murdered by their sons had existed at one remove, contained within the surface of the newspaper as if behind a looking glass. Now such dangers and terrors were spilling out into the world he occupied. He could vouch personally for their reality. Reading the paper was no longer a comfortable sensation; the anxieties it inspired, with its fulminating editorials against the new law courts, were no longer vicarious.

A murder investigation, that was what the policeman had said.

"Dangerous" was the word he had used.

In other words, Govorov was a murderer.

Tolkachenko swallowed back a dyspeptic, vinegary belch and read:

> There has never been any doubt as to Protopopov's guilt. On several occasions, in the presence of witnesses, he threatened to kill the victim. He was seen going into her apartment. A revolver was heard to discharge. When the police arrived, he was sitting calmly next to the dead body of his landlady with the murder weapon in his hand. He confessed immediately to the crime. And now, thanks jointly to the cleverness of his defense lawyer and the stupidity of the new juries—not to mention the incompetence of the police authorities— this man, a cold-blooded murderer, has walked free. In the process,

the victim has been transformed into the criminal. Subject to the vilest slander and innuendo, none of it material to the case, her character has been publicly traduced. The inference we are meant to draw is that she deserved everything that came to her. Naturally, she cannot speak in her own defense. (You may reasonably ask: Why should she have to?) She is dead. Protopopov murdered her. He has never denied it. But this same Protopopov is acquitted, and his acquittal is greeted with rapturous applause. This may be the way it is done in France, but when the innocent become the guilty, when murderers walk free, none of us is safe.

Tolkachenko heard the street door click. He sat up with a jolt and strained to listen. Footsteps reverberated on the stairs. The old boards shrieked and cracked like fireworks. Tolkachenko's senses tingled unpleasantly. He was used to listening to the comings and goings of the residents. He could recognize them each by their step. But this time it was difficult. Footfalls overlapped. He narrowed his eyes and discerned two separate step patterns. Was one of them Govorov's? It was hard to tell. He imagined, in fact, two Govorovs climbing the stairs.

Tolkachenko's arms began to ache from holding the paper still. He knew the footsteps were heading away from him. Even so, he was afraid of making the slightest sound. It could be a trick. Somehow the beat of his heart had fallen in rhythm with the steps. Every time there was a pause in the sounds of climbing, his heart seemed to stop beating. He imagined the two Govorovs turning around and coming back for him.

At last, a door above closed.

It was some time before Tolkachenko stirred. He folded the newspaper carefully and leaned forward to place it noiselessly on the floor. The throb of his pulse echoed in his head. His knees creaked as he rose from the seat. Partially digested pickled cucumbers gurgled in his stomach. He winced as if these minute interior noises were in danger of reaching the apartment above.

Tolkachenko moved slowly, lowering his feet with tense precision. He waited, listening, after each step. Then stood, listening, at his own door before grasping the handle with a grip that tightened the whole of his arm. He pushed his shoulder into the door as he eased it open.

Even in the dark he knew where to place his feet so that he could climb the stairs without setting off too many alarms from the floorboards. As he ascended, the low rumble of voices grew louder.

A light showed under Govorov's door. The voices he had heard were coming from inside. Tolkachenko couldn't make out what was being said, but he recognized Govorov's booming theatrical bass. There was one other man in there, he judged, whose voice was higher and lighter. They seemed to be arguing, but there was something detached, almost disjointed, about their exchange. It had not reached the point where both parties were shouting over each other.

Without questioning what he was doing, Tolkachenko took the heavy ring of keys from his pocket and fumbled for the key to Govorov's door. The metallic jangling prompted a break in the discussion within. But Tolkachenko moved quickly. He thrust the key into the lock and turned it. Then he slipped it off the chained ring and stepped back. He turned the key in the door so that it was at a slight angle to the keyhole. He heard footsteps hurry toward him. The door shook in the frame.

"Wha's this?" came Govorov's slurred cry.

"Murderer!" shouted Tolkachenko back.

"What are you talking about, you old fool? You've got no idea what you're talking about. It's not me who's the murderer. Besides, you can't lock me in."

Tolkachenko now heard Govorov try to insert his own key into the lock. But the keyhole was of course blocked.

"This is an outrage!"

"I'll tell you what an outrage is. Murder."

"There he is again with his murder. Good heavens! All he ever talks about is murder. Have you ever heard such a thing?" But there was no answer from whoever was in the apartment with Govorov.

"The police were here," cried Tolkachenko. "That's what I'm talking about. The police were here, looking for you. Let them come back and decide. That's what I say."

"Very well, let them come. I have nothing to——" Govorov's speech decayed abruptly into a strangled scream. There was a heavy, complicated crash, which resonated musically at the end. Now Tolkachenko heard a desperate thrashing about as if there was a struggle going on inside. Then a stifled gurgling of fluid in flesh and a panicked gasping for breath that would not come. It was a sound he could barely accept as human in origin. He wanted to run from it, to get as far away from that sound as he could. And yet the terrible novelty of it held him.

Then it stopped.

There was only silence now, or rather an oppressive buzzing emptiness.

Tolkachenko rapped his knuckles hesitantly on the door. When that produced no answer, he called out: "Hey! You! Konstantin Kirillovich! What are you up to?"

Tolkachenko heard footsteps behind him, coming down from the landing above. He turned and blinked into the gloom. At the same moment the door from the apartment across the landing opened, leaching a soft yellow light. Iakov Borodonich, the young civil servant who lived there, peered out nervously. The footsteps on the stairs had stopped. Whoever was there seemed to be hanging back.

"Leonid Simonovich?" Iakov Borodonich's face was white, his eyes wide with fear. He was a sickly, nervous young man at the best of times.

"Iakov Borodonich! You must go to the police station on Stolyarny Lane. Alert Lieutenant Salytov. Tell him that Tolkachenko sent you. Tell him I have captured Govorov."

"You have captured Konstantin Kirillovich? But why?"

"There isn't time to explain that now. You must go! Immediately!"

"But Leonid Simonovich, I'm unwell. I couldn't go to the ministry today. As you can see"—Iakov Borodonich stepped out onto the landing—"I'm still in my dressing gown."

"You must get dressed. It's the middle of the afternoon. You shouldn't be in your dressing gown in the middle of the afternoon."

"But I'm not well. It's the old problem. Nerves. I'm feeling terrifically depressed."

"Well, you must pull yourself together and go to the police station. Otherwise . . . he will murder us all."

There was a strange sound, a kind of rasping hiss, from the darkness above them. Iakov Borodonich leaped back into his apartment.

"What was that?"

"Who's there?" Tolkachenko called up the stairs.

There was no answer.

"You must go," Tolkachenko insisted to Iakov Borodonich. "Besides, I believe you will be safer at the police station than here."

There was a moment while Iakov Borodonich took this in. Then he nodded and hurried back inside.

As soon as the door was closed, the landing was plunged back into darkness. The footsteps on the stairs began again. Instinctively, Tolkachenko stepped back and pressed himself against the wall. He was able to make out an indistinct figure as it stepped down onto the landing, but the features remained obscure. The figure seemed to turn toward him and then bow. "Good day to you" came from it, in a light, ironic, and half-familiar voice.

Tolkachenko could say nothing in return. He felt a climactic churning in his besieged stomach. His cheeks bulged and a loud, reverberating burp escaped.

The figure crossed the landing and continued down the stairs.

T OLKACHENKO WAS STILL positioned outside Govorov's door when he heard Iakov Borodonich return. He felt as though the darkness had solidified around him.

"Leonid Simonovich!" cried the young civil servant from below. "It's

I, Iakov Borodonich. I have brought the policeman. And another gentleman."

"Can we not have a light here?" This voice was unknown to Tolkachenko. A moment later a match flared, and Iakov Borodonich lit the gas in the hall. The police lieutenant and the "other gentleman" came up the stairs. Their expressions denied Tolkachenko the reassurance he might have hoped for from their presence. Iakov Borodonich stayed downstairs, close to the front door.

"So he is in there?" whispered Salytov.

"Yes," confirmed Tolkachenko, also speaking in a low voice. "I have not moved from here. He has not come out. Neither of them has come out."

"Neither of them?" whispered the other man, whose colorless eyelashes flickered energetically. "So there are two men in there?"

"Yes," said Tolkachenko. "I heard two men come up the stairs. And two voices inside."

"Open the door," demanded Salytov.

Tolkachenko hesitated, deferring to the gentleman who had come with Salytov.

"One moment, Ilya Petrovich. Does it not occur to you that they might be armed?"

Lieutenant Salytov opened his greatcoat and pulled an American revolver from a holster. The gun's long barrel probed the air like a sleek snout. "I have come prepared, Porfiry Petrovich," he said.

"Oh!" moaned Tolkachenko.

"We should give them the chance to surrender, I think," said Porfiry Petrovich. "It is possible we may conclude this business without a shot being fired—or a drop of blood shed."

Salytov hammered on the door with the butt of his revolver. "You in there! This is the police. You are under arrest. Do you understand?"

There was no answer.

"I should tell you, I heard something," hissed Tolkachenko. "Before. It sounded like a struggle. A crash. Someone falling over." Tolkachenko fell silent. His eyes flitted desperately, as though fleeing from something that was forcing itself on his imagination. "Then nothing."

The frequency of Porfiry Petrovich's blinking increased sharply. "A fight?" he wondered aloud.

"We have given them a chance," said Salytov grimly, before Tolkachenko could answer.

Porfiry nodded. "First let us turn off the light out here."

Salytov nodded back and signaled to Iakov Borodonich, drawing a hand across his throat and pointing to the light. Iakov Borodonich stared back, stupefied by the brutality of the gesture. Finally he blinked his enlarged eyes and turned off the gaslight.

"Unlock the door, then stand aside" came Salytov's command from the darkness.

They waited as Tolkachenko fumbled with the key. They wanted the turning of the key to take forever, and at one moment it seemed as though it would. At last Tolkachenko moved out of the way, ducking into a huddle in the far corner of the landing. Salytov stood on one side of the door frame, Porfiry on the other. The lieutenant turned the handle and pushed the door in. Light from the flat gushed out.

Slowly, leading with the revolver held out in front of him, Salytov edged inside, followed by Porfiry. The room was cold and smelled strongly of vodka. Despite the burning gas, the atmosphere was undeniably lifeless.

They could tell that the man lying facedown on top of a smashed guitar was not going to get up. He was a big man who might have struggled to get to his feet at the best of times. But there was something final about the compact his bulk had made with gravity now.

Porfiry crossed to the body and crouched down to turn the head. The eyes were open but shrunken to dark slits under the frozen puffiness of his face. Salytov prowled the rest of the apartment, still with his revolver extended in front of him.

He came back a moment later, his demeanor perceptibly more relaxed.

"There's no one here."

"Are you sure?"

"I have searched the whole place. There is one room adjoining this one, a small kitchen."

"And the windows?"

"I have checked them all. Locked from the inside. Is that Govorov?" Salytov pointed his pistol toward the body.

Porfiry picked up and sniffed an empty vodka bottle that had been lying on its side near the body. "We will need our friend outside to confirm that. If it is, then I have to confess that this is not the first time I have encountered the elusive Konstantin Kirillovich Govorov."

One of Salytov's eyebrows rippled inquisitively.

"I met him once before, in Lyamshin's Pawnbroker's. He was pawning a guitar." Porfiry lifted the broken guitar neck attached by its strings to the crushed sounding box beneath the body. "It seems he found the funds he needed to redeem it."

Y ES, THAT'S GOVOROV," confirmed Tolkachenko. His expression was startled, almost outraged, as if he had been cheated by the man lying dead on the floor.

Porfiry nodded distractedly. "But you said there were two men in here? You said you heard two voices, did you not?"

"Yes. That's true."

Porfiry pointed at the body with an unlit cigarette. "One voice was his?"

Tolkachenko nodded.

"And the other? Did you recognize the other?"

"Well, here is a strange thing," said Tolkachenko. "I didn't recognize it. And then I did."

"What?" barked Salytov.

"I mean, there was this fellow. He came down the stairs. He spoke to me."

"What did he say?" asked Porfiry, scrutinizing his cigarette as if he had never seen one before.

"'Good day to you.' He said, 'Good day to you.'" This seemed to strike Tolkachenko as the most scandalous aspect of the whole affair.

"I see."

"Well, the thing is, the really strange thing . . . it was the same voice."

"What do you mean, it was the same voice?" Salytov's impatience showed in the rush of color over his face.

"I mean, it was *him*."

It looked for a moment as though Salytov would strike the yardkeeper.

Porfiry intervened quickly. "You mean the voice of the man on the stairs was the same as the voice of the man whom you had locked inside Govorov's flat with Govorov?"

"Yes!" cried Tolkachenko.

"But that's impossible!" Salytov thrashed the air in his frustration.

"Yes!" repeated Tolkachenko, smiling in amazement.

Porfiry finally put the cigarette in his mouth. "So, Ilya Petrovich," he said. He broke off to light the cigarette. "It seems we have a mystery on our hands." Porfiry let the smoke escape with his words. "The question is"— he inhaled deeply again and waited before exhaling and continuing— "who was this other person in the flat with Govorov?" Again he paused to draw deeply on the cigarette. "And even more perplexing, how could he be both locked inside the flat and coming down the stairs?" Porfiry smoked the cigarette through, only to be taken aback by the stub. He extinguished it between his thumb and forefinger and then handed it to Tolkachenko, with an absentminded "You may take that." Tolkachenko frowned at the stub as Porfiry lit a second cigarette. "It is a mystery, but"—Porfiry smoked with professional determination—"I feel confident we will get to the bottom of it. What do you say?"

Salytov didn't answer. He was lost in angry thought.

"Logic. We must apply logic," continued Porfiry. "Cold, dispassionate logic. Don't allow the puzzle to disturb your temper. You cannot solve it if you're annoyed at it."

"But it *is* impossible!" insisted Salytov crossly.

"No, patently it *is* possible." Porfiry's insistence was calm. "That is the first logically inevitable deduction we can make. It has happened, therefore it is possible. The actual is incontrovertibly possible."

Salytov shook his head impatiently.

"Think about it, Ilya Petrovich."

"You have worked it out?"

"A logical conclusion has forced itself on me."

"How? How could you have . . . from this?"

"Perhaps I have an unfair advantage over you. As I said, I have met this gentleman before."

"In the pawnbroker's. What of it?"

"He impressed me with a dramatic recitation from Gogol's *The Government Inspector*. He was once an actor, you see. His style was very natural. He seemed to become the character he was playing."

Salytov's face clouded in confusion. He looked from Porfiry down to the body, then back to Porfiry. "But why?"

Porfiry shrugged. He had another cigarette stub to dispose of. Tolkachenko steadfastly ignored his eye. "One thing at a time, Ilya Petrovich. One thing at a time."

20

Govorov Speaks

PORFIRY LOOKED OUT the window of the *prokuror*'s chambers, down on to Gorokhovaya Street. He wanted very much to smoke. So he was gazing out of the window as a distraction. The street-lamps were lit, chains of illumination strung across the early morning gloom. Behind him he heard the riffle of papers and the *prokuror*'s deep sighs.

Porfiry turned to see Prokuror Liputin close the report he had submitted. It contained statements taken from Tolkachenko and Iakov Borodonich, together with a formal request from Porfiry for a medical examination to be conducted on the body now confirmed to be that of Konstantin Kirillovich Govorov.

Liputin's expression was not encouraging.

"So, Porfiry Petrovich, you truly believe that this constitutes sufficient grounds for an application of habeas corpus?"

"Indeed I do, your excellency. I would not have troubled you with the matter otherwise."

Liputin screwed up his nose dismissively. "The man died alone. In a locked room. In your report, you yourself state that there was no evidence of an attack. No blood, no wounds, no bruises. The epidermis is intact."

"I stated there was no *forensic* evidence of attack. However, the yard-keeper testified that he heard a struggle."

"No, no, no! We can't base a case on what someone thinks he heard through a locked door. Especially when it is not consistent with what is logically possible."

"But it *is* consistent with what is logically possible," insisted Porfiry. "If we suppose that Govorov was struggling not with a human assailant but with a chemical one."

Liputin masked his confusion with a frown of annoyance and shook his head impatiently.

"I suspect poisoning, your excellency, as in the case of—"

"You're not going to bring up the yardkeeper, are you?" cried the *prokuror* in an irritable drawl. "As you know, that case is closed."

"Leaving that aside, there is the dead man's connection to the missing actor, Ratazyayev. An autopsy would determine—"

"But are we really justified in seeking an autopsy? Is it not more likely that Govorov simply died from natural causes?"

"It is certainly a possibility. Though it would be a strange coincidence given the circumstances."

"What circumstances?" Liputin's look of distaste suggested that he immediately regretted asking the question.

"As you will have read in the relevant statement, the yardkeeper heard two people enter the building."

"So he says. He could simply have been mistaken. As for his tale of two voices inside the apartment, that is simply not sustainable."

"I agree. Given that the windows were locked from the inside and given also Tolkachenko's constant presence outside the locked door, the presence of a second person in Govorov's apartment is without doubt logically impossible."

"You agree?" Liputin seemed more surprised by this than by any aspect of the case before him. It was evidently something he needed to confirm: "You agree?" he asked again.

"I agree."

The startled bristling of Liputin's unruly eyebrows settled into a suspicious scowl. "In that case, how *do* you explain—?"

"The two voices in the flat?"

Prokuror Liputin nodded anxiously.

"Govorov was an actor, a skilled mimic. It is my belief that he was talking to himself. It is likely that he was drunk. If he had been poisoned, he was possibly also raving. We all rehearse or reenact arguments in our heads. Perhaps he was simply vocalizing the process."

"Exactly! You have explained it just as I would myself. Apart from the poisoning. I would not have hypothesized poisoning. It was just a drunken actor raving, preliminary to the extreme moment."

"But you are overlooking the mysterious individual on the stairs, whose presence was mentioned by both witnesses. Tolkachenko said that his voice sounded familiar. When pressed on this, he claimed that it was the same as the other voice he had heard in the flat, the voice that was not Govorov's. Or, if my theory is correct, the voice that Govorov was mimicking."

"What does that prove?" demanded Liputin antagonistically.

"It proves nothing. It suggests, perhaps, that Govorov had just been conversing with this individual and was playing the scene again, this time taking both parts. Perhaps rewriting the script so that he got the better of his interlocutor. In all likelihood, the two men had parted company at Govorov's door. But for some reason the mysterious man did not leave the building. He went up to the next landing and waited. What was he waiting for? Possibly for the sound of Govorov's fall."

"Perhaps this, possibly that, in all likelihood the other—"

"Very well. I will confine myself to those things I know for certain. The words that Govorov spoke, in his own voice, through the door to Tolkachenko. 'It's not me who's the murderer.' This is not simply a protestation of innocence. It is also the beginning of an accusation. It suggests he knows who the real murderer is. Providing someone with a motive for killing him. A reasonable supposition would be the individual waiting on the stairs."

"But you are forgetting one thing, Porfiry Petrovich. There is no real murderer because there has been no real murder. What murder? Not the dwarf, I hope? Because you know very well that the man who killed the dwarf died by his own hand."

"But the new evidence—"

"The new evidence concerned the disappearance of Ratazyayev. Do you have evidence that Ratazyayev has been murdered? Did his body turn up? If so, I am surprised you did not inform me of such a significant development." The *prokuror* couldn't help smirking at the cleverness of his satire.

"At the very least, in the case of the sudden demise of an otherwise healthy individual in the prime of his life—"

"That hardly describes this fellow Govorov."

"—the law requires we establish cause of death. A medical examination is required for that."

"A medical examination is not necessary for every old soak who drinks himself into the ground. Your own report mentions the empty bottle found near the body."

"But what if we were wrong to dismiss Dr. Pervoyedov's findings concerning the cause of death in the case of the yardkeeper? Let us allow, for one moment, that Borya was poisoned with contaminated vodka. Do we now have another instance of the same crime? Is this a modus operandi? Will it come out, will it be something we read about in the newspapers, that in our eagerness to close that case, we allowed a murderer to kill again? It is too late to prevent Govorov's death. But imagine the scandal there would be if we made the same mistake again."

"Porfiry Petrovich. I am not wrong. I am never wrong. It is impossible for the office of the *prokuror* to make mistakes. The law is quite clear on this. However"—Prokuror Liputin looked Porfiry in the eye—"it is certainly possible that you could have made a mistake. You could, for example, have misinterpreted my instructions."

"I am sure that that is what has happened."

"So I shall speak very clearly this time, in order that there should be no misunderstanding. You are to commission Dr. Pervoyedov to conduct a medical examination of the deceased Govorov forthwith. If the test for prussic acid poisoning is positive, you are to reopen the case of the dwarf—"

"Stepan Sergeyevich Goryanchikov."

"—and the yardkeeper. Is that understood?"

"Yes, Prokuror Liputin."

"Incidentally, if Dr. Pervoyedov does find that Govorov was poisoned by prussic acid, I will have no choice but to instigate disciplinary proceedings against you, Porfiry Petrovich."

"I understand, your excellency," said Porfiry, almost losing his balance through the depth of his bow.

THE BODY WAS wrapped in a green canvas sheet, rubberized on the inside. Two rubber-aproned orderlies lifted it from the trolley, one at either end. They grimaced noiselessly as they took the full weight. It seemed a point of pride to them not to utter a sound. The load did not sag or bend at any point. The orderlies seemed surprised by this rigidity, although they must have experienced it before. Perhaps it surprised them anew each time they encountered it. Or perhaps they were thinking of something else entirely.

They dropped it heavily on the waist-high examination table, the pine surface of which was as pitted and stained as a butcher's block. It had beveled edges and a drainage hole at one end over an enamel trough. There was another, smaller table to one side, with a large set of balancing scales on it.

"How extraordinary. What an extraordinarily novel idea," commented

Dr. Pervoyedov, as he opened the canvas sheet exposing the gray-faced cadaver beneath. "To conduct a medical examination in a hospital! That is to say, to arrange the medical examination to suit the convenience of the medical examiner. What is the world coming to? What indeed. I wonder if our beloved tsar, when he began to entertain the notion of reform, I wonder if he ever dreamed that it would lead to such, such . . . revolutionary *novelties!*" Dr. Pervoyedov seemed particularly pleased with this choice of word and so repeated it several times: "Novelties. Yes, novelties. Here at the Obukhovsky Hospital, novelties!"

Major General Volokonsky and Actual State Councilor Yepanchin were once again in attendance as official witnesses. They frowned disapprovingly at Pervoyedov's outburst.

Porfiry Petrovich smiled indulgently. "I was much struck by the *prokuror*'s use of the word 'forthwith.' Equally by his tone. There was an urgency to it. I took it upon myself to ensure that there would be no possibility of delay."

"Will Prokuror Liputin be joining us?"

"I think not," said Porfiry. His smile became tense. "I have the feeling that he wishes to maintain a certain distance from the proceedings until the outcome is clear."

"Would that we all had that luxury." After this comment Dr. Pervoyedov worked in silence. He was helped by one of the orderlies, who took upon himself the role of *diener*. Dr. Pervoyedov had not trained in Germany, but he had learned his pathology from professors who had and from the German textbooks they had brought back with them. The doctor communicated with his assistant—or "servant," to translate the German term more accurately—through a system of finely nuanced facial expressions and nods. First Pervoyedov examined the already exposed areas of the corpse, including the eyes and fingernails. Then he nodded to the *diener*, and they began between them to remove the clothes. There was something numbing about the dead man's open-eyed passivity as he was hefted to facilitate his last undressing.

Now the body lay naked on its back. The contaminating grayness of death had been released. The abdomen spread out to the sides in soft, un-even mounds. The penis was plump and stunted, shrunken into itself. It had the shamefaced air of a whipped dog. It was hard to think of anything more insignificant. Porfiry thought back to the time in the pawnbroker's when Govorov had accosted him. He felt himself blush and averted his gaze distastefully.

He heard them roll the body over.

"No external signs of traumata," Dr. Pervoyedov murmured.

After several silent minutes the body was rolled again onto its back.

"We are particularly interested to know if there is any evidence of poi-soning. For example, by prussic acid." Porfiry addressed the remark to the ceiling.

"Everything in due course, Porfiry Petrovich. Everything in due course."

Porfiry saw out of the corner of his eye that Pervoyedov had begun the deep, Y-shaped incision that would enable the skin to be pulled back.

Dr. Pervoyedov teased a long-bladed scalpel beneath the flesh with one hand, as he lifted a single thick sheet of skin and tissue away with the other. Porfiry was aware of the movement and the faint meaty smell that came when the body was opened up. The *diener* was already standing ready with the small curved shears that were used for severing ribs. Dr. Pervoyedov gave one of his communicative nods and then exchanged his scalpel for the rib-cutters.

He clipped methodically through the ribs on either side, with the ugly concentration of a man cutting his toenails. Each time the sharp metallic snip of the blades as they pinched together through the costal cartilages increased the startled determination angling the doctor's eyebrows.

At last the cutting was complete, and he once again exchanged the shears for a scalpel. The *diener*, prompted by a particularly emphatic nod from Dr. Pervoyedov, placed the rib-cutters on the other table. He then bowed over the open chest of the body and suddenly plunged the fingers of both hands between the exposed and severed ribs, closing his grip be-neath the sternum. He gave a sharp tug. Dr. Pervoyedov's scalpel licked into the dark opening created to release the last tethers of tissue. The chest plate came away and was placed on the other table.

"If I remember correctly, Dr. Pervoyedov, you mentioned that in the case of the yardkeeper, Borya, the covering of the lungs was inflamed. It was that, I believe, that first alerted you to the possibility of poisoning. I wonder if that is the case in this cadaver?"

"We shall have a look, Porfiry Petrovich. Fortunately for you, I follow the Virchow method." Dr. Pervoyedov drew his scalpel across the top of the abdomen. The skin fell away under pressure from the bloated internal organs. The doctor stepped back, giving way to his *diener,* who was now intent on some dark business involving string and scissors inside the body. Dr. Pervoyedov watched him with an expression of focused approval. "The Virchow method, you know, by which the organs are removed and examined separately." To the *diener* he added: "Give me the lungs first, will you?"

The *diener* plunged both hands into the cavity and removed them a moment later, cradling an elongated raw pinky mass.

"The left?" asked Dr. Pervoyedov.

The *diener* nodded.

"It looks very pink. Not healthy. Not healthy at all. Yes, I would describe that as inflamed, wouldn't you, Porfiry Petrovich?"

"You are the expert."

"Ha! I am the expert! That's nice. That's very nice." Dr. Pervoyedov shook his head. Then nodded for the *diener,* who placed the lung on the scales.

The weighing tray plummeted with a heavy clatter, as though angry at being disturbed. The *diener* gradually added weights to the opposing plate until the weighing tray rose and bobbed and settled. "Thirty-nine *lot,* zero *zolotnik,* and twenty *dolya,*" he announced, glancing to the doctor for his reaction.

"Within the parameters of normality," said Dr. Pervoyedov. "Put it on the dissecting table, and I'll take a section to look at under the microscope."

"Would it not be possible to test the stomach contents first?" There was a slight edge of impatience to Porfiry's voice. "I am eager to know if there is any evidence at all of poisoning."

Dr. Pervoyedov seemed genuinely shocked by this suggestion. "But that's not the Virchow method. By that method, I must complete my examination of the lungs before moving on to the next organ. What method are you suggesting I follow? It's not the Rokatinsky."

"I suggest you follow the"—Porfiry Petrovich hestitated only for fraction of a second—"the Pervoyedov method. By which you prioritize the order of examinations in order to confirm or refute the suspicions of the investigating magistrate as quickly as possible."

"The Pervoyedov method, you say?"

"You could write a learned article on it. For the *Russian Journal of Pathology*."

"Ah, but the thing to do is to be published in Germany. That's the thing," said Dr. Pervoyedov, waving a scalpel carelessly.

"Well, then. Write it in German."

"The Pervoyedov method . . . It has a certain ring to it." Dr. Pervoyedov grinned. "Unfortunately, the method you propose is, from a scientific point of view, utterly nonsensical. If I were to attach my name to it, it would very likely spell the end of my career as an academic pathologist."

"It would be looked upon very favorably by the judicial authorities."

"Ah, yes. I don't doubt it. That's the thing, you see. There you have it in a nutshell, Porfiry Petrovich. On the one hand, you have the interests of science. On the other, the interests of the office of the investigating magistrate. I had hoped they were the same. But the more I do this job, the more I learn they are not."

"I trust our interests are the same. Both parties want the truth."

"But you will insist on dictating which truth you want."

"That's unfair, Dr. Pervoyedov. I am merely seeking to influence the order in which the various truths concerning this case are discovered."

The *diener* had by now weighed the second lung and was waiting for instruction.

"You know he's proposing to fine me, don't you," said Dr. Pervoyedov with sudden and sincere bitterness.

"I'm sure Prokuror Liputin can be prevailed upon to drop the intended disciplinary proceedings against you."

Dr. Pervoyedov considered Porfiry briefly. He shook his head with an indulgent smile as he turned his attention back to the dead man. "Very well. Give me the stomach now," he said to the *diener*.

Crooked and bulging, the stomach was sluiced off and placed in an enamel bowl. Dr. Pervoyedov slit the finely veined sac along its tense convexity. A stinking, murky liquid spilled out, and the stomach collapsed into a wrinkled yellow skin.

"Be thankful, gentlemen," said Dr. Pervoyedov. "He has not eaten solids recently. But judging by the smell, he has drunk vodka."

"There was an empty vodka bottle found by the body," said Porfiry. "Some vodka from it appears to have been spilled onto the carpet."

"It would be as well to test that too."

Porfiry nodded.

Dr. Pervoyedov opened a drawer in one of the laboratory benches. "I regret that Prokuror Liputin is not here to oversee my actions," he said. He had in his hand a tab of litmus paper. The doctor dipped the litmus paper into the liquid. An intense red stain spread over it eagerly. He showed it to the official witnesses without comment. They were at a loss as how to meet his arch, questioning expression. Their nods were hesitant and solemn. "Ah well, at least you gentlemen are here to see that I do things properly this time."

The doctor drew a quantity of the liquid into a syringe, which he then siphoned into a glass retort. With its long tapered spout at the side, the vessel had something of the appearance of a capsized swan. Dr. Pervoyedov showed a large brown bottle to the witnesses, his expression again pointed. The bottle was labeled SULFURIC ACID. The witnesses smiled weakly, averting their eyes and shuffling their feet like reproached schoolboys. The doctor shook his head and turned his back on them. He added a few drops of the sulfuric acid by pipette and shook the retort lightly. He then transferred it to another bench in the laboratory where there was a deep metal tray filled with sand, nesting on a burning gas ring. He closed the retort with a glass stopper and twisted it into the hot sand. He carefully turned the screw of a clamp to hold it at the neck.

"Satisfied?" he asked, with a half turn to the official witnesses. They communicated in dumb show that they were. "Really? Are you trying to catch me out, gentlemen? That's very mischievous of you. Very mischievous indeed."

Dr. Pervoyedov nodded to the *diener*. The assistant picked up a glass tumbler and crossed to one of the high windows of the pathology lab. A slab of winter pressed against it, its vast blankness even swallowing the black iron bars on the outside. The *diener* swung open an inner pane, and the air became suddenly sharp and hostile, a splinter of the great destructive force that was ravaging the city. He worked the tumbler between the bars, scooping up the icy snow that had settled on the ledge. His movements, as he closed the window, had a nervous haste to them. He put Porfiry in mind of a jailer sealing the cell of a dangerous prisoner.

Dr. Pervoyedov attached a small receiving vessel to the end of the retort's long spout. He now bedded this into the tumbler of snow. He shook his head and chuckled to himself. "They tried to catch me out. Imagine! They thought I would forget to collect the distillate." When he was satisfied with the arrangement, he went back to the table where the empty stomach lay in a pool of slops.

With a deft and decisive manipulation, he turned the stomach through, revealing the furrowed musculature of its interior.

"The stomach lining shows no sign of being subject to any corrosive action." Dr. Pervoyedov sounded almost disappointed.

"Does that rule out prussic acid?" asked Porfiry anxiously.

Dr. Pervoyedov glanced at the official witnesses, as if to say, *Why don't you ask them?* But he contained his resentment. "No, no. Not at all. Oh no. Although it does rule out almost any other poison you might care to mention. In some ways, it makes prussic acid more likely. If poison has been used at all, that is. We must wait for the real test, however."

"And how long will that be?"

Tiny globules of condensation were beginning to show inside the receiving vessel.

"Not long now. Not long at all, Porfiry Petrovich."

W HAT DID HE DO, this man, in life?" asked Dr. Pervoyedov, as he removed the receiving vessel from the retort. Barely more than a meniscus of clear liquor had collected. Dr. Pervoyedov rotated the vessel as if he were appreciating a fine cognac.

"He was an actor once, I believe," said Porfiry.

The doctor raised his eyebrows. He poured the liquid into a test tube, which he placed in a wooden rack. He turned briskly to the *diener*. "I will need sulfate of iron, solution of potassa, and muriatic acid."

The *diener* nodded and crossed to a cabinet. He brought the bottles over one by one. Using both hands to tilt and steady the first of them, Pervoyedov tipped out a small quantity of glassy pale green granules onto a circle of filtration paper. He held the paper over the test tube and tapped until one of the grains fell in. He waited for it to dissolve, then added a few drops of the solution of potassa. He stirred the contents with a glass rod, his gaze challenging the official witnesses. "Let us see if, in death, he has any talent for ventriloquism."

He unscrewed the cap of the last bottle and inserted the nozzle of a long pipette. Holding this over the test tube, he released a rapid drizzle of droplets.

All at once, the contents of the test tube turned inky blue.

"Well, there you have it," said Dr. Pervoyedov. "Govorov speaks. Or rather, his stomach does."

21

The Lilac Stationery

PORFIRY PETROVICH extinguished the cigarette and threw it behind him as the door to 17 Bolshaya Morskaya Street was opened. Stepping inside, he felt a sudden unpleasant taste rampage through his mouth, metallic and cloyingly sweet. It was so strong, he felt for a moment he would be sick.

"What's that? Something in the air?" he asked Katya.

She looked at him neutrally. "We have been fumigating the mattresses. Marfa Denisovna has complained of being bitten."

"Fumigating? What do you use?"

"Did you really come here to talk about fumigating methods?"

"No. I came to talk to Anna Alexandrovna."

"Very well, I shall tell her you're here."

PORFIRY PETROVICH admired the smooth curve of Anna Alexandrovna's back as he followed her into the pale blue drawing room. *There is something that surprises and saddens in every part of her,* he thought.

"May I offer you some tea?" As she turned to him, he saw that this quality was most concentrated in her eyes.

Porfiry refused with a smile and a minute shake of his head. "I don't wish to detain you any more than is necessary," he said. "There are, however, one or two questions I must ask, in the light of some new evidence."

"New evidence?" Anna Alexandrovna's hand shook as she set down the redundant glass.

"Do you know a man called Konstantin Kirillovich Govorov?"

Relief expanded Anna Alexandrovna's beauty, chasing out the frown. She shook her head vehemently. *She is relieved because she is able to answer honestly,* thought Porfiry.

"He was an associate of Stepan Sergeyevich's," explained Porfiry. "He is dead now. Murdered. Poisoned, I believe, by the administration of the same substance that killed Borya."

"But I thought Borya hanged himself? That's what we read in the gazettes."

"That is what someone wished us to believe. Until recently I thought that person was Govorov. Now I must look for someone else."

"And you have come here to look?" Anna Alexandrovna's alarm contained a note of remonstration.

"I have some further questions, that's all. I wish to understand, clearly, fully, the argument between Borya and Goryanchikov."

Porfiry noted Anna Alexandrovna's flinch under the force of his uncompromising gaze.

"You've asked me about this before. Why are you asking me again? I told you everything I knew then."

"Did you?"

"Yes!" Her neck flushed patchily with the heat of her insistence. Her instinct for defiance showed in her eyes. But she couldn't hold the look.

"What was Stepan Sergeyevich Goryanchikov to you?" asked Porfiry abruptly.

"A lodger," she protested with outrage, then insisted: "He lodged in my house."

"And Borya?"

"My yardkeeper."

"Is that all?"

"What are you suggesting?"

"That the argument was about you."

"You are wrong." Her response was calmer than he might have expected.

Porfiry Petrovich bowed but kept his fluttering gaze fixed on her.

"Stepan Sergeyevich . . ." began Anna Alexandrovna but lost heart. Her voice cracked.

"The place where their bodies were found, in Petrovsky Park—"

Anna Alexandrovna shook her head, tight-lipped, forbidding.

Porfiry continued, "Last time we spoke, when I mentioned Petrovsky Park . . ."

"What of it?"

"I noticed . . . it was as if I had . . ."

"What?"

"I suppose the expression is 'touched a nerve.' "

"Is that so?"

"What happened there, in Petrovsky Park?"

"Is it really necessary to go into this?"

"I'm afraid so. Please, there's no need to be afraid of the truth. I realize . . ."

"What do you realize, Porfiry Petrovich?"

"These matters may be painful to you."

She answered him first with a narrowing of her eyes. "We went there once. In the summer. There was a performance in the open-air theater. We picnicked in the park beforehand."

"When you say 'we'?"

"Myself and my daughter, Sofiya Sergeyevna. Marfa Denisovna was with us." There was a slight beat before she added, "And Osip Maximovich."

"I see."

"Vadim Vasilyevich was there too." She added this hopefully.

"Please. Tell me what happened."

"Borya." Her voice was heavy as she said the name.

"I see."

"Borya was there. That is to say, I think he must have followed us. He was not of our party. Or perhaps it was a coincidence, meeting him there like that."

"Like what?"

"He was drunk. That is the only explanation there can be for his behavior."

"What did he do?"

"We had set up the picnic in a slight dip in the land, a hollow surrounded by birch. The others had gone for a walk. I was tired. I stayed to read my novel. Borya suddenly appeared. From nowhere. He stumbled and almost fell on top of me. He . . ."

"There is no need to be afraid. It can only help you if you tell the truth."

Anna Alexandrovna's expression was momentarily outraged. "He declared feelings for me. He told me he loved me."

"And how did you react to his declaration?"

"He was a yardkeeper!" Her eyes widened.

"He was a man."

"Please."

"You rebuffed him?"

"It was horrible! He was drunk. Am I to be the object of the yardkeeper's drunken affections?"

"Did anyone else see him?"

"No. No! Thankfully."

"Can you be sure?"

"I sincerely hope not."

"And what of Stepan Sergeyevich? Was he with you that day?"

"No."

"Stepan Sergeyevich . . ." Porfiry repeated the name musingly. Anna Alexandrovna frowned. "Your daughter's name is . . . ?"

"Sofiya."

"Sofiya Sergeyevna."

"Yes."

"Your husband, then, was Sergei?"

"Sergei Pavelovich. What are you suggesting?"

"Sergeyevna . . . Sergeyevich."

"This really is preposterous."

"The coincidence of patronyms is striking."

"It's just a coincidence."

"Is it not true that your husband felt some obligation toward Stepan Sergeyevich? That's why he had him come to live in the house, isn't it?"

"I really cannot answer for my husband."

Porfiry nodded decisively. "Do you think it possible that Stepan Sergeyevich taunted Borya about the feelings he felt toward you? Could that have been the cause of the argument?"

"I . . ." The angle of her averted face quickened his pulse.

"Or were they rivals, perhaps?"

"Please!" cried Anna Alexandrovna. "In one breath you are suggesting that he was my husband's son, in the next that he was my lover."

Porfiry's bow was very close to an affirmative nod.

Suddenly, the double doors to the drawing room parted, revealing the portly, bespectacled figure of Osip Maximovich Simonov. His face was determined, antagonistic. "What is the meaning of this?" he demanded.

"Osip Maximovich," gasped Anna Alexandrovna. "Thank God!" She rushed toward him as he came into the room. Her out-held hands came to nothing. She turned from him, almost chastened.

"Sir, I demand an explanation," said Osip Maximovich, and closed the doors behind him.

"I am conducting an investigation into the murders of three people."

"And you suspect Anna Alexandrovna?"

"It is important to establish the truth. You should know that, sir, as the publisher of philosophical works."

"Anna Alexandrovna is a respectable woman. You have no right to come here with your insinuating questions."

"How do you know my questions were insinuating? Were you listening at the door?" asked Porfiry with a smile that strained to be pleasant.

"I am not a fool, sir. I can very well imagine the kind of filthy questions you were asking."

"Believe me, please, when I say that no one regrets the necessity of asking such questions more than I."

"Then do not ask them."

"I'm afraid it's my job."

"It is not a job for a gentleman."

"Perhaps not. It is a necessary job, all the same."

"But to persecute Anna Alexandrovna!"

A thought seemed to occur suddenly to Porfiry. "I wonder, Osip Maximovich, do you believe a gentleman would be capable of murder?"

"There is no saying what any one of us is capable of, I am sure," Osip Maximovich answered huffily. "It would be absurd to deny that murders have been committed by members of the gentry."

"But would a gentleman use an axe?" Porfiry's tone was arch.

"Wasn't there indeed such a case recently? The student who took an axe to those sisters."

"But the axe is more a weapon we would associate with the peasantry, do you not agree? More the sort of weapon someone like Borya would choose?"

"I suppose so."

"I wonder what weapon a gentleman would choose. Or a gentlewoman, for that matter."

"I take it you have finished questioning Anna Alexandrovna. In which case, may I suggest that it is time that you left?"

"I have one more question and a request. Anna Alexandrovna, do you have any idea how Borya came to be in possession of six thousand rubles?"

"Borya? I do not—" Her eyes flitted in confusion. The color drained from her face. "I have no idea," she added without conviction, her gaze plummeting.

"He must have stolen it. It's as simple as that," said Osip Maximovich. He tried to flash reassurance toward her.

Porfiry made no comment on this theory, except to say, "It is a lot of money." He watched Anna Alexandrovna closely, noting her discomfiture.

"Have you finished?" asked Osip Maximovich curtly.

"Yes, except for my request. I would like Anna Alexandrovna to write something for me."

"You really do suspect her! Meanwhile the real murderer—"

"What do you wish me to write?" asked Anna Alexandrovna. Although she spoke decisively, there was once again a fatalistic weight to her voice.

"It really doesn't matter. My only requirement is that you write it on your own personal stationery."

"Osip Maximovich," said Anna Alexandrovna, placing a hand to her forehead. "Will you ring for Katya, please?"

KATYA BROUGHT the paper on a wooden tray. Immediately Porfiry noticed that the stationery's lilac shade matched exactly that of the envelope in which the six thousand rubles had been found.

Katya's step was brisk and disapproving. She did not look at Porfiry. In her wake, held back by her timidity but drawn despite it into the room, was a girl of about thirteen or fourteen. Porfiry saw the imprint of Anna Alexandrovna in her features. But youth made her beauty heedless.

The girl rushed out from behind Katya toward her mother and cried, "Mamma!"

"It's all right, darling." Anna Alexandrovna reached an arm around her daughter's shawled shoulders. She stooped to kiss her forehead, then nodded firmly and released her.

At Sofiya Sergeyevna's entrance, Osip Maximovich turned his back and moved away to a window. He gave the impression of losing interest.

Katya placed the tray on the low mahogany table from which Porfiry had once drunk tea. There was a pen and a pot of ink on the tray with the paper.

"So I may write anything?" said Anna Alexandrovna, taking her seat on the sofa by the table.

Porfiry bowed.

"But I can think of nothing," she confessed.

"In that case, may I suggest, 'Do you remember the summer?'" said Porfiry Petrovich.

Anna Alexandrovna looked up at him questioningly but without reproach. She then looked to Osip Maximovich, only to find he still had his back to her. Her head bowed hesitantly, and she took up the pen. She handed the note to Porfiry. He studied it briefly before pocketing it.

"And so this farce is at an end?" said Osip Maximovich, returning abruptly from the window. "You have all you need?"

"I have all I need from Anna Alexandrovna," confirmed Porfiry.

"And what have you decided? Is it enough to have her arrested?"

"Not quite."

"Not quite. I see. Not quite. And do you think it is enough, this 'not quite'? Do you think it is good enough to justify this persecution?" Osip Maximovich didn't wait for Porfiry to answer. "And while we are on the subject of your persecutions, would it be possible for me to request the return of the Proudhon translation that you confiscated from Stepan Sergeyevich's room?"

"I can't return it yet. I haven't finished examining it."

"What is there to examine? It is the translation of a philosophical text. What possible bearing could it have on the case?"

"There are a number of discrepancies in it. Sections in the translation that do not occur in the original."

Osip Maximovich frowned angrily. "What do you know about discrepancies? What do you know about translating philosophy? It is impossible to do it literally. Stepan Sergeyevich had a genius for interpretive translation."

"Why is it so important to you to have it back?" asked Porfiry mildly.

"Because it belongs to me!" exploded Osip Maximovich. "And I have found a translator for the rest of it. I wish to know how much Stepan Sergeyevich was able to complete before his death."

"I will return it to you as soon as I am able. But now I would like to talk to one other member of the household."

MARFA DENISOVNA HEARD the door to her apartment open and close. She didn't look up from the cards but tightened her warty fingers around the pack.

"So you have come to speak to me at last," she said. There was something like a smile on the lipless gash of her mouth.

"Do you know who I am?" asked Porfiry Petrovich.

"You're the one who asks questions."

Porfiry nodded. "My name is Porfiry Petrovich. I am an investigating magistrate. I am investigating the deaths of Stepan Sergeyevich Goryanchikov and Borya the yardkeeper. As well as the death of another individual called Konstantin Kirillovich Govorov."

Marfa Denisovna moved the ace of diamonds up to the top.

"How long have you been with the family, Marfa Denisovna?"

The old woman chuckled. "All my life."

"You were born a serf?"

"Yes. I belonged to Sergei Pavelovich's father's estate."

"And you stayed on after emancipation?"

"Where else would I go? Besides, I had my little Soneshka to look after."

"Sofiya Sergeyevna?"

"Of course."

"I'd like to talk to you about Stepan Sergeyevich." Marfa Denisovna nodded assent. "He owed your mistress money, didn't he?"

"It didn't matter."

"Why do you say that?"

Marfa Denisovna's hard little body jerked up and down in an overdone shrug.

"It was only money. Some things are more important than money. So he was behind on his rent? But he would pay it when he was able."

"You suggest some kind of bond between Stepan Sergeyevich and Anna Alexandrovna."

Marfa Denisovna moved a row of cards, the eight of hearts down to the three of clubs, over to a nine of clubs. She turned over a jack of hearts.

"Shall I tell you a story? My darling Soneshka loves it when I tell her stories. Babushka, tell me a story, she says. Even now that she is nearly grown."

"Yes, Babushka. Tell me a story," said Porfiry, smiling.

"There was once a young and handsome man of noble birth. He came from a rich family. The family owned nearly a thousand souls. One day the young man saw a beautiful girl washing clothes in the river. And as she worked the clothes in the river, it was as if she were wringing his heart in her hands. The young man came out from his hiding place, for he had been spying on her in secret. And he knew from the look on the girl's face that his love was returned. But the girl was the daughter of one of his father's serfs. Their love could not be. And yet it was. A child was born, a boy. They christened the baby Stepan. Then in the night, while his mother slept, baby Stepan was taken to the Foundling Hospital in St. Petersburg. Years passed. The young, handsome man grew older and moved to the city, away from the beautiful girl he had loved. Abandoned, her heart turned to stone. She continued to serve his family and even came to the city to serve him when his new, young wife bore him a baby girl. Remembering the baby that had been taken from her, she nursed that little darling as if she were her own. In the meantime, baby Stepan grew up, though not as much as he might have done! The sins of his parents were there for all to see in his little arms and legs. But he was a clever boy. As you might expect, his father being a clever man and his mother nobody's fool. He had been left at the Foundling Hospital with a signet ring around his neck on a cord. There was a family emblem engraved on the signet ring. That was all that the clever boy needed. Well, a man now, though no taller than an infant, he tracked his father down. The father wept tears of regret and remorse and took in his son. Though to keep up appearances, he called him a lodger and said nothing to his young wife. And within a year of his long-lost son's arrival, the father died, suddenly and quite mysteriously." With an impatient shake of her head, Marfa Denisovna scooped the cards together. "It won't come out!"

"Does she know now?" Porfiry asked quietly. "Anna Alexandrovna?"

"Oh, yes. I told her. I had to tell her."

"Why?"

"You will find it hard to understand. You never knew Stepan Sergeyevich. Not when he was alive. You never saw his eyes. There was something undeniable about his eyes. A woman who would find the idea of it quite ridiculous, who would laugh if you were to suggest such a thing to her—even such a woman, when she saw his eyes, would begin to wonder. Such things she would begin to wonder! There is a part of all of us that we only see when we look in eyes like Stepan Sergeyevich had. That he was a dwarf did not come into it."

"What happened when you told her?"

"Hah! Poor dearie. She was sick. I mean, she vomited up her dinner. And all she had to reproach herself with were idle wonderings. But some women take such things harder than others. And she could see now how he was looking at her little Sofiya. There was something devilish in Stepan Sergeyevich, there's no denying it. Something more than ordinary mischief."

"Do you think she could have killed him to prevent . . . the unthinkable?"

Marfa Denisovna dealt out the cards for another game. She didn't answer Porfiry Petrovich's question and didn't look up when he closed the door behind him.

22

⸸

The Holiest Man
in Russia

A S THE DAY BEGAN, eight hundred versts south of St. Petersburg, in the town of Kaluga, a young deputy investigating magistrate pulled himself up into the box seat of an open sleigh. Yevgeny Nikolaevich Ulitin settled next to the driver and carelessly arranged a sheepskin over his legs. He was already wearing two fur coats, thick fur mittens, and a heavy *ushanka*. His blue eyes were bleary from lack of sleep, and his face was shimmeringly pale. He had been up half the night discussing *zemstvo* politics, the freedom of the press, the existence (or otherwise) of the soul, insanity (from both a legal and a strictly psychiatric point of view), ignorance, education, the church, the state of the peasantry, the emancipation of the serfs, the legal reforms, the tsar, the tsarina, the woman problem, the comparative beauty of two sisters, actresses both in the Kaluga Provincial Theater, beauty in the abstract, art, literature, architecture, St. Petersburg . . .

His partner in these often circular and invariably unsatisfying debates was Dr. Artemy Vsevolodovich Drozdov, whom Ulitin frequently de-

clared to be the only other civilized being in Kaluga. Ulitin licked a metallic taste from his teeth. The fine wisps of his beard were plastered crustily
around his mouth, and he resisted the temptation to send his tongue out to
test the whiskers of his mustache. A vague memory of champagne—how
many bottles had they opened?—prompted him to clamp one mittened
hand over his mouth, as if he had just let slip an indiscretion. Whatever
subjects they touched upon in their discussions, the two friends always returned to the same eternal theme. St. Petersburg. It was a mystery to each
of them how he came to be rotting away in this provincial backwater
when all his friends and associates from university days were undoubt-
edly carving out glorious careers for themselves, close to the heart of all
that was worthwhile and invigorating. Sometimes these discussions
lapsed into mere recitals of the streets and place-names of the great capital,
culminating in a rapturous chorus of "Nevsky Prospect! Ah, the Nevsky
Prospect!" There would then follow a meditative silence, during which
the evening's opened bottles would stare back at them sullenly. The night
would break up soon after that, as memories of the pressing duties of the
following day came back to claim them.

Nikita, his driver, was busy lighting a pipe. When this was securely
completed, he turned stiffly toward Ulitin, at the same time leaning away
from the younger man. It was a complicated posture, not without conde-
scension. "Where are we going today, your honor?" asked Nikita as he
took up the reins. Ulitin thought he detected an ironic tone in the peasant's deference.

"Optina Pustyn."

"Optina Pustyn?" Nikita threw the name back with astonishment. He
put the reins down again.

"Yes."

"It's a long way."

"I know. Which is why we should not waste another moment."

"We may not make it before nightfall."

"I think we will."

"We may not make it at all, if there is a storm."

"So what do you suggest, my friend? That we stay here? I have official business at the monastery. Should I telegram back to the authorities in St. Petersburg who have instructed me in this commission that I cannot go there because Nikita says it is a long way?"

"But if we get caught in a snowstorm and we lose the road, you will not thank me."

"I will thank you if you get me to Optina Pustyn safely. I have to speak to Father Amvrosy on a very important matter."

"Father Amvrosy?"

"Yes."

"The holy man?"

"They say he is holy."

"He is holy. There was this girl. The daughter of one of my wife's relatives. Her sister's mother-in-law's brother's daughter, or some such. Or perhaps it was someone else. Anyhow, he cured her."

"Yes. I have heard similar stories."

"The doctors couldn't do a thing for her. She was just wasting away before their eyes. She couldn't keep anything down, you see." Nikita mimed vomiting. Ulitin closed his eyes and turned away. "They say he's dying," added Nikita. "Father Amvrosy. Doesn't have long left in this world. Ah well, he is sure to be going to a better one."

"All the more reason to hasten our journey," said Ulitin.

Nikita stared at the deputy investigating magistrate for a long time, as if he had just said something incomprehensibly stupid. He then shrugged and took up the reins again. He shook his head and allowed the energy of his bewilderment to pass down the reins. The two horses shouldered heavily into the day, snorting their own reluctance back to their driver.

WHEN THE FIRST FLAKES touched their faces, Nikita turned briefly in the same stiff, backward-leaning way toward Ulitin. But he said nothing. Neither of them had spoken for a long time.

Before long the air was filled with swirling flakes. They looped and spiraled but most of all fell, with a frantic and dizzying insistence. First the woods on either side disappeared from view. Then the posts that marked the road. Now all that Ulitin could see, apart from the teeming rush of the blizzard, was the back of the trace horse.

Nikita pulled on the reins, and they slid to a halt.

"We've lost the road," he said, shielding his eyes and peering through the constantly shifting layers.

Ulitin said nothing.

Without warning Nikita jumped down from the box seat. He clapped his hands, nodded, then bustled off into the storm. In a moment he had vanished from sight.

Ulitin felt suddenly very alone. He heard the horses shift and shiver uneasily. Last night, with Drozdov, he had talked of the soul and of the question of its survival after death. With the abstract confidence of young men, they had resolved the issue beyond dispute. Drozdov was a doctor. He had vouched for the physiological basis of personality. The argument was irrefutable. If a subject's personality could become changed through morbid disease, as in the case of dementia praecox, it was logical to argue that it did not have its basis in anything eternal and immutable. And if disease can mutate the subjective self, it is also logical to conclude that death will terminate it.

Now, sitting lost and abandoned in the middle of a furious snowstorm, Ulitin was not so sure. Or rather, he wished he had not been so sure.

He closed his eyes. It was as if he did not wish to catch himself in the act of saying a prayer.

The sleigh shook. Nikita clambered up next to him. Ulitin had never been so pleased to see another human.

"Stavrogin's Copse. If we keep that to our right, we should find Kozelsk."

Ulitin peered in the direction Nikita indicated. But all he could see was the maddening dance of snowflakes in front of his eyes.

· · ·

THEY GOT TEA and something to eat at the *zemstvo* hut in Kozelsk. As they ate, they kept a close eye on the window, watching the storm intensify its rage. Ulitin became suddenly depressed and could bear it no longer. He looked away from the window and took out the telegram he had received the previous day.

GO TO OPTINA PUSTYN QUESTION F AMVROSY VERIFY
OSIP MAXIMOVICH SIMONOV AT OPT PUST 29 NOV TO
11 DEC INC STOP

Ulitin handled the flimsy paper forlornly. The telegram had been sent by one Porfiry Petrovich, an investigating magistrate with the Department of the Investigation of Criminal Causes in St. Petersburg. As he touched the words, he seemed to feel a direct contact with the city, or at least with the dreams of his that it represented. His heart had quickened when he'd received it. He had seen it as an opportunity to impress important personages in the capital. Perhaps a transfer would follow. But now his ambitions had been swallowed up by the snow, and he was trapped in the *zemstvo* hut in Kozelsk.

He tried to imagine Porfiry Petrovich. When this proved impossible, he imagined himself walking down the Nevsky in summer.

"Well, your honor, will you look at that!"

Ulitin looked up. Nikita was pointing at the window. The storm had stopped. The sky was clear.

"Get the horses ready!"

"You're not thinking of going now?"

"We have no time to lose," cried Ulitin, rising to his feet.

Nikita shook his head regretfully. "No, no, no, your honor. It will be dark before I have a chance to get the sleigh out. It would be as well to wait until the morning. We will see how it is in the morning."

Remembering how he had felt when Nikita had come back to him in the storm, Ulitin did not insist. He looked down at the telegram and felt a lump of self-pity in his throat. He blinked away the threat of tears.

THEY APPROACHED THE monastery on the frozen river Zhidra. Ulitin saw the gold crosses floating in the sky, the clear winter sunlight exulting on them. His heart leaped and he reproached it. *They are only painted crossbeams of wood!* But he could not deny that at first he had stared in amazement. For just an instant their appearance had seemed miraculous. *How can that be?* There was some trick, there had to be . . . Then they drew nearer. As the course of the river twisted their path, the crosses bobbed from one side to the other as if engaged in stately dance. And of course, it became clear. The crosses were mounted on cupolas, the blue of which had, from a distance, been indistinguishable from the sky. Gradually the domes had appeared, like a slow solidifying of the sky, forming beneath the crosses.

From the gatehouse by the river to the convent was a steep walk up a forested mountain. Ulitin had heard that some pilgrims completed it on their knees. He left Nikita and the horses at the gatehouse and set out on foot with a young monk who gave every impression of expecting him.

It's just a way they have, thought Ulitin. *They like to make a mystery out of everything.*

The young monk was excitable and garrulous and seemed unable to look Ulitin in the eye. His talk was trivial, at times almost hysterical. He reminded Ulitin of a child on the eve of a holiday.

Perhaps he's simpleminded, he thought.

"You've come to see Father Amvrosy," said the young monk, whose name was Brother Innokentiy. Although he was dressed only in a monastic cassock, he didn't seem to feel the cold. He walked quickly, despite the deep snow and the treacherous path.

Ulitin frowned in annoyance and hurried to keep up.

Brother Innokentiy smiled enigmatically. "Why else would you come? There are many who have already made the pilgrimage. Every day someone arrives. You will have to wait your turn to see him."

"I'm not a pilgrim. I'm here on official business. I'm an investigating magistrate."

"He won't see you. He's not interested in earthly affairs."

"It's a very important matter. I have orders from St. Petersburg. From the police authorities. It is to do with a criminal investigation."

"He won't talk about it. He doesn't care about such things now. The time has gone for him to talk about such things." Brother Innokentiy flashed one of his questing, sly glances. "What is it about? Perhaps I can help you." His smile was insinuating.

"I have been directed to talk to Father Amvrosy."

"But he won't see you, I tell you. Not about this. If it was about your soul, perhaps." Brother Innokentiy giggled unpleasantly as if he had just made a very funny, though slightly risqué joke. "He may die any moment. What if he dies before we reach the convent? You'll have to ask me then." One side of the monk's mouth snagged up in a leering grin.

Ulitin slowed his pace. He was tired. But he wanted to let the monk get ahead of him. He wanted a respite from his chatter.

Brother Innokentiy waited for him to catch up. His welcoming smile had a gloating edge.

B ROTHER INNOKENTIY SHOWED him into a room that was crowded with well-to-do pilgrims. Everyone seemed to be affected by the same talkative excitement that Ulitin had sensed in the monk. As they entered, every face turned to them expectantly, there was a momentary hush, and then the din picked up again.

Ulitin felt aggrieved on the old, dying monk's behalf. *They are expecting a miracle,* he thought. *They have come for a miracle, but they look like vultures.*

A group of landowners, the men in immaculate frock coats, the women already in shining black, made straight for Brother Innokentiy. Their faces were set with sanctimony. "How is he now?" was the question they all wanted to know the answer to.

"I don't know," said Brother Innokentiy. "I've come from the gate-house." He seemed delighted not to have any news for them.

"The end is near though, isn't it?" The middle-aged woman who spoke couldn't keep the eagerness out of her question, though her face was a solemn mask. She scrutinized Brother Innokentiy through a lorgnette.

A stout red-faced man pushing a girl of about eighteen in a wheelchair forced his way to the front. "He must see her. He must see my Lana. Please, you must make him see her." The girl blushed. *She is quite beautiful when she blushes*, thought Ulitin. Her eyes sought his, then looked away.

"He knows you are here. He knows you are all here. He asks for those he wants to see," said Brother Innokentiy.

"It is not as if I haven't been generous to the brothers," insisted the stout man, short of breath.

"Daddy!" protested Lana.

"Your generosity has not gone unnoticed. But perhaps there are others in greater spiritual need. There is so little time left. He can't see everyone."

"He will see me," said Yevgeny Nikolaevich Ulitin abruptly.

Brother Innokentiy looked Ulitin up and down thoroughly. "Perhaps he will," he said at last, quietly, and left.

He is not simpleminded after all, thought Ulitin.

The stout landowner took hold of Ulitin's arm. He had seen something in the young monk's look. "Make him see my Lana, before it's too late," he pleaded.

F OR A MOMENT Ulitin thought the man on the bed was already dead. His long white hair lay haloed about his head. The skin on his face was drawn back skeletally. His body was motionless, a minimal disruption in the blankets. It was hard to believe there really was a body under them. His eyes were open, but they didn't seem to see anyone in the room. They were fixed on a point beyond the ceiling.

The small bedroom was filled with monks, all of them standing. Some were dressed imposingly in robes embroidered with scriptural passages. Every one of them was reciting from the gospel, their gentle murmurs lapping over the dying man, like a kind of final baptism of voices before death.

"He has moments of remarkable lucidity and long spells when he is lost to us," explained Brother Innokentiy in an excited whisper. "The Lord is already calling to him. I was able to tell him about you. That an important magistrate has come on official business."

"I am not important," said Ulitin, and blushed. It was the last thing he would have thought he was going to say.

It is false, he thought. *That's why I blushed. Because it was false. I have been affected by all of this.*

"But still he wouldn't see you," went on Brother Innokentiy gleefully. "It was only when I told him that you were a nonbeliever that he asked for you to be brought."

"How do you know I'm a nonbeliever?"

"It's in your eyes." Brother Innokentiy smiled provokingly. "You must kneel beside his bed and wait for him to notice you. Do not speak until he speaks to you. If he closes his eyes, you must go."

Ulitin did as he was directed. At the same time Brother Innokentiy leaned intimately close to the old monk's face, as if he would kiss him, but instead whispered something in his ear. Brother Innokentiy moved away. Ulitin almost thought he winked at him.

Close to the dying man, Ulitin remembered how he had felt the day before when Nikita had left him alone on the sleigh, his rationalist certainties battered by the storm.

The old man's eyes rolled heavily toward Ulitin. The expression was infinitely pleading. "What do you want to ask me?" The voice seemed to come from far away, and as the monk's lips barely moved, it was tempting to believe that someone else was speaking for him.

Ulitin felt suddenly ashamed. "I am sorry to trouble you at this time," he said uselessly.

Father Amvrosy closed his eyes. Ulitin's heart sank. He did not want the audience to end, even though it was not important to him to ask the questions anymore. It was the privilege of the moment that he wanted to hold on to. He was about to get up when Father Amvrosy opened his eyes again.

"So you do not believe in God?"

"Not in God, not in the soul, not in eternal life."

Ulitin thought he saw a gentle smile form beneath the monk's massive beard. Perhaps it was a mild twinge of pain. "So why does it matter to you?"

"What?"

"Your investigation. If you don't believe in God, what does it matter?"

"Because there must be laws. A legal framework. Men must respect one another's rights. The right to life, for example. It is a question of social order. It is quite rational." Ulitin paused and added, "But it is not *my* investigation. I'm under instruction from a magistrate in St. Petersburg."

"A higher authority?"

"Yes."

"What does he want to know, this higher authority of yours?"

"He wants to know if one Osip Maximovich Simonov was here at Optina Pustyn from the twenty-ninth of November to the eleventh of December."

"You could have asked Brother Innokentiy that. It was he who looked after the gentleman. He took him his food every day and talked to him."

"I was ordered to ask you."

The elder's eyes rolled away from Ulitin, it seemed in disappointment. Ulitin feared he had pushed the monk too far. "Someone by that name was here."

"Between those dates?"

The old monk gave a barely perceptible nod. "The convent register will confirm it."

"Thank you." Ulitin made to rise. The eyes came back to hold him. These little movements of the eyes seemed to require every last calorie of energy the dying man possessed. They had to be important to him. Any one might be his last.

"Is there nothing else you wish to ask me?"

Ulitin hesitated. "Why did you agree to see me?"

Father Amvrosy swallowed epically. "I wanted to be sure," he said at last, when the swallowing was finally done. "I wanted to look an atheist in the eye one last time." As he spoke, the elder was staring fixedly into Ulitin's eyes. His gaze was as tender and consoling as a lover's.

"What do you see?" asked Ulitin, hardly daring to breathe.

"Fear," said Father Amvrosy. With that he closed his eyes. After a moment he murmured something that sounded like "I'm not afraid."

Ulitin felt himself raised and led from the bedroom. "But I am a believer!" he cried in sudden protest, and the outburst did not seem to surprise anyone.

B ACK IN THE room with the wealthy devout, Ulitin guiltily avoided the eyes of the girl in the wheelchair. He felt as though there was something between them, and he had betrayed her.

Her father accosted him. "Did you mention Lana to the elder? Did you tell him he has to see her?"

Ulitin shook his head.

Brother Innokentiy came in. The smile that occupied his lips now transcended all the others Ulitin had seen there. "Father Amvrosy is at peace," he called, his voice cracking with emotion.

All around Ulitin people fell to their knees and began praying. Yevgeny Nikolaevich Ulitin did the same. The girl in the wheelchair was weeping.

23

Jupiter's Bastards

I
S IT TRUE?" Nikodim Fomich closed the door to Porfiry's chambers but seemed unwilling to advance into the room. He was waiting on Porfiry's reply.

Porfiry blew out a funnel of smoke and flicked the ash from his cigarette. "Is what true?" He looked up from the papers he was studying and hyperblinked.

"Liputin's latest insanity?"

Porfiry handed the chief superintendent a letter bearing the crest of the *prokuror*'s office. "I'm to hand over the file relating to the deaths under suspicious circumstances of Stepan Sergeyevich Goryanchikov, Boris Borisich Kutuzov, and Konstantin Kirillovich Govorov to Prokuror Yaroslav Nikolaevich Liputin. He will take over the handling of the case personally. I am expecting his high excellency at any moment."

Nikodim Fomich read the note and threw it down on Porfiry's desk. "But this is absurd. 'Serious procedural irregularities.' 'Misinterpretation and misreporting of medical evidence.' You told him exactly what Pervoyedov had found. He chose to ignore it."

"The office of the *prokuror* is never wrong."

"But the man's an idiot. He doesn't stand a chance of solving the case."

"I think he believes that I have already solved it."

"And have you?"

Porfiry shrugged. "I have some theories. I have narrowed down the field of suspects."

"To how many?"

Porfiry's eyes rolled upward as he counted in his head. "About six."

"That's hardly narrowing the field, Porfiry Petrovich."

"Or seven."

"Well, I must say, you seem to be taking it very calmly." Nikodim Fomich was indignant.

"What can I do about it?"

"You can appeal."

Porfiry smiled weakly. "I must accept my fate. That's the Russian way, is it not?"

"No, it isn't," objected Nikodim Fomich petulantly. "I don't believe stoicism is a true Russian trait at all. I deplore it!"

"I must do all I can to help Prokuror Liputin uncover the identity of the murderer. That's the important thing now. My own personal disappointment is irrelevant." After a moment, Porfiry added, "Whoever is responsible for these deaths is certainly capable of killing again."

"Exactly! That's why you must stay on the case until it's solved."

The door opened suddenly. "Prokuror Liputin is here to see you," said the chief clerk, Zamyotov. He made no attempt to mask his pleasure.

Now the *prokuror* himself strode into the room. Liputin didn't acknowledge Nikodim Fomich and dismissed Zamyotov with a curt nod. "Porfiry Petrovich, you have the file I requested?" He held out a hand.

"Of course, your excellency." Porfiry gathered together the papers on his desk and placed them in a cardboard wallet that he handed to Liputin.

"You will wait until I have studied these papers, then you will answer any questions I put to you. Then you will consider yourself suspended until further notice."

"Yaroslav Nikolaevich!" cried Nikodim Fomich. "I really must protest. This is hardly just—or sensible."

Liputin still refused to look in Nikodim Fomich's direction. His head was bowed as he scanned the contents of the file. "Good day, Nikodim Fomich. Your presence is not required here. I trust you have police matters to attend to."

"I shall be entering a formal appeal on Porfiry Petrovich's behalf."

"Which I shall look forward to processing." The corner of Liputin's mouth went into spasm.

Porfiry Petrovich released his friend from the room with a gentle smile.

T HE *PROKUROR* TOOK over Porfiry's desk. Every now and then, for instance when he was studying the pornographic photographs found in Govorov's apartment, he would look across disapprovingly at Porfiry, as if he were responsible. Porfiry was sitting on the brown fake-leather sofa, chain-smoking. Occasionally the *prokuror* seemed about to say something but always thought better of it. At last he placed the final piece of paper, the line written by Anna Alexandrovna, back into the file and sat back in Porfiry's chair.

His eyes were fixed on Porfiry, who sat up expectantly and stubbed out the cigarette he was smoking in the crystal ashtray that was resting on the arm of the sofa.

"So, Porfiry Petrovich," began Liputin, "you think that Anna Alexandrovna is the murderer? Is that really likely? A woman? And a woman of her class too? Do you not think she would be restrained by modesty and a sense of shame?"

"She could equally be motivated by them. Or rather by a false modesty and a distorted sense of shame. To keep certain things secret. Poison is a notoriously female weapon."

"But she would have to have had a man working with her. If only to string up the yardkeeper."

Porfiry shrugged. "I have my theories about that. More of a problem is the fact that her hand does not match the note I found in the box in Borya's shed. I believe it was that note that led him to his death."

"It does not match?" asked Liputin, somewhat surprised. He searched quickly through the file to produce the two sheets of paper. "The paper is different, of course. But that means nothing."

"The paper is different. And that means nothing, as you say. But there are differences in the handwriting. Anna Alexandrovna's is more rounded and, I would say, feminine. I believe the other note was written by a man attempting to copy her hand."

"You can't possibly be sure of that!"

"You're right. I can't be sure it was a man. But I am sure it is a forgery."

"But you did identify the scent on the paper as hers?"

"Yes. However, anyone can buy a bottle of scent."

"It would have to be someone who knows what scent she uses."

Porfiry Petrovich nodded.

"For instance, her maid," suggested Liputin.

Porfiry Petrovich pursed his lips, as if impressed. "When I called at the Widow Ivolgina's house the other day, I noticed a particularly unpleasant taste in the air. I had just extinguished a cigarette. It is known that smoking cigarettes in the proximity of prussic acid can lead to such a reaction. I asked the maid about it, and she said that they had been fumigating mattresses. Fumigation is one of the domestic uses of prussic acid. She certainly would have had access to the substance."

"So it is the maid?"

Now Porfiry raised his eyebrows doubtfully. "But then again, anyone in the house would have had the same access. The old nursemaid, Marfa Denisovna, for example. Or the cook, Lizaveta. Then there are the two gentlemen who lodge there. Osip Maximovich and his secretary, Vadim Vasilyevich. We know that Goryanchikov did work for Osip Maximovich's publishing firm."

"Yes, but I see that Osip Maximovich's alibi is vouched for by the late Father Amvrosy of Optina Pustyn. The telegram from that fellow in Kaluga confirms it."

"It would appear so." Porfiry read from Ulitin's telegram: "'Someone by that name was here,' were the elder's exact words."

"There you have it," said Liputin carelessly.

"An interesting choice of words, do you not think?"

"The reverend father was dying. I don't think we can read too much into his exact choice of words. We were fortunate to get a testimony out of him at all. And besides, there was the convent register."

"A simple yes or no would have answered the magistrate's question more decisively, without expending undue energy."

"These old mystics like to talk in riddles," said Liputin conclusively. "So where are we? What of Vadim Vasilyevich? He has no alibi."

"And no motive, as far as we can ascertain."

"Oh, really, Porfiry Petrovich! You are really most infuriating! Will you not simply tell me who the murderer is?"

"Please be assured that if I knew, I would not hesitate to tell you."

Liputin leafed through the documents of the file. "You released the student Virginsky."

"Yes."

"So you have at least discounted him?"

"To some extent, I had discounted him, insofar as I had discounted anyone. You will know from the report that I had him tailed. And that he was seen to enter Friedlander's the apothecary. This was the day before Govorov's death."

"You questioned the apothecary?"

"Lieutenant Salytov did."

Liputin searched through the papers to find the relevant statement. "'He attempted to purchase laudanum. And failed.'" Liputin looked up, suddenly inspired. "Perhaps he was testing the apothecary. Someone who was lax enough to sell laudanum to an undernourished student might be amenable to even more questionable transactions. Your spy lost him. He may have tried again, somewhere else, and succeeded."

"But the murderer already had a source for prussic acid," argued Porfiry, "as Borya's death testifies."

"But to purchase too much from one source would certainly arouse suspicion." Liputin spoke as if the matter were settled.

"There is something else to consider," said Porfiry. "Money. Virginsky never has much of it. If he wanted prussic acid, I do not believe he would ask for laudanum. It's hardly consistent with the economics of poverty."

"Well, the apothecary may be lying. He would hardly be likely to admit selling a deadly poison to a suspected murderer."

"He did not know his customer was a suspected murderer. Perhaps he thought he was a butterfly collector."

"One does not collect butterflies in December in Petersburg, Porfiry Petrovich."

"What I mean is he could have justified the sale to himself—or to a jury."

"Juries!" cried Liputin with heat. "Don't talk to me about juries. Even so, we should bring Virginsky in. He has the motive. The bizarre contract conferring ownership of his soul on Goryanchikov. While we're at it, we should bring in the apothecary too. I'm sure Lieutenant Salytov would get the truth out of them."

Porfiry Petrovich bowed. "The investigation is in your hands now, your excellency." Something about the way Porfiry said this seemed to give Liputin pause.

"Yes, it is," said the *prokuror* uncertainly. "What is all this business with the philosophy translation?" he asked abruptly.

"I believe Goryanchikov knew his life to be in danger. I believe he also knew from whom. He has left clues in the text. Interposed sections that are not in the original."

"These are the passages you have drawn attention to?"

"That's right, your excellency. The first passage I noticed was the one that reads: 'The father of Faith will be the destroyer of Wisdom.' Since then I have discovered two other interpolations. One is a reference to Alcibiades and Socrates. You know who Alcibiades was?"

Liputin moved his head ambiguously. It could have been a nod or a shake of denial, or simply an involuntary tic.

"The great and, some would say, wholly immoral Athenian general," continued Porfiry. "As famous for his debauched and sacreligious acts as for his military exploits. The reference is from Plato's *Symposium*. The passage in Goryanchikov's text reads, 'Did not Alcibiades sleep with Socrates, under the same cloak, and wrap his sinful arms around a spiritual man?'"

"Yes, yes, yes, Porfiry Petrovich. I am well aware of the loathsome practices the ancient Greeks indulged in."

"There is no such mention of Alcibiades and Socrates in Proudhon. The third interpolation . . ."

Liputin raised a hand to silence Porfiry while he read the final passage that Porfiry had copied out:

> As everyone knows, Minerva was the daughter of Jupiter. She sprang directly from her father's head. This miracle was achieved only after her father had devoured her pregnant mother whole. It should not surprise us that such a deity was also the father of many bastards. With an irony the ancients would have appreciated, the name of one of Jupiter's bastards is Fides.

"So what does it mean?" asked Liputin, laying down the note and confronting Porfiry with a severe gaze.

"As yet I don't know."

"You don't know?" Liputin's tone was indignant.

"Do *you* know, your excellency? You have now had a chance to study all the evidence we have collected."

"Of course I don't know. This farrago of nonsense is no help. Good grief, Porfiry Petrovich! What have you been doing all this time?"

"I have been pursuing leads."

"And where has it got you?"

Porfiry held his palms upward, half in supplication, half in apology.

"It's just as well I'm taking over."

Porfiry nodded meekly. "What will your next step be, your excellency?"

Liputin seemed to be distracted by a scratch on the corner of Porfiry's desk. At last he threw a shy, almost abashed glance toward Porfiry. "What would *your* next step be?"

"I would go back to where the whole thing started. The girl. Lilya Ivanovna."

"The prostitute?"

Porfiry nodded.

"You think she is the murderer?" asked Liputin uncertainly.

"No. But I think she may be the reason for the murders. If I may make one further suggestion, your excellency. I fully accept the disciplinary action that you have initiated against me. However, I would propose that you postpone my suspension."

"That's out of the question. I do not go back on my decisions."

"Do you ever gamble, Yaroslav Nikolaevich?"

The *prokuror* regarded Porfiry with as much affront as if he had spat in his face.

"I propose a wager—that's all," pressed Porfiry. "Delay my suspension for two days. If I have not solved the case, you may suspend me, indefinitely—without pay. If I have solved the case, I ask you to take no action against me. My success will redound to your credit. My failure will give you a scapegoat."

Prokuror Liputin pinched his lower lip pensively. "I am a Russian, Porfiry Petrovich. Of course I gamble."

24

While the Girl Slept

THE SUDDEN INTRUSION of green on the snow-covered pavement startled Porfiry. Perhaps he was the only man in St. Petersburg who had forgotten what time of the year it was. But the depth of the green and the darkness of it shocked him into remembering.

Christmas trees of various sizes tumbled out from the Gostinny Dvor indoor market. The trees came from Finland. Some of them were still unadorned, others already decked with ribbons and painted baubles. The traders walked between them, hawking for business.

Porfiry tapped the driver's shoulder. "Here." To Salytov, he added, "Give me a moment. It's important."

He jumped down from the *drozhki*. It was half an hour before he returned. He was carrying a small package wrapped in gaudy paper.

"I wanted to get something for the child. She has a child, you know. A daughter."

"The whore?" answered Lieutenant Salytov sullenly, looking straight ahead as the driver's whip snapped the air.

A slight smile showed on Porfiry's lips.

"What a temper you were in that morning, Ilya Petrovich!" Porfiry cast a wary glance toward Salytov. The lieutenant's face was already pink from the cold air. It darkened at Porfiry's words, clashing violently with his orange whiskers. Porfiry saw and continued: "We could hear your shouting throughout the headquarters. If only you hadn't let Govorov get away, perhaps we would have solved the case by now."

Salytov brought his fur-sheathed fist down on the edge of the *drozhki*. "I didn't *let* him get away! It wasn't a question of letting him get away. He wasn't in custody. He was the aggrieved party. The one pressing charges. No one expected him to go missing like that. And besides, we didn't know he was Govorov then. We didn't know who he was at all." Salytov caught Porfiry's smile out of the corner of his eye. "Damn you, Porfiry Petrovich!"

"I'm sorry. I was being mischievous, I admit. But with a purpose. I want you to frighten her—Lilya Ivanovna—the whore, as you called her. I want you to bully her as you have never bullied anyone. Then, when I tell you, I want you to leave her to me." Porfiry held up the present he had bought for Lilya's daughter. "I shall take over."

"Does it ever occur to you, Porfiry Petrovich, that your methods may one day backfire on you?"

Porfiry's answering smile was unperturbed.

P ORFIRY RAPPED BRIGHTLY on the door, holding the gift he had bought for Vera in his other hand. He was still smiling as he said to Salytov, "Remember, be severe."

"Do you really feel the need to prompt me?" answered Salytov, and then blushed.

"My goodness, Ilya Petrovich! Is that a joke? A joke at your own expense?"

"Have the good grace not to—" Salytov broke off, flustered. A kind of flinching shudder gripped him. He looked away from Porfiry and continued to flex his neck in the aftermath of his convulsion.

"No jokes when we're inside, please. Leave that to me."

"If we ever get inside." Salytov pounded on the door with a clenched hand. The silence that followed seemed enlarged by the violence of the blows.

"Perhaps they've moved," wondered Porfiry aloud, after a moment.

Salytov tried the handle, which turned. The door opened inward but soon came up against something.

Salytov leaned his shoulder into the door and pushed hard. The unseen obstacle yielded with a sigh as it was moved along the floor.

"My God. My Christ," murmured Porfiry, closing his eyes. His fingers tightened around the little present. He followed Salytov into the room.

"This has just happened," said Salytov, his own eyes greedy for the havoc. "The blood is fresh."

"No!" cried Porfiry. "Don't say it."

"If we had come straight here—"

"How did this happen? How could this happen?"

The child, Vera, lay on the bed. Her body was in the typical pose of a sleeping child, the disposition of her hands angled by dreams. On her face, they wanted to see an innocent pout, perhaps a shadow of childhood anxieties, or even a hint of willful petulance. Anything but the bloody pulp, the mess of blood and bone and tissue, that confronted them. It seemed that someone had deliberately and laboriously obliterated her face.

"God help us. God help us. God help us." Porfiry felt his knees begin to buckle. He lurched backward. A flailing arm struck the door. It swung to. He fell back against it. "This is not right," he groaned.

"Let us hope she was asleep," said Salytov grimly.

"Why would anyone do this?"

"It is the act of a madman."

Porfiry shook his head. "No. There is reason behind this. Cold reason.

Did you see what he has done to her face? Why does he not want us to see her face?"

And now they saw the girl's mother. Lilya Ivanovna was lying on the floor near the stove, her head pooled in blood, her hair clotted in dark, damp ringlets. Her eyes and mouth were open. As if she had seen and named her attacker at the same moment. Her wound was not immediately evident.

Salytov crossed the floor and dropped to one knee beside Lilya's body, examining her head where it touched the blood-drenched floor. "She must have been struck in the back of the head," he said. "And then turned over post-mortem. Or perhaps she turned herself over before dying. There is blood all over the stove. And on the walls. The little girl was asleep. She must have been asleep. Let's say she was asleep. Let's pray she was. The mother turned her back for a moment and was struck down. Suggesting her assailant was someone known to her. The murderer then turned his attention to the girl." Salytov looked back, tracing the murderer's movements. He gasped and reared back and pointed. He was pointing at the floor next to Porfiry.

Porfiry looked down. Now that the door was closed, they could see what had been blocking it: Zoya Nikolaevna, in a silver fox fur coat that was stained with her own blood at the shoulders and down one side. That side of her head was glistening and red and wrong.

All around, the painted saints and the beautiful gilded Christs averted their gaze. But this turning away had not saved them from defilement. Streaks and spots of blood added a new garishness to their colors.

"He killed the mother while the girl slept," Salytov insisted. "Then he killed the girl. Then the old woman came back. And he killed her as soon as she stepped inside. No time even to scream."

"God, no!" said Porfiry. He stood and tottered and fell back against the door. He looked down again at the package in his hand. "This is my fault. This is all my fault. If we hadn't stopped—"

"You weren't to know," said Salytov unconvincingly.

"Who has done this?" Porfiry's stricken gaze demanded the answer of Salytov.

The policeman's expression seemed almost insolent. He held his back and neck very straight. "Pull yourself together, Porfiry Petrovich." Salytov nodded sharply, as if in approval of his own words. Then he suddenly seemed at a loss.

Porfiry pushed himself away from the door and staggered like a drunk toward Salytov. Salytov watched him in horror, unsure whether he was coming to throttle or embrace him. At the very end Porfiry veered to one side and stooped sharply, as if he would throw himself headlong onto the floor. One arm shot out in front of him and clutched at something. He somehow managed to keep his balance and stand up.

"What have you there?" said Salytov. He could not make his voice sound natural.

Porfiry held toward him the hand that contained the present for Vera.

"I meant the other hand."

"Don't you want to know what I got for her? I chose it very carefully." Salytov didn't answer.

"Look! Look at it!"

Salytov stood up to open the package. It contained a pair of painted wooden figures, a hussar and his lady, with crudely carved but cheerful faces. "What's in your other hand?" demanded Salytov, without commenting on the toys.

Porfiry opened his palm to reveal a small glass vial. The label said LAUDANUM.

THE CABINETMAKER KEZEL'S wife opened the door. Her face was bruised and swollen. Her nose had become a broad glistening mound of purple and yellow.

Salytov pushed past her. "Where's Virginsky?" He possessed the apartment with his straight posture and searching glance. The place was immaculately clean, the furniture simple but new, solid and well made. "No sign of blood," said Salytov to no one.

Porfiry came in more hesitantly. He looked into the woman's eyes for a long time, finding something there that he almost understood.

"He isn't here." Her voice was empty.

"Why does your husband beat you?" Porfiry asked. He sounded startled by his own words.

Fear and perplexity rippled her face.

"You would be pretty if he didn't beat you."

"When was he here last? Virginsky?" Salytov barked. "Come on! Come on!"

"Just now." She was still looking at Porfiry as she answered, as if she couldn't tear her eyes away from him. She had found something answering in his eyes.

"What state was he in? Did you notice anything unusual about him?" demanded Salytov.

The woman looked to Porfiry for an explanation.

"Was there any blood on him? Did he have to clean himself up?"

Kezel's wife nodded numbly. "He had blood on his hands."

"Just on his hands?" asked Porfiry. "What about his clothes? Did he have to change his clothes?"

The woman flinched, as if expecting a blow. She closed her eyes and forced out, "I don't know." Her voice was high and strained, on the edge of tears. "I don't think so," she squeezed out.

"It's all right," said Porfiry softly. "But tell me, why did he hit you this last time? Was it to do with Virginsky?"

Her eyes swelled with panic. "It was the samovar."

"The samovar?"

"It went missing. Someone stole it."

"Someone stole your samovar?" Porfiry was incredulous. He couldn't understand how he came to be having a conversation about a stolen samovar so soon after what he had just seen. He sensed Salytov's impatience. Meeting it with a glance, he nodded as Salytov indicated that he was going into Virginsky's room. "He beat you because someone stole your samovar?" Porfiry welcomed the rage that he felt rushing through him. He said to himself that if Kezel came home now, he would kill the man without regret. He imagined closing his hands around the cabinet-maker's neck.

Porfiry was suddenly disgusted by his own self-pity and self-delusion.

"Do you know who stole the samovar?" Porfiry felt a strange hilarity threatening to burst out. He had to struggle to keep his face straight.

The woman shook her head tensely.

Porfiry closed his eyes. The image of blood-splashed icons forced itself on him. "Who did your husband think had taken the samovar?" He saw Vera playing in the snow with her friends. But her face was smashed and bloody. She came toward him and tried to speak. Her nose flapped loosely every time she opened the raw gash that had been her mouth. No words came out, but she dribbled bloody mucus. Porfiry opened his eyes and studied the bruises on Madame Kezel's face. He wanted to touch the places where her skin had ruptured.

"Pavel Pavelovich," she answered at last.

"Virginsky," Porfiry nodded. "And was he right?"

Kezel's wife looked down at the floor.

"He didn't steal it though, did he? You gave it to him. You gave it to him knowing that your husband would miss it—how could he not miss it?—and knowing that your husband would take it out on you. My dear, you love Virginsky almost as much as you hate yourself."

"I don't hate myself," she answered firmly. "I hate my husband."

"Of course. Like every good Russian, he loves his tea. What a perfect way to punish him, to give away the samovar. So tell me, what did Pavel Pavelovich want with the samovar?"

"He pawned it. He said he would get it back. He was going to get it back now. When he saw what Kezel had done to me."

"He was going to the pawnbroker's?"

Salytov came out of Virginsky's room. "I found more vials of laudanum. And this." He handed Porfiry a scribbled note.

Father,

I am your son. I see that now and cannot deny it. I am as foul and as loathsome and as capable of crime as you. I have proved myself capable of the worst crimes imaginable. And I hate myself more than I have ever hated you. I can't live with what I have become. A criminal and a coward. I shall throw myself in front of a galloping troika. It is the only way for a Russian to kill himself. I will be free of you and you will be free of me.

But you shouldn't have beaten her. How could you beat her?

Your son, Pavel Pavelovich.

T HE BELL COMPLAINED fussily as Salytov threw open the door to Lyamshin's. Porfiry was aware that he was allowing the policeman to take the lead now. Remembering his exchange with the Jewish pawnbroker, he had an uneasy feeling.

The last time he had set foot in the shop, the objects around him had seemed enticing. He had chosen to invest them with mystery and desire. He had plunged his fingers between some of them. Even the sense of tragedy they had inspired was romantic. It moved without touching him. Now the feeling they provoked in him was more visceral and stifling. These were not neutral everyday objects; they were the forms of despair. Despair was the one raw material from which they had all been shaped, not porcelain or brass or Karelian birch. And they were imbued with a destructive malevolence.

Porfiry recognized the man behind the counter and could tell that he had been recognized. Distrust closed the man's features.

Porfiry put a restraining hand on Salytov's shoulder. "Please, Ilya Petrovich, let me talk to him," he said in an undertone.

Salytov writhed away from his touch. "What does it matter?" he said angrily.

Porfiry walked past Salytov, up to the counter. The pawnbroker shifted uncomfortably, waiting. "You remember me," said Porfiry.

The pawnbroker nodded.

"The last time I was here, we talked about the student Virginsky. Have you seen him recently?"

"He came in yesterday." The man's eyes darted from side to side, as if looking for escape.

"To pawn a samovar."

"That's right." Surprise and a reluctant admiration showed in the man's eyes.

"Did he not come in today, just now, to redeem it?"

The pawnbroker shook his head. "I haven't seen him since yesterday."

"Perhaps one of your assistants dealt with him?"

"But the samovar is still here. He hasn't redeemed the pledge."

"Can you show it to me?"

The pawnbroker pointed high up behind Porfiry. Porfiry turned to see a shelf of samovars. "It's the one on the end. The end nearest you."

Porfiry winced to think that Madame Kezel had received a beating over the loss of such a tarnished and battered object. It was an ugly, ordinary samovar. He signaled his dejection to Salytov. They left the shop without further questions.

T HEY CAME OUT into the echo and blur of the flea market and the excited bustle of the great Apraxin Arcade. The scent of pine trees and spiced pastries rushed them. Porfiry felt weak and suddenly hungry and nauseous at the same time.

"What will you do?" asked Salytov.

"Stay here. Watch."

"You think he'll come here?"

Porfiry shrugged. "It depends if he has the money to redeem the samovar."

"Perhaps he took money from them. That may have been the motive."

"No." Porfiry shook his head impatiently, almost angrily. "He may have taken money, but it wasn't the motive. There is more than money to this."

"What do you want me to do?" asked Salytov.

"Go back to the station. Wait for me there."

Salytov seemed reluctant to take his leave. "He may be dangerous," he said. "If you try to apprehend him, he may—"

"I'm not going to apprehend him. I just want to talk to him."

"But you can't let him go, if you see him."

"I hope to persuade him to give himself up."

"I should stay with you," said Salytov after a slight pause.

Porfiry smiled weakly. "Really, Ilya Petrovich. There is no need. He won't do anything here. Not with all these people around." Porfiry gestured vaguely to the rushing crowds.

"He may panic. Who knows what he will do if he panics."

"But I can't believe it's him. I've looked into his eyes. They were not the eyes of a murderer."

"You can't know that!"

Porfiry was shaking his head insistently. "He is not the murderer. How could he be the murderer and be moved by Madame Kezel's wounds?"

"He had blood on his hands! The note. It was as good as a confession."

"But it was not a confession. Not to murder. Perhaps it was a confession to some other crime. The crime of taking the samovar. The crime of causing Madame Kezel's beating."

"Then explain the vial of laudanum we found."

"He was there!" Porfiry's cry was anguished. "But so were we, were we not?" he pleaded desperately.

"We had reason to be."

"Go," commanded Porfiry.

Salytov nodded tersely and turned his back on the investigating magistrate.

T HERE WAS A bookstall near the entrance to Lyamshin's. Porfiry positioned himself on the far side of it, so he could keep an eye on the door to the pawnbroker's without being seen by anyone who went in or out of the shop. He pretended to browse the books and nourished himself on the fumes from the bookseller's samovar.

He had no definite plan. It was hard to shake off the feeling that he was wasting his time. But he had to be somewhere. It seemed to fulfill some deep consoling need that he was here. Dimly, he sensed that this surveillance exercise was not strictly rational.

An hour passed. Porfiry had gone from watching for Virginsky to simply willing him to appear. He tried to superimpose the student's face on everyone who came into view. He began to ask himself how much longer he would give it. The tenuous sense of purpose he had felt initially had evaporated. All that kept him there now was the lethargy of depression.

He looked down at the book in his hands. The words communicated nothing to him.

When he looked up, there were tears in his eyes.

"Do you want that book, or what?" demanded the bookseller roughly. Porfiry nodded. "Fifty kopeks."

He handed over the money, still without knowing what book he was buying. *It is as senseless as any of my other acts.*

He took one last look at the door to Lyamshin's. A man of more than average height was just pushing it open. Something about this figure's back struck Porfiry as familiar. He watched as the man cast a furtive glance over his shoulder before going inside. That quick glimpse was all that Porfiry needed. The pallor of the man's face was unmistakable, as were his thin compressed lips and his cold gray eyes.

"Porfiry Petrovich!" Porfiry frowned to hear his name called. Lieutenant Salytov was running up to him. His shout drew the attention of more than a few passersby.

"Shhh!" Porfiry beat the air with an outstretched palm, signaling Salytov to be quiet.

Salytov stopped a pace in front of him, out of breath. "But there's something you need to know. I came straight over to tell you. I hoped I would find you here. We've had a report of a student trampled to death on the Kazansky Bridge."

"Virginsky?"

"It's impossible to say for certain. The head was mangled by the horses' hooves. But the rest of the victim's appearance fits Virginsky's description."

Porfiry looked back at the door to the pawnbroker's. "Nothing makes sense," he said. "There is no logic to any of this."

"I am going there now," said Salytov, squinting as if into the sun. But there was no sun, of course, in the gloomy arcade. "Will you come with me?"

Porfiry heard the agitated jangle of the bell to the pawnbroker's. "Look," he said, indicating the tall, thin gentleman with the pinched mouth who was coming out.

"Vadim Vasilyevich," murmured Salytov.

Porfiry nodded in confirmation.

The publisher's secretary was holding a small and densely ornamented gold box. He sheltered it protectively in both hands, as though it were a damaged bird he had rescued.

"Vadim Vasilyevich!" Porfiry raised a hand as he called out.

The secretary looked up at his name. For a moment, he seemed to contemplate making a run for it, but the sight of Salytov bearing down on him deterred him.

"May I see what you have there?" asked Porfiry, as he strode up to him.

Vadim Vasilyevich handed the box over without a word. It was heavy in Porfiry's hands. He tried the lid, but it was locked.

"Do you have the key?"

"I do not." Vadim Vasilyevich's bass voice resounded with antagonism.

"You have just redeemed this?" Porfiry turned the elaborate box in his hands.

"You spied me coming out of the pawnbroker's, I believe."

"Why would a gentleman like yourself have need of the services of a pawnbroker?"

Vadim Vasilyevich hesitated before answering. "I have redeemed it on behalf of a friend."

"Osip Maximovich?"

The secretary's silence was answer enough.

"The question is even more pertinent. Why would a gentleman like Osip Maximovich have need of the services of a pawnbroker?"

"I really do not know. Except to say, even a gentleman may find himself in pressing circumstances."

"The business is failing?"

"No. There is no question of that. It is just, sometimes, it pleases Osip Maximovich to engage in eccentricities. I really do not know why he pawned this object. I only know that he was most desirous of having it returned to him."

"He commissioned you to redeem it on his behalf?"

"You may put it like that, but it was not so formal."

"What were his words to you when he asked you to undertake this commission?"

"I cannot recall."

"Cannot? Or will not?"

"He said it was time for him to have it back. That was all."

"I see." Porfiry handed the box back to the secretary. "Then please, return it to him with my compliments."

Vadim Vasilyevich looked uncertainly at Porfiry. "May I go now?"

Porfiry nodded tersely. Vadim Vasilyevich clutched the ornamental box to his chest and hurried away.

Porfiry's gaze scoured Salytov's bewildered face. "Lead the way," he said at last.

There was feverish excitement in his gaze as he followed Salytov across the flea market toward the Nevsky Prospect exit.

I T WAS A FINE DAY, cold but clear. The city glistened in the frost-refracted sunlight, like a newly forged weapon.

Porfiry dawdled as if he wanted the short walk to the Kazansky Bridge to last forever. Salytov repeatedly had to stop and wait for him, frowning severely as he bit the inside of his cheek. Then he would nod and turn as Porfiry drew level, and walk ahead again. They did not speak.

The Kazansky Bridge rose in an angular peak over the frozen Yeka-terinsky Canal. As they approached it, they could see the stooped backs of the small crowd that clustered on the incline, defying the repulsive effects of the sloping, icy pavement. A *polizyeisky* shouted and scowled discour-agement, but the stubborn voyeurs refused to disperse. They gazed with desperate fixity at a point on the ground, beyond the sharp ridge, as yet unseen by Porfiry and Salytov. Another *polizyeisky* could be seen turning away traffic.

A private closed carriage, fitted with winter runners, was pulled up just in front of the bridge. The horses stamped and snorted, their eyes bulging with wild indignation. The liveried driver took a sly swig from a flask. In-side, a dark, indeterminate figure sat motionless and withdrawn.

As Porfiry stepped onto the bridge, he felt his feet slide from under him. A firm hand caught him under the armpit and prevented him from falling. It was hard to see solicitude in Salytov's expression. He unhanded Porfiry quickly, as though with some distaste.

Now that he was in among them, Porfiry could tell that it was more than fascination that held the onlookers. A kind of profane and callous awe was evident in their faces. They were mostly poor folk, servants, seamstresses, prostitutes, ragpickers, and low-grade civil servants, shiver-ing with grim excitement in threadbare coats. It seemed that for the mo-ment they had found relief from their own misery by contemplating the fate of someone worse off than themselves. And yet there was a sense of community, solidarity even, in their gaze. Although the victim was in all probability a stranger to them, it seemed they took the death personally, and they directed sly, resentful glances toward the waiting carriage. At the same time, however, a flicker of triumph, which they could not suppress but dared not acknowledge, showed in their eyes. It was the triumph of the living over the dead, and for the moment that they were possessed by it, there was no room for any other feeling, not even pity.

Their shoulders, as Porfiry and Salytov pushed through them, were hard but unresisting. Salytov negotiated briskly with the *polizyeisky,* who seemed both relieved and embarrassed to see them. "They are like dogs, sir. Like dogs in heat," he explained, gesturing to the crowd.

Salytov got details of the accident from a witness whom the *polizyeisky* had detained, a cavalry officer who happened to be on the bridge at the time. His rank and bearing lent authority to his account, and there was an immediate understanding between the two men. He spoke clearly and unhurriedly, neither agitated nor bored. He had seen worse, was the impression he gave, but he recognized the necessity of due process and was respectful of that, if not of the dead. It seemed he felt more pity for the horses than for the trampled man.

Porfiry paid only scant attention to the officer and found himself looking at the obscure figure in the closed carriage. Finally he walked over. The black and highly polished lacquer of the coach's bodywork shone impenetrably. It reflected back the tragedy of the day, without allowing it to touch the passenger within. Porfiry looked through the window. A girl of about nineteen or twenty stared back at him. The spreading bulk of her furs set off the fine, haughty beauty of her face. Her expression communicated outrage at Porfiry's presumed insolence.

For an instant he wanted to drag her out of the carriage and manhandle her over to where he knew the dead man lay. Instead he simply bowed his head and looked down at the family crest laid in gold leaf on the carriage door.

He turned away and, at last, surmounted the crest of the bridge. With sudden decisiveness, as if to emphasize the independence of his actions, he looked down.

Inevitably, his gaze went first to the head, which had exploded like a trampled fruit. The snow around the sprawl of flesh, bone, hair, and brains was a dirty pink slush. Madly, Porfiry stared at the mangled center of this dark vortex, as if he really believed he would be able to recognize Virginsky's features there. And when he could not, he cast about desperately over the rest of the body. All the limbs had a rag-bag casualness to them, as if they had been arranged by someone in a hurry, or with only a partial understanding of how the human body fitted together. Even the shape of the dark overcoat failed to impose any form or coherence.

At the bottom of the coat, two brown, worn boots, cracked uppers and gaping soles advertising their antiquity, projected at impossible angles.

Porfiry's heart began to pound. But then he felt a guilty sickness at his own jubilant excitement. Here was a man driven to death by poverty and despair, or possibly in an alcoholic stupor, which amounted to the same thing. He deserved better than Porfiry's selfish relief.

Suddenly, from a clear sky, it began to snow.

Porfiry turned his back on the dead man and broke into a brisk walk away from the bridge. This time it was Salytov who had to hurry to keep up.

25

Wild Surmises

THE BRIGHTLY PAINTED facades of the wine cellars and delicatessens on the Nevsky Prospect beckoned cheerily. Porfiry felt a fleeting, childish wonder at the oversize representations of grapes, charcuterie, and caviar. All he wanted to do was go inside one of those shops and never come out.

Instead he went into the three-story office building on the corner of the Nevsky Prospect and Bolshaya Konyushennaya Street, across from the Lutheran church.

He declined the wiry commissionaire's offer to escort him to the office of Athene Publishing.

He didn't wait for his single, sharp knuckle rap to be answered but went straight in, signaling to Salytov to wait outside. Osip Maximovich Simonov, seated at his desk, looked up over his spectacles. Their lenses shone, veiling his eyes with a film of silver. There was not a speck on his black frock coat. His beard had a sculptural perfection to it, and his long hair presented a helmetlike solidity. His neatness went deep.

"May I sit down?" Porfiry bowed from the waist as he made the request.

The other man nodded guardedly.

Porfiry took a seat on the other side of the desk and fixed Osip Maximovich steadily. "I'd like to get to know you better, Osip Maximovich. I feel we have a lot in common."

"You do?"

"Yes. I was educated at a seminary as well, you know."

"Indeed? I didn't know."

"Couldn't you tell?"

"I hadn't really thought about it."

"I will never forget the monks who taught me."

"Of course."

"I sometimes wonder if they would remember me."

Osip Maximovich seemed to shrug.

"I like to think they would," continued Porfiry.

"I'm sure you were a memorable youth."

"Yes, but I'm a man now, am I not? The thing is, would they think of the child now when they saw the man?"

"Possibly. Possibly not. Porfiry Petrovich, I hate to—"

"I will never forget what they taught me too."

"Then your education wasn't wasted."

"I was thinking more of my moral education."

"I too." Osip Maximovich's smile revealed his straining patience.

"Do you believe in the soul, Osip Maximovich?"

"You already know that I am a believer."

"Then I am afraid for you."

"Please don't be."

"My friend Pavel Pavelovich Virginsky claims he doesn't believe in the soul."

"I'm surprised to hear you describe such a fellow as your friend."

"Why do you say that?"

"Oh, I know all about Pavel Pavelovich Virginsky," said Osip Maximovich quickly. "I know all about his addiction to laudanum. And his habit of stealing other people's possessions to pawn them. I also know about that blasphemous contract he drew up with Goryanchikov."

"You do?"

"Yes, Goryanchikov showed it to me."

"An interesting document, wouldn't you say?"

"Such a man is capable of anything."

"Why?"

"Because he has no soul. He has surrendered it to another."

"But if you don't believe in the soul—as Virginsky did not—it follows that you don't believe in the contract," said Porfiry. "Such a document is meaningless. In fact, it only makes sense if you are a believer."

"I suppose you're right."

"How is Anna Alexandrovna?" asked Porfiry abruptly.

"She's very well." Osip Maximovich took off his spectacles. A small twinge of a smile quivered on his lips. "We are to be married, you know. Our engagement will be announced on New Year's Eve."

"Ah," said Porfiry. "Now I know you did it. I know you did it all. You killed all of them. Starting with Goryanchikov. Then Borya. Then Govorov. Then Lilya, Vera, and Zoya. You killed them all, Osip Maximovich. I only needed your motive, and now you have given it to me."

Osip Maximovich didn't seem surprised. He didn't even attempt to feign surprise. He simply said, "Nonsense," then put his spectacles back on. "But tell me, how have you worked all this out?" There was mockery in his tone.

"Let's start with Borya."

"Why start with him?"

"Because he was where my suspicions started. Borya didn't hang himself. Someone else did that for him. There was oil on the collar of his greatcoat. How did the oil get there? It was when I came to see you here that it came to me. I noticed the shop selling mechanical devices on the ground floor of this building. Of course! He must have been hoisted up by a block and tackle. You tied a length of rope around the bough of the tree, high up, with a loop hanging off it. Through the loop you threaded the rope that was tied around Borya's midriff, which was attached at the other end to the block and tackle, itself secured to one of the other trees. At this point he was still alive, just, though he was rapidly dying from the poisoned vodka you had given him. We know he was alive because of the bruising we found around the middle of his body. You probably already had a halter loosely in place around his neck. When he was high enough, you tied this rope around the bough. You then untied the rope around Borya's middle and used Borya's axe to cut down the rope with the loop. It left the nick in the bark, which I admit puzzled us for some time. Now Borya was hanging by his neck, but he was already dead. The blood had ceased to circulate. That's why there was no bruising around his throat."

"But you haven't explained why I should want poor Borya dead."

"It wasn't Borya you wanted dead so much as Goryanchikov. Borya was simply there to take the blame. He wouldn't do it willingly, of course. So you staged his suicide to make it look like he had been overcome by guilt after murdering Stepan Sergeyevich for the six thousand rubles you stuffed into his pocket."

"An interesting theory. I admit to being a collector of interesting theories. I find them entertaining. So I will hear you out. And then I shall refute you."

Porfiry nodded. "You wanted Stepan Sergeyevich Goryanchikov dead because he knew your secret; or rather, secrets. The first secret is that you, Osip Maximovich, are the publisher of both the Athene and the Priapos imprints. That is to say, a publisher of both reputable philosophy texts and disgusting obscenities. Goryanchikov knew this because he worked for you in both capacities. That was the meaning of one of the quotes in the extraneous passage of the translation. 'Did not Alcibiades sleep with Socrates, under the same cloak, and wrap his sinful arms around a spiritual man?' Alcibiades was the pen name Goryanchikov used when translating pornography. 'Socrates' refers simply to the philosophical content of the Athene books."

"Now I really have had enough of this tiresome nonsense. The fact is, Porfiry Petrovich, I can't have been Borya's murderer, or Goryanchikov's. I was a thousand versts away in Optina Pustyn. If you had taken the trouble to check my alibi, you would have saved yourself the embarrassment of making these preposterous and quite unfounded charges."

"I did check your alibi. I am always suspicious of people who are at pains to produce an alibi before they have been accused of anything, as you did. So I had the deputy investigating magistrate of Kaluga speak to Father Amvrosy in person. Fortunately he was granted an audience with the saintly man shortly before he died."

"There was no need to do that. You could have simply looked in the convent records."

"But I wanted, so to speak, to hear it from Father Amvrosy. Father Amvrosy was, after all, your old teacher from the seminary."

"And?" The word came out bullishly impatient.

"Fortunately, the young gentleman whom I directed to gather this information was very thorough. He sent me a transcript of Father Amvrosy's exact words."

"Which were?"

"He said, 'Someone by that name was here.'"

"There you are."

"But don't you think it's a revealing choice of words? It suggests to me he was expecting a different Osip Maximovich Simonov from the one he received. Certainly, these are not exactly the words you would expect an old teacher to use of a former pupil."

"But I took the train to Moscow. Vadim Vasilyevich saw me off."

"To begin a journey is not the same thing as to complete it. I believe you did take the train to Moscow, in the first stage of a journey to Optina Pustyn. But you got off at Tosno. The first station on the route. In the meantime, you had exchanged luggage with an actor called Ratazyayev. Who then went on to Optina Pustyn and impersonated you."

"Why should this fellow do this for me?"

"Because you had a hold over him. Your knowledge of his homosexuality. The crime of sodomy carries a sentence of exile, hard labor, and complete loss of civic rights. Of course, between consenting adults and behind closed doors, the legal prohibition of this act is difficult to enforce. The only successful prosecutions come as a result of denunciation. You threatened him with this."

"Where is he now? Has he confirmed this? If so, he is a liar."

"As yet we haven't found Ratazyayev."

"That is both convenient and inconvenient for you. Convenient, because it allows you to fit him into this jigsaw puzzle of accusations, in whatever way suits your purposes. Inconvenient, because you can't prove anything."

"Allow me to continue. Disembarking from the train at Tosno, where incidentally you were seen by Ratazyayev's—by his dear friend, Prince Bykov, you were able to return incognito to St. Petersburg on the first available train heading back. You took a room at the Hotel Adrianopole, under the name of Govorov. This Govorov was an agent of yours, known to Goryanchikov. You then sent a note via the bellboy to Goryanchikov, tricking him into coming to the hotel to see Govorov. You charged the bellboy with a second delivery, a forged billet-doux to Borya, supposedly from Anna Alexandrovna, enticing him to Petrovsky Park that same night. In your room at the Hotel Adrianopole you overpowered Goryanchikov and suffocated him with a pillow. You put his body in Ratazyayev's case, having had the foresight to tell him to leave it empty. You couldn't close the case with Goryanchikov wearing his fur *shuba*, so you removed that garment and concealed it in the mattress. You simply told the hotel that Goryanchikov was taking over your room, paying them in advance, to buy a little time before they went snooping. Something they would not be overly inclined to do anyway, although you had piqued the curiosity of the bellboy. You took the case to Petrovsky Park for your midnight rendezvous with Borya. Of course, Borya was expecting to meet Anna Alexandrovna. Instead, you were there. He must have been surprised, to say the least. How did the conversation go? Something like this, I imagine. 'Where is Anna Alexandrovna?' To which you reply: 'She couldn't come herself. She sent me in her stead.' 'She sent *you*? To this place?'"

"Please!" cut in Osip Maximovich.

"Was it not like that?"

"This is a farce."

"At some point, you looked Borya straight in the eye and said, 'Anna Alexandrovna has need of your help.' To which he replied something along the lines of, 'I will do anything for Anna Alexandrovna.'"

Osip Maximovich looked away sharply.

"Perhaps I am on the right lines after all," said Porfiry.

Now Osip Maximovich faced him and shook his head.

"At that point, perhaps," continued Porfiry, "or at some point soon after, you showed him the contents of the suitcase. That is to say, the dead body of Stepan Sergeyevich Goryanchikov. You told him about the filthy advances the dwarf had made toward his beloved Anna Alexandrovna, a lustful attention that was now being transferred to Sofiya Sergeyevna. And now you revealed the terrible act you claimed Anna Alexandrovna had been driven to commit in order to prevent an even worse crime. In absolute terror, Borya swears that he will do whatever you ask of him. 'We must make it look like suicide,' you say. 'Help me tie this rope around this tree. Lift me up. That's right. Put me on your shoulders. That's right. That's good. I just have to tie this. Don't worry, I know what I'm doing. You can put me down now. My goodness, you're shaking, Borya. Here, have some vodka, I've brought some vodka.' And when he offered your flask back to you, you naturally declined. 'One of us must keep a clear head,' you say. Was it something like that, Osip Maximovich?"

"What? All because I am supposed to have published a few smutty novels?"

"No. Not all because of that. I'm getting to the real reason. Would you like me to continue?"

"You can't prove any of this." Osip Maximovich seemed almost saddened to have to point this out to Porfiry.

"After Borya was strung up and dead, you used his axe to smash in Goryanchikov's head. You then slipped the axe into the yardkeeper's belt. While all this was going on, you had the real Konstantin Kirillovich Govorov incriminate Lilya. Why? In order to get her out of the way. Deportation to Siberia with her daughter. Isn't that what you wanted? Unhappily for Lilya and Vera, unhappily for Zoya too, Govorov failed."

"I have no idea what you're talking about. Who is this Lilya?"

"A prostitute, now. But she had not always been. Once she was the daughter of a respectable family. But I'll come to that. You killed Govorov because he was your creature. Not just the distribution agent for your pornographic publications. It was he who found you Ratazyayev. It was he you had entrusted to get rid of Lilya. Like all servants, he knew too much about his master. He knew enough to ruin you. Perhaps he was beginning to blackmail you. Or perhaps you had simply lost patience with him because he'd failed you. It no doubt irked you that you were forced to take matters into your own hands concerning Lilya and the child. You were forced to destroy all the evidence of your earlier crime, the rape of Lilya. You killed Lilya. And you killed her daughter, little Vera—your daughter too."

Osip Maximovich held his index finger vertically over his lips, as if to silence Porfiry. The side of his finger touched the tip of his nose and nestled momentarily in the indentation there.

"Yes. You are her father. You may deny it, but it's written in your features, and it was written in hers too. Her nose, in particular, it has the distinctive cleft that is evident on your own. Or rather I should say, it had. There is nothing left of her nose now."

Osip Maximovich dropped his hand hastily. "I wish I knew what you were talking about."

"And it's also written in Goryanchikov's text. You are the founder of the Athene imprint. You could be said to be the father of Athene—or Minerva, to give her Roman name. According to Goryanchikov, in a reference to Jupiter's bastards, the father of Minerva is also the father of Fides. A name we might translate in Russian as Vera."

"Really, this is the worst kind of argument, made from piling speculation on top of speculation. You take one away, and the whole edifice tumbles."

"It's interesting coincidence though, isn't it, that the name on Lilya's prostitution license is Semenova. Very similar to your family name of Simonov. Perhaps she considered herself in some way to be almost your wife, a kind of bastard wife with a bastardized name. It was you who had taken her virginity."

"Or perhaps it was simply her name, and as you say, it is a coincidence."

"I have learned not to trust coincidences."

"Instead you put your faith in wild guesswork! Even if all this is true, which I by no means admit, you can't prove a word of it. What is supposed to be my motive in all this?"

"To maintain your respectability, which became acute once you had conceived the plan to marry Anna Alexandrovna."

"What a strange way to put it! A plan indeed!"

"Yes, a plan. Because you had a hidden purpose in wanting to marry Anna Alexandrovna. You're marrying her not because you love her but because she has something you covet."

"I don't need her money!"

"I'm not talking about her money. But I'm getting ahead of myself. Goryanchikov found out about your relationship to Lilya from Lilya herself. He was a client of hers. He came to you and confronted you with it. Perhaps he even demanded that you make amends to Lilya. That would be typical of a freethinking liberal, full of all the modern ideas, one perhaps with an especially heightened sense of society's injustice, given his own personal circumstances. Perhaps Goryanchikov threatened to tell Anna Alexandrovna everything. That you had raped Lilya—or would you rather I used the word *seduced?* At any rate you abandoned her. She was pregnant. You denied that it was anything to do with you. Her family cast her off. Were you engaged to her? Did you break off the engagement when you learned of her condition? No one could blame you. You had been promised a virgin. But look at the hussy. Of course no one listened to Lilya's side of the story, if she had the courage to voice it. So you had to imagine Anna Alexandrovna hearing all this from Stepan Sergeyevich. It didn't bear thinking about. It couldn't be allowed to happen. Not to mention the fact that you are a pornographer, although I admit that rather pales into insignificance next to your other crimes. If Anna Alexandrovna knew the truth about you, if she were able to see your character in its true light, I wonder if she would be as willing to marry you? And if she called off the marriage, that would be an immense disappointment to you, wouldn't it, Osip Maximovich?"

"What are you talking about? I mean, yes, of course I would be disappointed. But why do you say it in that obnoxious way?"

"You're not marrying Anna Alexandrovna for herself. You're marrying her for her daughter. That's why Goryanchikov wrote, 'The father of Faith will be the destroyer of Wisdom.' Faith is a translation of Fides, which we have already identified as Vera, Lilya's daughter, your daughter. And as for Wisdom—well, the meaning of the name Sofiya is of course 'wisdom.' Goryanchikov is clearly indicating that you are a threat to Sofiya. You have a taste for young girls, don't you, Osip Maximovich? And that taste has dictated the photographs that Govorov produced for you. You even had him photograph Lilya, even after all that had happened. Though I expect that by then she had already lost her charms as far as you were concerned."

Osip Maximovich said nothing.

"But you're right," said Porfiry. "I can't prove any of this. This is just a conversation between two former seminarians. I've let myself get carried away. I've indulged in wild surmises. So I must leave you a free man. And besides, we already have a killer. A conveniently dead one, we are led to believe. So you are lucky—if indeed anything that I have said is true. Pavel Pavelovich Virginsky has written a suicide note, which, if genuine, appears to be a confession of guilt. A bottle of laudanum, similar to bottles found in his room, was found at the scene of the latest crime. He was even seen to have blood on his hands. It was clever of you to change your method, by the way, to switch to the axe for these final murders. Not the weapon of a gentleman. But the weapon of peasants—and deranged students, as you once hinted to me. The fact is, however, that anyone can buy an axe at a hardware store. The note spoke of his intention to kill himself by throwing himself under a *troika*. And someone more or less answering his description has been killed in that way. It seems to be a closed case. The possession of his soul by Goryanchikov also provides a motive there. Virginsky may say he doesn't believe in the soul, but we shouldn't forget he is a Russian."

"So why did you come here?" asked Osip Maximovich in genuine bewilderment.

"Because I can't accept that Virginsky is a murderer. I can't allow it."

"But why should he confess to the killing if he isn't the killer?"

"That's precisely the question I asked myself," said Porfiry. "Perhaps he's trying to protect someone."

"Who?"

"You."

Osip Maximovich looked at Porfiry for a moment, as if to confirm that he was serious. When he saw that he was, he began laughing. His laughter was loud and harsh and stopped as abruptly as it had started. "Why on earth would he be trying to protect me?"

"So that we won't arrest you. So that you will remain free. So that he can track you down and kill you. He went to Lilya's apartment. He found her as she was dying. He held her bloody head in his hands and tried to make her comfortable. She named her killer. According to this hypothesis, Virginsky isn't dead. The body that has turned up belongs to someone else."

"Ratazyayev perhaps?" suggested Osip Maximovich archly.

"I have no reason to believe that," said Porfiry. He didn't smile. "It could be anyone. There are a lot of emaciated students in St. Petersburg. Virginsky simply wants us to think he is dead."

"What do you intend to do about it?" For the first time in the interview, Osip Maximovich seemed genuinely shaken.

"Nothing," said Porfiry. "There is nothing I can do, even if I wanted to. It's all speculation. I have no proof of anything. The only way we will find out for sure is if you are killed." Porfiry got to his feet.

The emotion on Osip Maximovich's face took a step up to fear. "You're leaving me to my death," he said, his voice rising in startled outrage.

Suddenly, to the surprise of both men, the door to the adjoining room slowly opened. Vadim Vasilyevich came in. His face was more than usually pale, almost glowing. A strange excitement showed in his eyes, which were fixed on Osip Maximovich. His lips were tightly clamped. Porfiry saw that he was holding the gold box he had carried out of Lyamshin's.

"Hypocrite!" He whispered the word. But the force of his anger carried.

"Calm yourself, Vadim Vasilyevich."

"Did you think this would save you?" The artificial baritone was gone. Vadim Vasilyevich's natural voice was thin and reedy. He spoke quickly, breathlessly.

"What *are* you talking about?" Osip Maximovich attempted an amiable smile. But his eyes flashed hatred at Porfiry.

"Don't lie. It's too late for lying. I heard it all."

"You heard nothing. Now please give me the box. It doesn't belong to you. I thank you for retrieving it. But it's mine."

"I believed in you. You betrayed me. You betrayed yourself."

"On the contrary. I found a way to be true to myself."

Vadim Vasilyevich opened the lid of the little box and took out a folded piece of paper. He threw the box down. It fell apart as it hit the floor. "Did you really think this would save you?" He waved the paper in the air.

"Give it to me."

Vadim Vasilyevich began to laugh. "You really do believe in this, don't you? But God isn't a lawyer. It's the devil who's the lawyer, you fool!"

"No matter. I will negotiate with the devil then." Osip Maximovich rose from his seat and stalked toward his secretary. Vadim Vasilyevich was far taller than Osip Maximovich. He held the paper tauntingly over his head, at arm's length. The shorter man jumped comically but failed to reach it.

"I ought to—" Vadim Vasilyevich's face suddenly lit up with malign pleasure. "I know what I ought to do." He turned his back on Osip Maximovich and ran back into the adjoining room, slamming the door behind him. He evidently locked it, or blocked it in some way, as Osip Maximovich turned the handle uselessly.

A moment later the door opened, and Vadim Vasilyevich came back in. He was still holding the paper above his head, but it was alight. Jags of lambent orange leaped from his hand.

"You monster!" cried Osip Maximovich, desperately reaching for the flame-lapped document.

"What is that?" asked Porfiry Petrovich, who until now had been content to allow the scene to play out in front of him.

"It's his soul," cried Vadim Vasilyevich gleefully. "Or at least he thinks it is. It is a document conferring ownership of his soul to whoever is in possession of this paper. He placed his soul in the possession of the pawn-broker, the Jew Lyamshin. He believed that because he was no longer in possession of it, his soul would be untouched by his crimes." Vadim Vasilyevich gave a cry of pain and dropped the burning paper. But he moved forward to prevent Osip Maximovich from getting close to it.

"My soul is innocent. My soul is spotless," protested Osip Maximovich. "You saw the contract between Virginsky and Goryanchikov. We talked about it. You agreed—the logic is faultless. If a man is not in possession of his soul, his soul cannot be affected by anything he does. You yourself said it."

"But I was—" Vadim Vasilyevich's eyes rolled upward as he searched for the right word. "Amusing myself! I thought it was a joke. You couldn't possibly take it seriously." He broke into anguished sobbing laughter. "We talk about all sorts of things. That's what we do! All the day long. Idle talk! And we publish whole books full of other men's idle talk."

Osip Maximovich's eyes stared indignantly. He turned to Porfiry. "He's destroyed a legally binding document. Pure vandalism. Can't you arrest him?"

Porfiry turned toward the door. "Lieutenant Salytov!" he called out.

Salytov stepped into the office.

"Arrest this man," said Porfiry, indicating Osip Maximovich.

"What!" cried Osip Maximovich, in sudden rage. "That was not our deal! You were going to leave me to face Virginsky. You were going to let Virginsky kill me. That's what we agreed. I was willing to accept that. I wanted that. You cheated me."

"I don't care a jot about your soul," said Porfiry. "But I do care about Virginsky's."

26

The Cellar on Sadovaya Street

PORFIRY PETROVICH looked up from his desk as he heard the door to his chambers open. He stubbed out a half-smoked cigarette and rose slowly from his seat. "Pavel Pavelovich!" Porfiry said the name warmly. He invested it with a surprise that he did not entirely feel.

"Porfiry Petrovich." Virginsky looked away, shamefaced.

"You gave us quite a scare." Porfiry gave a quick moue of rebuke. "Until I saw the boots on the dead man, I was convinced it was you."

"Ah, yes." Virginsky flashed a tentative glance toward Porfiry. "I'm sorry about that. That note . . . it was stupid. Although at the time I fully intended to. I . . . saw the accident on the Kazansky Bridge. He looked just like me. It was like I was watching myself. That's what I should do, I thought. That's the answer. But I couldn't go through with it. Perhaps I should have. I wish to God I had gone through with it. I may still."

"Don't talk like that!"

"I should have killed him. That was my other plan. That was the only reason to keep myself alive. But I couldn't go through with that either." Virginsky hung his head. "I'm a coward."

"No."

"Yes. I should have killed him. And when I realized I didn't have it in me to do that, I should have killed myself. She——" Virginsky broke off and hid his face in his hands.

"What is it, Pavel Pavelovich?"

"She asked me to pray for his soul." Virginsky dropped his hands, revealing the appalled confusion on his face. "For Osip Maximovich's soul."

Porfiry blinked his agitation. "And can you?"

"Can you?"

"I am a believer," said Porfiry. "And yet I find it difficult to think of troubling God with that prayer."

"I've tried. For her sake." Virginsky lapsed into thought. He suddenly remembered something. "She gave me this." Virginsky handed Porfiry a sealed envelope, addressed to one Yekaterina Romanovna Lebedyeva. The name seemed familiar to Porfiry, though he could not think from where. "It's a letter to her mother that she has never sent."

"This woman is her mother?" Porfiry's voice sounded startled. He thought perhaps he could place the name after all.

"Apparently. Lilya carried the letter about with her always. She was holding it when he killed her. Perhaps it gave her strength, or hope . . . or something. She asked me to deliver it. I can't. I can't conceive of looking that woman in the eye."

"I will take it," said Porfiry, noting the address. "What will you do now?"

"I don't know. I've written to my father. A different letter. Not the one you found."

Porfiry nodded his approval. "Do you wish me to destroy that?"

Virginsky nodded.

Porfiry came out from behind his desk and held out his hand. Pavel Pavelovich took it. "This is a hard time," said Porfiry. "A terrible time.

You need your father. You need to forgive him and to allow him to forgive you."

Virginsky sighed deeply and looked away.

T HE ADDRESS ON the envelope was for an apartment building in Sadovaya Street. He tracked the Lebedyevs down to a frigid cellar. There was no door. The light seeped in through barely translucent half-windows cut off by the ceiling. There was a layer of ice on the walls.

Madame Lebedyeva lay in bed. As soon as he saw her—even before that, as soon as he heard her constant, almost mechanical keening—Porfiry knew for certain why her name had been familiar to him. This was the woman who had come to his chambers and given a statement declaring herself "guilty of everything." Her husband, Lebedyev, sat close by. His face retained its air of protected dignity.

"Yekaterina Romanovna," said Porfiry, aware suddenly of a dull ache in his chest. "I have something for you." He crossed to the bed and held out the letter.

The woman did not look at him. She simply continued her endless cycle of lamentation. It rose and fell and shook her.

"It's from Lilya," Porfiry went on. "Your daughter."

Yekaterina Romanovna broke off to declare, "I have no daughter."

"You're right. I'm sorry to say you're right, at last. But you did have. Lilya is dead now."

Yekaterina Romanovna struck her breast with a clenched fist.

"Dearest, dearest," began Lebedyev. But he had nothing else to offer.

"Listen to me," said Porfiry sternly. "Listen to the truth. It's time you listened to the truth. She *was* murdered. As was her daughter, your granddaughter. By a man called Osip Maximovich Simonov."

"No, sir!" protested Lebedyev, rising to his feet. He sat back down immediately. "Osip Maximovich is a gentleman. Retract that slander now, sir, or you will have to answer to me."

"So you do know Osip Maximovich?" demanded Porfiry.

There was a sudden wail from the bed. Madame Lebedyeva began tearing at her face with her nails. Porfiry watched in horror as the blood broke through her cheeks. At last he stirred himself and lurched forward to restrain her. She was stronger than he expected. But he used his weight to wrestle her into stillness, pulling her hands away from her face. He could see from her eyes that she understood. The guilt that she had been waiting for had finally come to her.

"Osip Maximovich was to have been my son-in-law," continued Lebedyev. "We had an arrangement. It was all decided. We were honored. And it would have been . . . the end of all our troubles. She had come to his attention. He—he was willing to condescend to take her hand. The hand of a foolish girl. And she—she threw it away! She, she, she . . . I cannot bring myself to speak of it."

"Then allow me. She was raped by a man she trusted."

"No! It was some boy, some filthy boy. Quite naturally Osip Maximovich broke off the engagement. Do you know how much he was going to pay us? And normally it is the bride's family that must provide a dowry!"

"But he raped her," insisted Porfiry.

Lebedyev shook his head violently. "Some boy, some filthy boy," he repeated. "She was faithless. How could you expect a respectable gentleman like Osip Maximovich to marry a whore like that? She ruined this family!" raged Lebedyev, again rising from his seat only to fall back onto it. "Look what she did to her mother! Broke her poor mother's heart! Shattered the balance of her mind! She is responsible for everything! I never touched a drop before that day. And now I have lost my position, lost everything . . ."

Yekaterina Romanovna's wailing intensified. She screamed and writhed beneath Porfiry's restraint. Eventually she calmed and looked into Porfiry's face. Her expression was pleading but lucid. "I believed her. I always believed her. But I said nothing. That's how I killed her. By my silence."

Porfiry answered her with a fit of blinking. He threw the letter onto the bed and stood up. He crossed to Lebedyev and pulled him up by his lapels so that he could say into his face, which stank of vodka, "She was your daughter." The former civil servant met this assertion with his usual mask of anaesthetized dignity. "Lilya Ivanovna. Ivanovna. Lilya Ivanovna," continued Porfiry, stressing the patronymic. "Even if she was all that you accuse her of, she was still your daughter." He released the man's lapels. Lebedyev swayed but remained on his feet. "I am Titular Councilor Ivan Filomonovich Lebedyev. I have a position. I have standing. I have a reputation."

"You have nothing," said Porfiry.

Lebedyev frowned, as if he were struggling to understand Porfiry's point.

Porfiry pushed him back into his seat and left. He heard Yekaterina Romanovna's wailing begin with renewed force.

P RINCE BYKOV ROSE to his feet as he saw Porfiry approach, gripping the rim of his fur-covered top hat tightly. Porfiry began coughing and fumbled automatically for his cigarettes.

Zamyotov was hovering in the background. Porfiry sensed the look of angry reproach on his face and did not take out the enameled case.

"Prince Bykov," murmured Porfiry with a bow.

"Alexander Grigorevich informs me that the case is closed." Prince Bykov spoke stiffly.

Porfiry deepened his bow, then rose slowly.

"But you haven't found Ratazyayev?"

Porfiry met the prince's anguish with a carefully judged smile. He cleared his throat and spoke with deliberate clarity. "I dearly wish we had. There are many questions I would like to put to him."

"This is Russia. A man cannot simply disappear!"

"Even in Russia. Sometimes a man doesn't want to be found. Perhaps that is the case with your friend. He is a consummate actor, after all." Porfiry gave the prince a long, significant look.

Prince Bykov's tone became accusatory: "You have given up on him."

"All the requisite agencies and bureaus have been alerted. The image that you kindly provided has been circulated. However, I have to say, it would be better for your friend if we did not find him. He is, after all, an accomplice to murder, however unwitting the part he played."

"Exactly! You must hunt him down. He must be brought to justice. He must be made to face up to what he has done. You must find him!"

"It is a question of resources, your excellency. And priorities."

"Are you saying Ratazyayev is not a priority?"

"We may not find him today, or tomorrow, but if he ever comes to our notice again, we will know him. Policemen have long memories. *I* have a long memory."

Prince Bykov gulped in air, as if he had suddenly forgotten how to breathe. "What if he is dead? That man, the man who killed all those others, may have killed him."

"We don't know that." Porfiry's voice softened. His posture slumped a little, as if in defeat. "We have every right to hope that he is still alive."

"But I will never see him again."

"I advise you to forget about him," said Porfiry.

"But how can I? Everywhere I go I am reminded of him."

"Then leave St. Petersburg. Travel is often an aid to recovery in cases like this."

"Switzerland," murmured the prince distractedly. "We once talked of going to Switzerland together."

"Wherever he is, I'm sure that he thinks of you—with warmth and affection." Porfiry felt a sudden stabbing ache in his frontal lobe. "And love." He allowed himself to blink. He couldn't stop. He felt that he would never be able to stop.

Porfiry closed his eyes tightly and placed one hand over them. When he took his hand away and opened his eyes, he saw that the prince was gone. His fit of blinking had passed too.

He bowed again, to the empty space where the prince had stood. Without looking at Zamyotov, he went into his chambers.

Porfiry leaned his back against the closed door and finally took out his cigarette case. He busied himself in lighting a cigarette. The headache eased as quickly as it had come. He gazed across the room at the window. A low sun blinded him to the details of his chambers. All he could see was the cloud of exhaled smoke, a swirling trap for sunlight.

He tried to remember what day it was. He could not shake off the feeling that there was something he should be doing. And yet whatever it was, it was not as important to him as leaning against this door and watching the smoke from his cigarette.

The ash fell unheeded to the floor. Porfiry was absorbed in the shifting smoke, studying it as if it were a mystery that could be solved. When he had finished the cigarette, he squeezed the glowing tip, feeling its sharp heat between his thumb and forefinger, and strode away from the door. The room became visible to him, and he knew it was New Year's Eve. Later, he would be expected at Nikodim Fomich's house.